"SUBCOMMANDER, DESTROY THAT SHIP."

"Yes, sir." Dimetris lifted her voice and began belting out orders. "Helm, set intercept course, maximum warp. Weapons, stand by for a snap shot. Target their center mass. Centurion, stand by to drop the cloak on my mark."

Curt acknowledgments came back to her in quick succession, and Centurion Akhisar nodded once to indicate he was ready. Commander H'kaan watched the tactical display in front of him and felt his pulse quicken with anticipation as the *Valkaya* closed to attack position on the *Sagittarius*. When they reached optimal firing range for torpedoes, he said simply, "Now."

Akhisar dropped the bird-of-prey's cloak, and the weapons officer unleashed a burst of charged plasma that slammed into the small Starfleet scout ship and knocked it out of warp.

"Helm," Dimetris called out, "come about and drop to impulse. Sublieutenant Pelor, charge disruptors and ready another plasma charge. Centurion, raise shields."

Pelor replied, "Weapons locked!"

Dimetris crowed, "Fire!"

In the scant moments between the order and the action, H'kaan glimpsed the sparking, smoldering mass of the *Sagittarius* on the bridge's main viewscreen. *Looks like we scored a direct hit with the first shot,* he observed with pride. *All those battle drills finally paid off.*

Then a pair of disruptor beams lanced through the smoldering the *Sagittarius,* and the ship erupted in a massive fireball ckly dissipated, vanishing into the insatiable vacuum of pace. When the afterglow faded, all that remained was g debris.

cure from general quarte Much as he tried to remain not resist the urge to glo ral Inaros, 'Starfleet vess

D1285700

THE SAGA OF

STAR TREK®
VANGUARD

STAR TREK®
VANGUARD

STORMING HEAVEN

DAVID MACK

Story by
David Mack and
Dayton Ward & Kevin Dilmore

Based upon *Star Trek*
created by Gene Roddenberry

POCKET BOOKS

New York   London   Toronto   Sydney   New Delhi   Eremar

Pocket Books
A Division of Simon & Schuster, Inc.
1230 Avenue of the Americas
New York, NY 10020

This book is a work of fiction. Names, characters, places, and incidents either are products of the author's imagination or are used fictitiously. Any resemblance to actual events or locales or persons, living or dead, is entirely coincidental.

First Pocket Books paperback edition April 2012

POCKET and colophon are registered trademarks of Simon & Schuster, Inc.

For information about special discounts for bulk purchases, please contact Simon & Schuster Special Sales at 1-866-506-1949 or business@simonandschuster.com.

The Simon & Schuster Speakers Bureau can bring authors to your live event. For more information or to book an event, contact the Simon & Schuster Speakers Bureau at 1-866-248-3049 or visit our website at www.simonspeakers.com.

Manufactured in the United States of America

10 9 8 7 6 5 4 3 2 1

ISBN 978-1-4516-5070-9
ISBN 978-1-4516-5071-6 (ebook)

*For Dayton and Kevin, who made this journey to
the final frontier more fun than I could ever have imagined,
and for Marco, who brought us all together for the trip.*

Historian's Note

The prologue and epilogue of this story are set in April 2270. The rest of the narrative transpires in 2268, coinciding with the events of the latter half of *Star Trek*'s third season.

Wisdom begins at the end.
　　　—John Webster, *The Duchess of Malfi* (1623)

PROLOGUE

THE SENSE OF RECKONING

APRIL 2270

CALDOS II

Diego Reyes stared through the amber lens of a short glass of whiskey in his hand. "How long did you stay on the station after I left?"

Tim Pennington's answer was low and fraught with grim remembrance. "I was there till the end, mate. The bitter, bloody end."

The two men sat in reclining chairs that faced the gradually rekindling embers in Reyes's stone fireplace. A silence yawned between them, broken only by random pops from fresh logs splintering atop the banked fire and tossing short-lived sparks across the broad hearth. Reyes tilted his head back, splaying his shoulder-length black-and-gray hair across his headrest, and enjoyed the quietude. They had been conversing for hours, ever since the journalist's unannounced arrival on the shore of Reyes's private island, just before sundown. The former Starfleet commodore had done most of the talking, of course, filling in gaps and illuminating secrets of what had gone on behind closed doors during his final days at Starbase 47, which had become better known, within Starfleet and to the public, as Vanguard. Now it was late, and the air in the room felt heavy from the surfeit of conversation.

Pennington tucked in his chair's footrest and pulled himself to his feet. The lean, fair-haired Scotsman straightened and stretched his arms toward the high, open-frame ceiling, whose rough-hewn beams gave off a fragrance reminiscent of fresh cedar. As the writer lowered his arms, he paused to massage his right shoulder, where his cybernetic prosthetic met his torso. He had been plagued with a persistent ache, he'd confided, ever since losing his arm in a furious Starfleet-Orion crossfire on Starbase 47 a couple of years earlier.

Reyes watched him pick up his glass and carry it to a frost-bordered window that overlooked the lake. Dappled by wind and moonlight, the black water seemed to stretch away forever into the night. There were no lights along the lake's shore—at least, none visible from Reyes's home—so at night the heavily wooded mainland became a distant memory, swallowed by darkness until the stars wheeled away to their daytime hiding places.

The younger man nursed his drink and stared out the window. "I'm not sure how much I'm really allowed to say about what I saw."

Another sip from his own glass rewarded Reyes with a mouthful of smoky warmth and a complex sweetness that mingled notes of caramel, cherry, and oak. He savored the pleasant burn of the small-batch whiskey as he swallowed, then he fixed his gaze on a pair of dueling flames inside the fireplace. "If it helps, you were never here, and we never spoke."

"I'd figured as much." He spent a moment looking into his glass. In the ruddy firelight and dancing shadows, he looked much older to Reyes than he had just two years earlier. Reyes imagined that whatever events Pennington had lived through since then were to blame for the crow's-feet that framed his blue eyes and the worry lines that creased his high forehead.

Poor bastard, Reyes reflected with dark humor. *He's starting to look like me.*

Pennington turned away from the window and drifted back to the empty recliner. He stood beside it and watched sparks float from the fire and disappear up the chimney. "What was the last thing you heard from Vanguard before the news blackout?"

"I seem to recall something about a civilian shipping accident."

That drew a crooked, wry grimace from Pennington. "Ah, yes. The warp-core breach on the *Omari-Ekon*." He shook his head, then looked askance at Reyes. "I'd always wondered why it was allowed to leave the station, after what happened."

Reyes avoided his guest's accusatory stare. "I didn't." He recalled his escape from the Orion merchantman—the same incident that had cost Pennington his arm. With a little help from Starfleet Intelligence officer Lieutenant T'Prynn, Reyes had hacked the Orion ship's navigational records and stolen the coordinates for the source of an artifact that Starfleet had learned could be used as a weapon against the Shedai, an ancient race that possessed fearsome power and mysterious abilities. Although his and T'Prynn's exit from the ship had resulted in a bloodbath, the Federation had defused the ensuing political fallout by exonerating the ship's owner, Neera, of culpability for the firefight and sending her and her crew on their way.

What none of the admirals at Starfleet Command had said aloud was that there was no way they were going to permit the *Omari-Ekon* to leave Vanguard's jurisdiction with that kind of intel aboard as a lure for the Klingons, the Romulans, the Tholians, and whoever else might be vying for control over the Taurus Reach and its terrible secrets. Consequently, shortly after moving beyond the station's patrol zone, the *Omari-Ekon* had suffered a sudden, disastrous mechanical failure, and, just as Reyes had suspected, the first ship to reach its smoldering wreckage had reported there were no survivors.

He scratched an itch on his chin through his neatly trimmed salt-and-pepper beard and cast a wary look at Pennington. "So, what now?"

"Fair's fair, right? You told me your secrets, so now I tell you mine?"

"Only if you're planning on drinking any more of my whiskey."

Pennington looked at his glass for a moment, or perhaps he was staring through it while his thoughts roamed light-years away; Reyes couldn't tell for certain. The man pursed his lips. "There are some things I know only secondhand. Some of it's from witnesses, some's nothing more than hearsay. I've got signal intercepts and transcripts, sensor logs and declassified reports. But a few of the holes I had to fill in with educated guesswork.

I'm pretty sure what I'm about to tell you is the truth, but I can't be a hundred percent certain that some of it's not spun from cobwebs. You get what I'm telling you?"

Reyes nodded. "I take your meaning."

"Good." Pennington settled back onto the empty recliner with a tired grunt. He leaned over, grabbed the bottle of whiskey, uncorked it, and refilled his glass. Then he nudged the open bottle across the small table toward Reyes. "I'd top off if I were you, mate. When you hear the story I'm about to tell . . . you're gonna need it."

PART 1

MORTAL INSTRUMENTS

2268

1

The *Telinaruul* have wronged us for the last time.

The Shedai Wanderer made her telepathic declaration of war to the thousands of her kin who surrounded her atop a basalt mountain on a world of fire. All around them, a sea of molten rock churned and belched superheated gases into the tenuous atmosphere of the newly formed planet. Overhead, a penumbral moon blazed with its own inner fires and dominated the black sky, its infernal glow blotting out the cold sparks of starlight around its edges.

They have stolen what is ours, as if they had any right to our legacy. She shared with her fellow members of the *Serrataal* her memories of the crystalline prison in which she had recently been snared. **Now they arm themselves with the weapons of our old enemies, the Tkon.** Waves of antipathy surged from the host gathered below her when they heard the name of their long-extinct foes. **If they master this instrument of terror, none of us will be safe. Even now, the *Telinaruul* hold captive none other than the Progenitor himself.**

Shock and dismay coursed through the shared mindspace of their ad hoc Colloquium. Ripples of disbelief shimmered back to the Wanderer, and the Warden's protesting response was steeped in shades of incredulity. **The Progenitor was a myth! A piece of lore to explain our forgotten origins.**

He exists, the Wanderer insisted, offering up her memory of fleeting contact with the creator of their race of interstellar dynasts. **The first and greatest of our kind lies yoked to the weapon our enemies would turn against us. We must punish these impudent upstarts who would call themselves our peers.**

Resistance surged upward from the Adjudicator. **Do not be so quick to pit us against these new *Telinaruul*,** he cautioned. **They grew mighty while we slept. Have you already forgotten the culling of our numbers on Avainenoran? Or the losses inflicted upon us by the Apostate's treachery?**

The Wanderer seethed. **I have forgotten nothing. But even alone, I cut through their so-called fortress with ease. Our numbers are more than sufficient to lay waste all the worlds they control and make their peoples ours to command.**

Her declaration was met with hues of doubt, most profoundly from the Avenger. He elevated his essence above the throng to address the Wanderer. **Tell us, youngling: How would you have us face this new foe that dwells in deep space, light-years from the nearest Conduit? Should we permit them to capture us all and hope for a moment of providence such as the one that liberated you?**

His question sparked a storm of panic. Fear washed over the Wanderer like a tide of poison and left her reeling and sickened. This was not the way of the Shedai, not the voice of the people she had known for hundreds of centuries. What had become of them? Had the Apostate been right to condemn them? Had the Shedai become moribund and degenerate? She refused to accept that. Marshaling her strength, she quelled the others' rising tide of anxiety with an overpowering exhortation: **Silence!** The chaotic clamor fell away, and she continued. **We waged war against distant powers in ages past, and we will do so again. Our folly in the age before the Grim Awakening was that we contented ourselves with fighting through proxies. No more. I will see justice done upon the *Telinaruul* by my own touch. I will hear their wailing pleas for mercy, their desperate cries of surrender, and ignore them all as they perish in darkness and silence, in the cold void they should never have dared to cross.**

Many of the *Serrataal* reflected the Wanderer's aura, signaling their support for the war she was committed to wage. Yet islands of defiance remained. Radiating skepticism of her rhetoric were the Herald and the Sage—persons of consequence, former members of the Maker's inner circle, the elite corps within the elder caste of named Shedai, the Enumerated Ones.

Exuding rich tones of disdain, the Sage asked, **Why should we follow you to war? We pledged our loyalty to the Maker, not to you.**

I, too, swore fealty to the Maker, but she is gone now, lost beyond the farthest Conduit. And the _Telinaruul_'s error that set me free also made me stronger than I have ever been. Perhaps even stronger than you, Old One.

The Sage's essence darkened with resentment. **I will not give my oath to a youngling—not even one so obviously powerful as you.**

His rebuff enraged the Wanderer. **Do _you_ mean to lead us, then?**

Seniority has always been our way, the Herald interjected. **The Warden is the oldest of us who remain.**

Taking the Herald's cue, the Wanderer aimed her fury at the Warden. **And what say you? Will you sanction war for the sake of preserving order? Or counsel a galactic cycle of sleep while the _Telinaruul_ turn our secrets against us and one another?**

Anticipation swelled as the assembled minds focused themselves upon the Warden. Perhaps sensing the terrible gravity of the moment, he remained silent for a long moment while pondering his answer. **If the decision is mine to make,** he told the Wanderer, **I would have your answer to the Avenger's question. How are we to strike at these new enemies? Do you propose we lure them into reach?**

She mustered her confidence to lend her words the force of authority. **No. We will take our fight to the _Telinaruul_ and slay them where they think themselves safest and most secure. We will crush their puny starships and rend their vaunted starbase into scrap. Then we shall free the Progenitor and let him show us how to cleanse the galaxy of these vermin—starting with the ones who call themselves _the Federation_.**

Massed on the black slope, the last of the Shedai hegemons

waited for the Warden's pronouncement, for the declaration that would define the fate of their race, their legacy, and the galaxy at large. High above, the dark moon passed the midheaven in slow degrees; far below, a sea of magma and fire roiled beneath a Stygian sky. A distant eruption trembled the planet from its molten core to its obsidian crust. Then came the moment of decision.

The Warden was incandescent with pride.

To war.

2

Admiral Heihachiro Nogura stood alone, looking down through a pane of transparent aluminum that sloped outward, affording him an unobstructed view of a wide arc of Starbase 47's main docking bay. Dozens of meters directly beneath his vantage point, the Starfleet scout vessel *Sagittarius* was tethered at the airlock for Bay 2. Its pristine hull was a testament to the skills of its chief engineer and the starbase's repair personnel, who had expertly removed all trace of the many and varied horrors the fast little ship had endured in the past few years.

All so I can send it back out to get mauled again.

Sending the ship and its crew into danger didn't bother Nogura. If he'd had his way, the *Archer*-class starship would have been deployed weeks earlier. What made him livid was that, for reasons beyond his control, it was still here instead of on its way to one of the most vital missions it had ever been assigned, and that he had no other vessels suited to assume its role.

Distant footsteps echoed in the empty corridor and slowly drew closer. He glanced to his right, but the source of the footfalls was not yet visible, still somewhere beyond the long curve of the passageway that ringed the station's core, one level above the cathedral-like main concourse of the docking level. Nogura preferred to admire the ships under his command from this more isolated location, a service level free of the random pedestrian traffic and bustling activity of the main level's gangways. The service level was rarely visited by more than a handful of station personnel. Most of its interior sections were sealed off to serve as airspace above the cavernous repair bays that occupied more than a dozen decks inside the main core adjacent to the docking bay, which occupied the lower half of the station's massive saucer.

The footsteps were close now, snapping crisply on the gleaming duranium floor, which reeked of pine and ammonia, thanks to a recent pass by a crewman with a mop, a bucket, and punishment-detail work orders. Nogura's visitor cleared the bend in the corridor, and he noted with a sidelong glance that it was Lieutenant T'Prynn, the station's acting liaison to Starfleet Intelligence. The tall, athletically trim Vulcan woman wore a red minidress uniform and knee-high black boots, and her insignia bore the emblem for the security division. Her straight sable hair reached to the middle of her back and was cinched in a simple ponytail above her shoulders. She carried a data slate tucked close at her side, and walked with her chin up, her bearing proud.

Nogura turned his attention back to the *Sagittarius* until T'Prynn stepped up beside him. She waited until he acknowledged her arrival by making eye contact with her reflection in the transparent aluminum window, and then she said simply, "Admiral."

The diminutive, square-jawed flag officer's voice was as deep as the sea and had a rasping growl like a power saw. "What's the excuse this time?"

His brusque query seemed to surprise T'Prynn, and for a brief moment she appeared to be formulating a response steeped in classic Vulcan dry sarcasm. Then she answered him plainly. "The Romulans and the Klingons have both increased their patrols in the sectors surrounding Vanguard, and they appear to be coordinating their activities."

"In other words, the same excuse as last time." He shook his head, frustrated by the prospect of another indefinite delay. "We can't just sit and wait for the Klingons and the Romulans to let their guard down. That escaped Shedai could come back at any time—and if it brings friends, we'll be in real trouble."

T'Prynn relaxed her pose. "I agree. If Eremar is the source of the Mirdonyae Artifacts, it's imperative we investigate it before anyone else finds it."

"Exactly," Nogura said. "But it won't do us any good if the Klingons or the Romulans follow the *Sagittarius* to that pulsar.

Best-case scenario, they'd swoop in and steal the artifacts out from under us. Worst-case scenario, they'd destroy the *Sagittarius* in the process. It's not enough to get Nassir and his ship there. We also need to bring them home with the prize."

She proffered the data slate to Nogura. "I have a plan that may accomplish the first part of our mission objective."

He took the slate and skimmed its contents. "Just the high points, if you please."

"An act of subterfuge. First, we disguise a small craft as a replica of the *Sagittarius,* one capable of high-warp speed. Then we launch it as a decoy on a heading away from Eremar."

Nogura scowled at the Vulcan. "And where, exactly, will we find the spare duranium, fuel, and warp nacelles to make this drone?"

"We already have them. They're in Repair Bay One, awaiting assembly."

Getting the sense that he was being read into a plan already set in motion, he harrumphed and resumed perusing the slate's contents. "Go on."

"We conceal the *Sagittarius*'s deployment by hiding it inside the main cargo bay of a larger vessel, which will carry it to the Iremal Cluster, a stellar phenomenon known for scrambling short- and long-range sensors. Once the ship reaches the cluster, the *Sagittarius* deploys on a new course while its transport continues on its original heading. There is a high probability the *Sagittarius* will reach Eremar undetected if it can reach Iremal without incident."

Nogura exhaled slowly; it was not so much a sigh as a prolonged huff of irritation. "I see several things wrong with your plan, Lieutenant."

T'Prynn cocked her head, and her face betrayed a hint of curiosity. "Could you be more specific, Admiral?"

"For starters, whatever ship you dress up as your decoy will have a dozen Klingon and Romulan warships hunting it from the moment it leaves our patrol zone."

She pointed at the slate in his hand. "I've accounted for that, sir. The decoy will, in fact, be an unmanned drone, equipped with sensor feedback systems to create the illusion of a living crew. As noted on page six of my proposal."

He paged forward in her briefing and saw that she was telling the truth. "Very well. Now maybe you can tell me how you plan to fit the *Sagittarius* inside another ship's cargo hold. Don't most ships usually leave here packed stem to stern?"

"Under normal circumstances, yes. We would need to take the extraordinary measure of commandeering a civilian vessel of sufficient capacity to execute the ruse. As a result, whatever ship we select would be deprived of its cargo and civilian passengers."

Nogura regarded her with naked suspicion. "I presume the ship of 'sufficient capacity' you have in mind is the freighter *Ephialtes*?"

"In fact it is."

"I trust you know Captain Alodae won't go along without a fight." He waited for T'Prynn to reply, but she said nothing. Despite all her claims of having rededicated herself to logic devoid of emotion during her long recovery from a mental breakdown, he suspected that on some level she was enjoying this at his expense. "All we need is for him to go crying to the JAG Office."

She lowered her chin, lending her mien a conspiratorial air. "I don't claim to be a legal expert, but I sincerely doubt Captain Alodae would prevail in such a dispute."

"You have an answer for everything, don't you?"

"I strive to be prepared, sir."

Unable to shake off his skepticism, he pored over a few more paragraphs of T'Prynn's mission plan. "Let's say we proceed with this scheme of yours, whether Captain Alodae likes it or not. Sending one of our ships out of here as luggage on a superfreighter, straight into a sensor blind spot that has 'ambush' written all over it, might be just as dangerous as letting the *Sagittarius* leave here undisguised. And even if this absurd ruse works, I don't see anything in your plan for how to bring our people home safely from Eremar."

A grudging half nod. "I admit, I'm still working to resolve a few details."

His thick, graying brows knit together as he glowered up at the statuesque Vulcan. "This is one of the most reckless, dangerous mission plans I've ever seen, in all my years in Starfleet."

She met his hard, scathing gaze with one eyebrow arched in elegant mockery. "Is that a 'yes,' Admiral?"

He handed back the data slate. "Make it happen."

3

There were few luxuries that were as sorely underappreciated as that of a good meal, in the opinion of Captain Kutal. He sat alone at the officers' table in the mess hall of the *I.K.S. Zin'za*, savoring a mouthful of succulent *gagh*. The tiny worms were young and fresh, having just been stocked into the ship's larder a few days earlier, during a brief port call at Tythor, just over the border inside the Empire. He always made a point of enjoying such delicacies while they lasted. Before long, the *gagh* would grow large and tough, until not even the hardiest Klingon warrior could chew them, and then they would be useless, just more raw mass consigned to the ship's waste-processing system.

We must take our pleasures where we can, he reminded himself as he downed a long draught from his stein of *warnog*, a potent alcohol with a bracing kick and a sharp aftertaste.

A knot of enlisted crewmen sat on the other side of the compartment, hunched over their trays slopped with second-rate blood pies, saying little but filling the air with wet smacks of mastication. Kutal could tell they were behaving self-consciously because he was there, refraining from whatever conversation would normally fill the spaces in their midday meal. The reason for their discomfort was of no interest to Kutal. He simply enjoyed the silence.

He plucked a generous pinch of *gagh* from his dull gray bowl and stuffed the wriggling delicacy into his sharp-toothed maw. Biting down, he was rewarded with their frantic dying squirms and a delectable squirt of warm blood rich with salt and minerals. The delight it brought him verged on the religious, and he shut his eyes to drink in the moment free of distraction. Then he heard the heavy footfalls of his first officer, BelHoQ, and Kutal knew even before the man spoke that his perfect lunch was about to be ruined.

"We have new orders from the High Command, Captain."

The captain shot a murderous look over his shoulder at his black-bearded, wild-maned brute of a first officer. "I'm *eating*, damn you!"

BelHoQ stepped around the table and sat across from Kutal. "*Priority* orders."

Kutal shoved aside his tray. "If you knew good *gagh* from *kesh*, you'd have waited for me to come to the bridge." He reached out and demanded with twitching fingers, "Give it to me." The second-in-command reached under a fold in his tunic and pulled out a data tablet, then shoved it into Kutal's waiting hand. Just as the captain had expected, it contained nothing but bad news. "When did this come in?"

"A few minutes ago."

"It could have waited." He stood, tossed the tablet back to BelHoQ, then abandoned his tray and strode toward the door. BelHoQ followed him out to the corridor and forward, toward the bridge. The two warriors walked side by side through the dim, musky passageways of the *Zin'za*, whose deck plates thrummed with the steady pulse of its warp engines.

BelHoQ grumbled, "*Fek'lhr* take those *petaQpu'* at the High Command. I'd rather be whipped naked against the gate of Gre'thor than trust a Romulan to watch my back."

"Not that we have much choice, now, do we?" They side-stepped past a pair of mechanics effecting repairs at an open bulkhead, then Kutal continued. "I get the feeling someone very high up is in league with the Romulans, and not just for the sake of spiting the Federation."

A low grunt presaged BelHoQ's reply. "I think the Romulans traded their cloaking secrets for safe passage through the Empire so they could gather intelligence for an invasion."

"Maybe. But if so, that's a long way off. Right now, I think their agenda leans more toward corruption than conquest." The port hatch to the bridge slid open ahead of them. Kutal marched to his command chair and shouldered aside Lieutenant Krom, the ship's second officer, along the way. "Krom, report!"

Krom had almost regained his footing when BelHoQ shoved past him and left the shorter soldier off balance and half-sitting on a deactivated gunner's console. Straightening, the young lieutenant tried to act as if neither slight had just happened. "We're continuing on course for the Gonmog Sector, Captain. Standing by to execute course change based on our new orders."

Kutal turned a sour scowl on BelHoQ, silently reproaching him for failing to keep word of the ship's new mission profile from being prematurely leaked to the rank and file. "Helm, set course for our rendezvous with the Romulan cruiser *Kenestra*, in the Hujok system."

Qlar, the helm officer, keyed commands into his console. "Plotted and ready."

"Engage." Kutal swiveled his elevated chair toward the weapons officer. "Tonar! Make sure you read the report on Romulan tactical protocols. We've been ordered to conduct joint operations with our new allies, harassing Federation shipping, until further notice." A curt nod signaled Tonar's understanding, and he set himself to his task without speaking—a habit Kutal wished more of his crew would emulate. Turning forward, Kutal punched his left palm a few times while he pondered the shifting currents of power coursing through the Empire. Then he glanced left, toward BelHoQ, who stood, waiting on the captain's next words. "No good will come of speaking our minds to the High Command. They won't hear ill words spoken against the providers of the great and mighty cloaking device."

"A cowardly invention," BelHoQ sneered.

Waving away the criticism, Kutal replied, "A weapon is neither cowardly nor brave. What matters is how it's used. And I think the Romulans are using it to seduce our leaders—the generals inside the High Command, the heads of the Great Houses, and who knows who else. The point is, we need to choose our friends very carefully."

"With all respect," BelHoQ protested, "we know who our friends are."

"Do we? Just because we've trusted someone in the past doesn't mean we should trust them now. Do some digging. See what secrets our good friends on Qo'noS have buried, and make sure they really are still our friends before we start making new enemies."

A low growl of frustration rumbled deep inside BelHoQ's barrel chest. "Why must we waste time while *novpu'* move freely through our space? Why not take action now?"

"Because we're not preparing for a duel, we're preparing for a war. Which means our first action must be to prepare the battlefield. Remember the lessons of Kahless: the victorious warrior wins first and then goes to war, while the defeated warrior goes to war and only then seeks to win." He met the first officer's sullen gaze with a stare that brooked no dissent. "I will fight this war when I'm ready to win it, my friend—and not a moment sooner."

The rank perfume of coitus assaulted Duras's sensitive nose as he traversed the brothel hallway, passing one curtained partition after another on his way to a clandestine rendezvous.

It struck him as particularly ironic that, of all the possible locations for a meeting in the First City, his contact should choose this one. Normally, as a scion of a Great House, Duras would never come within a hundred *qelIqam*s of such an establishment; if he desired companionship, it would be his for the asking, in the privacy of his own home. Only offworlders and those without honor frequented these places.

As he noted the way in which everyone he passed made a point of avoiding eye contact with him or one another, however, he realized there was a certain perverse logic to this plan. The single most important element of the social contract in a brothel was discretion, making it the one place where people actively avoided remembering, or being remembered by, those around them. It was the most anonymous place in the capital, making it a far more discreet meeting place than his office within the Great Hall, or his estate, which was always under surveillance by operatives employed by his rivals.

He reached the end of the hallway and stopped in front of the drawn curtain on his right. Assured by a furtive glance back the way he'd come that he hadn't been followed, he knocked lightly on the door frame and whispered, "The hunter stands ready."

From within the alcove, a hand jerked the curtain aside. Valina, a striking young Romulan woman of unusual height and beauty, was clad in a sheer negligee that left precious little to Duras's imagination. She flashed a salacious smile. "The prey awaits." With her free hand she pulled Duras to her and met him in a ferocious kiss. Despite her lean physique, her strength never failed to impress him, and though her species resembled the stoic Vulcans, their hearts burned with passions worthy of Klingons. Pulling free of the kiss, she bit Duras's lip, a playful nip just hard enough to break the skin and draw blood.

Duras pushed her aside. "Business first." He turned and pulled the curtain shut behind him. As he stepped farther inside the small room, she stood with her back to the wall, twirling a lock of her long, wavy black hair around one finger and following him with her customary come-hither leer. He wondered if her brazenly sexual demeanor was all an act for his benefit. The first time he met her, she had seemed arch and aloof, just as one would expect of an attaché of the Romulan ambassador to the Klingon Empire. Or had that icy façade been the act, the mask she wore to conceal a lustful inner life? The only way to know for certain would be to untangle Valina's intricate web of lies, a task that Duras suspected could take most men years, and an abundance of time was a luxury he did not have. "You know what I need."

Her leer transformed into a steely glare. "And you know what I *want,* Duras."

"I have it." He reached into an inner pocket of his jacket and took out a data card. On it was a smattering of raw intelligence gathered by the Klingon Defense Forces about the beings known as the Shedai, and the technology their extinct civilization had left strewn throughout the Gonmog Sector. Valina reached for the card, then frowned as Duras pulled it away, teasing her. "This is top-secret information, Valina. I need something of equal value in return."

She narrowed her eyes and lifted her chin, and in the span of a breath she reverted to being the cold-eyed predator he had met months earlier, when the High Council had welcomed the Romulan ambassador and his retinue to Qo'noS. "What do you want?"

"I need to ensure my House's rise within the Empire."

Hostility shone in her dark eyes, betraying her waning patience. "Be specific."

He stepped past her to the bed and ran his finger along the hard, smooth slab, which was surprisingly clean, considering its surroundings. "If an accident were to befall Chancellor Sturka, it could pave the way for my family's advancement inside the High Council."

Valina crossed her arms. "An accident? Or an assassination?"

"Let's not quibble over semantics."

His glib deflection of her query was met by a hard stare. "The Tal Shiar won't do your dirty work for you. If you want Sturka dead, have the spine to do it yourself."

Duras noted the undercurrent of pride in Valina's voice as she'd said "Tal Shiar," and he made two immediate mental connections. First, he inferred from the context that it was likely a proper name for the Romulan Star Empire's military intelligence apparatus, or at least a part of it; second, he surmised that Valina was likely an undercover operative for the organization.

Both useful things to know.

He expunged all aggression from his voice. "In that case, what *can* you do for me?"

"I can give you what you really came for." She flashed an arrogant smirk. "Did you actually think you were being crafty? By asking for something you knew I'd refuse, just to make the thing you really wanted seem reasonable by comparison? If you plan on making a career of lies and deception, you need to work on your conversational tactics." She reached over to a stack of rough towels in the corner by the bed, plucked out the one second from the bottom, and unfolded it to reveal a concealed data card. "It contains all the technical information your House will need to figure out why your attempts to convert our cloaking devices to your ships haven't been working—and how to fix it. With control over this vital tactical asset, the House of Duras can rise in stature through its public actions, and earn the thanks and praise of the Empire."

Duras reached for the card on the towel, but Valina pulled it back and tsk-tsked at him. "You first, my love."

He held up his card of stolen data in two fingers. "Both at the same time." He waited for her to mimic his pose. "On three. One. Two. Three." Their hands struck like serpents, each of them seizing their prize before the other decided to renege on the deal. Then they stood, facing each other, and smiled. "Well," Duras said, "now that that's over. . . ."

They flung the cards aside, and then Valina tackled him to the floor, where Duras found what he had really come for in the first place.

4

Master Chief Petty Officer Mike Ilucci leaned forward—his hands on his knees, sweat running in steady streams from beneath his uncombed black hair, nausea twisting in his gut—and groaned.

Even though Ilucci had been careful to moderate his drinking in recent weeks, since technically the *Sagittarius* crew was not on leave but rather awaiting an opportunity to ship out, he had not been so careful in his choice of cuisines, and his epicurean tendencies seemed to have finally caught up with him. He couldn't say whether the culprit responsible for his current gastrointestinal distress was the highly acidic Pacifican ceviche on which he'd gorged himself the night before, the overly spicy eggs Benedict with chipotle hollandaise sauce over Tabasco-marinated skirt steak he'd enjoyed for breakfast, or the huge portion of obscenely rich linguine carbonara he'd devoured for lunch that afternoon. Or perhaps some combination of the three.

It didn't matter, he decided. Hot swirling pain moved through his gut, and it hurt so badly that he imagined he must have swallowed a plasma drill set on overdrive. All he wanted at that moment was a few minutes of peace to let the agony subside.

A moving shadow intruded upon his view of the deck, and then he saw the feet that trailed behind it. From above his bowed head, he heard the familiar voice of enlisted engineer Crewman Torvin. "You all right, Master Chief?"

Grotesque discomfort put an edge on Ilucci's reply. "Do I *look* all right, Tor?"

The young Tiburonian sounded nervous and concerned. "Anything I can do to help?"

"Yeah. Kill me."

Torvin shuffled his feet, apparently at a loss for a reply. "Um . . ."

"What do you need, Tor?"

The lean, boyish engineer doubled over so he could look Ilucci in the eye. His voice cracked as if he were suffering a relapse of puberty. "Before I kill you, can I get you to sign off on the repulsor grid?"

A tired moan and a grudging nod. "Help me up."

With one hand pushing against Ilucci's shoulder and the other hovering behind the husky chief engineer's back, Torvin guided Ilucci back to an upright stance. The chief cleared his throat and lumbered across the main cargo hold of the civilian super-freighter *S.S. Ephialtes,* with Torvin a few steps ahead of him. Above and around them, teams of engineers and starship repair crews from Vanguard worked under the direction of Ilucci's engineers, installing a host of new systems inside the freighter's recently emptied, titanic main cargo hold. Several decks had been torn out, along with most of the ship's cargo-handling machinery, such as cranes and hoists. The result was a vast, oblong cavity that accounted for the center third of the ship's interior volume.

Torvin led Ilucci to the center of the deck, where he had installed a gray metal hexagonal platform that stood just over a meter tall and measured two meters on each side. The top of the platform was festooned with an array of smaller hexagons composed of a dark, glasslike substance. The enlisted man lifted a tricorder that he wore slung at his hip, keyed in a command, and powered up the repulsor grid. An ominous low hum filled the air for a moment, and then it faded to a barely audible purr. Shrugging out from under the tricorder's strap, Torvin handed the device to Ilucci. "I set the amplitude, frequency, and angles according to your specs." He pointed around the cavernous hold at five other devices: one on the overhead and one on each of the four main bulkheads—forward, aft, port, and starboard. "The load's balanced on a six-point axis, has two redundant fail-safes, and can support five times the mass of the *Sagittarius.*"

Ilucci scrolled through the benchmark tests Torvin had run, then nodded. "Nice work, but if this tub drops too fast from warp to impulse we could plow right through its forward bulkhead and end up as a hood ornament." He shut off the tricorder and handed it back to Torvin. "Do me a favor: hop back to the salvage bay and bring back some more inertial dampers."

"Just me?" Torvin fidgeted and looked over his shoulder.

"Yeah, just you." He paused and eyed his flummoxed engineer. "Why? What's the problem? Afraid you'll get lost?"

The youth palmed the sweat from his shaved head and absent-mindedly tugged on one of his oversized, finlike Tiburonian earlobes. "No, I, um . . ." He took a breath and calmed himself. "I don't think the civvies on this ship are too thrilled about us ripping up their hold."

The chief couldn't suppress a sympathetic frown. "I wouldn't be, either, if I was them." Noting the fearful look on Torvin's face, he lowered his voice. "Did someone threaten you?"

"Let's just say I think it might be a good idea if we moved in pairs for a while."

He gave Torvin a reassuring pat on the shoulder. "Noted." Then he turned and waved to get the attention of the *Sagittarius*'s senior engineer's mate, Petty Officer First Class Salagho Threx. The hulking, hirsute Denobulan nodded back, then crossed the cargo hold at an awkward jog until he joined Torvin and Ilucci, both of whom he dwarfed with ease. "Yeah, Chief?"

"Tor says the civvies have a bug up their collective ass about us gutting their boat, and he thinks they might be looking for a bit of payback on any Starfleet folks they catch alone in the passageways between here and the station."

Threx looked unsurprised. "I get the same feeling, Master Chief."

"Okay. Go with Tor and get a pallet of inertial dampers to beef up this repulsor grid. And if any of those grease monkeys start some shit, you have my permission to kick their asses."

"Copy that, Master Chief." The bearded giant of a Denobulan beckoned Torvin with a tilt of his head. "Let's roll." The two engineers walked toward the exit, both keeping their heads on swivels, looking out for trouble from whatever direction it might come.

Ilucci turned, hoping he might slip away to some dark corner of the freighter to collapse into a coma until his stomach cramps abated, but instead found himself face-to-face with another of his engineers, Petty Officer Second Class Karen Cahow. The short, indefatigable tomboy had grease on her standard-issue olive-green jumpsuit and grime in her dark blond hair, but she looked ecstatically happy. "I figured out how to mask us from sensors in transit!"

The bedraggled chief engineer tried to shuffle past her. "Good job. I'll put your name in for a medal." His escape was halted by her hand grasping the upper half of his rolled-up sleeve.

"Don't you want to hear how I did it?"

Overcoming his urge to retch, he turned and smiled. "Are you sure it works?"

Her face was bright with pride. "Positive."

"Then I'll look forward to reading your report." The perky polymath started to protest, so he cut her off. "Later. *Capisce?*"

His urgency seemed to drive the point home for her. "Got it."

"Good. Now go make sure this boat's ventral doors are rigged for rapid deployment. And if you need me, just follow the stench till you find my shallow grave."

"Will do, Master Chief." Cahow bounded away, a bundle of energy so infused with optimism that it made Ilucci want to drink himself stupid and spend a week asleep.

He made it to the cargo hold's exit, where he collided with the first officer of the *Sagittarius,* Commander Clark Terrell. The lanky, brown-skinned XO had the muscled physique of a prizefighter and the razor-sharp, lightning-quick intellect of a scientist.

Probably because he's both, Ilucci mused. During their years of service together on the *Sagittarius,* he'd learned that Terrell, in addition to having double-specialized in xenobiology and impulse propulsion systems, had been one of the stars of the Starfleet Academy boxing team.

Terrell cracked a brilliantly white grin. "How goes it, Master Chief?"

"By the numbers, sir. We'll be ready to vent the hold and move our boat in here by 0300 tomorrow." He rapped one knuckle against the top of his head. "Knock on wood."

"Outstanding, Chief." He studied Ilucci with a critical eye. "Are you all right?"

Ilucci swallowed hard, forcing a surge of sour bile back whence it came. "Nothing a year in the tropics wouldn't fix, sir." Eager to change the subject, he glanced upward and asked, "How's Captain Alodae taking the news?"

The query drew a snort and a chortle from the commander, who shook his head in glum amusement. "Let's just say I'm glad I'm down here with you right now."

"That well, huh?"

"Master Chief, you don't even want to know."

Nogura stood his ground as Captain Alodae jabbed him in the chest with his index finger and raged, "I'm not signing anything! You people have no right to take my ship or my cargo!"

The thick-middled, heavily jowled Rigelian drew his hand back to poke Nogura a second time, only to find his wrist seized mid-thrust by the cobralike grab of T'Prynn, whose gaze was as fearsomely cold as her voice. "Control yourself, Captain."

Watching from just beyond arm's reach, the other officers at the meeting—Captain Adelard Nassir of the *Sagittarius* and Lieutenant Commander Holly Moyer from Vanguard's office of the Starfleet Judge Advocate General, or JAG—tensed in anticipation of violence.

Alodae retreated half a step from Nogura and jerked his hand free of T'Prynn's grip. A flurry of emotions distorted his tattooed face, then his nostrils flared as he drew a deep breath. Features still crinkled with anger, he bowed his head to Nogura. "My apologies, Admiral."

Nogura replied with curt formality, "Apology accepted, Captain."

Though he was obviously still furious, Alodae reined in his temper enough to lower his voice to just less than a shout. "My point stands. This is a violation of my rights, as well as the rights of my crew, passengers, and employer. You can't just press us into service and use us any way you like. The Federation has laws against this kind of thing."

"Very true," Nogura said. "Unfortunately, we're not inside the Federation."

Looking as if he'd just been slapped with a dead fish, Alodae stammered, "Huh—what?"

Moyer stepped in from the conversational sideline. "I'm afraid that's technically correct, Captain." The svelte redhead flinched slightly as the fuming Rigelian turned his ire toward her, but she rallied her confidence and continued. "Despite the presence of Starbase 47 as a hub for colonization, commerce, and exploration, formal jurisdiction over this sector remains in dispute. And because this is a Starfleet facility rather than a civilian one, the only law in effect here is the Starfleet Code of Military Justice, which does, in fact, authorize us to commandeer vessels and personnel when required to defend Federation security." She handed Alodae a data slate.

He glanced at it, then at the Starfleet officers surrounding him. "What if I refuse and tell you to get your people off my ship so we can leave?"

Nogura shrugged. "Then we'd continue this discussion in the brig."

Moyer added, "You and your crew would be placed under arrest, and Starfleet would impound your vessel. Then we'd issue your ship a military registration, crew it with our own people, and proceed with the operation we've already described to you."

The Rigelian merchant captain's visage was a taut mask of

contempt. "I see. So, that's it? You hijack my ship and my crew, and we just have to roll over and take it?"

"Well, Starfleet would compensate your employer for the ship, if it came to that," Moyer said. "Also, you and your crew and passengers would be provided with transport to the nearest Federation port of call and given vouchers for whatever destinations you choose beyond that."

Alodae narrowed his eyes. "How generous of you."

"However," T'Prynn cut in, "if you comply with our requests, you would nominally retain command of your vessel, and after the *Sagittarius* separates from yours at the Iremal Cluster, you would be free to continue on your way."

Swiveling his head toward the Vulcan, Alodae asked, "And what about my lost profits, Lieutenant? An empty ship might use less fuel than a full one, but flying empty also burns up time and money. Our margins were razor thin *before* you folks forced us to do charity work."

Nogura traded a look with Moyer, then he said to Alodae, "If it's purely a matter of remuneration, I'm sure we can negotiate a fair settlement."

"I'll take you up on that, but it's not just about the money." Alodae aimed his ire at Nassir. "If I use my ship to sneak yours away from this station, that puts my ship and crew at risk. We'd stop being civilians and become legitimate military targets."

The short, bald, and slightly built Deltan starship captain projected placidity as he answered the beefy Rigelian. "Respectfully, Captain, you and your ship are already targets, every time you cross the Federation border into the Taurus Reach. The Klingons and the Tholians don't care about the legal niceties of your ship's status. If they decide to board you or blow you to kingdom come, they will. The only difference between this trip and any other you've made in this sector is that, this time, Starfleet will be watching over you every step of the way."

Alodae surrendered to the inevitable. "Fine. Do what you

want. But you'd better believe I plan to lodge a formal complaint with the Federation Council after I get my ship home."

"We would expect nothing less," said Nogura.

The Rigelian frowned at Moyer. "Let's go set a price for this little adventure of yours."

As the JAG officer turned to lead Alodae out of Nogura's office, Nassir took half a step toward the man. "Captain, I just want to thank you on behalf of—"

"Blow it out your ass," Alodae groused. "And tell your crew that once we're on our way, I don't want to see you or any of them inside *my* ship."

Nassir mustered a polite smile. "You won't even know we're there."

"Somehow, I doubt that." Alodae turned and motioned for Moyer to continue, and the two of them left the office. The hum of activity from the operations center briefly filtered in through the open doorway as they made their exit, then the door hushed closed, and silence reigned inside the admiral's sanctum.

"Well," Nassir said to no one in particular, "that went better than I expected."

Nogura walked to his desk and sat down. "Alodae says he'll cooperate, but I don't trust him. He's willful. And proud." He steepled his fingers while he considered the situation, and Nassir and T'Prynn waited quietly for him to continue. Then he made up his mind, pressed his palms on the desktop, and pushed himself back to his feet as he looked at Nassir. "Have your chief engineer make sure your bridge crew controls the cargo hold doors on the *Ephialtes*. I don't want Alodae or his crew ejecting your ship without permission."

"Yes, sir."

He shifted his gaze to T'Prynn. "Post a security team on the *Ephialtes* to make sure its crew don't do anything to jeopardize the mission."

"Understood, Admiral. What rationale shall I give Captain Alodae for their presence?"

Nogura stroked his chin. "Tell him they're just passengers,

heading home now that they've finished their tours of duty. And add their fares to his compensation package."

"Very good. Shall I book them in the first-class cabins?" She noted the incredulous stares of both Nogura and Nassir, then arched one brow in sardonic understanding. "No, of course not. Such generosity by Starfleet would be certain to draw suspicion. Steerage it is, then."

5

Reality was a muddy blur as Cervantes Quinn blundered through the cobblestone lanes of Stars Landing, a cluster of residential and commercial buildings tucked inside the expansive terrestrial enclosure that occupied the upper half of Vanguard's saucer hull. Every step he took was a dare to the station's artificial gravity to pull him down and drop him on his face. His vision and his memory both were dulled by bourbon, a result entirely of his own design. For a few blessed seconds, he could neither see where he was nor remember where he was going.

Such moments had become all that he lived for, the holy grail of his existence. In the months since he had come back from the mission that claimed his beloved Bridy, he had become a surgeon with a shot glass, and whiskey was his scalpel: He used it to carve away his sorrows.

Stumbling half-blind, he relished the near-constant sensation of free fall, the feeling that at any moment he might plunge down a rabbit hole into endless darkness. He longed for such oblivion, for a total divorce from his memories. Then he recalled where he was going: back to his apartment, a depressing hovel adorned by only a few meager furnishings and an ever-growing number of carpet stains. There he would slip into a dreamless and fitful slumber and pray this might be the night when he finally choked to death on his own vomit.

Best not to get my hopes up, he cautioned himself. *Otherwise I'll just be sad when I wake up tomorrow, alive and feeling like hammered crap.*

He was in no hurry to get home—or anywhere else for that matter. Most of the reputable drinking establishments in Stars Landing had long since eighty-sixed him for one thing or another.

Starting fights, or not paying his tab, or urinating on the bar; it was always something.

Bereft of hope as well as a destination, he spent most of his days hiding from the station's simulated daylight, and most of his nights dragging his sorry ass from one joint to another in an ever more difficult search for someone who'd serve him a goddamned drink. Morose and at a loss for any other reason to go on, he drifted alone through the twisted wreckage of his life, turning in steadily shrinking circles while waiting for the Great Drain of Time to suck him whole into its infinite abyss and put an end to his misery.

Quinn's toe caught on the edge of a cobblestone. His elbows hit the road, followed a moment later by his face, and he thought perhaps he'd finally gotten his wish. Then the sharp pain of impact faded to a dull ache of bruises and the steady throb of a fresh gash on his chin. He reached up with one dirty hand and palmed away the bright red blood running in a thick stream over his Adam's apple, and he chuckled at the hopeless stupidity of his life.

He was still gathering the will to stand when a pair of feet edged into his sharply limited field of vision. A few hard blinks and a deep breath improved his sight from triplicate to duplicate, and he lifted his head to see who was looming over him. It came as little surprise to find freelance journalist Tim Pennington looking back at him. "Hey, Newsboy," he slurred.

The fair-haired, Scotland-born writer looked annoyingly fit, in a yogurt-and-yoga kind of way. His smile felt condescending. "Quinn. I see you found the fast track back to the gutter."

"Yeah, but I'm looking up at the stars."

Pennington looked up. "Those are holograms." Back down at Quinn. "Can you even see them through those whiskey goggles you call eyes?"

"No, but I know they're there. And they're lookin' back at me." *And laughing.*

The younger man kneeled and tried to snake his hands under Quinn's armpits, but the grizzled old pilot and soldier of fortune shook him off with a violent spasm of twists and jerks.

"Let me help you up," Pennington said. "We need to get you home." He reached out again, and this time Quinn was too tired to struggle, so he let his body go limp and transform into dead weight in Pennington's hands. "Come on, you stupid tosser, get up."

Drool spilled from the corner of Quinn's mouth and ran down his shirt as he mumbled in a pathetic monotone, "Leave me here."

Pennington's voice cracked from exertion. "Not a chance."

Exhibiting a degree of stubbornness Quinn hadn't known the man had, Pennington snuck under Quinn's arm and draped it across his shoulders, then forced him to his feet. Despite thinking he would passively resist, Quinn found his feet keeping step with Tim's as the writer lurched forward and led Quinn down a street of blurry lights and murky shadows. "You're doing great, mate," he said. "Just a bit farther."

They might have been lumbering along for seconds or minutes—Quinn couldn't really tell—but he lost hold of his anger and sank into maudlin gratitude. "Thanks."

Pennington's voice was taut from the strain of carrying Quinn. "You're welcome."

Not certain he'd made his point, Quinn added, following a wet and odiferous belch, "No, really, I mean it, thanks. I'm glad you found me instead of . . . instead of those security goons."

Pennington guided Quinn around a corner. "They aren't looking for you."

"The hell they ain't. Busted up some shit real good down at Shannon's."

"I squared that, mate. Paid for what you broke. Got the charges dropped." As they started up some stairs, Quinn's head dipped forward, and he found himself hypnotized by the off-sync spectacle of their moving shoes. Pennington's feet stepped straight and sure, Quinn's splayed in a pigeon-toed pantomime of alcoholic ineptitude.

Weaving and staggering down an open-air promenade, Quinn began to recognize familiar details of the residential building in which he lived. Even in his deeply sotted state, he knew that without Pennington's guidance, he would never have been able to tell one of the station's prefabricated living modules from any other, much less have found his own door in this rat's maze from hell. Then he caught up with the conversation of a minute earlier. *Newsboy's probably the only reason I ain't in the brig right now.* "How 'bout my other bar tabs?"

"Settled," Pennington said.

They stopped in front of a door that Quinn assumed must be his own. With effort, he swiveled his head toward Pennington, only to find the man's face too close for him to focus on. "So, does that mean I can go back to Tom Walker's place?"

"No. It just means he won't press charges." The door opened, and Pennington dragged Quinn inside. He led him to a sofa whose upholstery had already suffered a terrifying number of indignities caused by Quinn's headlong plunge off the wagon of sobriety, and then he slipped out from under Quinn's arm and let him collapse onto the sofa.

"Home sweet home," Quinn mumbled into the cushion.

Pennington took a moment to prop Quinn on his side, using pillows to prevent him from rolling onto his back. Then he fetched a small trash can from the kitchenette and placed it next to the sofa. He ran a hand through his sweat-soaked hair. "Need anything else?"

Quinn thought he should find some way to thank Pennington, some way to reward him for playing the part of his guardian angel despite all the stupid crap Quinn had said to him, for being such a good friend to him despite all the misery Quinn had brought into his life, most of it unintentional but a catastrophe nonetheless. Of all the people he had ever known, Pennington was one of the few he still knew who hadn't written him off as a lost cause. That deserved some kind of recognition. At the very least, it merited a sincere word of thanks. Something.

"Tim . . . ," he began.

His stomach twisted in a knot, his chest heaved, and he puked a gutful of half-digested food and bile that reeked of sour mash, all over Pennington's feet.

He was almost grateful to lose consciousness before having to say he was sorry.

Doctor Carol Marcus was on the move and in no mood to stop for anyone or anything. She passed one of her colleagues after another as she circled the main isolation chamber located in the center of the Vault. The recently rebuilt, state-of-the-art top-secret research facility lay deep inside the core of Starbase 47, and it was the most heavily shielded and redundantly equipped section of the entire Watchtower-class space station.

"Watch those power levels," she said to Doctor Hofstadter as she passed his console. "We can't afford a spike." The dark-haired, bespectacled researcher nodded once in confirmation of Marcus's instruction, then he resumed his work. Striding past another station, Marcus paused long enough to lean past Doctor Tarcoh, a spindly, soft-spoken Deltan man of middle years. She activated a function on his panel. "Remember to keep the sensors in passive mode. I don't want to feed this thing any signals it can use. You saw what happened last time." Tarcoh continued his work, duly chastised for his error.

The "last time" Marcus had spoken of, and which every scientist on her team recalled all too vividly, was a disastrous attempt to make contact with a Shedai trapped inside a Mirdonyae Artifact identical to the one still housed inside the Vault's main isolation chamber. The steps that had been necessary to transmit a signal through the artifact's baffling subatomic lattices had also enabled the creature snared inside it to replenish its power and exploit damage the Federation researchers had unwittingly wrought in the artifact. That error had led to an explosive episode of escape and the violent destruction of the Starfleet Corps of Engineers vessel *U.S.S. Lovell*.

As she moved around the laboratory, checking status gauges and second-guessing all her colleagues' work, her Starfleet counterpart, Lieutenant Ming Xiong, fell into step beside her. "He's still waiting for you in your office," Xiong said.

The reminder turned her mood into thin ice—cold and brittle. "Let him wait."

Marcus kept moving, and Xiong followed her. "He's showing you a courtesy by coming down here. He could've had you hauled up to his office."

She ignored Xiong's warning and took a moment to sidle up to Doctor Koothrappali. "Keep an eye on the plasma capacitors. If they redline, dump the charge through the station's main deflector dish. Don't ask for permission, don't wait to be told. Just do it."

The longer Marcus pretended nothing was wrong, the more apparent Xiong's anxiety became. "This isn't a joke, Doctor. And it's not some mere formality."

"When did *you* become such a stickler for rules and regulations?" As soon as she'd said it, she felt a pang of regret, because Xiong's reflexive wince told her she'd struck a nerve. The young lieutenant had once enjoyed a reputation on Vanguard as a maverick and iconoclast. The last few years, however, had broken his spirit by slow degrees; the final straw had been the recent demise of his friend Lieutenant Commander Bridget McLellan, known to her friends as Bridy Mac. The former second officer of the *Sagittarius,* McLellan had been reassigned to Starfleet Intelligence as a covert operative attached to Operation Vanguard. Xiong had often spoken of her as his "big sister." Her death in the line of duty, while on a mission to which he had assigned her, had left him emotionally devastated for weeks.

She reached out, gently grasped his upper arm, and stepped away from the workstations with him. "I'm sorry. I wasn't trying to say that . . . you know . . ."

"I know what you were trying to say."

Realizing there was no quick fix for the hurt she'd just inflicted, Marcus chose to change the subject. "All right, you win. Let's go talk to him." Over her shoulder, she called to the other scientists, "Everyone, I'll just be a minute. Don't start the procedure till I get back."

Neither she nor Xiong spoke as they walked to her office. The door whished open ahead of her, and she entered her tidy private work space to find the station's chief of security, Lieutenant Haniff Jackson, standing in front of her desk, facing the door, waiting for her. The broad-shouldered man looked decidedly displeased by the prolonged wait she had inflicted on him. "Doctor. Nice of you to join me. I was beginning to think you'd fled the station."

"Are you kidding me?" She edged past him to get behind her desk and reclaim the room's sole power position. Turning back to face him, she continued. "This whole place has been turned into a fortress. Armed guards at the only entrance, weapons systems inside the lab waiting to unleash holy hell, all on the word of someone up in ops. I doubt I could escape if I wanted to."

The zeal with which she'd delivered her harangue seemed to have embarrassed Xiong, who avoided her gaze, choosing instead to stare at his shoes as if they were the most interesting things he had ever seen. Jackson, meanwhile, seemed not the least bit put off by her tirade. "Doctor, I understand that the enhanced security measures we've installed here in the Vault might seem a bit excessive—"

She was livid. "A bit? Reactor-grade reinforced bulkheads? Fast-acting antimatter self-destruct packages built into the floors? Why would I find that excessive?"

"I appreciate your sarcasm, Doctor. Really, I do. But you need to understand that Admiral Nogura doesn't share my carefree sense of humor. Especially when it comes to violations of the security protocols regarding off-station communications."

"You mean when I decide my rights to free expression trump your right to censor me."

Palms upturned, Jackson said, "That's one way of putting it."

"I am so sick of Starfleet and its euphemisms," Marcus said. "Call it what it is: censorship. I, for one, won't stand for it. I have rights as a Federation citizen."

Her declaration left Jackson looking pained. "Actually, ma'am, out here, you don't. Right now you're on a Starfleet base, which means you need to live and work by our rules."

Marcus felt a wave of heat prickle her scalp and knew her face had flushed with anger. "That is *not* what I signed on for, Lieutenant. I never agreed to those terms."

"It doesn't matter what you agreed to or think you agreed to. I'm just telling you how it is." He leaned forward and tapped a data slate that he had left in the center of her desktop. "This is an official warning from Admiral Nogura. Do not share *any* of your research data with anyone off this station, no matter how innocuous or generic you think that data is."

"You've got to be kidding me." She looked to Xiong, hoping, perhaps irrationally, that he might leap to her defense if prompted. "Xiong, explain to this man that independent peer review is an essential component of all serious research."

Xiong lifted his eyes from the floor long enough to glance sheepishly into Jackson's unyielding stare, then he cast an apologetic look at Marcus. "I'm sorry, Doctor, but I have to agree with Starfleet on this one. We can't let even one shred of this data out of here. Not yet."

Jaw agape, Marcus shouted at her colleague, "Are you serious? That's it? You're just going to roll over and play dead? I thought you were a scientist, Ming!"

An awkward hush filled the room. Jackson cleared his throat and stiffened his posture. "Please read the memo from Admiral Nogura, ma'am. If you violate the station's security protocols again, we'll reserve the right to impose punitive measures in order—"

"Screw your security protocols. And get the hell out of my office. *Now*."

Jackson forced a polite if joyless smile onto his face. "As you wish, Doctor." He dipped his chin toward Xiong. "Lieutenant." Then he turned on his heel and left the office.

The moment the door closed behind him, Xiong looked up at Marcus with pleading eyes. "Are you crazy? What the hell are you thinking, provoking him like that?"

Disgusted with Starfleet in general and Xiong in particular, she flashed an angry look as she marched past him on her way back to work. "Isn't it obvious? I'm trying to get fired."

• • •

The night life in Stars Landing was winding down as Pennington ambled homeward, stopping every few paces to kick some newly discovered fleck of Quinn's emesis from his shoes.

It was late, just after 0215 according to the station's chronometer, to which he'd synchronized his wrist chrono. Most of the commercial businesses in Stars Landing had closed hours earlier, and now the restaurants and drinking establishments were ejecting their patrons, the courtesies of last call fulfilled. Watching the ordinary folks of Vanguard—enlisted personnel, civilian residents, transient colonists waiting for a chance to depart for some new life—he imagined that Quinn must once have counted himself among their number. Watching his friend and former accomplice in adventure accelerate into a downward spiral saddened him. Quinn's grief was so raw that it resurrected Pennington's memories of Oriana D'Amato, his own lost love, who had perished years earlier when the Tholians destroyed the *U.S.S. Bombay*.

He had thought his own experiences would give him some insight into Quinn's state, some clue how to guide the man through his labyrinth of mourning and back to the world of the still-living. Instead, he'd discovered the hard way that each person's path through the valley of the shadow was as unique as their own soul, and that everyone had to make the journey alone.

All I can do is be there and keep him from ending up dead or in jail, he decided. *The rest has to be up to him.*

Submerged in his own thoughts, he almost failed to notice the faint echo of music from somewhere nearby. He stopped and looked around, and saw that he was outside the front door of Manón's cabaret, an upscale establishment that had become one of Stars Landing's most popular nightspots as well as Vanguard's de facto officers' club. The cabaret was closed and dark, and its front entrance was locked when he tried it. Then he put his ear against a window and listened.

Through the glass, he heard a few awkward notes from the cabaret's baby grand piano. *Plink. Plunk.* There was no melody, no rhythm to them. They conjured for Pennington the image of someone who didn't know how to play tapping distractedly at the keys. Despite the haphazard nature of the sound, he was certain he could still sense some kind of emotion behind it—a quiet despair, a longing. He lifted his ear from the glass and tried to peek inside, but the interior blinds were drawn shut, denying him a view of the player.

His curiosity aroused, Pennington circled the building and slipped down the alleyway that ran behind it. Moving in careful, light steps, he approached the restaurant's rear service entrance and was pleased to discover it slightly ajar. He pulled the door open just wide enough to slip inside, then he eased it back to the way he'd found it.

Once inside, he heard the atonal playing more clearly. He skulked across the kitchen and stopped at the door to the dining room. Peering through its small, eye-level window, he saw T'Prynn sitting at the piano, her fingers hesitating above the keys as if she had never touched the instrument before. Her back was to him, so he couldn't see her face, but the way she bowed her head and half clenched her right hand spoke volumes to Pennington about the frustration the Vulcan woman must be feeling. Most members of her species were psychologically inscrutable to him, but he had spent several months traveling incognito with T'Prynn after helping her escape Starfleet custody on Vulcan—a ruse that had involved her adopting a fake identity and then marrying Pennington to claim the legal benefits of Earth citizenship, in order to exempt herself from some of her homeworld's more draconian security policies. As a result of the time they had spent together, he had learned to read the subtle cues of her moods in a way that very few others on the station ever had, or likely ever would.

He recalled watching her play that piano, on that stage, just a couple of years earlier. Her virtuosity had stunned him as much as her choice of portfolio—songs drawn from catalogs of up-tempo Terran blues and jazz, music of tremendous complexity and expressiveness. She had been able to inspire crowds to standing ovations after performing a single number. Her long, graceful fingers had tickled those keys with subtlety or pounded them without mercy, but always with passion and precision. Now she hunched over the immaculately polished Steinway and poked at it like a child prodding a dead animal with a stick, a portrait of uncertainty and sorrow.

Pennington nudged open the kitchen's swinging door and sidled into the dining room, hoping to approach a bit closer before announcing himself. As soon as he let the kitchen door close, T'Prynn stopped, turned her head, and stared directly at him.

He was annoyed at being found out so easily. *Damn that Vulcan hearing.*

T'Prynn stood and hurried down the stage steps, then slalomed through the tables and chairs toward him. "What are you doing here, Mister Pennington?"

Hooking his thumb backward, he said, "I heard the music from outside."

"And you used it as a rationale for trespassing?"

He recoiled from the accusation. "What about you?"

She stopped in front of him. "I'm here with Manón's permission."

Looking up slightly to meet her confrontational stare, he was struck by the imposing quality of her dark beauty. "I'm sorry, I didn't mean to intrude."

She took him by the arm and pulled him back the way he'd come, through the kitchen. "If you have no further business here, I'd suggest—"

"Hang on," he cut in, stumbling to keep up with her. "Maybe I can help."

"I don't need your help." She pushed open the rear exit and shoved Pennington through the doorway, back out to the alley behind the cabaret.

He spun back to face her and grabbed the door's edge. "I remember how you used to play. You stopped after your breakdown. They're connected, aren't they?"

"Most insightful," T'Prynn said. "But I don't wish to discuss it." She tried to shut the door, but he held it open, albeit with great difficulty. "Let me go."

He shook his head. "Not till you talk to me. I was there the day you saw the *Malacca* get bombed. I saw the look on your face, and I knew it, 'cause I'd seen it on mine the day I lost someone I loved." His words seemed to crack T'Prynn's stern façade, and he saw a fleeting instant of vulnerability in her eyes. Remembering her sexual orientation, he took a chance on a wild guess. "What was her name, T'Prynn?"

She didn't answer him, but the momentary anguish that possessed her features told him he had deduced the nature of her distress. Visibly struggling to recover her composure, she succeeded only in transforming grief to fury. "Go home, Tim." Then she yanked the door closed with overwhelming force, and Pennington let it go to prevent her from amputating his fingers.

The door slammed shut, and he heard its lock click into place.

Everyone makes their journey alone.

6

Nogura set the data slate on his desk, reclined his chair, and rubbed his eyes. It was the middle of the night, close to 0300, the scheduled launch time of the *Ephialtes,* and he was burning the midnight oil so that the *Sagittarius* and her crew would not embark for danger while he slept.

There was no shortage of work demanding his attention. He had asked for a steady stream of hot tea and productive distractions, and his three yeomen had obliged him, one duty shift at a time. From 0800 to 1600, Lieutenant Toby Greenfield had piled his desk high with the latest news and administrative paperwork from the Federation's numerous colonies throughout the Taurus Reach. From 1600 to midnight, Ensign Suzie Finneran had buried Nogura beneath an avalanche of reports from the station's department heads, including maintenance, security, and engineering, as well as an update from Starfleet Command on the latest fleet deployments. He had found the criminal-activity reports especially entertaining reading, and so had saved most of them to enjoy while he ate his dinner.

For the past three hours, he had been attended by his gamma shift yeoman, Lieutenant Lisa McMullan, a cherub-cheeked woman in her twenties. She managed to convey both joviality and professionalism with her easy manner and quick smile, and she had been intuitive enough to sense that as Nogura's day dragged into its twenty-first hour it might be time to fill his docket with lighter fare. She had loaded a slate with all his unread personal correspondence from home and had even been savvy enough to secure the latest recording from his favorite jazz quartet back on Earth, an album of music that fused classical jazz styles with the Mardi Gras chants of New Orleans' traditional Creole Indians. It was utterly unlike anything else Nogura had ever heard. Listening to it inside the refuge of his office, he marveled at the way a single piece of music could bridge the gulfs between centuries, cultures, and ideas.

The buzz of his intercom broke the music's enthralling spell. He turned down the volume and then opened the channel. "Yes?"

McMullan replied, *"You have a visitor, sir."*

He furrowed his brow in disbelief. "At this hour?"

"It's Doctor Fisher, sir."

That was two bits of unexpected news in quick succession. "Send him in."

The door opened with a soft pneumatic hiss, and Doctor Ezekiel Fisher, the station's chief medical officer, walked in and saluted Nogura with a data slate. "Evening, Admiral."

"Doctor. Everything all right?"

Fisher stopped in front of Nogura's desk, looking quite mellow. "Couldn't be righter."

Nogura leaned forward and folded his hands on the desktop. "So. What brings you here at oh-dark-hundred?" He held up his hand to forestall Fisher's response. "No, wait, let me guess." After a pause for dramatic effect, he added, "I'm overdue for my annual physical."

The elderly surgeon grinned, his perfectly white teeth brilliant in the middle of his deep brown face. "Probably. But that's no skin off my nose. Care to guess again?"

"An outbreak of Typerian meningitis aboard the station?"

Amused, Fisher shook his head. "Not that I've heard."

Nogura was too fatigued to continue with guessing or small talk. "Out with it, then."

Fisher handed him a data slate and waited until the admiral activated it before he spoke. "I'm resigning my commission and my post, effective immediately."

The news left Nogura dumbfounded. He put down the slate. "Why?"

"The simple truth?" Fisher looked tired. "There's nothing left here to make me want to stay." He gestured at one of the chairs in front of Nogura's desk. "May I?" Nogura motioned for the man to sit down, and once Fisher had settled into a chair, he continued. "I was halfway out the door to my retirement when this assignment landed in my lap. The only reason I took it was to be there for Diego. After all we'd been through, I felt like I owed it to him."

A veteran of many such obligations born of shared service, Nogura sympathized. "I understand. You and Commodore Reyes served together for a long time."

"Yes, we did." Fisher turned thoughtful. "After I thought he'd been killed in the ambush on the *Nowlan,* I stayed here to look after Rana. I knew how much she'd meant to him, and I couldn't leave until I knew she'd be okay."

Nogura had known that Fisher and Captain Rana Desai, the former ranking officer of the station's JAG division, were friends, but he hadn't really understood the context of their relationship until that moment. "I'm sure Captain Desai was grateful for your support."

A sad smile. "She was, in her own way." His leaden sigh conveyed the totality of his exhaustion. "But now she and Diego are both gone—her back to Earth, and him to God knows where. And I'm here all alone." He reacted as if to a private joke. "Isn't that a funny thing to say? Sitting here, surrounded by thousands of people, and I feel *alone.*"

"It's not such a strange concept. Trust me: I speak from experience."

The surgeon leaned back and folded his hands in his lap. "Bottom line: I'm too old for this kind of work. It's time for me to go home and spend the rest of my life with my family."

The admiral nodded in approval. "As noble a goal as any. Where's home for you?"

"These days? Mars. My daughter has a medical practice in Cydonia."

"Very nice." Nogura picked up the data slate and skimmed its terse letter of resignation. "I'll be sorry to lose you, Doctor. But I can't fault your reasons. I'll approve your resignation on an interim basis, but I can't arrange your transfer home until Starfleet Command and Starfleet Medical sign off."

Fisher nodded. "I understand. There's nothing harder to shake off than bureaucracy." He eyed the slate. "I included a short list of attending physicians at Vanguard Hospital who I think would be qualified to take my place. For the time being, I've appointed my chief attending as acting CMO. You can decide for yourself whether you want to keep him or not."

"Fine." Nogura hoped the advisory he was about to give didn't prove too disappointing. "Just so you know, the Klingons and the Romulans have been playing hell with our commercial and civilian traffic out here lately. Everyone's running behind schedule as a result. It might take a few weeks or even longer to book you a spot on a transport headed home."

The bad news drew a good-natured chortle from Fisher. "That's all right," he said. "Now I'll have a chance to catch up on my reading."

Sleep eluded Captain Adelard Nassir. It had always been that way for him on the eve of a mission, but this assignment left him grappling with a peculiar blend of anxiety and restlessness. He tried to chalk it up to encroaching middle age, but he knew the root cause was his temporary lack of control over his circumstances. Shipping out, even into grave peril, was an exciting time for any starship commander. Occupying the center seat, with the universe stretching past on the main viewscreen, gave one a sense of possibilities, of facing one's destiny head-on.

On this occasion, however, the *Sagittarius* was being carried off in the belly of a great metal leviathan. Trapped inside the cargo hold of the *Ephialtes,* there was nothing Nassir or his crew could do. They weren't in control of their fate, they were just passengers, and their ship naught but freight. It was a humbling experience, exacerbated by the open resentment and hostility of the civilian crew that had been pressed into portering them.

Agitated and wide awake, the slim and short Deltan captain

stepped out of his private quarters—a privilege limited to himself and the first officer—into his ship's circular main passageway. He drank in the sounds of routine life aboard the tiny scout ship. To his right was the bridge, located at the leading edge of the ship's saucer. He went left, past the unisex head and showers. Water was running in one of the stalls, and clouds of vapor billowed out of the open doorway, accompanied by deep and melodious singing. The voice belonged to the senior engineer's mate, Salagho Threx. Nassir had been enthralled the first time he overheard the man belt out what he assumed were Denobulan folk tunes. Then he'd asked Threx to translate the lyrics and had been appalled to find the songs he'd so admired were positively obscene.

Cabin 3—which was assigned to Doctor Lisa Babitz, the chief medical officer, and Lieutenant Celerasayna zh'Firro, the second officer and senior pilot—was silent. Cabin 4, on the other hand, rumbled with the sawing snore of Master Chief Ilucci. Nassir wondered how Ilucci's cabinmates could stand it—especially Sorak, the elderly Vulcan senior recon scout, with those supersensitive ears of his.

I guess people can learn to adapt to anything, Nassir figured.

He kept on walking, past the lifeboat he prayed he'd never have to use, and then past the open space of the ship's mess, which doubled as its conference room. Medical technician Ensign Nguyen Tan Bao sat alone at one table, picking at what appeared to be a reconstituted bowl of tofu stir-fry. Lieutenant Dastin sat on the other side of the mess, nursing a mug of something hot while reading a well-worn copy of the interstellar bestselling novel *Sunrise on Zeta Minor.* Each man wore the ship's standard uniform, an olive green utility jumpsuit that had the crew member's name stitched above the left breast and a *Sagittarius* insignia patch on the right shoulder, but no rank insignia. Because the ship's typical mission profile was based on long-range pathfinding and reconnaissance, its fourteen-person crew survived long missions in tight quarters by taking a relaxed and highly informal approach to uniforms and protocol. Each member of the crew also had to be cross-trained in multiple mission specialties in order to qualify for a spot on the *Archer*-class vessel—even Nassir himself, who, in addition to being skilled in starship combat tactics, had trained in both cryptography and warp propulsion at Starfleet Academy.

Passing beneath the ladder that led up to the transporter bay and engineering deck, as well as down to the cargo hold, Nassir heard sounds of life from both directions. From above came the voices of engineer Karen Cahow and science officer Lieutenant Vanessa Theriault. He couldn't discern what they were saying, but the two women clearly found their discussion hilarious: Cahow's effervescent, unabashed laughter pealed down the ladder-way, drowning out Theriault's more demure but still enthusiastic chortling.

Wafting up from below was the huffing and puffing of exertion at a regular tempo. At first, Nassir worried he might be eavesdropping on a private moment between two of his crew—not something that had been an issue yet under his command, but neither was it verboten—but then he realized he was hearing one person exhaling with the rhythm of hard exercise. Stealing a look down the ladderway, he spied a scaly arm and leg practicing martial-arts forms and wondered whether his Saurian recon scout, Senior Chief Petty Officer Razka, ever got tired.

He wandered on, past the dark alcove of sickbay, and then past cabins 10 and 11, which were both quiet. As Nassir neared Commander Terrell's quarters, Threx passed by on the way to his cabin—stark naked in all his beefy, hairy splendor, a standard-issue white towel draped around his neck. The Denobulan smiled and nodded without a hint of self-consciousness. "Captain."

"Threx," the captain said, keeping a straight face only through effort and practice. Unclothed flesh usually didn't bother Deltans in general or Nassir in particular, but when it came to Threx, he wished the Denobulan hadn't been raised in a subculture without a nudity taboo.

Not seeing any point to another lap around the deck, Nassir drifted onto the bridge. All the duty stations were powered down and unmanned. Lieutenant zh'Firro was alone on the bridge, seated in the command chair and scribbling with a stylus on a data slate. She glanced at Nassir as he entered, and she tensed to stand. He held up one hand. "Don't get up. I'm just roaming."

The beautiful young Andorian *zhen* smiled. "I understand."

He ambled over to her and peeked at the slate. "What're you working on?"

"Poetry." She lifted the tablet with one blue hand and turned it toward him.

A memory nagged at him. "You had some poems published last year, didn't you?"

"Yes, on Andor." A humble shrug. "The critics liked them, but most people don't seem to care. I guess I won't be retiring on my royalties."

"Still, I'm envious. At least you have something to occupy your mind." He folded his hands behind his back and looked around, at nothing in particular. "Without work, all I have right now is too much time to think."

She set down her slate. "What are you thinking about?"

"This mission. Other missions. Philosophical quandaries." A crooked, embarrassed smile. "Those and a hundred other dusty thoughts that roll around this dry old brain of mine."

Her stare was keen. To Nassir, it felt as if she could look right through his pretenses and evasions and know that what he wasn't saying—what he was really afraid of—was that this mission might go wrong the way the Jinoteur mission had. That ill-fated adventure had cost the life of one of his recon scouts, and it had very nearly led to his ship's destruction by the Shedai, followed immediately by a close brush with capture by the Klingons. Nassir was not by nature a superstitious man, but lately he had begun to feel as if his luck was running out.

Finally, zh'Firro released him from the bonds of her gaze. Tapping her stylus on the side of the data slate, she asked, "Would it help if you had something else on which to focus?"

The implication of her query intrigued him. "Such as?"

She cocked her head and twitched her antennae in an utterly

affected but still totally charming way that was uniquely hers. "I need a Vulcan word that rhymes with *Uzaveh*."

Nassir pondered that, feeling both amused and vexed at the same time. "Well," he said, "that ought to keep me busy for the next few decades till I retire."

Standing in the center of the supervisors' deck in Vanguard's operations center felt to Nogura like standing in the center of the universe. That impression wasn't a product of the sheer size of the room, though Vanguard's nerve center was quite cavernous compared to most command decks; rather, it was the towering walls of interactive viewscreens that wrapped two hundred seventy degrees around the expansive circular compartment. At any given moment, a few of those screens might be tasked to monitoring complex shipping traffic or displaying important tactical updates from Starfleet Command, but most of them showed the endless reach of space surrounding the station.

The one that held Nogura's attention at that moment, however, showed a large, oblong block of a ship slowly maneuvering away from Vanguard and adjusting its heading as it prepared to accelerate to full impulse and, eventually, to warp speed. Seeing the vessel in motion, Nogura realized for the first time how slow and vulnerable-looking the *Ephialtes* really was, and he felt a pang of regret for having ordered the *Sagittarius* entombed inside the lumbering bulk of the *Antaeus*-class superfreighter. Watching it head out into space, he couldn't help but think of some enormous sea creature being released into the wild only to find itself a fat and easy target for predators.

What if Alodae was right? What if I've just doomed him and his crew? Reason reasserted itself in his thoughts. He knew the *Ephialtes* was in no greater danger than it would be on any other return trip to Federation space. Instead, he reserved his concerns for the *Sagittarius* and her crew. The ship had survived its tour of duty in the Taurus Reach by exploiting its two chief advantages: tremendous speed and a low profile.

And I just locked them inside a huge, sluggish target. What have I done?

Before Nogura could silently berate himself any further, the station's executive officer, Commander Jon Cooper, crossed the supervisors' deck to stand at his side. In a muted but professional tone, the lanky, salt-and-pepper-haired XO said, "Sir, the *Ephialtes* has cleared the approach lanes and is free to navigate. All her readings appear nominal."

"Thank you, Commander." As Cooper stepped away to resume his duties, Nogura allowed himself a small moment of relief. "Nominal" had been a code word chosen to indicate that the station's sensors—which were formidable—had been unable to penetrate the sensor camouflage the engineering teams had installed inside the *Ephialtes* to mask the presence of the *Sagittarius*. Though there was no guarantee that the Klingons or the Romulans hadn't improved their sensors in some unexpected way that would negate this defensive measure, Nogura knew he should take good news wherever he might find it. *Now all we have to do is hope the freighter doesn't get attacked at random by the Klingons, or raided by some Orion corsair, or blunder into some exotic Tholian trap.* He scolded himself. *Stop that. Stay positive.* His years in Starfleet had made him understand how important his disposition was to the morale of those under his command. If he wanted to inspire optimism and courage and openness to new ideas, he had to exhibit those qualities himself. If he gave in to negativity, to defeatism, he would only drag his people down with him. *It all starts at the top,* one of his former commanding officers had told him when he was but a newly minted ensign. *A commander gets the crew he deserves.*

Watching the *Ephialtes* cruise away into danger, however, he found it hard to put a positive spin on the situation. He wondered if the twist of dread he felt knotting his innards at that moment was anything like what Reyes had felt when he first sent the *Sagittarius* and her crew all alone to Jinoteur, straight into the heart of the beast, just a few short years earlier. The more he thought about it, the more likely it sounded, but knowing that others had experienced this brand of anxiety did nothing to alleviate the suffocating pressure in his chest.

He descended the stairs to the main level and walked to the turbolift. The doors opened as someone called from behind him, "Admiral?" Nogura turned to see a short, fiftyish man with close-cropped steel gray hair and a narrowly trimmed mustache walking toward him. The man wore the blue tunic and insignia of the Medical Division, and he carried a data slate. He offered a genial smile and extended his hand as he caught up to Nogura. "Hello, sir. I'm Doctor Gonzalo Robles, the new acting chief medical officer."

"Good evening, Doctor," Nogura said, motioning for Robles to follow him as he stepped inside the turbolift. "What can I do for you?"

Robles used one hand to hold the lift doors open. "Actually, sir, I came up to let you know that you missed your mandatory physical four weeks ago."

"I what?"

A conciliatory shrug. "Doctor Fisher let a lot of paperwork slide over the last few weeks. I guess he had a case of short-timer's disease, if you know what I mean." He held out his data slate toward Nogura. "Anyway, as you can see, I need to complete your physical so I can certify you for duty. It's really kind of an embarrassment that it's been allowed to slip this long."

Nogura took the slate from Robles and looked over its contents. It displayed an order from Robles, as acting CMO, for Nogura to report immediately to Vanguard Hospital for his physical. Looking up at the physician, Nogura said, "Can this wait until tomorrow?"

"Technically, sir, it shouldn't have waited this long. It'll only take an hour. If you—"

"*Doctor.*" Heads turned throughout ops as Nogura's voice rose in volume, dropped in pitch, coarsened with exhaustion, and echoed off the high ceiling and surrounding bulkheads. "I have been awake for twenty-one hours. I've not had a decent meal since yesterday. And as busy as I know you are, I assure you: I am busier. So I am going back to my quarters to log six hours of rack time. When I get up, I will come to your office, and you can do your tests. But if you say so much as *one more word* before these turbolift doors close, I will have you pushed out an airlock without a spacesuit. Do I make myself clear?" The lack of a response from Robles made it clear to Nogura, and to everyone else, that he had done exactly that. "Good night, Doctor."

Robles removed his hand from the turbolift doors, which hissed shut. Nogura grasped the control bar. "Level Fifteen, Section Bravo." As the lift coursed into motion with a hypnotic hum, Nogura shook his head. *I should have told Fisher to leave his job vacant.*

7

Unemployment suited Ambassador Jetanien. Sequestered inside his nondescript but also heavily fortified and comm-secure residence on Nimbus III, the Chelon diplomat enjoyed a measure of solitude and tranquility unlike any he had known since his childhood.

Months had passed since he and his staff had been forced to evacuate and abandon the Federation Embassy in Paradise City, the nominal capital of Nimbus III. The riot that had engulfed the city and toppled the embassy also had claimed the life of Senator D'tran of Romulus. To the Federation, the senator's murder had been a public embarrassment, since it had occurred inside the Federation Embassy. For Jetanien, D'tran's death was an aching loss and a lingering shadow over all he had accomplished in life; he had considered the man a friend, and could not disabuse himself of the suspicion that he had failed him in his final moments.

Hiding his profound dismay from his colleagues and acquaintances had been easy, thanks to the limited expressive range of Chelon faces. Having evolved from an amphibian ancestor on Chelar—known within the Federation by the far blander appellation Rigel III—the Chelons had leathery features and beaklike proboscises. Consequently, their emotional cues often went overlooked by non-Chelons, except for a few who had taken the time to learn their ways.

For his own benefit, Jetanien had taken up the practice of meditation to quell his tempest of self-recrimination, and as a positive reinforcement he had coupled his periods of reflection with sessions of sunbathing. Stretched prone across a heated artificial boulder, he basked in solar rays magnified by special panes in the glass roof above the chamber on the top floor of his villa.

To the casual observer, he would appear to be just another layabout on that backwater world, and that was precisely how he wished to be perceived. Officially, he had been indefinitely furloughed from the Federation Diplomatic Corps following the loss of the Federation Embassy. Unofficially, it was understood by a handful of very highly placed individuals within Starfleet and the Federation government that Jetanien now served as a clandestine diplomatic back channel to both the Klingon Empire and the Romulan Star Empire. Even if all other political relations between the powers should be severed, this secret pipeline of communication would remain, in the hope of someday brokering a true and lasting peace.

He reached down with one clawed manus, pressed a control disguised as a nub on the boulder's surface, and filled his basking chamber with a fresh blast of steam. The cleansing moist heat soothed his tough hide as it seeped beneath the edges of his dorsal carapace. A sensation much like bliss began to suffuse Jetanien's being.

Then he heard the buzz of an incoming signal on his private comm channel. *Naturally,* he thought, simultaneously appreciating and resenting the irony of the moment. He gave himself a gentle nudge and slid down the curved slope of the ersatz boulder. When his feet touched the floor, he pushed himself upright, then plodded across the room to the companel on the wall near the door. It was a local signal, from the outskirts of Paradise City. Knuckling open the channel, he grumbled, "This is Jetanien."

A gruff male voice replied, *"What took you so long, you old turtle?"*

"Lugok," Jetanien said, his mood lifted by contact with his Klingon counterpart. "Forgive me. After all this time, I thought you'd forgotten how to use the comm."

A deep belly laugh. *"Hardly, old friend. To be honest, it feels like I never get a moment away from it. My new master is almost as long-winded as you are."*

"If you dislike long-distance conversations, go home to Qo'noS."

Lugok became a touch defensive. *"I've lost my patience for the tempo of life in the First City. Compared to Vanguard or this overcooked trash ball, Qo'noS is a madhouse."*

"No doubt."

"So, are the pundits still calling for your head because you lost your embassy?"

Jetanien didn't know which surprised him more: the fact that Lugok was deigning to engage in casual conversation, or that he was managing to sound as if he was interested in Jetanien's replies. Choosing not to jinx the rare moment of social grace by the Klingon by questioning it, he restrained himself to answering the direct query. "I try not to heed the reactionary tirades of the chattering classes. For the moment, I've worked a bit of political judo and turned our setback to my advantage. I'm content to be the punch line of their snide jokes, because it serves to conceal the true nature of my ongoing work. So long as the cause of peace is served, my public disgrace is of little consequence—and possibly even of value."

"You haven't changed," Lugok said wistfully. *"You still use fifty words where five will do."* He exhaled heavily, as if he were deflating. *"I wish I could be as blasé. Since the riots, my House's honor has been smeared, and the political elites treat me like a pariah."*

Feeling a deep empathy for Lugok's predicament, Jetanien said, "I'm sorry to hear that."

"Don't be," Lugok said. *"It wasn't until the powerful hated me that I realized how much I hated them back. And that, as it turns out, is why I've contacted you today."*

That sounded promising. "Go on."

"I'm acting as a confidential adviser to Councillor Gorkon. I trust you know of him."

"Most assuredly." In addition to being Chancellor Sturka's right-hand man on the Klingon High Council, Gorkon was the only high-ranking member of the Klingon government who was sympathetic to the diplomatic initiative Jetanien, Lugok, and their current Romulan contact, S'anra, had undertaken. Gorkon

had even gone to great effort and personal risk to extend a hand
in truce to his former nemesis, Diego Reyes, in the hope of per-
suading the Klingon chancellor to make an overture of peace to
the Federation. His efforts had withered and died on the vine, but
Jetanien still had admired the audacity behind them.

"Gorkon wants to ask a favor of you." After the briefest
pause, Lugok continued. *"He wants you to ask your contacts inside the Federation's various intelligence services to look for
hard evidence that the Romulans are forging secret alliances
with some of the Great Houses of the Empire, in order to corrupt
our government and turn it into a puppet of their own."*

A low rumble born of doubt resonated inside Jetanien's chest.
"I'm not dismissing Gorkon's request, but I need to ask: doesn't
the Klingon Empire have its own internal intelligence and security apparatus for matters such as this?"

*"Gorkon fears those services have already been compro-
mised. And if his suspicions are correct, the Romulans have
friends on the High Council, which means we can't launch a
formal investigation without risking serious political consequences—up to and including execution."*

It was a bleak picture, but Jetanien understood Lugok's concern. If elements within the Romulan Star Empire—most likely
operatives and directors of its intelligence service and secret po-
lice bureau, the Tal Shiar—were co-opting the Klingon High
Council, the diplomatic triumvirate he had established with
Lugok and S'anra would be rendered moot. Worse, the Romulans, who already possessed a significant tactical advantage in
the form of their cloaking devices, would be in a position to
marry that technology to the considerable military, industrial,
and economic resources of the Klingon Empire. It was a daunting
prospect.

"This is a tall order," Jetanien said, "but I will set myself to it
immediately. I expect my contacts inside Starfleet Intelligence
will prove more helpful and forthcoming than their civilian
counterparts. As soon as I have some intelligence of note, I'll
contact you to set up a meeting."

Lugok sounded suspicious. *"Just like that? Is this some kind of trick?"*

"Why would you think that?"

"Because you haven't asked for anything in return."

Jetanien's exasperation manifested itself as a grinding of his bony mandible. "Lugok, my friend, ours is not some simple quid pro quo arrangement. We are not hagglers in a market. This is how a relationship of trust is built: one act of goodwill at a time."

The Klingon chuckled cynically. *"I don't know whether to thank you or pity you."*

"Start by thanking me," Jetanien said. "We'll see how the rest goes from there."

8

A battle alert blared from the *Valkaya*'s overhead speakers. Commander H'kaan leapt from his shower and scrambled into his uniform without bothering to towel himself dry. He pulled on his boots, and raced from his quarters to the bird-of-prey's bridge to find his first officer, Subcommander Dimetris, and senior noncommissioned officer, Centurion Akhisar, conferring in low voices as they hunched over the shoulders of the tactical officer. Straightening the line of his red sash across his right shoulder with a small tug, he said, "Dimetris. Report."

The sharp-featured woman turned and saluted H'kaan. "Commander, we've sighted the Starfleet vessel *Sagittarius,* cruising at warp eight-point-five on bearing one-eleven mark six." She moved aside as H'kaan stepped forward to see the sensor readings for himself.

"Who made the identification?"

Akhisar looked him in the eye. "I did, Commander." There was neither pride nor defensiveness in the gray-haired man's declaration. "Hull configuration and energy signatures are a match, and preliminary readings suggest its usual crew complement is aboard."

Eyeing the star chart for the sectors ahead of the Starfleet ship, H'kaan asked, "What seems to be her destination?"

The centurion deflected the question with a glance to Dimetris, who replied, "Unknown. That heading takes her into uncharted space." She was quick to add, "We're still close enough to intercept her, but if we don't attack soon—"

"I can read the chart." H'kaan respected Dimetris; in many regards she was an excellent first officer. Her most serious shortcoming, however, was impatience. He turned to Akhisar. "Centurion, did you notify the fleet commander about this contact?"

"Yes, sir. We're still awaiting his reply."

Dimetris shot a hard look at the sensor image of the *Sagittarius*. "And while we wait, our prey widens its lead. We should strike now."

H'kaan was dismayed by her hotheadedness. "Attacking a Federation vessel could spark a war. We don't make such decisions. That privilege belongs to our betters."

His answer only stoked the lithe woman's frustration. "If we aren't meant to destroy this ship, why was it designated a target of interest by fleet command?"

"Don't ask so many questions," H'kaan counseled her. "You'll live longer." He understood her hunger for revenge, and he knew that many members of the crew shared the sentiments she'd voiced. Animosity toward the Federation, and in particular toward Starfleet, had been running high since the crew of the *Enterprise* had breached the Neutral Zone and entered Romulan space, engaged in a blatant act of espionage, and escaped with a stolen cloaking device. It was not just a public embarrassment for the Romulan Star Empire but a major setback in its ongoing arms race against both the Federation and the Klingon Empire. The "*Enterprise* incident," as it had come to be known, had afflicted the Romulan military's psyche like an open, festering wound. Any opportunity for revenge was now embraced with great relish.

An electronic chirping from the subspace radio console prompted H'kaan, Dimetris, and Akhisar to huddle around the communications officer. Dimetris said, "Kiris, report."

Sublieutenant Kiris checked the readings on his panel. "Encrypted traffic from fleet command. Decoding now." He engaged several preprogrammed functions, whose specific workings were classified, and downloaded the new orders to a ciphered data card, which he handed to Dimetris. The subcommander turned to face the centurion, who held up a small device used for deciphering classified directives. He and Dimetris looked at the device's screen as the orders appeared.

"Commander, we have new orders from Admiral Inaros," Akhisar said. " 'Engage and destroy Starfleet vessel *Sagittarius* with extreme prejudice. Authentication code: *Tisar, Jolan, Kolet,* nine, four, seven, *Seetha*.' " He looked up at H'kaan. "Message is authentic, sir."

H'kaan looked at Dimetris, who added, "I concur, sir. Message is authentic."

"All hands to battle stations," H'kaan said, stepping smartly to his command console. Dimetris and Akhisar took their places at the other two sides of the triangular station in the center of the bridge. "Subcommander, destroy that ship."

"Yes, sir." She lifted her voice and began belting out orders. "Helm, set intercept course, maximum warp. Weapons, stand by for a snap shot. Target their center mass. Centurion, stand by to drop the cloak on my mark."

Curt acknowledgments came back to her in quick succession, and Akhisar nodded once to indicate he was ready. H'kaan watched the tactical display in front of him and felt his pulse quicken with anticipation as the *Valkaya* closed to attack position on the *Sagittarius*. When they reached optimal firing range for torpedoes, he said simply, "Now."

Akhisar dropped the bird-of-prey's cloak, and the weapons officer unleashed a burst of charged plasma that slammed into the small Starfleet scout ship and knocked it out of warp.

"Helm," Dimetris called out, "come about and drop to impulse. Sublieutenant Pelor, charge disruptors and ready another plasma charge. Centurion, raise shields."

Pelor replied, "Weapons locked!"

Dimetris crowed, "Fire!"

In the scant moments between the order and the action, H'kaan glimpsed the sparking, smoldering mass of the *Sagittarius* on the bridge's main viewscreen. *Looks like we scored a direct hit with the first shot,* he observed with pride. *All those battle drills finally paid off.*

Then a pair of disruptor beams lanced through the smoldering husk of the *Sagittarius,* and the ship erupted in a massive fireball that quickly dissipated, vanishing into the insatiable vacuum of deep space. When the afterglow faded, all that remained was glowing debris.

"Secure from general quarters," H'kaan said. "Well done, all of you." Much as he tried to remain detached and professional, H'kaan could not resist the urge to gloat over his victory. "Kiris! Send to Admiral Inaros, 'Starfleet vessel *Sagittarius* destroyed. Continuing patrol.' And make sure to notify our friends at the Klingon High Command. I want them to know we've just scored the victory that's eluded them for years."

Akhisar sidled up to the commander and asked confidentially, "Are you sure you wish to rub their noses in our triumph so boldly?"

"Absolutely. I just wish I could be there to see the looks on their faces."

A dull and distant buzzing, like a million bees at the bottom of the sea. That was all Nogura heard, all he could latch on to. He felt like a synesthete, seeing the steady, angry sound as if it were an anchor line sunk into the depths to serve as his guidepost, a filament of focus to lead him up out of the oceanic fathoms of sleep, back into the twilight of semiconsciousness.

Slumber's murky curtain parted, and the waking world flooded into Nogura's mind, smothering him with its overwhelming, concrete reality. He blinked as he turned his head toward the companel on the end table beside his bed. Despite still being so groggy that he felt as if he were bobbing on a storm swell, he swatted open the comm channel. "Nogura."

"Admiral, this is Lieutenant Commander Dohan."

Nogura visualized Yael Dohan as he honed in on her voice. He imagined the swarthy, athletically toned Israeli woman with her short-cropped coal-black hair standing over the Hub, the octagonal situation table on the supervisors' deck inside the operations center. "Go ahead."

"The Romulans took the bait, sir. At approximately 0356

station time, a bird-of-prey uncloaked and opened fire, destroying our Sagittarius *decoy drone."*

Pinching the sleep from the inner corners of his eyes, he asked, "Are we sure they didn't know it was a decoy?"

"As sure as we can be, sir. The drone's sensors picked up a fair amount of encrypted signal traffic before the attack, and our long-range sensors picked up major chatter on the secure Klingon and Romulan frequencies just afterward."

The admiral covered his mouth as he yawned and hoped the sound didn't carry over the open channel. "All right," he said. "What time is it now, Commander?"

"Just after 0438, sir."

"Hrm. Cut new orders to the *Endeavour.* Have them divert and proceed to the drone's last known coordinates at maximum warp."

"Acknowledged. Dohan out." There was a soft click as the channel closed.

Collapsing back onto his bed, Nogura hoped this convoluted deception didn't turn out to be a waste of time, or worse. If the enemy really believed it had destroyed the *Sagittarius,* then the Klingon and Romulan patrols in the sectors adjoining Vanguard might let up just enough for the real *Sagittarius* to be safely on its way to Eremar. But if the enemy knew that they'd just destroyed a drone, then every patrol ship in the Taurus Reach would be on high alert.

Let the lie live just a few hours longer, he prayed, *that's all I ask.*

Captain Droga considered the news his first officer had just given him and felt torn between jubilation and envy. To make sure his revels weren't premature, he asked, "This is confirmed?"

"Yes, sir." Tarpek pointed at the communications officer. "Magron showed me the message from High Command. The *Sagittarius* was destroyed fourteen hours ago by one of our Romulan allies, roughly fifty-nine light-years from our current position."

Droga swiveled his chair on its elevated dais until he faced the weapons officer. "Rothgar! What's been Starfleet's response to the attack?"

The portly lieutenant looked over his shoulder at the captain. "The battle cruiser *Endeavour* has been diverted from its regular patrol route. It's on a direct heading for the coordinates where the *Valkaya* reported the *Sagittarius* destroyed."

"Glorious!" The broad-shouldered, hard-muscled captain stood and hopped down to the main deck beside his burn-and-shrapnel-scarred first officer. "Now we're free to plunder the prey we've been tracking since last night." He pointed to the slow, hulking vessel on the bridge's main viewscreen. "Have we figured out what that is?"

Tarpek reached over to a command console and keyed in a few commands. A string of data appeared on the screen, superimposed over the image of the ship: registry, tonnage figures, and other technical gibberish Droga didn't feel like making time to read. That was the job of the first officer, who reported, "The Federation freighter *Ephialtes*. Twenty-five crew and officers, maximum speed warp six. Primary function: colony support."

Stroking his brown-and-gray-bearded chin, Droga could see with his own eyes that the vessel was unarmed and likely had only the most perfunctory shielding. "Is it carrying anything worth stealing?"

"Perhaps," Tarpek said. "Our scans suggest it's fully loaded with unrefined minerals."

The captain nodded. "Probably bound for the refinery on Benecia." He gave Tarpek's shoulder a hard, fraternal slap. "Let's make sure it never gets there. Are we set?"

"Yes, sir. The target is now fully inside the blind spot created by the qul'mIn star cluster, and there's no indication its crew has detected our presence. The cloaking device appears to be working—for now."

Droga understood the grievance implicit in Tarpek's last remark. Their ship, the *I.K.S. vaQjoH,* was a Klingon bird-of-prey, so far the only class of ship that the Klingon Defense Force had succeeded in equipping with the Romulan invention known as the cloaking device. Even aboard the *vaQjoH* and ships like her, however, the new technology was plagued by overloads, spontaneous failures, and other potentially disastrous malfunctions. As much as Droga enjoyed being able to creep up on his prey in deep space like a hunter stalking *targ* in the deep forest, he hated the unreliability of the new system and had serious doubts that it would ever really earn widespread acceptance by the great mass of Klingon warriors. *That's a problem for future generations,* he decided as he climbed back into his command chair. Once he settled in, he pointed at the ship on the main screen. "Commander, seize that vessel. I want its cargo."

"Yes, Captain." Tarpek moved from station to station, handing out orders and back-slaps as he went. "Garthog, prepare to sweep in from their starboard side. Hold position at five hundred *qelIqam*s. Kopar, stand ready to drop the cloak, on my command. Rothgar, target their engines, but do not fire unless I give the order. We want to board this ship, not destroy it." Returning to the captain's side, he shouted, "Drop cloak and come to attack position!"

The bridge lights switched from a dull, ruddy background glow to a harsh white glare as the cloaking device disengaged and the ship's crew switched into combat mode.

Garthog declared, "In position!"

The weapons officer added, "Torpedoes locked!"

"Magron," Tarpek said, "open a hailing frequency." A moment later, the communications officer nodded to Tarpek that the channel was open, and the first officer nodded at Droga.

"Attention, Federation vessel *Ephialtes*. This is the Imperial Klingon warship *vaQjoH*. Drop to impulse, surrender, and prepare to be boarded." Droga waited several seconds while watching the slow mountain of a ship on his viewscreen. Then, to his satisfaction, the enormous cargo vessel slowed to impulse just shy of an intimidating-looking planetary debris field. The *vaQjoH* circled the freighter once, then took up a prime firing position off the ship's aft starboard quarter. Looking toward Magron, Droga asked, "Have they surrendered yet?"

Holding up one hand to signal that he needed a moment, Magron first looked perplexed, then alarmed. Slowly, he turned to face the captain. "Sir, we're being hailed by a *different* ship."

"*Another* ship?" Droga spun toward Tarpek. "Where is it?"

From the weapons console, Rothgar answered, "Behind us, sir." Anticipating the captain's next order, he patched the aft angle to the viewscreen, and the image of the *Ephialtes* was replaced by that of a *Constitution*-class Starfleet battle cruiser. "They have a full weapons lock," he added with a note of submission that Droga found distasteful.

"They're hailing us again," Magron said.

Bloodlust had Droga's pulse thundering in his ears, but for once his wisdom prevailed over his passion. He took a deep breath, then said in an even voice, "On speakers."

"*Attention, Klingon vessel* vaQjoH. *This is Captain James T. Kirk, commanding the Federation starship* Enterprise. *Power down your weapons immediately, or we will fire upon you. Acknowledge.*"

Droga pointed at Magron, who opened the response channel. "Captain Kirk, this is Captain Droga of the Klingon warship *vaQjoH*. Apparently, there has been some misunderstanding. We—"

"*There's been no misunderstanding,*" Kirk interrupted, his words sharp and quick. "*You intercepted a Federation vessel and ordered it to surrender and prepare to be boarded. You armed your weapons and locked them on an unarmed civilian ship. That's an unprovoked act of aggression, Captain.*"

Shooting a glare at Rothgar, Droga pointed at the man's console and then pulled one finger across his throat in a slashing motion. Rothgar released the weapons locks on the *Ephialtes* and began powering down the weapons. Droga had played his fair share of games of chance, and he had earned a reputation as a skilled gambler. He knew a bluff when he heard one—and this man Kirk was not bluffing. Though the crew of the *vaQjoH* enjoyed a battle as much as any band of Klingon warriors, Droga was certain none of them were in the mood to commit suicide, and it would do the Empire no service to lose a warship for no good reason.

"We've complied with your directive, *Enterprise*. With your permission, we'll depart."

"Yes, you will—on a course we'll specify, with my ship's weapons locked onto your warp core. And if you try to engage that cloaking device or go to warp speed before I give you permission to do so, I will blast your ship to bits. Is that understood?"

Humiliation churned into rage deep inside Droga's gut, but he knew he was in no position to dictate terms. Kirk's reputation, earned over just the last few years, preceded him. There was no doubt in Droga's mind that a thoughtless act of bravado at that moment would accomplish nothing except the near-instantaneous destruction of his ship and crew.

"Understood, *Enterprise*. We await your approved flight plan. Droga out." Magron cut the channel, and the rest of the crew sagged into their chairs. It was obvious that no songs would be sung over that night's meal aboard the *vaQjoH*. Staring at the massive gray battle cruiser lurking on their aft quarter, Droga understood all too well why many of his fellow starship commanders had begun using Kirk's name as a curse and the word *Enterprise* as an obscenity.

Discreetly savoring the sweet taste of victory, Captain James T. Kirk watched the *Enterprise*'s main viewscreen, which showed the aft end of the Klingon bird-of-prey *vaQjoH* as it retreated toward Klingon space with the *Enterprise* close behind it. All around Kirk, the sounds of the bridge and the hum of the ship's impulse engines were a welcome aural backdrop after nearly a full day of eerie silence. Acting on orders from the sector's ranking officer, the *Enterprise* had been lurking near a planetary debris field, lying in ambush with its key systems running at minimum levels and all nonessential systems powered down. Now the *Constitution*-class starship was under way at full power, as Kirk preferred.

Kirk got up from his command chair and strode to the forward console, which was manned by helmsman Lieutenant Hikaru Sulu and navigator Ensign Pavel Chekov. "Keep that ship within optimal firing range, Mister Sulu."

"Aye, sir," Sulu said, his baritone cool and professional.

To Chekov, Kirk added, "Make sure you keep the heat on them, Ensign."

Chekov looked over his shoulder and up at Kirk. "All weapons still locked, sir."

As he stepped away, he gave the boyish Russian a friendly pat on the shoulder. "Good work." He climbed the short steps out of the bridge's command well to its upper ring and joined his first officer, Commander Spock, who peered intently into the cerulean glow emanating from the hooded sensor display. "Spock, any sign the Klingons have armed weapons?"

"None, Captain." Spock straightened and turned to face Kirk. "They appear to have taken our warning at face value."

"As well they should." Kirk looked across the bridge toward the communications console. "Lieutenant Uhura, inform Vanguard that our objective has been accomplished, and we await further orders."

Uhura nodded. "Aye, sir." She turned to her panel and sent the message.

The half-Vulcan, half-human first officer leaned closer to Kirk and looked at the image of the Klingon ship on the main viewscreen. "The advance intelligence Vanguard provided about this attack was surprisingly accurate, Captain. Their mission briefing predicted not only the coordinates of the Klingons' ambush, but its time and likely attack vector."

Spock's observations stoked Kirk's curiosity—and his suspicions. "You think they had something to do with arranging the attack?"

The question prompted Spock to recoil slightly and cock one eyebrow in mild surprise. "Not at all. I was merely remarking on the admirable degree of precision in their report. In retrospect, it appears to be well grounded in logical assumptions."

Kirk frowned. "Right down to the Klingons starting to use cloaking devices."

"A troubling development, to be certain. A Klingon-Romulan alliance could alter the balance of power throughout known space."

As always, Spock's knack for understatement fueled Kirk's cynicism. "That's a nice way of saying they'd be writing the Federation's epitaph inside of a year, Spock."

Brow creased with thought, Spock replied, "I doubt the situation would become so dire so quickly. And, while such a development would prove less than advantageous to the Federation, it would not significantly alter our current security status."

Anxiety put an edge on Kirk's voice. "How do you figure?"

Spock folded his arms. "We already find ourselves in adversarial relationships with most of the other powers in local space. Apart from the Klingons and the Romulans, we also face opposition from the Gorn, the Tholians, and, to a lesser degree, the Orions." His eyebrows arched upward as he added, "While it is not in our interest for the Klingons and the Romulans to pool their resources, share their technologies, and coordinate their actions, I suspect this new alliance they've forged will be short-lived."

"Based on what?"

The first officer cocked his head slightly. "A great many factors. However, I think both peoples will eventually find their respective worldviews . . . *incompatible*. And I suspect the Klingons will quickly realize their current arrangement benefits the Romulans far more than it helps the Klingon Empire."

Before the captain could ask Spock to elaborate, Uhura called out, "Captain? We're receiving a priority signal from Vanguard. It's Admiral Nogura, sir."

Kirk and Spock exchanged looks of intrigued surprise. Descending the steps to the command well, Kirk replied, "Put him on-screen, Lieutenant." As he settled into his chair, the image of the *vaQjoH* was replaced by the lean, angular features of Admiral Nogura. Striking a relaxed but confident pose, Kirk greeted his superior with a half nod. "Admiral."

The gravel-voiced admiral's comportment was stern. *"Captain Kirk. Before I begin, let me remind you that Starfleet considers all transmissions in this sector vulnerable to interception—an assessment with which I concur."*

"Understood."

"Have you held on to your official mission logs, as I ordered?"

"Yes, sir. Though I have to say, Admiral Comstock is starting to insist that we transmit our logs back to Starfleet Command for analysis. He hasn't yet gone so far as to countermand your order, but—"

"I've informed Admiral Comstock your logs will be relayed from here," Nogura said. *"As soon as you finish escorting that Klingon ship out of the Iremal Cluster, set your course for Vanguard. I'll debrief you in person after you arrive. Understood?"*

Masking his unease at Nogura's gruff manner, Kirk replied with a straight face and not a hint of emotion, "Perfectly, sir."

"Good. Send us your ETA once you're en route. Nogura out." The image on the screen reverted to that of the *vaQjoH,* cruising at full impulse ahead of the *Enterprise.*

Kirk leaned forward. "Sulu, how long until we cut that Klingon ship loose?"

Sulu glanced down at his console. "Seven hours and twenty-six minutes, sir."

Rising from his chair, Kirk said, "Very well. Keep me apprised of any changes."

"Aye, sir."

Turning toward Spock, Kirk saw his second-in-command seated at the sensor station, his expression grave as he seemed to pierce the bulkhead with a thousand-meter stare. Kirk climbed the steps to the upper ring, then edged slowly toward his friend. He kept his voice low. "Spock?" No reply. Kirk raised his voice ever so slightly as he inched closer. "Spock?"

Spock blinked, then turned his head to look at Kirk. His manner was even more subdued than normal. "Yes, Captain?"

"Is everything all right? You look troubled."

The half-Vulcan's brows furrowed. "Not exactly. I was merely recalling our last visit to Vanguard, approximately three years ago. I departed the station with an important personal matter unresolved."

Taxing his memory for three-year-old details of the *Enterprise*'s first visit to Starbase 47, Kirk recalled Spock's unusual encounter with another Vulcan in some kind of cabaret-bar. "Does this have anything to do with that woman you met at the nightclub inside the station?"

"If you mean T'Prynn," Spock said, reminding Kirk of the woman's name, "yes, it does."

Kirk wondered if she was another past romantic acquaintance of Spock's, like Leila Kalomi, or some link to his mysterious Vulcan heritage, like his former fiancée, T'Pring. Hedging his bets, he asked, "Hoping to pick up where you left off three years ago, Spock?"

Steepling his index fingers as he folded his hands in front of his chest, Spock replied, "For T'Prynn's sake . . . I sincerely hope not."

As the senior officers of the *Endeavour* impatiently went through the motions of a search-and-recovery operation, Captain Atish Khatami leaned forward, perched on the edge of her command chair. The main viewscreen showed little except infrequent glimpses of scorched wreckage tumbling across the star-flecked emptiness of interstellar space, but Khatami's focus was on the chronometer mounted on the base of the forward console, between the Arcturian helm officer, Lieutenant Neelakanta, and the irksomely chipper young navigator, Lieutenant Marielise McCormack.

Time's passage preoccupied Khatami's thoughts. The *Endeavour* crew needed to stay long enough at these coordinates, retrieving the debris of the unmanned drone, to convince any Klingon or Romulan vessels that might be observing them that this was a recovery of wreckage from the real *Sagittarius,* but Khatami didn't want to spend one moment longer on this charade than necessary. *Every second we're not on patrol, we're asking for trouble,* she worried.

Lieutenant Commander Katherine Stano conferred quietly with science officer Lieutenant Stephen Klisiewicz. Khatami shook her head at the younger woman's new beehive hairstyle. Stano's dark hair and alabaster skin made the beehive look good, but Khatami still questioned her first officer's adoption of the fad that had swept through Starfleet during the past few years. Ever wedded to practicality, Khatami had chosen (over her husband Kenji's desperate objections) to have her own raven hair styled into a short but elegant coiffure that she could wash in sixty seconds and towel dry just as quickly. *To each her own,* she decided.

The shy-natured first officer stepped down into the command well and crossed to Khatami's chair. "We've reeled in almost every piece large enough to get our hands on," she said. "If we keep at this much longer, we'll be chasing dust motes."

"We still need to stretch this out a bit," Khatami said. "Vanguard just confirmed the *Enterprise* intercepted a Klingon attack on the *Ephialtes* inside the Iremal Cluster nine hours ago. Another couple of hours and the *Sagittarius* will be in the clear."

Doubt animated Stano's youthful features with a lopsided grimace, an arched brow, and a roll of her deep brown eyes, all at the same time. "I think we've milked this for all it's worth, Captain. Even if this had been the *Sagittarius,* we'd be done by now. There's nothing left here."

Despite sharing the XO's opinion, Khatami paused before she replied, lest she seem too eager to agree or too easily swayed from her opinions. Then she looked at Stano. "All right. File your report with Starfleet Command, as per the mission briefing."

Stano nodded. "No survivors, no sign of the culprit. Got it." She moved quickly aft to the comm station, where she directed communications officer Lieutenant Hector Estrada to load up and transmit, on a less-than-secure coded frequency, the *Endeavour*'s prewritten, phony after-action report—setting into place yet another piece of Vanguard's carefully crafted puzzle of disinformation. *If this is what's going to be expected of us from now on,* Khatami grumped to herself, *Starfleet Academy will have to start teaching cadets about sleight-of-hand.*

A few moments later, Stano returned to Khatami's side. "Message sent, Captain."

"Very well. Helm, set a course for—"

"Captain," Klisiewicz interrupted. The lean, dark-haired young man looked up from his sensor hood. "I have something here that you and Commander Stano need to see."

Khatami and Stano exchanged keen glances of alarm. They both knew that Klisiewicz was not prone to emotional outbursts or hyperbole for effect, which meant whatever he'd just found was serious. Khatami sprang from her chair and hurried up to the sensor console, where Klisiewicz remained hunched over the hooded display, and she loomed over his left shoulder while Stano leaned in over the man's right. The captain asked, "What've you got?"

"A massive signal on long-range sensors." He stepped back to allow Khatami and Stano to take turns confirming his discovery with their own eyes. "Major fleet movements inside Tholian space, all of them heading toward the border zone closest to Vanguard."

Khatami was still studying the sketchy data being compiled by the sensors and analyzed by the ship's computer as Stano asked, "Could it be a training exercise?"

Klisiewicz shook his head. "I've never heard of the Tholians doing anything like this, not on this scale. If I'm reading that thing right, we're looking at battle group deployments."

"You're reading it right," Khatami said. "Those are heavy warships massing on the border." She leaned back to let Stano have a look as she added, "Those aren't recon units looking to harass border worlds. If I had to make a bet, I'd say that's a major expeditionary force."

Gazing into the azure light of the sensor display, Stano looked perplexed. "None of them are crossing the border, even though there's nothing ahead of them. What're they waiting for?"

The science officer shrugged. "Maybe they're waiting for final orders?"

"More ships would be my guess." Khatami's already fretful mood darkened. "Either way, we need to get a warning back to Vanguard immediately. It looks like the Tholians are gearing up for war in the Taurus Reach."

Stano and Klisiewicz swapped nervous glances, then the first officer mustered the will to ask, "War against who?"

"That's what we need to find out." Khatami descended into the command well and strode back to the center seat. "Neelakanta, set course for the Tholian border. Estrada, inform Vanguard of the change in our flight plan, warn them about the Tholian fleet, and ask if they have any idea what's got the Tholians riled up this time. Klisiewicz, keep an eye on that fleet and let me know if you read any more ships moving to join it."

The bridge crew swung into action. Watching one last, lonely piece of debris tumble-spin past on the main viewscreen, Khatami sensed she was witnessing a disaster take shape.

Stano moved back to Khatami's right side. "What are *my* orders, Captain?"

Khatami hardened her heart for the days to come. "Start running battle drills."

9

"You perplex me, Jetanien."

The Chelon diplomat lowered his bowl of *N'va'a* and shot a questioning look across the table at his young Romulan hostess, who reclined lazily in her chair and held a tall-stemmed cocktail glass brimming with the blue ale of her homeworld. "In what regard, S'anra?"

S'anra met his stare. "You've always struck me as a creature of refined tastes and educated sensibilities. So I find it impossible to fathom how you tolerate that odiferous swill."

"On my world, *N'va'a* is considered a beverage of rare quality."

Her coy smile threatened to stretch into a smirk. "On my world, we'd call it compost."

Jetanien lifted his bowl of fermented fruit juice in a jaunty faux salute. "Your loss."

The former aide to Senator D'tran of Romulus favored Jetanien with a brief glimmer of amusement, then sipped her drink. As the pair enjoyed a moment of silence, Jetanien noted the tasteful appointments of S'anra's villa. They sat in the center of an interior courtyard, beside a small swimming pool ringed by tall trees that offered her shade from the powerful rays of the late-afternoon summer sun. The rooms of the villa all had been decorated with works of art, such as sculptures and paintings, that were as beautiful as they were subdued. Like his own residence, S'anra's home on Nimbus III was located outside of Paradise City, and, despite its obvious attention to creature comforts, it was equipped with a variety of potent concealed defenses. *It would seem she's taken the same lessons from D'tran's death that I have,* Jetanien concluded.

She set down her drink. "Since you took the liberty of arriving

with an ample supply of your own beverage, I presume your visit
is not about availing yourself of my hospitality."

"Not entirely, no," he confessed. "Though who could resist
your charming company?"

Her gaze sharpened as she studied him. He could tell that, far
from the eager young naïf she had presented herself as months
earlier to his assistant, Sergio Moreno, S'anra was a shrewd if
inexperienced player in the political arena. "What are we really
here to talk about?"

"Any number of topics present themselves." Jetanien kept her
waiting a few moments by taking another swig of *N'va'a* and then
setting down his bowl before sitting back against his portable
glenget, a special type of kneeling chair designed to accommo-
date his unusual anatomy. "Your assumption of D'tran's mantle
of diplomacy here on Nimbus III; the need to defuse tensions
between our two governments following that unfortunate incident with the *Enterprise* and one of your birds-of-prey; the Romulan Star Empire's new accord with the Klingons; the rumors
of a new praetor rising to power on Romulus in the next year; my
suspicion that you've initiated a sexual relationship with my assistant, Sergio, as a means of compromising my privacy. Many
things are in short supply on Nimbus III these days, my dear, but
worthy topics of conversation we possess in abundance."

She tapped her index finger twice on the tabletop and narrowed her eyes. "I saw what you did there, Jetanien. You muddied the waters with an excess of verbiage to conceal which
subject really matters most to you. It was an especially deft
gambit to finish with a personal accusation designed to make
me feel defensive and vulnerable, so that I would dismiss the
rest of your prattle as preamble. But I think it's the new accord
with the Klingons that sparks your interest."

"What a curious presumption," Jetanien dissembled. "Why
would you think that?"

Projecting her suspicion like a rebuke, S'anra said, "Off the
top of my head? There's no reason to discuss my succession of
D'tran as your clandestine channel to Romulus; it's a fait accom-

pli. The *Enterprise* fiasco is far too public to merit our attention, and any rumors of a new praetor are woefully premature—as I'm sure you already know. And you should have more faith in your man Sergio. His only virtue greater than his stamina is his phenomenal discretion. Your secrets are safe with him, Jetanien—but you already knew that, too, or else you would certainly have forbidden him to become my lover."

"Actually, I did forbid it. When I took him to task for his disobedience, his only defense was the rather cryptic human expression, '*È l'amore.*'" Jetanien had to stop himself from grinding the halves of his mandible in frustration. "If he weren't such an exemplary attaché in every other respect, I'd have fired him on the spot. I might do so yet."

S'anra threw her head back and laughed, then half covered her mouth with her fingers. "Please don't," she said with a teasing lilt. "I rather enjoy him."

"You mean you enjoy his company."

A rakish tilt of her head. "That, too." Putting on a more serious air, she continued. "In any event, that leaves the Romulan-Klingon accord as the sole remaining topic of interest."

"If you say so," Jetanien replied, feigning disinterest. "I suspect your alliance will be short-lived."

She picked up her drink and lounged back, affecting a casual air. "Alliance? That's quite a loaded word. I think you might be overstating our relationship with the Klingons."

"What would you call it?"

A small shrug. "A détente, perhaps. A beneficial exchange of technology in return for certain logistical considerations."

"In other words, you traded the secrets of cloaking technology for a handful of warships and . . . what else? Passage through Klingon space to the Taurus Reach? Those hardly seem like a recompense worth surrendering your monopoly on the cloaking device."

She swallowed a sip of Romulan ale. "Our monopoly lost some of its value after the *Enterprise* absconded with one of our devices."

"Ah. I see." He reached out with one clawed manus and lifted his bowl of *N'va'a* to his mandible, then inhaled its heady fragrance while he waited for S'anra's patience to crumble. He did not have to wait very long.

Simmering behind dark eyes, S'anra asked, "What do you see, Jetanien?"

"Now that Starfleet has one of your devices, you're afraid you can no longer traipse undetected through Federation space. You've lost your advantage against us because you were tricked, so rather than risk creating a second enemy on your doorstep, you bribed the Klingons to let you travel through their Empire, and to provide you with more powerful ships that you think can keep Starfleet on its side of the Neutral Zone." He clicked his mandible in an approximation of the *tsk-tsk* noise some humanoids made. "Still, it's a terrible price to pay for that privilege . . . unless you happen to be close to rolling out a newer, better version of that technology."

Noting with satisfaction that S'anra's mood had taken a turn for the petulant, Jetanien rewarded himself with another draught of the *N'va'a.*

The young Romulan took a calming breath and forced herself back into a semblance of composure. "An interesting hypothesis. Most imaginative."

"Thank you. I do strive to entertain with my prognostications and analyses." At the first sign that S'anra was starting to relax, he added, "But even those boons would not yield a sufficient return on Romulus's investment, would they? No, it seems to me your praetor and Senate must be angling for a far greater reward, something valuable enough to merit currying favor with the Klingon High Council. Or part of it, at least."

His speculation pushed S'anra back into an agitated state. "Such as?"

"Who's to say? But given what I know of your praetor and the Klingons' Chancellor Sturka, I find the notion of them sharing common ground less than plausible."

As Jetanien had hoped, his verbal feint enticed S'anra to

smugness. "Sturka is not the only member of the High Council."

He leaned forward, as if to share a confidence. "Of course not, but he and Gorkon hold most of the others in line. Now, if you can get to Gorkon—well, that would be a very different scenario. But it's not likely your people could offer him anything better than what Sturka has already promised him and his House."

Mimicking his body language, S'anra shifted forward and lowered her voice. "And what, exactly, do you think Sturka's promised to Gorkon?"

"The Empire. Gorkon seems likely to succeed Sturka as chancellor."

S'anra's eyes shone with a conspiratorial gleam. "I wouldn't be so certain."

"I didn't say I was certain, my dear, only that I thought it likely. Pray tell, who do you predict will be the next to sit upon the throne of Kahless?"

She sat back and waggled a finger at him. "That would be telling."

"So it would. And I'd hate for you to incur the wrath of someone like Duras."

Jetanien paid careful attention to S'anra's lack of a reaction. Her face was a blank slate—perfect for playing poker but ill-suited to brazen mendacity or fervent denial. Had she pretended to confusion or surprise, he might have had a harder time gauging whether his educated guess had struck the mark. Instead, she had made such an effort to bury her surprise that she had simply frozen. *She may as well have indicted Duras herself,* he gloated silently behind his leathery physiognomy. All that remained now was to play out the conversation according to its unwritten rules before retiring to his residence and passing the news along to Lugok.

"In any event," the Chelon said, "even with your help, Duras is a long shot at best. And considering the wealth and influence his House already wields, he can't have been an easy mark for your people to exploit. Still, I can't fault your—what do you call them? ah, yes, the Tal Shiar—for their forward thinking in this matter. Though I doubt the Federation has anything worth trading for someone of his stature, perhaps we should look into buying a few lesser figures on the Klingon High Council. No doubt the return on investment would be quite stellar."

The Romulan leaned back in her chair and sulked while staring at her empty glass. "There are no words equal to the depth of my contempt for you right now."

"No doubt a passing phase." He picked up the bottle of Romulan ale from the table, reached over, and refilled her glass. "Have another drink, and I'm sure you'll find the words you seek soon enough."

10

The intercom buzzed at precisely 0830, exactly the time Admiral Nogura had specified. He noted the detail with approval. There were many qualities he admired in other people, but punctuality was one upon which he placed particular importance; he did not like to be kept waiting. He thumbed open the channel to his yeoman. "Yes?"

Lieutenant Greenfield answered, *"Captain Kirk is here for his debriefing, Admiral."*

"Send him in." The door swished open and Kirk strode in carrying a data slate. Nogura stood and stepped around his desk to greet the younger, taller man. "Good morning, Captain."

They shook hands. "Good morning, sir."

Nogura gestured to the chairs in front of the desk as he returned to his own. "Have a seat." They sat facing each other. "Can my yeoman bring you anything? Coffee, perhaps?"

"No, thank you."

"All business, eh? I see your reputation is well earned." The admiral reclined his chair a few degrees. "Half of Starfleet is buzzing about you these days, you know."

Kirk responded with a disarmingly modest smile. "I can't imagine why."

"I've followed your career since you took over the center seat on the *Enterprise,*" Nogura confessed. "Three years ago, I was one of those who doubted you could ever emerge from the shadow of the great Christopher Pike. Now I hear officers talk as if you're some kind of modern-day Magellan, and dropping Pike's name makes the new cadets ask, 'Who?' "

The captain rolled his eyes, as if to deflect the praise. "I can't control what others say—but whatever praise they think I've earned probably belongs to my crew."

"No doubt there's some truth to that," Nogura said. "A commanding officer has to have good people in order to be effective. But a real leader inspires good people to greatness—and the *Enterprise* crew has excelled under your command, Kirk. Take pride in that."

The commendation seemed to bring out a tendency for self-effacement in Kirk, who mustered an embarrassed smile. "I do, sir. Every day."

"Good. Just don't do anything stupid—like get yourself promoted to the admiralty. Large bureaucracies tend to reward their best people with desk jobs where they can't be of any use to anyone, and in your case, I can't imagine a greater waste of talent."

That drew a small chuckle from Kirk. "I'll try to remember that." He leaned forward and handed the data slate across the desk to Nogura. "Our logs, hand-delivered as ordered, sir."

Nogura activated the slate and perused the long index of entries. "Your log for stardate 5693.2 indicates you found the *Defiant* trapped in—I'm sorry, what is *interphase*?"

"A rip in space-time, like a torn membrane between two universes," Kirk said. "The space between the universes is like . . ." He paused to conjure the right word. "Well, it's a kind of limbo, I guess. My first officer could explain it better."

Even a cursory skimming of the accounts by Kirk and Commander Spock made it clear to Nogura just how harrowing the *Enterprise*'s attempt to rescue the *Defiant* had been. "Your first officer's log says he and the rest of the crew thought you had died when the *Defiant* slipped out of phase and vanished."

Kirk's mood turned somber. "If not for my crew, I *would* be dead."

Nogura respected the toll that mission had taken on Kirk. "Well, we're all glad you're still with us. It's unfortunate you weren't able to recover the *Defiant,* but from what I see here, you and your crew went above and beyond in your attempt." He lowered the data slate. "Let me ask you, Captain: Do you or your senior officers think the Tholians had anything to do with creating the spatial interphase that snared the *Defiant*?"

"No. None of their weapons seemed to function in any way that would account for the phenomenon. Commander Spock speculated the interphase might have been a natural occurrence, but now that it's dissipated, there's no way to be sure what caused it."

"Very well." With regret, he closed the file on the search for the *Defiant*, resigned to accepting its loss in the line of duty as another of Starfleet's everyday tragedies.

After what seemed like a moment's hesitation, Kirk asked, "Sir, can you tell me what happened after my crew and I finished our first-contact mission with the Melkots?"

"They admitted they're curious about us, but they've chosen to remain in seclusion."

"Damn. Powers like theirs might've been useful against the Shedai."

"Technically, Captain, you—"

"I guess we could have asked the Metrons for help, but I get the impression they won't think we're worth talking to for another millennium or so. If Trelane wasn't so damned impetuous, I'd almost be tempted to—"

"*Captain*." Nogura spoke the word with such force that it silenced Kirk in mid-sentence. "I appreciate your input, but you need to refrain from discussing the Shedai—or any other aspect of our mission here."

All at once, the captain's humble bearing was replaced by a steely confidence. "Admiral, my senior officers and I stand ready to help you and your team. You might not be aware of this, but three years ago we were the ones who unlocked a key part of the mystery that had the research team here completely baffled. No one told us exactly *what* we'd discovered, but I think we've proved that we can be trusted with sensitive intelligence. Let us help."

Yes, Nogura thought, *this is how I imagined Kirk the starship commander. Aggressive, direct—and in need of an ego check.*

"Captain, unless there's been a radical change in Starfleet's chain of command, starship commanders don't get to decide for themselves when they should be read into classified operations."

"We've already been read into Operation Vanguard, for the mission to Ravanar IV."

Nogura held up one hand, palm out. "All details of which you were ordered to purge from the *Enterprise*'s databanks. I'm sorry, Captain, but Operation Vanguard remains on a strictly need-to-know basis, and right now there's no reason for you or your crew to be in the loop."

A sour frown expressed Kirk's resignation to the inevitable. "I see." After a calming breath, he asked, "How soon can the *Enterprise* depart?"

"I'm afraid we need you to linger awhile," Nogura said. "With our other ships deployed to the far ends of the Taurus Reach, we'd all feel better with the *Enterprise* standing by for short-range tactical deployments."

A curt nod. "Of course." His shifting posture telegraphed his desire to be anywhere other than Nogura's office at that moment.

"Dismissed." The captain rose and strode to the door. Before he got there, Nogura called out, "You should know that one of our resident scientists is Doctor Carol Marcus." Kirk halted shy of the door, turned back, and glared at Nogura, who added, "Your son, David, is here, too. Maybe you could pay the boy a visit before you ship out again."

Kirk seemed on the verge of an irate reply to Nogura's benignly intentioned suggestion, but then the captain reined in his anger and walked briskly out of the office without another word. The door slid shut behind him, leaving Nogura alone in his office. Sitting at his desk, he stared at the closed door and tried to make sense of Kirk's reaction.

I guess he's not much of a family man.

Spock exited the gangway from the *Enterprise* and joined the steady flow of pedestrian traffic in Vanguard's main docking bay concourse. The broad thoroughfare consisted of a single, vertiginously high-ceilinged passageway that ringed the station's core and linked the four internal docking bays in the lower half of the station's mushroom-cap saucer. Well lit and immaculately clean, it betrayed no evidence of the damage it had sustained in two separate incidents: a bombing inside the docking bay, three years earlier, and a Shedai attack just a few months before the *Enterprise*'s return visit. The latter had resulted in hull breaches to both the saucer and the core and had penetrated all the way down into the station's most fortified areas.

The opposing currents of pedestrian traffic that slipped past each other in the wide concourse resembled a cross section of the Federation's population. Most of the people Spock saw looked like humans, but there also were Vulcans, Tellarites, Andorians, Caitians, Arcturians, Rigelians, and Denobulans. He also noted a handful of individuals from species whose homeworlds were not yet full members of the Federation, including a Bolian and a Grazerite—the latter of which Spock had, until that moment, only ever read about.

Navigating through the flow of bodies, he made his way toward a nearby turbolift. His intention was to pay a visit to the Stars Landing establishment know as Manón's, located inside the station's terrestrial enclosure, and inquire after T'Prynn. Her peculiar predicament—involuntary possession by the *katra* of her former fiancé, Sten, whom she had slain in the *Kal-if-fee* decades earlier—had made a profound impact upon him, though out of respect for her privacy he had never discussed it with anyone else. Despite their extremely brief acquaintance, he felt an obligation to seek her out and once again offer whatever succor he might be able to provide.

He had already pressed the tubolift's call button when he noticed, at the periphery of his vision and through a brief gap in the river of pedestrians coursing past him, a lone figure standing at the towering wall of transparent aluminum in the observation lounge opposite. Looking more closely, he observed that it was a tall Vulcan woman, her jet hair pulled back in a loose ponytail that revealed the elegant upward curve of her ears. As if she sensed his attention from more than fifteen meters away, she turned her head slightly, enough for him to take in her striking, angular profile. Certain that it was T'Prynn, he slipped and dodged through the busy passageway and then crossed the empty lounge until he stood behind her shoulder.

She stared out the window into the docking bay, as if deep in thought. Several seconds later she acknowledged his presence. Her reflection looked at him. "Hello, Spock." There was a placid quality to her manner that he did not recall from their last encounter.

"T'Prynn."

With slow grace, she turned and faced him. "I read of your part in the capture of the Romulan cloaking device," she said. "It would seem you took to heart my advice regarding the occasional tactical necessity of falsehood."

He recalled their discussion about the ethics of a Starfleet officer—in particular, a Vulcan—employing lies in the line of duty, especially when doing so harmed others. They had left the matter unresolved when they last parted ways. Though her accusation was correct, in that he had misled a female Romulan starship commander so that Captain Kirk could steal the newest cloaking device prototype, he was not yet prepared to cede his entire argument. For the time being, he contented himself with a rhetorical evasion. "I did as I was ordered to do."

"A convenient rationalization. One I know all too well." She softened. "Forgive me. I meant no offense, and I doubt you've come in search of a debate. May I be of service?"

He lifted one eyebrow. "I had thought to ask you the same question." Looking into her eyes, he could see that her once turbulent psyche had been calmed. "When last we spoke, you were a *val'reth,* beyond the help of the Seleyan Order."

"Much has changed." She averted her eyes and looked back out at the docking bay. "A few months after you left, while standing on this very spot, I suffered a psychological collapse. I nearly died." There was no pathos in her voice, only cold truth. "I was made whole again on Vulcan, by a healer in my native village of Kren'than."

The mention of the small, technology-free commune stoked Spock's curiosity. "You lived among the L-langon mystics?"

"For a time. With my sister, T'Nel, when we were young." Her gaze took on a faraway quality, as though she were peering through a needle's eye into the distant past. "But after I slew Sten in the *Kal-if-fee,* maintaining my psionic defenses became too difficult in that place. So, I left Vulcan." Shifting back into the present, she looked at Spock. "A shipmate of yours brought me to Healer Sobon. A Doctor M'Benga."

Spock noted the coincidence with curiosity. "Then it would seem we are both in his debt. Doctor M'Benga was instrumental in saving my life on two occasions."

"Most fortuitous."

Shifting to an at-ease stance, Spock said, "I presume that Healer Sobon was successful in removing Sten's *katra* from your mind?"

A subtle tilt of her head signaled agreement. "He was. The process was difficult and not without risk, but my liberation was more than worth the cost of those hardships."

"Most agreeable news. . . . Yet your mind remains troubled." It was only a guess on Spock's part, but one he'd made with confidence. For all her affectations of serenity, he divined shades of melancholy in her fleeting microexpressions and the subtle intonations of her voice.

An ephemeral flush of shame deepened the green tint of her exquisite features. She was unable, or perhaps simply unwilling, to meet Spock's gaze as she answered him. "My freedom came at a price, one that I did not expect but in retrospect seems inevitable." She turned her palms upward and looked at them. "After I awoke, I gave no thought to my art. It wasn't until I came back here and sat down at the piano that I realized I no longer knew how to play."

The implications of her statement were intriguing. "All your learned ability was gone?"

"No. I remember the notes, but when I play, the melodies no longer flow. There is no beauty in them. No truth." She paused. "For most of my life, music was my refuge. My salvation. Now I'm forced to find sanctuary in the silence that follows. It's a poor substitute."

Spock thought for a moment. "Have you spoken of this to anyone else?" T'Prynn shook her head. Might this be an opportunity to be of service? "I, too, am a musician. Perhaps, if we were to try playing music together, I might help you find that which you have lost."

She studied him with a frank curiosity. "You would do this for me? Even though we're little more than passing acquaintances?"

"You are in need, and I may be able to help you. It seems the logical course of action."

For the briefest moment, her emotional control seemed to waver, as if a bittersweet smile desperately yearned to be seen on her face. Then her composure returned, and she restrained her reaction to a polite bow of her head. "Most generous of you, Spock. I would be honored to accept your help, and to share in your music."

Though he would have been hard-pressed to explain why, Spock found T'Prynn's quiet gratitude most agreeable, indeed.

Packing it in. Doctor Ezekiel Fisher, M.D.—Zeke, to his friends—figured he must have used that phrase hundreds of times over the years, but it had never seemed so apt a description as it did now, as he prepared to vacate his office at Vanguard Hospital. He resisted the urge to indulge in nostalgia over each knickknack and personal effect as he stuffed them all into boxes. Some items, such as his assorted family holographs, he had removed to his quarters a few at a time, in anticipation of filing his resignation. Others, such as the various gag gifts his friends or subordinates had given him over the years, he had waited until today to box up.

A familiar, squarish head topped with gray hair and fronted by an ashen mustache leaned in around the corner of the office's open doorway. "Excuse me, Zeke," said Doctor Robles, "I don't mean to rush you, but—"

"Yes, you do," Fisher said. He flashed a teasing grin he'd spent a lifetime perfecting. "Hold your horses, Gonzalo. I'll be out of your hair soon enough."

Robles scratched absently at his snowy temple. "That's what you said three days ago."

"I have a lot of things." Sensing that the new CMO was about to reach the limits of his patience with the already unconscionable delay in claiming his new office, Fisher held up a hand to forestall any argument. "No more jokes. I'll just be a few more minutes, I promise."

Making a V of his index and middle fingers, Robles pointed first at his eyes, then at Fisher, miming the message, *I'm keeping an eye on you.* Then the fiftyish man slipped away, back to the frantic hustle and deadly drudgery of running Vanguard Hospital on an average day.

Fisher tucked a jawless, cast-resin skull that he had used for close to thirty years as a candy dish into his lightweight carbon-fiber box of bric-a-brac. For a moment he considered leaving "Yorick" as an office-warming gift for Robles, but then he decided that inheriting the prime piece of Vanguard Hospital real estate would be reward enough for the soft-spoken internist. Besides, without it, where would Fisher keep his mints?

As he excavated three years of detritus from the bottom drawer of his desk, he heard a knock at the open doorway. Laboring to push himself back up to a standing position, he grouched, "Dammit, Gonzalo, when I said 'a few minutes,' I didn't think you'd take it so literally." Then he turned and saw not his successor but his former protégé, his professional prodigal son, looking back at him. "Well, I'll be damned."

Doctor Jabilo M'Benga smiled, adding warmth to his kind face. "I hear I almost missed you." He stepped inside the office, and Fisher met him halfway. They embraced like brothers, and then Fisher clasped the younger man's broad shoulders. "Look at you. I hate to admit it, but starship duty agrees with you."

"You don't know the half of it," M'Benga said as they parted. He strolled in slow steps around the nearly empty office. "Hard to imagine this place without you in it."

Fisher shrugged. "Not *that* hard. I've been doing it for months, and it gets easier all the time." He continued wedging the last of his private effects into the box. "Sometimes you see the storm coming and you just know it's time to get out. Know what I mean?"

"I suppose." M'Benga tucked his hands into the pockets of his blue lab coat. "Though I have to wonder: After more than fifty years in Starfleet, do you think you're still fit for civilian life? I can't help but picture you getting home and going stir crazy in about a week."

That made Fisher chortle. "Oh, I don't think so. Let me find a seat by a baseball diamond, or a soccer pitch, or a tennis court, and I'll be right as rain. You'll see."

M'Benga mirrored Fisher's smile. "So. No regrets?"

"Honestly? Only one." Fisher closed the box. The lid locked with a soft magnetic click. "I'd always hoped you'd be the one to succeed me in this office." He hefted the box with a grunt, set it atop two others that he'd already sealed for the quartermaster's office to deliver to him later, then clapped his hands clean and stood beside M'Benga. "But I can see now that you'd never have been happy here. Not really. And I'm glad you found your calling on the *Enterprise*."

"So am I. But I'm glad I got the chance to work here with you first."

"Come with me," Fisher said. "I want to tell you something." Moving with the slow, steady gait of a man blessed with good health but burdened by old age, he led M'Benga out of the office and down a corridor through the administrative level of Vanguard Hospital. The younger man walked at his side, close enough for them to converse in the hushed tones considered appropriate in a medical setting. "Be glad for all the places you get to be, and everyone you meet along the way. It's human nature to focus on beginnings or endings, and that's why we often lose sight of where we are and what we're doing, in the moment. But the present moment—the ever-present *now*—is all we ever really have. Our past is already lost, gone forever. Our future might never come. And as you get older and time feels like it's speeding up, you even start to feel the *now* slipping away. And that's when you realize just how quickly things can end—when you're busy thinking about what was or what'll never be."

M'Benga aimed an amused but admiring sidelong look at Fisher. "All right, Doctor. Let's put your philosophy to work. What's your prescription for this moment of *now*?"

"I thought you'd never ask." Fisher draped his arm across M'Benga's shoulders. "How would you like to watch a few dozen Tellarites try to reinvent the sport of rugby out on Fontana Meadow?"

"That depends. Will there be beer?"

"Of course," Fisher said, as if M'Benga were a Philistine just for asking. "Just because we're hundreds of light-years from civilization, that doesn't mean we live like savages."

The younger man laughed. "Okay, count me in."

They reached the turbolift, Fisher pushed the call button, and they waited for a lift to arrive. "Let me test your memory, Doctor. What's the first and only rule of rugby?"

M'Benga put on a thoughtful intensity, and Fisher imagined it was because the young physician was recalling one of the many afternoons they'd spent watching sports together on the meadow years earlier. Then M'Benga smiled and looked at him. "No autopsy, no foul."

"Good man," Fisher said, patting him on the back. "First round's on me."

PART 2

A MUSE OF FIRE

11

A pale dot on the *Sagittarius*'s main viewscreen, Eremar looked like nothing special to Captain Nassir's naked eye. Bereft of planets, it was a dim and tiny ember, a lonely spark in the barren emptiness of the cosmos. The *Sagittarius* was half a billion kilometers from the pulsar, which, without the benefit of a false-spectrum sensor overlay, looked to Nassir like any other star. He knew better, of course. Incredibly dense, it was a neutron star rotating at a phenomenal rate, and its intense electromagnetic field emitted invisible bursts of extremely powerful and potentially dangerous radiation from its magnetic poles at regular intervals of 1.438 seconds.

Commander Terrell stood beside Nassir's chair, arms folded, looming over the captain, who hunched forward and did his best imitation of Rodin's iconic sculpture, *The Thinker*. Around them the bridge officers worked quietly, each one keeping a close watch for any sign of danger. At the helm, zh'Firro guided the *Sagittarius* into a standard orbital approach and recon pattern. Sorak monitored the communications panel, Dastin fidgeted nervously as he leaned against the weapons console, and Theriault had her face pressed to the hood over the primary sensor display. The ship hummed along, the deck under Nassir's feet alive with a steady vibration from the impulse engines pushed to full output.

Nassir had no idea what he and his crew were supposed to be looking for. The pulsar had no planets. Were they seeking a derelict spacecraft? An abandoned space station? What if the Orions had simply used this isolated, hazardous place as a rendezvous point? He pushed that last pessimistic speculation from his mind. The *Omari-Ekon*'s navigational logs had not indicated any contact with other vessels in proximity to Eremar. They had, however, indicated a number of peculiar maneuvers, and unless a more promising lead presented itself soon, Nassir's orders were to copy the Orions' flight path and see where it led.

Theriault dispelled the leaden hush with a brief exclamation of surprise and elation, transforming herself into the focus of attention on the bridge. She looked up from the sensor hood, her youthful face bright with excitement. "I found something! Something really *weird*!" Before either Nassir or Terrell had the chance to ask her to elaborate, she punched commands into her console and routed her findings to the main screen. A computer model of Eremar was superimposed over the image of the star, and several seemingly random points in close orbit of the pulsar were highlighted. "There's a network of artificial objects around the pulsar, including one directly in the path of its emission axis."

Everyone fixed intense stares on the viewscreen, and Nassir rose from his chair. "What in the name of Kasor is *that*?"

Trembling with barely contained glee, Theriault said, "I have a hypothesis."

Terrell shot a curious stare her way. "Let's hear it."

"I think these objects used to be part of a Dyson bubble," Theriault said. "They're all composed of ultralight carbon compounds the sensors don't recognize." More commands tapped into the science console conjured a web of arcing lines connecting the far-flung dots to the one at the top. "Based on their positions, I think there used to be a lot more of them, hundreds of thousands, all around this pulsar. Now there are maybe a few hundred left."

Sorak arched one gray brow. "Most remarkable."

Getting up from the tactical panel, Dastin asked, "What do those lines represent?"

"Subspace distortions," Theriault replied. "Tiny tunnels through space-time."

Nassir began to imagine what this construct must have looked like when it was whole. "Could those subspace tunnels have been transmission conduits for energy and data?"

The perky science officer nodded. "Absolutely."

Zh'Firro leaned forward until she'd practically draped herself over the helm. "Are they orbiting the pulsar?"

"No," Theriault said. "They're statites, not satellites." She thumbed a switch on her panel and enlarged the sensor image of one of the nearest objects. It resembled a massive disk surrounded by enormous, diaphanous fins. "They maintain their positions by using light sails and radiation pressure to counteract the pulsar's gravity."

Terrell's brow wrinkled with confusion. "But what about the one that lies on the pulsar's emission axis? How does it hold its position when it gets zapped?"

Theriault shrugged. "No idea."

"I think we're about to find out," zh'Firro said. She looked back at Nassir. "If we follow the *Omari-Ekon*'s flight plan, we'll have to make a roughly half-second warp jump into that statite's shadow. It's the only way to get there without being fried by a blast from the pulsar."

Shrinking back into his seat, Dastin muttered, "I don't like the sound of that."

"Neither do I," Nassir said, "but she's right. If that's the end point of the Orions' trip to Eremar, there's a good chance that's where they found the artifact."

That news didn't seem to sit well with Terrell. "Is it safe for us to go there?"

Theriault's sunny disposition gave way to trepidation. "Mostly."

Sorak stepped forward, toward Nassir and Terrell. "To elaborate on Lieutenant Theriault's response, the statite would shield us from the majority of the pulsar's immediately damaging emissions—but not all of them. Even in its shadow, we'd still be subjected to dangerous levels of cosmic radiation and electromagnetic effects. Inside the ship, with shields raised, we would have little to worry about. But anyone venturing outside would need to limit their exposure to no more than four hours at a time. They would also require antiradiation therapy upon their return to the ship."

Dastin shot a dubious look at the Vulcan. "Isn't that a decision for the doctor?"

"I am a medical doctor," Sorak said.

Terrell quipped to the new tactical officer, "He also holds doctorates in archaeology and xenobotany. So, if you get the urge to debate him about fossils or flowers . . . don't." The gentle rebuke was enough to persuade Dastin to turn his attention back to his own console. Turning back, Terrell asked Sorak, "How long will it take to prep a landing party?"

"Twenty minutes," Sorak said. "However, there is one further complication."

Anticipating the Vulcan's news, Nassir said, "No transporters."

"Correct, sir." To the others he explained, "Despite the protection offered by the statite, inside the pulsar's emission axis the transporter will be inoperable. We'll need to land the ship and deploy either on foot or in the rovers, depending upon the local gravity and terrain."

Nassir returned to his chair and sat down, feeling as if a black hole had taken hold of his spirit. He recalled the hyperbolic slogan of a Starfleet recruitment poster he'd seen as a youth on Delta IV: "It's not just a job, it's an adventure."

Isn't that the truth.

"Sayna, plot a warp jump to the statite. Clark, take Sorak, Theriault, and Ilucci, and suit up down in the cargo hold. We'll let you know when it's safe to go ashore." He thumbed open an intraship channel from his chair's armrest. "Ensign Taryl, report to the bridge. Doctor Babitz, report to the cargo deck, and bring antiradiation hyposprays for the landing party."

As Sorak, Theriault, and Terrell left the bridge, Nassir watched the pulsar loom large on the main viewscreen. He couldn't see the relativistic jets of supercharged particles bursting out of it at regular intervals of less than two seconds, but he knew they were there—just as surely as he knew that even the most infinitesimal miscalculation by zh'Firro would see the *Sagittarius* reduced to ionized gas before any of them had time to realize they were dead.

He clutched his armrest a little tighter and put on his mask of calm.

It's not just a job, he reminded himself, *it's an adventure.*

• • •

The *Sagittarius* touched down with a rough bump, and Ilucci felt the impact rattle his bones.

Commander Terrell sealed the hatch to the main deck and the centenarian Lieutenant Sorak primed the depressurization sequence for the hold, both acting in preparation for the unsealing of the aft exterior hatch. Ilucci had never enjoyed stuffing his portly form inside an environmental suit, one of the least forgiving of all garments. As the landing party's departure became imminent, the chief engineer tugged at his suit's inseam, desperate to relieve its overly snug fit and give himself enough slack to walk with a normal stride. He wondered why the pressure gear always seemed cut for people with stick-figure bodies.

Overcome with what he believed was a reasonable degree of paranoia, he rechecked the settings on his suit: Oxygen level: check. Reserve power: check. Radiation barrier at full: check.

Everything was the same as it had been sixty seconds earlier.

He had almost succeeded in calming his frazzled nerves when the aft ramp began to fold down, away from the underside of the ship's saucer, toward the ground below. As the sliver-thin crack between ramp and bulkhead widened, Ilucci took in the barren sprawl that awaited the landing party: a tenebrous, trackless waste on the dark side of a radiation-bathed disk blasted sterile by millions of years of bombardment by a pulsar.

Terrell led the landing party down the ramp and out into the forbidding darkness. Despite the small size and supposed low density of the statite, its gravity felt close to Terran normal.

Theriault jumped up and landed almost immediately, displacing the regolith beneath her booted feet. Over the shared helmet comm channel, Ilucci heard her say, *"Artificial gravity?"*

"That'd be my guess," he said. "If it's consistent, we might be able to use the rovers."

Sorak stepped away from the team and moved a few strides beyond the sheltering overhang of the *Sagittarius*' saucer. Ilucci, Theriault, and Terrell followed him. Standing in the open, Ilucci turned in a slow circle, observing his surroundings.

The graceful off-white form of the *Sagittarius* was veiled in shadow because its running lights were off. Over a hundred kilometers away in every direction, but still clearly visible thanks to the absence of an atmosphere to obscure the view with haze, the horizon curved upward by the slightest degree, making Ilucci hyperaware that they were on the shallowly concave side of the circular statite. Beneath that close horizon, he knew, light sails fanned around the statite's edge, transforming the pulsar's regular bursts of lethal energy into power and lift. Overhead, the stars burned with cold, steady fires, offering minimal illumination and no warmth.

He noticed that the others all were facing in the same direction. Turning himself toward the same bearing, he saw why.

An enormous structure stood several kilometers away, at the apparent center of the statite. It looked like a ruptured blister, a gigantic splashing droplet of molten black glass frozen in time. Its shapes and protrusions made it seem simultaneously biological and mechanical. The simple act of looking upon it, even from this distance, filled Ilucci with a cold dread. Everything about the construct made him want to retreat inside the ship; the last thing he wanted to do was move closer to it. Which made it very easy for him to predict what Terrell's next order would be.

"Master Chief, let's power up the rovers and head over to that structure, on the double."

"Aye, sir," Ilucci said, jogging back up the ramp and inside the ship's cargo hold, in a hurry not to comply but to turn his back on the biomechanoid horror dominating the bleak nightscape. He took his time powering up one of the two terrestrial rovers, a pair of off-white, six-wheeled all-terrain vehicles optimized for moving personnel but powerful enough to haul cargo. Stenciled on the back panel of each rover was its nickname. "Roxy" was the faster of the two, but "Ziggy" had proved on many occasions to be more maneuverable, particularly at speed or in tight quarters. Roxy started up with no difficulty, and Ilucci hopped behind the controls and guided it in reverse down the ramp. A quick jerk of the wheel and a tap on the brakes, and he spun it to a halt beside the landing party, facing the alien structure. He hooked his gloved thumb over his shoulder at the empty seats. "Meter's runnin'. Hop in."

Terrell took the front passenger seat. Sorak sat behind Ilucci, and Theriault climbed into the seat behind Terrell's. All four of them took a moment to secure their safety straps, and Ilucci gave the rover's protective roll cage a firm tug to make certain it was secure. "And away we go." Against his better judgment and natural instincts, he stepped on the accelerator and sped the landing party toward the obsidian nightmare ahead.

The drive across the statite's surface was eerily silent. No one spoke; they all simply stared at their destination. The rover's electric motor was quiet even in terrestrial settings, but in an airless environment such as this, it made no sound at all. No motor hum, and almost no appreciable vibration of acceleration. All that Ilucci heard during the drive to the structure was his own shallow breathing, hot and close inside his helmet. He watched the *Sagittarius* grow steadily more distant in the rover's side-view mirror.

As they neared to within a hundred meters of the structure, its details became clear and all the more terrifying. It was almost obscenely black. A wall ten meters high ringed its base, and from it a dozen looming towers rose at thirty-degree intervals and curled inward toward its center, like the retracting legs of a burning insect. Every square centimeter of its exterior that Ilucci could see was either mirror-perfect, fissured with cracks, or ringed with tubes that made him think of veins. Small tendrils of violet energy crept up the ebon talon-towers, and when the creepers met at the apex, they coalesced into bolts of blue lightning that stabbed down into the heart of the machine. The design was strongly reminiscent of the Shedai-built Conduits that Operation Vanguard had uncovered throughout the Taurus Reach, but this was clearly the product of a different culture wielding a less organic technology than the Shedai's.

Terrell nudged Ilucci and pointed to the right. His voice crackled softly over the helmet comm. *"Circle its perimeter, Chief. Let's find an entrance."*

"Copy that, sir." Ilucci steered right, off their collision course, and followed the curve of the structure. Within a minute it became obvious that the stadium-sized facility was round and highly symmetrical in its design.

They were two-thirds of the way around the wall when Sorak pointed at a subtle variation in the shadows-on-darkness surface of the wall. *"There. That looks like an opening."*

"All right," Terrell said. *"Chief, take us in. Sorak, set your phaser for heavy stun and stand by to scout the entrance."*

Ilucci drove the rover toward the wall and slowed to a gradual halt less than ten meters from the opening. Sorak freed himself from his safety harness, leapt from the rover, and dashed forward until he was beside the entrance. He peeked around the corner, then stole into the shadows with his phaser level and aimed straight ahead. Darkness swallowed him in seconds.

"Theriault," said Terrell, *"run a tricorder scan."*

The science officer fumbled with gloved hands to retrieve her tricorder from her suit's thigh pocket, then she poked clumsily at its controls. A few moments later, she lowered it and shot a flustered look at Terrell. *"No good, sir. Too much interference from the pulsar."*

The first officer balled his right hand into a fist. *"Meaning we'll have to go in there blind. I was afraid of that."*

Sorak returned to the doorway and signaled the rest of the team to follow him. Ilucci and the others unfastened their harnesses and clambered out of the rover. As they joined Sorak at the entrance, the Vulcan recon scout said to Terrell, *"It appears to be deserted, but I think you and I should do a full search while Theriault and the Master Chief inspect the device."*

"All right." Terrell motioned for Sorak to head inside. *"Lead the way."*

They followed Sorak through a long, zigzagging trapezoidal corridor whose glistening surfaces were all ridged and scaled. It felt to Ilucci like passing through an organic orifice.

Marching into the belly of the beast.

They emerged from its far end inside the aphotic arena, which at first glance resembled a shallow crater of dark volcanic glass. Long tubes radiated from its center, like longitudinal markings on a map, guiding Ilucci's eye immediately to the pit's nadir. Forks of sapphire lightning zapped down from the overarching talon-towers, illuminating the spokes of a wheel-shaped onyx frame that held several thousand skull-sized, dodecahedronal crystals identical to the Mirdonyae Artifact secured inside Vanguard's research lab. Unlike that captured prize, however, these crystals all were perfectly clear, rather than swirling with the eldritch energies of an imprisoned alien life force. Though Ilucci had no words to say why, the very sight of the alien contraption filled him with a sick sense of foreboding.

As Sorak and Terrell split up and began conducting a thorough search of the upper tiers of the stadium's interior, Theriault shouldered past Ilucci and hurried down the slope of the pit, on a beeline for the crystal wheel. Seeing her rush headlong into peril made Ilucci's gut twist, reminding him that he'd never really purged himself of his infatuation with the impulsive young Martian woman. Her energetic curiosity was a key ingredient of her charm, and as an officer she was expected to lead by bold example, but he worried about her more than he could ever say. All he could do was pick up his feet and run after her.

By the time he caught up to her, she was circling the thing, trying in vain to scan it with her tricorder. She cursed under her breath, but each profanity was perfectly audible over the comm channel. Ilucci cleared his throat, and she stopped abruptly. *"Sorry,"* she said. *"But I can't get much on this thing except straight-up visual scans, and even those are coming out pretty rough from all the radiation."* She pointed at the wheel's hub, a thick trunk of onyxlike stone that appeared to be fused to the ground. *"It looks pretty well anchored. I can't imagine how we'll ever get this thing out of here. Or fit it into the ship, for that matter."*

He scrunched his brows. "Why the hell would we want to do that?"

A grimace made her lips thin and disappear, then she mustered a weak and unconvincing smile. *"Because we were ordered to recover anything we found and bring it back for analysis."*

Ilucci raised his voice in anger as he turned and looked up toward the distant Terrell. "Nice of somebody to tell me!"

"Chief," Terrell said, sounding diplomatic but not the least apologetic, *"we were under strict secrecy protocols. This whole operation's been on a need-to-know basis."*

The military cliché lit the fuse on Ilucci's temper. "And why would I need to know, right? I mean, I'm only the goddamned chief engineer! Just the tool-pusher who has to figure out how to cut this thing free and turn it into cargo! Why tell me anything, right?"

Theriault sounded oddly chipper. *"Chief, it might not be that bad—look."* He turned back toward her. She was pointing at an empty nook on one of the wheel's spokes. *"This might be where one of the Mirdonyae Artifacts came from. Which suggests . . ."* She stepped forward, clutched the nearest crystal on the wheel with both hands, and pulled it free with ease. Stumbling backward, she was filled with innocent glee. *"Easy peasy!"*

He shouted, "What's the matter with you? Are you crazy?" The impetuous redhead held out the artifact toward Ilucci. Staring at the glibly plucked forbidden fruit being proffered by the object of his unrequited affections, Ilucci thought of Adam in the Garden of Eden. He held up a hand and shook his head. "No, thanks. You keep it."

"Suit yourself, Master Chief." She turned to look in Terrell's direction. *"Commander? I can't get a reading on these things. What do you want me to do next?"*

The first officer and Sorak were both on the way down to regroup with Ilucci and Theriault. *"Take that crystal back to the rover and find some way to pack it safely for the ride back,"* Terrell said. *"We'll dump some of the ship's cargo so we can use the empty crates to box up the other crystals. Master Chief, we'll need both rovers to move them to the ship, so have your team get Ziggy ready to roll. We'll come back with Threx, zh'Firro, Dastin, and Cahow."*

Ilucci stared at the huge wheel, its spokes clustered with artifacts. "This could take days."

"I estimate it will take us four days and twenty-one hours," Sorak said.

"Then we'd best get started," Terrell said. *"The sooner we finish, the sooner we leave."*

Ilucci plucked an artifact from its cradle, tucked it under his arm, and started walking back to the rover. He said nothing, but his gut told him this mission would not end well.

12

Captain Khatami jolted awake in her quarters at 0418, instantly aware that something was amiss. The drone of the *Endeavour*'s warp engines had pitched upward by an octave, and she had felt a subtle moment of disorientation as the ship's inertial dampers lagged a few thousandths of a second behind the change. She threw aside her bedcovers and was crossing the room to her desk when the intraship comm split the silence with an electronic boatswain's whistle, which was followed by the voice of the ship's second officer and gamma shift commander, Lieutenant Commander Paul Norton. *"Bridge to Captain Khatami."*

A jab of her thumb on the comm's controls made it a two-way conversation. "Khatami here. Report."

"That Tholian battle fleet we've been shadowing since it crossed the border just took off at high warp, destination unknown."

For several days, the *Endeavour* had maintained a close watch on the Tholian fleet, which until that moment had followed a course parallel to their territory's border, albeit a few dozen light-years outside it, through the unclaimed sectors of the Taurus Reach. Khatami didn't know what the sudden change meant, but she suspected it would not be good news.

"Set a pursuit course, then wake up Stano and Klisiewicz. I'm on my way." She closed the channel and dressed in a hurry without bothering to turn on the lights. In less than a minute she was out the door and squinting against the harsh light in the corridor while she pushed her unwashed sable hair out of her eyes and smoothed it with her hands. A pair of ensigns, one human and the other Vulcan, held the turbolift for her as they stepped out of it.

She sprinted into the waiting lift, gripped its control handle, and guided it toward Deck 1.

The doors parted with a pneumatic hiss, and she strode onto the bridge, which was as busy with comm chatter and routine shipboard activity in the middle of the night shift as it was during the day. Norton, a very tall and gangly man whose bald, narrow head reminded Khatami of a Crenshaw melon, vacated the command chair as he noted Khatami's entrance.

"The Tholians are still pulling away," he said. "Warp seven and accelerating."

Moving with a grace that came from practice, Khatami stepped past Norton, pivoted on her right foot, and spun herself onto her chair. "Helm, increase to warp eight."

Ensign Sliney answered, "Warp eight, aye." The engines' whining pitched up another note as the rail-thin Irish helmsman tested their limits.

The turbolift door opened again, and from it emerged Commander Stano and Lieutenant Klisiewicz. The lieutenant relieved his gamma shift counterpart at the sensor post, while Stano situated herself on Khatami's right, opposite Norton, who handed a data slate to the captain. "We've been monitoring their communications," he said, "but they've maintained subspace radio silence. Not a peep in or out."

Khatami wondered aloud, "So, what changed?"

"Whatever it was," Stano chimed in, "it lit a fire under them. Wherever they're headed, they're in a hell of a hurry to get there."

Klisiewicz backed away from the sensor hood and shook his head. "It just doesn't make sense. The Tholians are isolationists and xenophobes. They're almost never this bold."

"Except when they're on the warpath," Stano said. "Remember Ravanar IV." Her comment drew dour nods of remembrance from the other bridge officers. Three years had passed, but no one had forgotten the Tholians' ambush and destruction of the *U.S.S. Bombay.*

"I just hope we're not being suckered off our patrol route,"

Norton said. "This battle group is only a fraction of the armada we detected massing at the border. Who knows what the rest of those ships are doing while we're chasing these?"

Realizing that Norton's concern was sensible, Khatami asked Klisiewicz, "What possible destinations lie within a week's travel on the Tholians' current heading?"

"Too many to know which one might be their target. At least two dozen colony planets—some of them ours, some the Klingons', and a few independents." He seemed befuddled. "I'd say warn them all, but I can't see what that'll do besides start a panic."

Stano frowned. "I'd have to agree, Captain. Until we know what the Tholians are after, there's not much point sounding the alarm. After all, the Taurus Reach is still mostly unclaimed space. They have as much right to haul ass through here at warp eight as we do."

"Be that as it may," Khatami said, "I still think it's worth sending up a red flag. Log the Tholians' current speed and heading, and send that data on a priority channel to Vanguard."

Norton lowered his voice to ask, "What if that fleet attacks one of our colonies?"

Khatami clenched her left hand into a fist. "Then we'll have to step in."

"But, Captain, they outnumber us twelve to one."

A rakish smile. "What? Are you worried it won't be a fair fight?"

His eyes widened, and he cocked his head nervously. "A bit, yes."

"So am I," Khatami said, "but I won't just wait around while they look for more ships to even the odds. If twelve is all they've got, that's *their* problem."

Unshaven and out of uniform, Xiong bolted from the turbolift, crossed the operations center at a quick step, and ignored the shocked protest of Nogura's yeoman as he passed her and entered the admiral's office without breaking stride. T'Prynn and Nogura turned away from the large tactical display on the wall to face Xiong as he joined them. "Admiral? You said it was an emergency."

"It is." Nogura motioned for Finneran to stand down. "Lock my door, Ensign."

"Aye, sir," Finneran replied as the door slid closed.

Glancing at the admiral's icon-covered star map of the Taurus Reach, the nearly breathless Xiong asked, "What's going on, sir?"

"The Tholians know about Eremar," Nogura said in his sepulchral rasp.

Dread became a swirl of nausea in Xiong's gut. He looked at T'Prynn. "Are we sure?"

The Vulcan woman pointed at a cluster of orange icons shaped like slender isosceles triangles. "The *Endeavour* is pursuing twelve Tholian warships on a heading that leads directly to Eremar. The battle group is proceeding at what we believe is their maximum warp factor. We need to assume the Tholians know about the Tkon artifacts."

Xiong knew as well as T'Prynn and Nogura did that the Tholians were going to Eremar not to research the ancient artifacts but to obliterate them—and that they would not hesitate to destroy the *Sagittarius* and her crew in the process. He struggled to rein in his temper as he asked T'Prynn, "How did the Tholians find out about Eremar?"

"I suspect the Orion slave-mistress Neera sold the information to the Tholians after the *Omari-Ekon* left Vanguard, but before it met with its . . . unfortunate accident."

The admiral looked puzzled. "I thought Reyes wiped that data from the *Omari-Ekon*'s databanks after he copied it."

"He did. As I feared, Neera must have realized the data's potential value and kept a secret backup. In retrospect, it's regrettable that we didn't impound her vessel, but Starfleet regulations and political considerations made that . . . impractical."

Nogura grimaced. "The damage is done. So, what are we going to do about it?"

"We warn the *Sagittarius*," Xiong said. "Then we send the *Endeavour* to help them."

"It might not be that simple," T'Prynn said.

"Why not?"

"If we're mistaken about the Tholians' destination, sending a warning to the *Sagittarius* might alert them to our operation, and instigate exactly the sort of incident we wish to prevent."

Her icy detachment stoked Xiong's anger. "I think that's a risk we ought to take." He pointed at a huge cluster of triangular orange icons massed along the border of the Tholian Assembly's declared territory. "The Tholians are primed for a major offensive. I think the armada waiting at their border is meant as a warning. They're telling us not to mess with the battle group they've sent to Eremar." Waving his hand at the rest of the map, he added, "If they were planning to invade the Taurus Reach, they'd all have come across at once, right?" Neither T'Prynn nor Nogura answered, so he continued. "If that fleet's not heading to Eremar, where the hell is it going?" Fed up, he folded his arms. "We need to move on this before it's too late."

The admiral's aspect was grave. "Mister Xiong, I know how much you have invested in your research of the Shedai and now the Tkon artifacts, and you've made it clear to us more than once how vital it is to protect the unique alien antiquities—"

"Screw the artifacts," Xiong snapped. "I'm talking about saving our people. If the relics have to burn to get our ship back in one piece, so be it."

His outburst seemed to catch Nogura by surprise. It certainly had come as a shock to Xiong himself. Until that moment, he hadn't realized how much guilt he'd harbored over the death of his surrogate big sister, Bridy Mac. In many ways, the crew of the *Sagittarius* were like a second family to Xiong, and he couldn't bear the thought of losing any more of them—not in the name of science, security, or anything else.

He hung his head. "Sorry, sir. I guess I got a bit carried away there."

"Perhaps," Nogura said. "But that doesn't mean you were

wrong." He looked at T'Prynn. "I think Mister Xiong's point has merit. All the evidence says the Tholians are going to Eremar. At this point, I think we should assume our mission's secrecy is fatally compromised."

T'Prynn was silent for a moment, then her brows arched upward. "I concur. Given the facts in evidence, I suggest we direct the *Endeavour* to take any steps short of preemptive attack to enable the crew of the *Sagittarius* to abort their mission and escape. While the recovery of the Tkon artifacts should remain a mission objective, I believe it should now be considered secondary to the safe return of our ships and personnel."

"Then we're all in agreement," the admiral said. "Time to bring our people home." He walked to his desk as he added, "Lieutenant T'Prynn, get word to the *Endeavour,* and take every precaution to keep the contents of that message encrypted."

"Aye, sir." The Vulcan turned to leave, Nogura sat down in his chair, and Xiong stood alone in front of the star map, feeling as if he must have missed something.

"Hang on. What about warning the *Sagittarius*? That's our first priority, right?"

Nogura's face slackened, and with a look he delegated the task of answering Xiong to T'Prynn. "We have no means of warning the *Sagittarius* crew," she said. "Even if they hadn't been ordered to maintain subspace radio silence for the duration of their assignment, their flight plan indicates their destination lies inside the emission axis of a pulsar. Until they're clear of that high-energy phenomenon, we will be unable to reach them via subspace radio."

"In other words," Xiong said, "they're deaf, dumb, and blind, and they have no idea what's about to hit them."

T'Prynn averted her eyes from Xiong's. "Correct."

Too angry to respond, Xiong headed for the door and hoped his friends' homecoming wouldn't be in the form of a memorial service.

13

Vivid hues of patriotism coursed through the communal thoughtspace SubLink of the Tholian battle cruiser *Toj'k Tholis,* and its commanding officer, Tarskene [The Sallow] telepathically shared his own colors of confidence with his crew. As the leaders of the attack group that had been dispatched to rid the galaxy of a dangerous abomination, it was absolutely essential that he and his crew project unity and assurance to their caste-peers on the other ships of their fleet. At the moment of action, he could brook no hesitation, no dissent. All must act as one.

Brightening his mind-line to convey an aura of authority, he inquired of tactical officer Lostrene [The Sapphire], *Range to target?*

Lostrene momentarily attuned herself to the ship's sensing units, then she responded, *Six-point-three-one million and closing.* She relayed to the SubLink a kaleidoscopic array of images she had witnessed through the ship's systems—an irregular network of artificial objects in a stationary formation around the pulsar, and a connective web of energies linking them all to one node that lay directly in the path of the neutron star's radiation emissions.

According to intelligence sold to the Tholian Assembly by the now-deceased Orion merchant-princess Neera, that central node was their target—the source of the mysterious artifact she and her people had bartered to Starfleet in exchange for temporary safe haven at Vanguard, and which the Starfleet scientists allegedly had used to snare and yoke a Shedai to their will—until, predictably, the entity escaped in a fury of blood and flames, destroying their engineering vessel *Lovell* in the process. There were unconfirmed reports that there might be another such artifact on Vanguard, but Tarskene could not concern himself with that just yet. Studying the reports that Lostrene had shared, it appeared that all the other details of Neera's report had been confirmed by the sensing units, and this pleased him. It meant the victorious completion of his mission was imminent.

The tactical officer's mind-line darkened with shades of concern. *The Starfleet vessel* Endeavour *remains on an intercept course,* she warned.

Ignore them, Tarskene commanded, overpowering Lostrene's muted alarm with a flare of courage. *Arm all weapons and stand by to lock them on target as soon as we are in range.*

Disregarding the Starfleet heavy cruiser was a calculated risk. It had been trailing the fleet ever since they crossed the border but had not yet given any indication that it meant to attack. It was Tarskene's belief that the *Endeavour*'s commander was merely playing a futile game, harassing the fleet in the hope of intimidating Tarskene into abandoning his mission. That was not an outcome he would permit. At any cost, the Tkon artifacts had to be destroyed. And if the Starfleet vessel attempted to interfere in any way, his orders were to destroy it with prejudice.

Another shadow dulled the perfection of the SubLink. Tarskene opened his mind-line and sought out the lone voice of discontent. He was surprised to find its source was his first officer, Kezthene [The Gray]. In their many cycles of service together, she had never before challenged one of his priority directives. Crimson and violet tainted Tarskene's thought-colors, revealing his irritation with his second-in-command. He sequestered her thoughts with his inside a private SubLink so that their conflict would not agitate the rest of the crew. *Why do you resist unity?*

The first officer's thoughts coruscated with confusion. *We have insufficient information to justify this action,* she protested. *The Orion's intelligence specified neither the nature of her discovery nor what use it might be to the Federation. A military response seems premature.*

Irrelevant! Tarskene's fury turned his thoughts black. *We have our orders.*

Kezthene summoned the image from the sensing units. *The platforms orbiting the pulsar represent an unknown technology. They should be studied, not destroyed.*

He flooded her mind with facets of his memory. Heated debates among the members of the Elite Political Caste on Tholia. Moments of conflict against the Klingon and Federation interlopers. Worlds shattered, turned into clouds of debris. The message of his psionic montage was clear: this mission's importance was more than strategic, it was existential. *My directive from the Ruling Conclave is to destroy the source of those artifacts before Starfleet acquires any more of them. Their meddling with the Old Ones must be brought to an end.*

Defiant hues coursed through Kezthene's mind-line. *What if the Federation is using the artifacts as weapons against the Shedai? Should we not consider doing the same? We could at least try to capture one of the Tkon devices for analysis.*

Absolutely not, Tarskene fumed. *Those objects were made to imprison the Shedai, but no trap can hold the Old Ones forever. Such a risk must never be permitted on a Tholian world. For the good of the Great Castemoot, we must destroy those objects before the Federation's deluded scientists make the mistake of using them.* Infusing his mind-line with the brilliant luminance of the command caste, he asserted his absolute authority. *Will you join the crew in harmony?*

Kezthene's aura flickered briefly, telegraphing her uncertainty, but then her mind-line resolved into a steady pale hue of compliance. *I will attune myself with the others.*

Tarskene released her from the private SubLink, and she was true to her pledge. She calmed her thought-colors and synchronized them with his own. Together they guided the ship's communal thoughtspace to a uniform golden radiance. Firm and resolute, they were of one mind, one purpose. Within moments their harmony spread to the other ships of the fleet, and then Tarskene knew they all were ready to enact the will of the Ruling Conclave.

Lostrene quelled a pulsing alert from the sensing units. *The*

Starfleet vessel is receiving a transmission from the starbase, she advised. *I am unable to decrypt it.*

It is of no consequence, Tarskene assured her, and the others as well. *Charge all weapons to maximum, and let me know the moment we reach optimal firing distance from the target.*

Khatami reeled in dismay from the news Admiral Nogura had just delivered to her over the encrypted subspace channel. "Are you saying the *Sagittarius* is on . . . whatever that thing is?"

"That is exactly what I am telling you," the gravel-voiced flag officer said, his head magnified to epic proportions on the *Endeavour*'s bridge viewscreen. *"Their mission to Eremar is of vital importance, and we need you to escort them to safety."*

Lieutenant Thorsen looked back from the forward console at Khatami. His gloomy mood told Khatami the situation hadn't improved in the last thirty seconds. "That's going to be difficult," Khatami said. "All twelve Tholian ships are locking their weapons on the statite inside the pulsar's emission axis. There's no telling what'll happen when they open fire."

Nogura's fierce presence seemed to jump through the screen. *"You need to make them hold their fire until the* Sagittarius *is clear. After that, the Tholians can do as they like."*

"We're not exactly in a position to dictate terms, and the Tholians don't seem interested in talking, but I'll do what I can. Khatami out." She glanced at Estrada and made a throat-slashing gesture with her thumb. He took the cue and terminated the comm channel to Vanguard. "Yellow Alert! Hector, find a way to punch through the pulsar's interference and get a warning to the *Sagittarius*." Swiveling her chair to the right, she said to Stano, "Hail the Tholian fleet commander again. Tell him we're *demanding* a parley."

Tense seconds bled away while Estrada and Stano worked at adjacent consoles, trying to raise anyone involved in this fiasco on a comm channel. On the main viewscreen, the Tholian fleet fanned out into a formation optimized for group bombardment of the underside of the statite upon which sat the *Sagittarius,* unaware of and unprepared for the Tholians' impending assault. Obeying a gut instinct that told her this situation was likely to degenerate quickly, Khatami shot another look at Thorsen. "Charge shields, arm phasers, and load all torpedo bays."

He checked his readouts as he worked. "Ninety seconds to weapons range."

Khatami looked back in hope at Estrada, who shook his head.

Then Stano turned, one hand cupped over the Feinberger transceiver in her ear, and nodded. "I have the Tholian fleet commander."

"On-screen," Khatami said. The ring of Tholian warships on the viewscreen blinked to a fiery red haze, within which she discerned the faint outline of a Tholian. The multilimbed, crystalline arthropod gesticulated with his forelimbs and screeched like a drill bit grinding against neutronium. The universal translator rendered the noise into Federation Standard on a quarter-second delay. *"What is the meaning of this intrusion?"* It was a testament to the translator's superb programming that it preserved the tonal quality of the Tholian's outrage.

"Tholian fleet commander, this is Captain Atish Khatami, commanding the Federation starship *Endeavour.* We request that all vessels in your fleet power down their weapons so that we may carry out a rescue operation." It was an off-the-cuff lie, one for which she hadn't rehearsed her bridge crew. She hoped they would be able to improvise and keep up. "Another Federation vessel has crashed on the statite your fleet is targeting, and we have orders to render immediate aid to that vessel and its crew."

"Captain Khatami," said the radiant, nearly transparent creature on the screen, *"I am Commander Tarskene of the* Toj'k Tholis. *What is that ship doing on the statite?"*

"They were conducting a spectral survey of the pulsar when they experienced a malfunction in their navigational system."

Tarskene slowly rubbed his forelimbs together. It struck Khatami as a cogitative gesture. Then he lurched forward and loomed large on the screen. *"I do not believe you, Captain. If your lost vessel had successfully transmitted a distress signal, we, too, would have received it. But given the disruption the pulsar causes to subspace signals—especially within its emission field—I think it is extremely unlikely you have had any contact with a vessel on the statite. That leads me to two possible conclusions. First: There is a vessel on the statite, and you know about it because you are an accomplice to whatever covert mission led it there. Second: There is no vessel on the statite, and you are attempting to delay the completion of our assignment so that you may gain access to the statite. In either case, our course is clear: We proceed as ordered."*

Khatami sprang from her chair and strode toward the viewscreen, mimicking the Tholian's aggressive posturing. "Commander Tarskene, I assure you, there is a Starfleet vessel stranded on that statite. In the interest of interstellar amity, I am begging you to order your fleet to stand down until we have completed our rescue operation."

"Your petition is refused. If there is a Starfleet vessel on that statite, its destruction will be its just penalty for trespassing. Now I will advise you to stand down and withdraw, Captain. If you attempt to interfere in our mission, your ship will be destroyed."

The transmission ended, and the viewscreen reverted to the image of the dartlike Tholian ships deployed in a ring, their tapered bows all aimed at the statite. Khatami shot a look at Stano, who said, "They've closed the channel, Captain."

"Hector! Any luck hailing the *Sagittarius*?"

"Negative, Captain. I still can't break through the pulsar's interference."

Her pulse throbbing in her temples and clenched fists, Khatami felt the situation spiraling out of control. Her ship was outnumbered twelve to one, which made any solution predicated on the use of force perilous at best. Complicating the matter was the contentious political situation between the Federation and the Tholian Assembly; any act of overt aggression could instigate a full-scale war between the two powers. But if she stood by and did nothing, the *Sagittarius* would be destroyed, along with its crew and whatever they had been sent to find. Worse, she would have to live with knowing she had been a witness to mass murder, and had done nothing to stop it.

If only I had another minute, she realized. *We could jump into the statite's shadow and have a chance of hailing the* Sagittarius. *But what if they aren't ready to leave? How would we buy them more time? How do we convince Tarskene not to—*

Before she could finish weighing her options, the Tholian fleet opened fire.

Easy does it, Terrell cautioned himself as he lowered a Tkon crystal into the padded packing crate mounted on the back of his rover, Ziggy. Detaching the crystals from their spokes inside "the Pit," as Chief Ilucci had nicknamed it, and then carrying them up to the rovers wasn't strenuous work, but it was slow and tedious, and for once Terrell was glad that even on a tiny ship like the *Sagittarius,* rank still had its occasional privileges. As the designated driver for Ziggy, he got to break the monotony by making regular runs back to the *Sagittarius* to drop off each filled container and replace it with an empty one. He was pleased to see that Ziggy's latest crate was almost topped off.

Through the faceplates of their environmental suits, he had observed the anxiety etched on the crew's faces. None of them liked visiting the Pit, and a few of them—Ilucci, zh'Firro, and Threx—had said outright that it made them nervous. If the sinister aura that infused the alien arena was having any ill effect on Sorak or Razka, however, they were masking it expertly.

Razka and Threx emerged from the gap in the Pit's outer wall. Each of them clutched a single Tkon artifact in their gloved hands. The Saurian scout stowed his fragile cargo inside the container on Ziggy's rear flatbed, then the hulking Denobulan did the same. As they trudged back inside, Lieutenants Theriault and zh'Firro passed them, cautiously ferrying two more artifacts to the rover.

A glance toward the *Sagittarius* confirmed that Ilucci was on his way back in Roxy, having completed the delivery of another fully packed crate of artifacts to the ship's cargo hold. With an empty crate secured to Roxy's flatbed and only Ilucci aboard, the tough little rover sped and bounced across the barren waste that separated the ship from the Pit. Terrell thought the bleak vista reminiscent of a salt flat, minus the warmth and homey charm.

Theriault and zh'Firro packed away their latest contributions to Ziggy's hold, and Terrell made two more check marks on his data slate. That brought the total number of recovered artifacts to nearly fifty-five hundred. They had been working around the clock, six-person teams operating in four-hour shifts, for three days, yet they had harvested fewer than half the artifacts they'd found inside the Pit. The work would have gone faster had they been able to drive the rovers all the way down to the machine, and faster still had they been able to use the transporter, but since neither option was available, they had done the best they could.

While he watched Ilucci pull up and park Roxy, Terrell pondered ways to enable his people to haul more than one artifact at a time out of the Pit. Backpacks were a bit too cumbersome to add to their environmental suits, and trying to carry the orbs one-handed was too risky—they'd already dropped and damaged one due to careless handling. Terrell wondered if it might be practical to attach woven-net pouches to the ends of poles they could carry across their shoulders, or perhaps attach up to four pouches to a pole that would be carried by two people, thereby doubling their productivity. He was about to ask Ilucci if he could jury-rig one when the ground under their feet lurched violently, knocking both men off their feet.

Sprawled beside Terrell, Ilucci looked appropriately alarmed. *"What the hell is that?"*

"Feels like an earthquake," Terrell said, even though the notion was ludicrous. The statite was an artificial construct; it couldn't be geologically active. Could it?

Another jarring vibration rocked the statite, and the two rovers lurched several centimeters off the ground, as did Ilucci and

Terrell. The surface continued to shake and heave as the rest of the landing party scrambled empty-handed out of the Pit. Terrell looked up, fearful that one of the inward-curving towers above the Pit might have started to collapse, but the alien arena seemed unaffected by the tremors. The stars above, however, began to shift . . . and then he realized the stars weren't moving—the statite was. If it turned far enough to expose the landing party to the full force of the pulsar's fury, they would all die instantly.

"Everybody into the rovers! Now!" As the landing party sprinted back to the ATVs, Terrell closed and secured the partially full container on the back of Ziggy, then he hopped into the driver's seat and started the engine. Another quake trembled the vehicle and fissured the landscape between the Pit and the *Sagittarius*. He looked over his shoulder at his staggering landing party, who fought to keep their balance as they crossed the last few meters to the rovers. "Move it, people! Time to go!" Threx and zh'Firro piled into the back of Terrell's rover as Razka and Theriault clambered aboard Roxy with Ilucci. As the passengers raced to strap themselves in, Terrell stomped on Ziggy's accelerator. "Punch it, Master Chief!"

The two vehicles were off like shots, swerving and fishtailing through the superfine dust on the statite's surface as the ground rocked and the stars wheeled precariously overhead.

Over the helmet comms, Threx shouted, *"What's happening?"*

He was answered by a distant, eerily silent eruption of broken rock and twisted metal riding a plume of orange fire and blinding light, and then another explosion, and another, each closer than the last. As jets of fire tore up the ground between the rovers and the *Sagittarius,* Terrell and Ilucci were forced to swerve apart and chart new slalom routes back to the ship.

"Either we tripped a self-destruct switch," zh'Firro replied while hanging onto Ziggy's roll cage for dear life, *"or someone's shooting at us."*

Smoldering, glowing debris rained down and littered the path ahead of the rover, and Terrell fought to keep the vehicle from rolling as he swerved madly around one obstacle after another.

Huge chunks of superheated rock and metal rolled erratically, cutting deep gouges in the ground that threatened to snare the ATVs unless they were traversed at just the right angle. A steep dip into one smoking trench was followed by the scrape—felt but not heard—of Ziggy's front bumper striking the far slope and being torn off in the bargain. Two quick jolts shook the ATV as it ran over its own shed parts, leapt clear of the trench, and sped toward home.

The open aft ramp of the *Sagittarius* was less than fifty meters away, and the two ATVs were closing in fast—but so was a series of explosions that looked like chain reactions, tracing a fiery path across the shadowy surface toward the ship. Boulders trailing smoke slammed down onto the *Sagittarius,* denting its primary hull and warp nacelles.

Then a massive flare of light burst over the far horizon, and for a moment the terror of being exposed to the pulsar washed away every other thought in Terrell's mind. Then he saw the expanding debris cloud that followed the flash and realized what he was seeing was the destruction of three of the statite's solar sails. It took half a second before he asked himself why the *Sagittarius* was no longer between him and the horizon.

Twisting to his right, he realized that Ziggy, Roxy, and all their occupants had been sent aloft by a sudden interruption of the statite's artificial gravity. Both rovers were floating away into space, and their strapped-in passengers were along for the ride, wherever it might lead.

Watching the ground and the *Sagittarius* recede, Terrell hoped Captain Nassir would embrace cold reason, abandon the landing party, and save the ship. But as towers of flame ripped apart the statite around the stationary starship, Terrell feared it might already be too late.

Distant explosions flashed on the *Endeavour*'s viewscreen. Watching with her fists and jaw clenched in fury, Khatami felt like an overwound spring being twisted tighter by each new bit of bad news her bridge crew reported, torqued one step closer to breaking by every crimson bloom the Tholians' weapons ignited on the statite. Then, all at once, the Tholians' massive barrage ceased—but the statite continued to fracture and flare with internal eruptions.

"What am I looking at?" she demanded.

Klisiewicz stared into the blue glow of the sensor display. "The Tholians have deployed six devices onto the underside of the statite. The devices have embedded themselves on the surface at roughly equidistant points from the center, approximately sixty degrees apart."

She eyed the magnified image on the forward viewscreen. "What are they?"

The science officer straightened and turned toward her. "There's nothing like these things in the memory banks. They're generating harmonically reinforcing interphasic distortion fields. In about five minutes those things'll rip the statite to shreds."

"Did you say 'interphasic' distortion fields?" The word jogged Khatami's memory of a classified briefing disseminated recently to Starfleet captains throughout the fleet. The *Enterprise* had encountered an interphasic rift that had proved highly dangerous to navigation. Though a general alert would eventually go out to the public, so far the phenomenon was still classified as top secret while Starfleet investigated all its possible properties and effects. The report filed by the *Enterprise*'s captain had suggested the interphasic rift might be a natural anomaly, but if the Tholians were wielding such forces as weapons, this was valuable intelligence that needed to be relayed to Starfleet Command immediately. "Estrada, have you raised the *Sagittarius* yet?"

"Not yet, Captain. Still trying."

From the forward console, Ensign Sliney declared, "The Tholians are powering up their weapons, Captain!" Seconds later, six of the Tholian ships launched another sextet of the unknown devices into the underside of the statite, targeting them precisely to reduce the spaces between them to thirty degrees. Around them, the statite's disintegration accelerated, and sensor alarms shrilled from numerous stations on the *Endeavour*'s bridge.

Returning to her chair, Khatami felt her pulse pounding in her temples. "Estrada! Hail the Tholian commander! Order him to cease fire and deactivate those devices immediately!"

Keying in commands, the communications officer replied, "Transmitting now." The viewscreen flared momentarily as the Tholian fleet fired another barrage of charged plasma at the statite, which listed even more sharply off its axis. Then Estrada grimaced and swiveled around to face Khatami. "No answer from the Tholians, Captain."

"Red Alert," Khatami declared. "All hands to battle stations. Thorsen, raise shields. Sliney, move us into an attack posture."

Stano interposed herself between Khatami and the viewscreen. "Captain, if we fire on the Tholians, we might be starting a war."

Khatami protested, "They fired *first*."

"On an alien construct to which we have no claim. They can claim they didn't believe the *Sagittarius* was there. They have diplomatic cover on this. We don't."

Precious seconds bled away as Khatami weighed the lives of the *Sagittarius*'s fourteen crew members, her own ship's complement of more than four hundred personnel, and the potential casualties—military and civilian alike—that would be on her conscience if she gave the order that started a war. Then she look around Stano at Thorsen. "Target the twelve Tholian devices on the statite and fire phasers. Keep firing till they're gone."

"Aye, sir," Thorsen said, already turning her command into action. The high-pitched whoop of the *Endeavour*'s phaser banks resounded through the hull as blue beams slashed through the darkness and began vaporizing the interphasic generators.

Firing on the Tholians' weapons rather than their ships was a legal gray area. Khatami could argue her actions were not aggressive but defensive. If the Tholians chose to interpret this act as hostility and escalate this confrontation, the consequences would be on their collective conscience, not hers—but she was hoping they would take the hint and back off.

Klisiewicz checked the sensors, then aimed a wary glance at his captain and first officer. "The Tholian fleet is coming about and moving into an attack formation."

So much for hope.

"That didn't take long," Stano said.

Khatami forced an empty smile. "Good. Now they have something new to shoot at. Keep them busy as long as you can, and let's hope the *Sagittarius* can use this time to escape."

Stano's eyes widened as the Tholian fleet loomed large on the main screen. "Great plan, Captain. Now who's going to rescue us?"

Before Khatami could lighten the moment with a witty retort, the Tholians opened fire, and then all she could hear inside the *Endeavour* was a roar like thunder.

"On the count of three!" shouted Terrell, watching the rover's slow roll. "One! Two! Three!"

He and the other members of the landing party in his vehicle huddled together in the middle of the ATV's passenger area and fired their environmental suits' maneuvering thrusters straight up, holding open the thrust valves until he ordered, "Stop!"

Looking over the vehicle's edge, zh'Firro exclaimed, *"It worked! We're moving back toward the ground!"*

Terrell exulted but kept his relief to himself. The rover's descent was fast enough to get them back within less than ten seconds, but slow enough that the impact wouldn't inflict serious damage on the vehicle or them. "All right, Master Chief," he said over the open channel, "your turn. Look for a full burn of about six-point-one seconds."

"Copy that, sir." To his passengers, Ilucci added, *"Look sharp, guys."* Keeping one eye on the ground and the other on Ilucci's rover, Terrell heard Ilucci start his countdown right on

time. *"Five. Four."* He was just starting to say *three* when both rovers went into free fall.

Ziggy slammed to the ground hard, and Terrell, zh'Firro, and Threx held on to their unfastened harness straps as the vehicle tumbled sideways, tossing them like rag dolls in slow motion inside the roll cage before coming to rest upright inside a cloud of fast-settling dust. As the fine gray haze dissipated, Terrell saw Roxy lying on its side a few dozen meters behind them. Half-buried in the regolith were the unmoving forms of its passengers.

"Master Chief! Theriault! Razka! Someone respond!" Terrell tried to start Ziggy's engine, but the rover's controls remained dark.

Beside and behind him, Threx and zh'Firro stared mutely toward their fallen comrades. Then the burly Denobulan pointed. "They're moving!"

Boosting the gain to his suit's transceiver, Terrell said, "Master Chief? Are you mobile?"

In the distance, the portly chief engineer emerged from behind Roxy's bent chassis. *"I think we are, but Roxy's toast."*

The statite's horizon began to shatter and blow away in blinding flashes of light, one roughly every two seconds. Terrell shouted, "Back to the ship! Move!" He bailed out of Ziggy and forced his bruised, aching body to sprint toward the *Sagittarius*. In moments, zh'Firro had outpaced him, but Threx struggled to keep up; his beefy frame was made for power, not speed.

As they neared the ramp to the ship's cargo hold, Terrell heard Captain Nassir's voice crackling over the comm. *". . . to landing party, please respond!"*

"We're here, Captain," he replied, gasping for breath as he followed zh'Firro up the ramp. "A few more seconds and we'll all be aboard."

Nassir, who almost never raised his voice, shouted, *"We need to go, Clark!"*

Terrell looked back and windmilled his arm, signaling Ilucci, Theriault, and Razka to hurry. The Saurian scout was well ahead of the science officer and chief engineer when the ground between them heaved upward and then erupted in a blast of light, heat, and molten rock. A wall of flames and superheated gas slammed into Razka's back and launched him toward the *Sagittarius*. He landed, unconscious inside his smoldering environmental suit, mere meters from the ramp. Terrell ran to the fallen scout, grabbed him beneath his arms, and dragged him backward up the ramp into the ship. Threx and zh'Firro stood at the bottom of the ramp, both looking past Terrell for any sign of Ilucci or Theriault.

Over the comm, Nassir commanded, *"Close the aft hatch! We're taking off!"*

"No!" zh'Firro cried. *"Theriault and the chief are still out there!"*

"Close that hatch! That's an order!"

Terrell set down Razka and turned to see zh'Firro and Threx staring at him, their gazes feral and desperate, both pleading with their eyes for him to do something. Stealing a look out the open hatchway, he saw Ilucci and Theriault both down and not moving, surrounded by a hellscape of fire and fracturing ground. He made up his mind.

"The hatch won't close, sir," he lied. "The controls are jammed."

Nassir replied, *"Get inside, I'll close it from up here."*

Terrell slapped Threx's shoulder and pointed at a nearby locker for emergency gear. The senior engineer's mate nodded, understanding Terrell's intentions perfectly. Terrell motioned for zh'Firro to follow him, and she did so without hesitation. On his way down the ramp, he said, "Engineer Threx is fixing the ramp now, sir!" As he and zh'Firro hit the ground, Threx wedged a large, heavy tool into a critical segment of the ramp's hydraulics.

Even through his suit, Terrell could feel the heat and radiation that were tearing the statite to pieces under their feet. Every running stride was a fight to stay upright as the ground buckled and sagged, then expanded and erupted. Walls of fire burst randomly from growing fissures, and Terrell knew that he and zh'Firro wouldn't be able to count on taking the same route back to the ship, because it likely would no longer be there.

They reached Ilucci and Theriault. The engineer was face-down in the dirt, and the lieutenant was sprawled on her back in an awkward pose. Terrell didn't bother to check for vital signs. He'd come out here to bring his people home, dead or alive. He knelt and hefted Ilucci over his shoulder in a fireman's carry. He turned to see zh'Firro had done the same for Theriault. With a nod, he signaled her to lead the way back. The lithe Andorian wasted no time and began the hard run back to the ship.

Dodging the random hazards of the dying statite had been hard enough with his hands free, but struggling under Ilucci's dead weight, Terrell found the fiery maze insurmountable. Every turn he made led to a dead end, every path zh'Firro blazed turned to slag before he could follow it to safety. Within seconds he was ten meters behind her and turning in panicked circles, frantically searching for a way back to the ship. Steeling his nerve, he hoped the Starfleet environmental suits were as well insulated as their design specs claimed—and he made a straight dash through the flames toward the *Sagittarius*.

He regretted his choice almost immediately. He felt the sting of searing heat over his entire body, except where he was covered by Ilucci. Painful burning sensations prickled his face and back, jabbed his arms and legs like needles fresh from an acid bath, and filled his suit with the horrid stench of singed body hair. By the time he broke through the far side of the firewall and stumbled the last few meters to the ship, he was sure the bottoms of his feet were covered in broken blisters. He fell to his knees halfway up the ramp, and Threx and zh'Firro leapt forward to grab Ilucci and carry him inside to safety.

Terrell crawled up the ramp into the cargo hold. As he collapsed in exhaustion onto the deck, he felt a rumbling through the ship's hull and knew it wasn't another quake. The engines were powering up. He shot a look at Threx, who grabbed the bulky metal rod he'd wedged into the ramp's hydraulics and pulled on it—only to find it was jammed.

Goddammit, Terrell cursed to himself, *this is no time for irony!* He forced himself to stand, stumble across the shuddering deck to Threx's side, and grab the rod. Adding his strength to the Denobulan's, he gritted his teeth and pulled until he was sure he'd given himself a hernia. Then the rod broke free, and the sudden release sent Terrell crashing back to the deck. Lying beside Ilucci, Razka, and Theriault, he watched the ramp lift and close, and he keyed his suit's transceiver. "Terrell to bridge. Ramp closed."

"Clark, get up here, on the double." The captain sounded pissed off.

"On my way." He shut off his comm and groaned. *No rest for the wicked.*

The environmental status light beside the ramp switched from red to green, indicating the cargo hold had been repressurized. As Doctor Babitz and medical technician Tan Bao scrambled down the ladder with medkits in hand, Terrell gratefully emancipated himself from the stifling bulk of the headpiece, then stripped off the rest of his suit and left it on the deck. Dressed only in his regulation gray undergarments, he winced as he climbed the ladder to the main deck.

Seconds later, he stepped onto the bridge. Nassir was in the command chair, and Dastin was at the helm. On the main viewscreen, the crumbling disk of the statite was being pulverized by the pulsar's emissions as it tumbled downward on a collision course with the neutron star. The captain turned slowly to face Terrell and fixed him with a stinkeye glare. "A *jammed hatch,* Clark? Really? *That* was the best excuse you could come up with?"

Terrell shrugged. "Time was a factor."

Nassir reproached him with a look. "Try to come up with something better for the log."

"Yes, sir." Terrell felt himself sway, and he blinked to focus his eyes as he fought off an attack of vertigo. "Permission to go to sickbay and collapse?"

"Granted."

• • •

Bad news came to Khatami from every direction. On her right, Klisiewicz tore his eyes from the science console to warn, "Starboard shields buckling!" At the forward stations, Thorsen called out, "Enemy ships too close for torpedo lock!" Shouting over Thorsen, Sliney declared, "The Tholians have split into three groups and are flanking us!" Over the intraship comm, chief engineer Bersh glov Mog bellowed, *"Hull breaches on Decks Fourteen, Fifteen, and Sixteen!"*

"Thorsen, switch to phasers! Target the group off our port bow!"

Thunderstrokes of enemy fire pummeled the *Endeavour*'s hull and drowned out the angry screech of its phasers. A split-second of weightlessness was Khatami's only warning before the deck pitched, courtesy of a momentary overload of the inertial dampers. She clutched the arms of her chair while her bridge crew struggled not to be hurled from their seats. The overhead lights dimmed for several seconds as the bridge consoles stuttered and threatened to go dark, and for a moment the only light was the ruddy glow of the Red Alert panels on the bulkheads.

Systems all over the bridge flickered, then thrummed back into service. Another low shriek of the phasers reassured Khatami that her ship was still combat-worthy. "Helm, hard about! If you have to ram through the enemy formation, do it, but block their shot of the statite!"

Eyes fixed on the main viewer, a despondent Thorsen replied, "Too late, Captain."

The screen showed the splintered remains of the statite being blasted into dust by the pulsar's regular bolts of supercharged particles. With a majestic flash, the statite vanished.

Thorsen looked back at Khatami. "The Tholian fleet's disengaging, Captain. I guess they're calling this mission accomplished."

Klisiewicz checked his sensor readings. "The other nodes in the statite cloud are falling into the star, Captain. So much for studying the—" He let the sentence trail off as he worked furiously at his console, adjusting the settings on the sensors.

As impatient as Khatami was to know what had snared the science officer's attention, it was Stano who prodded, "Talk to me, Klisiewicz. What've you got?"

Joy widened his eyes and lifted his voice. "The *Sagittarius*! She's clear of the pulsar's emission axis and breaking orbit of the star at full impulse!"

Immediately quashing the good mood, Thorsen declared, "Tholian fleet coming about on an intercept course for the *Sagittarius*!"

Khatami seized the moment. "Helm, put us between the *Sagittarius* and the Tholians. Estrada, let *Sagittarius* know we'll guard their aft quarter. Thorsen, route all shield power to the aft emitters, and have all torpedoes transferred to the aft launchers, on the double." She keyed open an intraship channel. "Bridge to engineering. Stand by for maximum warp."

"We'll give you all we've got," Mog answered.

Holding one hand over the Feinberger transceiver in his ear, Estrada reported, "Captain? *Sagittarius* says, 'Thanks for the escort, and try to keep up.'"

"Tholian vessels closing fast and charging weapons," Thorsen interjected.

"Load aft torpedo tubes," Khatami said, "and stand by to fire a full spread, Pattern Romeo." With a look she cued Stano to step out of the command well to the upper deck, watch over Klisiewicz's shoulder, and let her know when the Tholians closed to optimal range.

Sliney locked in a set of coordinates on the helm console. *"Sagittarius* has set course for Vanguard. They're powering up their warp nacelles."

"Stay with them, Mister Sliney."

"Aye, sir." On the main screen, the *Sagittarius* went to warp speed in an iridescent flash, and Sliney jumped the *Endeavour* into subspace right behind the scout ship.

Thorsen noted with dry efficiency, "The Tholians are matching our course and speed."

Stano nodded at Khatami, indicating that the Tholian battle group was in range.

"Fire," Khatami said. "Aft angle on-screen." The viewscreen switched to show the volley of photon torpedoes that raced away from the *Endeavour* and detonated in the Tholians' path. She hoped a show of strength would discourage their pursuit, but when the blinding glare faded, the Tholian vessels were still there and closing with slow, steady menace.

"Their shields are holding," Thorsen said.

Klisiewicz raised his voice while keeping his eyes on the sensor readout. "Incoming!" Muffled explosions shook the *Endeavour* and reverberated for several seconds in the hull.

"Aft shields holding," Thorsen said. "For now."

Stano stepped back down into the command well and took her place beside Khatami. "It's a long run back to Vanguard. And it's gonna seem even longer with them shooting us in the back every step of the way."

Khatami swiveled left and looked back toward the comm station. "Estrada, let Vanguard know we're coming in hot and could use a helping hand."

Sliney cast a nervous look back at the captain and first officer. "How long do you think they'll keep chasing us?"

There was no point in lying to the anxious helmsman. "Until we turn and fight or run out of fuel," Khatami said, "whichever comes first."

14

Once the old melody had been familiar, a bastion of comfort; now all T'Prynn could hear in it were the echoes of old lies.

She masked her frustration behind a placid façade as her best efforts raised nothing from Manón's grand piano but graceless notes that embodied banality. Her only consolation was that the shadowy cabaret was empty except for her and Spock, who sat beside her with his Vulcan lyre perched on his thigh. His expression mirrored hers, fixed somewhere between neutral and dour, while he listened to her uninspired performance of Gene Harris's arrangement of "Summertime," a number that once had been her signature piece, and that he had heard her perform years earlier. She hit all the right notes in the right tempo, and yet the song no longer sounded right. Some element she couldn't define, some ineffable quality that differentiated mere competence from virtuosity, was absent. It left her feeling empty even as she filled the darkened nightclub with sound. She no longer found any meaning in it.

Less than halfway through the piece, she lost patience with it and stopped. The interrupted note decayed for several seconds until she lifted her foot from the sustain pedal, restoring the yawning silence that surrounded her and Spock.

He wore a contemplative look as he stared at the stage, his angular features accentuated by the hard shadows of the spotlight that illuminated them on the piano's bench. T'Prynn imagined he was choosing his words with care. "You learned to play this instrument on Earth," he said, posing the question with the flat inflection of a statement.

"Correct."

Cradling his lyre, he shifted to face her. "And your teacher was a human."

A minuscule nod. "Yes."

His upswept brows furrowed slightly. "Did you choose to study this style of music, or was it the only option available to you?"

"I chose it." She found it difficult not to succumb to defensiveness at his questions. "Why do you consider that relevant?"

He cocked an eyebrow. "The fact that you gravitated to styles as expressive as jazz and blues suggests that those genres resonated with your subconscious. However, they no longer seem suited to you—or, to be more precise, you no longer seem suited to them."

In no mood for riddles, T'Prynn said, "Speak plainly, Spock."

"Very well. You've told me you feel disconnected from your music. But these are styles and songs you learned and related to when you were, in a very real sense, a different person." He leaned closer and spoke more gently. "You learned to play this instrument when you were a *val'reth,* two living *katras* fused in psychic conflict. Though you denied it, I suspect that, for you, music served as a psychic outlet for emotions you dared not otherwise express."

She looked down at the keyboard. In the past, her pride would have impelled her to deny his assertion, but now, freed of the combative *katra* of her dead fiancé, Sten, she saw the logic of Spock's assumption. "Do you mean to suggest that I no longer need music?"

"That is not for me to say." He thought for a moment. "However, I think that it will be futile for you to continue trying to play as the person you were. I would suggest you change your approach to this instrument, and to music in general, to reflect the person you have become."

Trying to imagine how she would put his simple-sounding advice into practice, she felt paralyzed. "How can I put aside more than fifty years' worth of training and experience?"

"Let go of old patterns," Spock said. "What was once an emotional purgative can now become an act of meditation and pure creation. Don't think about what to play; just play."

"I'm not sure I know how," T'Prynn confessed.

His voice was deep and soothing. "Close your eyes." She did as he asked, and then he continued. "Clear your mind of all thought. Let your hands rest on the keys." She settled her fingers into the middle third of the keyboard. "Breathe, T'Prynn. Relax and listen."

As she emptied her mind of its chaotic flurry of concerns and anxieties, she heard the first faint notes rise from Spock's lyre, music floating on the air like a feather aloft on a spring breeze, slow and meandering, seemingly random yet entirely natural in its effect. "What song is that?"

"An improvisation," Spock said, his voice hushed as he continued to play. "Listen and join me when you feel the music you want to play."

She tensed with disapproval. "*Feel* the music? Isn't that rather *human*?"

"Logic doesn't ask us to deny that our emotions exist, but to control and channel them in productive ways. All I ask is that you confront your emotions honestly, T'Prynn."

Reassured by his interpretation of the Vulcan disciplines whose apparent internal contradictions had long baffled her, T'Prynn drew a deep breath and exhaled slowly, forcing herself to relax and let the sweet sound of the lyre free her mind from its endless tumult. Seconds slipped away and melted into minutes, and then she lost herself in Spock's carefree melody. It was deceptive in its simplicity, and soon her trained ear discovered subtleties in it, hints of a longing behind its innocent façade. Then she noted a new richness in the tune and realized it was the piano—with eyes still shut, she had begun to explore the tune with Spock by instinct alone.

At first she merely filled in harmonies or echoed passages that Spock had played. Soon, she settled into key and devised her own melody to complement Spock's. As her performance became more confident, Spock let the lyre become her accompaniment, and then he let his part fade away altogether as T'Prynn charted her own musical course.

The music emerging from the piano was a mystery to her. The melody was nothing she had ever heard or been taught. It was very different from the human jazz and blues that she had played for decades; this new style was slower, more fluid and yet just as complex as jazz and as rich with feeling as blues. At moments it skirted the edge of dissonance, but each time she felt the way to bring it back into harmony before it went too far. Hidden in its rhythms and chords, she was certain she could hear influences as varied as Terran classical and Vulcan sonatas, Deltan chamber music and Andorian concertos.

All at once she felt the improvisation draw to a close. The melody culminated artfully and found its ending with a quiet grace. The measured, dignified conclusion reverberated softly inside the deserted cabaret, and as the last note decayed into silence, T'Prynn opened her eyes. She understood then what Spock had meant. It had simply *felt right*.

Neither of them spoke for several seconds. They sat together, reverent in their respect for the silence and each other. Reflecting upon her inner state, T'Prynn discovered a feeling she had not truly known since her childhood: contentment.

Spock's communicator beeped twice. He tucked his lyre under his left arm, plucked his communicator from his belt, and opened its gold grille with a flick of his wrist. "Spock here."

A voice that T'Prynn recognized as James Kirk's responded, *"Spock, we need you back on the* Enterprise. *There's an emergency, and we're shipping out in twenty minutes."*

"On my way. Spock out." He closed the communicator and tucked it back onto his belt as he stood. "You must excuse me."

As he moved to step away from the piano, T'Prynn reached out and gently grasped his left wrist. He met her gaze as she said in a humble voice, "Thank you, Spock."

He turned to face her and raised his right hand, fingers spread in the Vulcan salute. "Live long and prosper, T'Prynn."

She stood and returned the salute. "Peace and long life, Spock."

He lowered his hand, then hurried down the stage's front steps and crossed the cabaret's main room at a quick step on his way to the rear kitchen entrance. As she watched him leave, she wondered how she would ever repay him for this great kindness.

Then she imagined what Spock would want her to do: He would want her to live a life worthy of such a gift. She didn't know if she was equal to such a goal, or if she ever would be.

But as he disappeared from her sight, she vowed to try.

15

I don't know whether to admire the Tholians' tenacity or pity them for it, Khatami brooded.

Two days had passed since the *Endeavour* and its Tholian pursuers both had run out of torpedoes, but the twelve wedge-shaped warships remained close behind, engines pushed to their limits in order to keep pace with the heavy cruiser and its speedy companion, the *Sagittarius*. The only way the Tholians would be able to continue their assault would be if one or both of the Starfleet vessels dropped from warp speed to impulse, enabling the Tholians to bring their beam weapons to bear, but that wasn't likely to happen before they reached Vanguard. And once *Endeavour* and *Sagittarius* reached the station, they would be under the protection of its formidable defenses, which would easily pulverize the twelve Tholian ships.

All we have to do now, Khatami reminded herself, *is not let the ship fall apart before we get back to Vanguard*.

Stano conferred with an engineering liaison officer at a console on the bridge's upper ring, updated some figures on her data slate, then stepped down to join Khatami. "Mog reports he and his people have salvaged enough working parts to keep the last shield emitter running until we get back to Vanguard, but to do that they'll need to seal off nonessential compartments and shut down a number of auxiliary systems to conserve power." She handed the slate to Khatami. "Also, I've approved his proposal to consolidate crew accommodations and seal off outer sections in the saucer to reduce the strain on the life-support systems."

"How long to get it all done?"

"About two hours. They've already started."

An approving nod. "Good. Keep me posted."

The first officer stepped away to continue coordinating the crew's seemingly Sisyphean tasks. Though damage-control operations on the *Endeavour* had continued around the clock since the first shots were exchanged with the Tholians days earlier, so many of the ship's systems had been overloaded, compromised, or simply destroyed that complete repairs would not be possible without the aid of a starbase. Only the tireless efforts of the crew, guided by the unorthodox solutions of their Tellarite chief engineer, had kept the ship cruising at warp speed.

Fortunately, the *Sagittarius* had suffered only moderate damage before escaping from the statite, and that was due in large part to the *Endeavour* serving as its shield for the entire marathon run for home. Whatever they might have found or learned on the statite apparently had been important enough for Admiral Nogura to make its safe return to Vanguard a top priority. Unfortunately, the numbers on the data slate in Khatami's hand made it clear that her ship was one mishap away from a total warp core failure, and she had no doubt that if the *Endeavour* fell behind, the Tholians would scream past it and continue chasing the *Sagittarius*.

Her grave ponderings were interrupted by the anxious voice of Lieutenant Klisiewicz. "Captain? Long-range sensors detect a ship ahead of us, moving at warp eight, on an intercept trajectory. Whatever it is, it's big."

Stano crossed the bridge to look over his shoulder. "Can you identify it?"

"Not yet. I'll keep scanning for an energy signature."

Neelakanta turned his chair to look back at Khatami. "Captain, if the Tholians have flanked us with a battleship, and our only functional shield emitter is angled aft—"

"I'm aware of our tactical predicament, Lieutenant."

The Arcturian navigator's red eyes widened with alarm. "I should also remind you, Captain, that we can't use phasers at warp, or power them without dropping the shields."

"Luckily," Khatami replied, "we're not alone out here. Estrada, hail Captain Nassir and let him know we need the *Sagit-*

tarius to cover our bow. Whatever shield power they have should be angled forward, and if they still carry a pair of photon torpedoes, they should get ready to use them." The communications officer nodded and set to work relaying the message.

Khatami took a deep breath and forced herself to present a calm front to her crew as the minutes ticked down, bringing the *Endeavour* and the *Sagittarius* closer to whatever was heading their way. She was contemplating turning the *Endeavour*'s shuttlecraft into bombs and launching them on autopilot at the pursuing Tholian fleet when Klisiewicz suddenly exclaimed at the top of his lungs, "Yes!" All eyes turned toward the lieutenant, who looked up, eyes bright and wide. "Sir, I've identified the incoming vessel! It's the *Enterprise*!"

A loud cheer erupted from around the bridge, and if not for the demands of propriety, Khatami would gladly have joined them. She raised her voice to be heard above the noisy celebration. "Estrada, tell Captain Nassir to belay my last, then hail the Tholian fleet commander. Let him know he's about to meet our reinforcements."

"With pleasure, Captain," Estrada said, already at work.

As she expected, there was no immediate response from the Tholian fleet commander, though she wasn't sure if it was merely posturing or the fact that the Tholians' sensors hadn't yet confirmed the identity of the approaching Starfleet vessel—a *Constitution*-class heavy cruiser like the *Endeavour*. Once the *Enterprise* closed to visual range, however, the Tholian fleet abruptly dropped out of warp and began a hasty course correction, back toward Tholian space.

"Not a moment too soon," Stano said under her breath.

Before Khatami could reply, Estrada said, "The Tholian commander's hailing us."

"Put him on," Khatami said.

The image on the main viewer shifted from an aft view of the Tholian fleet to a hazy crimson glow, within which Khatami could barely discern the outline of the Tholian fleet commander's arthropodal crystalline body. His metallic shriek of a voice came through the universal translator charged with fury. *"This is not over,"* he said. *"You have meddled with forces you do not understand—and you will all pay for your interference."*

Then the transmission ended, and the screen reverted to the image of the alien fleet as it finished its course change and leapt to warp speed, en route to regroup with its waiting armada.

Stano crossed her arms. "Charming fellow. Real smooth talker."

"For a Tholian, he's practically a diplomat," Khatami said.

Estrada looked up from his console. *"Enterprise* is hailing us, Captain."

"On-screen." Khatami watched the forward screen snap to an image of the *Enterprise*'s dashing young commanding officer, a lean and fair-haired man in his mid-thirties. "Captain Kirk, I presume?"

"And you must be Captain Khatami."

She favored him with a grateful smile. "Thanks for rolling out the red carpet."

"Our pleasure, Captain." Kirk turned serious. *"What's your status? Do you need assistance?"*

"More than I'd like to admit. We got beat up pretty badly over the last few days."

Kirk nodded. *"Understood. We'll be in transporter range in a few minutes. Once we're all at impulse, we'll beam over engineers, supplies, and whatever else you need."*

"Glad to hear it," Khatami said. A glance from Stano confirmed that she was passing the good news to Mog. Turning her attention back to Kirk, she added, "Maybe then we'll be able to keep up with you on the way back to Vanguard."

"We'll only be with you for half the trip, I'm afraid. About an hour ago, we received a distress signal from the planet Ariannus. We'll have to leave you after we pass Kessik. But don't worry— the latest intel from Starfleet says the rest of that sector is clear, and the Buenos Aires *is en route to meet you at Al Nath. They'll be your escort from there back to Vanguard."*

"Acknowledged." Khatami was about to sign off, but she

didn't know when she might get another chance to speak with Kirk, and her curiosity was too intense to be denied. "Captain, if it wouldn't be too impertinent, could I ask you a personal question?"

The young captain looked amused by her carefully couched inquiry. *"Be my guest."*

"I read a report from Starfleet Command last year that said you'd met the Greek deity Apollo. I was just wondering . . . did that *really* happen?"

Kirk glanced at someone off-screen, then his mouth curled upward with playful mischief. *"I prefer to think that Apollo met me. . . . Enterprise out."*

16

Jetanien kneeled on his portable *glenget* opposite Lugok, at a table in a secluded corner of Ventus, one of the few restaurants still operating within the limits of Paradise City. The narrow, low-ceilinged dining room's deeply subdued illumination did little to conceal its filthy floors and bare walls. If not for the dim shaded bulb hanging directly above their table, Jetanien doubted he would even be able to read the menu. He looked around the dingy eatery with suspicion. "Lugok, are you quite certain this establishment is open for business?"

"Quite certain," the Klingon replied without lifting his eyes from his menu.

Tapping the digits of one scaly manus on the tabletop, Jetanien wasn't convinced. "If that's the case, old friend, shouldn't someone be attending us? Had we not found menus on our table when we arrived, I suspect we would still be waiting for them."

Lugok looked mildly irritated as he peeked over the top of his menu. "Be patient. Maybe they're busy."

"Oh, really?" He waved broadly at the sea of empty tables surrounding them. "With whom? If this restaurant is a going concern, why do we appear to be its only patrons?"

The Klingon answered with a glum frown, "Its cuisine isn't very popular."

"Nonsense," Jetanien huffed. "I've already seen several items on the menu that sound delectable to my rather discerning palate."

"As I said."

Jetanien ground his mandible for a moment, then set down his menu. "I suppose we can at least be grateful that by meeting here, we are unlikely to fall victim to eavesdroppers. Or the temptation to overeat. Or eat at all." He leaned back and strained to divine any sound or motion from the kitchen, but detected nothing. "Perhaps this is a self-service automat."

"I am quite sure it's not."

Leaning away from the table, Jetanien grumbled, "Maybe if I go back there, I could get their attention."

Lugok harrumphed. It was a deep but muffled sound, hidden under his thick beard and fleshy torso. "Like the way Captain Khatami got the Tholians' attention at Eremar?"

"So, you heard about that, did you?"

A sadistic chuckle animated the Klingon's swarthy face. "Half the quadrant's heard about it by now. The Tholians all but called it a war crime."

"Ridiculous. Captain Khatami's actions were entirely proportional and in accordance with accepted interstellar law. She did not fire on their ships until they fired upon hers."

"You speak as if the Tholians give a damn about such distinctions. At a time when the Gonmog Sector—"

"We prefer to call it the Taurus Reach."

"Good for you," Lugok continued, unfazed by the interruption. "At a time when the Gonmog Sector is teetering on the brink of all-out war, Khatami should have known better."

A derisive snort escaped Jetanien's nasal aperture. "It's just more Tholian saber-rattling."

"Yes, just like that empty gesture they made when they destroyed the *Bombay*." Lugok looked up and studied Jetanien's face, perhaps hoping to provoke some kind of response. After several seconds passed without Jetanien taking the bait, the Klingon moved on. "So, what was your little scout ship looking for on Eremar, anyway?"

"I have absolutely no idea," Jetanien said. "You might recall that I'm officially no longer cleared for sensitive operational intelligence from Starfleet." He knew that Lugok understood the key word in that sentence had been *officially*. The two "retired" diplomats had become quite adept at reading between the lines of each other's statements. It was simply a matter of professional courtesy that they tended to refrain from calling each other out on their lies. "If, by some thermodynamic miracle, a server should ever appear to take our orders, I believe I should like to sample their assortment of fried beetles."

"With any luck, this place will burn to the ground, with us in it, before I have to endure the spectacle of watching you eat that." He perused the menu again. "The *thrakas* carpaccio sounds like it might be edible, if I can get a decent stein of *warnog* to wash it down."

Inhaling deeply, Jetanien thought for a moment that he caught the scent of smoke from the kitchen, but then it was gone, and silence reigned once more inside Ventus. "I suppose now is as good a time as any to mention that I conferred with our friend from Romulus."

"And . . . ?"

"The conversation was less than fully illuminating."

Lugok chortled softly. "I presume you're exercising your talent for understatement." He shook his head. "So, you've learned nothing pertinent to my inquiry?"

"That was not what I said." Jetanien reached under the folds of his tunic and took a data card from an inside pocket. He put it on the table and pushed it across to Lugok, who picked it up and tucked it inside his own jacket as Jetanien spoke. "Apparently, both Starfleet Intelligence and their civilian counterparts have been investigating this matter for some time. It seems your suspicions are correct: one of your empire's noble Houses is being courted to act as a proxy for Romulan interests, perhaps as a prelude to seizing the chancellorship."

The Klingon's voice was a low rumble. "Which one?"

"Duras. One of the more bellicose voices on your High Council at the moment, and not one the Federation would be keen to see wield power as a head of state."

Lugok nodded. "That is a desire you share with Councillor Gorkon and Chancellor Sturka." He leaned closer, and Jetanien mirrored the gesture. "Of course, the chancellor's animus toward Duras is personal, rooted in old House rivalries. Gorkon's enmity for the man is political. Hotheads like Duras make it difficult to cultivate more moderate voices on the High Council."

"It's our hope that assisting you in this matter will foster such moderate voices in the future, for our mutual benefit," Jetanien said.

A broad grin exposed jagged teeth. "And the fact that it screws the Romulans . . . ?"

"Is merely an added incentive."

The two comrades in exile shared a hearty laugh that gradually tapered off, leaving them once again enveloped in silence.

Then Lugok pounded his fist on the table. "Where in Gre'thor is our waiter?"

Jetanien stood and folded up his portable *glenget*. "Did I mention that on my walk over here, I saw a street vendor selling grilled *pleeka* lizards on sticks?"

The Klingon got up and gave Jetanien a fraternal slap on the back.

"Lead the way, old friend."

The ruby glow of the transporter faded from Kutal's sight as he materialized alone aboard the *I.K.S. baS'jev*. The ship's commanding officer, Captain Chang, moved forward and extended his hand as Kutal stepped off the transporter platform. "Welcome aboard, Captain," Chang said.

Kutal and Chang clasped each other's forearms, their grips firm and manners guarded. "Captain Chang." Kutal looked down at his shorter, slightly built peer. Unlike most Klingon warriors, who took pride in their manes of hair and ragged beards, Chang had shaved his head bald and limited his facial hair to a pair of tusklike growths above the corners of his mouth. His baldness called attention to his suppressed cranial crest and emphasized his status as one of the *QuchHa'*, a caste of Klingons descended from the victims of the previous century's Augment Virus, which had transformed proud Klingons into pathetically human-looking weaklings that the Empire had decided were good for little but cannon fodder. Kutal knew not to judge Chang by his appearance, however. No one rose to command of an imperial warship without great reserves of strength and cunning, and he was certain that Chang, whose lineage included ties to some of the Great Houses, was no exception.

Chang released Kutal's arm and directed him toward the small compartment's open doorway. "Let's repair to a more private location."

"As you wish." He followed Kutal out to the corridor and then forward. The *baS'jev* was a vessel of the same class as the *Zin'za*, and except for a few minor details and the unfamiliar faces of the crew in the passageways, its interior was identical to that of Kutal's ship—right down to the musky, acrid odors that rendered its humid air richly palpable. The two captains walked in silence until Chang entered his quarters and summoned Kutal inside.

The door slid shut behind Kutal, and then Chang spoke. "It would appear that we both count Councillor Gorkon as a friend and ally."

Kutal didn't like the way Chang spoke. He used too many words, like a human. It made Kutal wonder whether the man was showing off or trying to hide something—or both. "Yes," Kutal said as he slowly circuited the room's perimeter. "Gorkon is a friend." He paused long enough to shoot a cautionary look at Chang. "If he were not, I would not be here."

"True enough." Chang crossed the room to his desk, opened a drawer, and took out a bottle of very old *warnog* that Kutal knew to be obscenely expensive. He removed the stopper and held the bottle out toward Kutal. "Shall we drink to our new acquaintance?"

The more he speaks, the less I like him. He buried his contempt deep. "I'll drink."

Chang filled two goblets half full, handed one to Kutal, and set down the bottle. "How much were you told by Gorkon?"

"Only that I was to meet your ship here. The rest he left to you."

The other captain's smile was cold. "I see." He guzzled half his beverage in one tip, sleeved the excess from his chin, and grinned at Kutal. "Drink, my friend. I give you my word the *warnog*'s not poisoned."

"I never said it was." Kutal downed a mouthful of the potent libation. It lived up to its reputation: it was some of the finest *warnog* he'd ever tasted. "What have you been told?"

"Gorkon suspects the House of Duras is in league with the Romulans, trading the Empire's security for their own enrichment."

If true, it was a damning accusation. "Based on what evidence?"

Chang's icy smile remained frozen in place. "He didn't say. I didn't ask. Far be it from me to question the word of a member of the High Council."

Kutal continued to wander the room's periphery. He stopped when he noticed a row of unusual tomes on the shelf above Chang's bunk. Leaning closer, he scrutinized the titles, then turned a curious eye toward his host. "You read *human* literature."

"Only the playwright known as Shakespeare." He added with a sly hint of conspiracy, "Between you and me, I think his plays read better in the original *tlhIngan Hol*."

It was hard for Kutal to know whether Chang had spoken in jest or sincerity. He decided to give the man the benefit of the doubt. "Know your enemy through his art, eh?"

"If you like. But for the moment, our enemy lies not without but within."

Kutal nodded. "How do we proceed? I trust you don't need to be reminded that Duras and his House are among the wealthiest and most powerful members of the Empire?"

All traces of mirth fled Chang's face. "I'm well aware, yes. It falls to us to turn the strengths of the Duras clan into their weaknesses. They have numbers but lack discipline. Their patriarch is temperamental and susceptible to provocation. With time and observation, I am certain we will divine an exploitable weakness and then seek our moment of opportunity."

A dismissive grunt telegraphed Kutal's incredulity. "In my experience, opportunities multiply only when seized."

"Quite right," Chang said. "So it is that Gorkon has seized such an opportunity for us." He stepped over to his desk and rotated the computer screen so that it faced Kutal. Then he activated the display, which showed a set of orders from the High Command. "Brakk, son of Duras, commands the battle cruiser *Qu'vang*. It recently lost its two primary combat escorts in a battle on our rimward border. Gorkon has arranged for our two vessels to be reassigned as the *Qu'vang*'s new escorts—putting us in position to monitor Brakk's communications with Duras."

"A waste of time." Kutal guzzled the rest of his *warnog* and set the empty goblet on Chang's desk. "Spying on that *taHqeq* will gain us nothing."

"Perhaps." Chang's frigid smile returned. "Though I suspect Gorkon already knows that."

Momentarily dumbfounded, Kutal wondered aloud, "Then why make us wing guards to that sniveling—" He caught himself as the councillor's likely rationale became clear to him. "We're being used as bait. To see if Duras moves against us as a prelude to attacking Gorkon."

"My supposition exactly. However, we have the advantage of knowing our part ahead of time—and as every hunter knows, sometimes the prey wins."

"And if spying on Brakk uncovers proof of the Durases' treachery, what then?"

Chang refilled Kutal's glass. "In that case, my friend, on behalf of the Empire, we shall make medicines of our great revenge."

17

Hands folded atop his desk and his face cast in a portrait of stern rebuke, Nogura watched Captain Khatami enter his office and halt at attention in front of him. The tall, olive-skinned woman of Iranian ancestry held her chin up proudly. "You asked to see me, sir?"

"Indeed, I did." His voice had an edge that could cut through steel. "Do you have any idea how much damage control Starfleet has had to do because of your actions at Eremar? The Tholians have filed formal protests with the Federation Council! Half the members of the Security Council are calling for your stripes." He stood and stepped around his desk, then circled slowly behind her as he continued. "You damned near put us into an all-out shooting war with the Tholians. In the last seven days, I've had my head handed to me by everyone from the C-in-C to the president's chief of staff! If they had their way, you'd be swabbing decks aboard a sublight garbage scow on an endless loop through the Rigel colonies." He stopped in front of her and trained his stare on her brown eyes, which were fixed on the rear wall of his office. "Well? What do you have to say for yourself, Captain?"

Khatami's demeanor was cool and composed. "Permission to speak freely, Admiral?"

"Granted."

She turned and met his gaze. "If you've read my report, sir, then you know that I did absolutely everything I could to resolve the situation without the use of force. The Tholian fleet commander refused to negotiate in good faith or even permit the *Sagittarius* to withdraw safely. Once they began bombarding the statite, and refused our requests to cease fire, they left me no choice but to take armed action. In keeping with both the letter and spirit of your orders, I restrained our initial response to targeting the interphasic generators the Tholians had deployed. Legally, we acted in defense of the *Sagittarius,* and under the terms of the Selonis Accords, we were fully within our rights to do so. Subsequently, the Tholian fleet opened fire on us, and I took such action as I deemed necessary to defend my ship and crew, as well as the *Sagittarius.* Our tactical responses were designed to be proportional, not lethal." She paused, drew a deep breath, and looked away from Nogura. "If placed in the same situation again, I would respond *exactly* the same way. If that means you need to take my stripes and relieve me of my command, so be it. But I stand by my decision, whether the paper-pushers back on Earth like it or not."

Holding his poker face steady, Nogura paced back to his chair and sat down. He folded his hands and leaned forward. "No one's taking your stripes, Captain. Or your command. Not if I have anything to say about it." She registered the news with a wide-eyed stare, and Nogura smiled. "Of course you did the right thing. But the president yells at Starfleet Command, and Starfleet Command tells me to yell at you. So, this is me yelling at you. After all, orders are orders. And now that I've obeyed my orders, I can tell you what I *really* want to say: Well done, Captain. You and your crew have an open tab tonight at Manón's."

"Thank you, sir."

"Don't thank me yet. Take a seat. There's something else we need to talk about." Khatami sat down in a guest chair and crossed her legs at the knee—a relaxed pose made possible by her preference for wearing the standard duty uniform of tunic and trousers rather than the minidress variation some personnel had adopted. She raised her brow, cueing Nogura to continue. "I'm afraid it's going to take a bit longer than usual for us to complete your ship's repairs. We used up a lot of resources refitting a superfreighter to sneak the *Sagittarius* out to the Iremal Cluster, and what we didn't pour into that went into building the decoy whose wreckage you recovered. We have a shipment of spare parts on order, and we're doing our best to fabricate what we can, but I'm afraid the *Endeavour* will have to spend at least the next few weeks in the docking bay—and maybe longer, depending on whether our shipment gets delayed by piracy."

Khatami's features tightened. "Putting aside my own feelings about the matter, how will this affect the station's tactical posture?"

"I've ordered the *Akhiel* and the *Buenos Aires* to tighten their patrol routes, but with *Defiant* gone and the *Endeavour* down for maintenance, we're more vulnerable than ever before. I'd hoped we could count on the *Enterprise* to cover the gap, but Starfleet insists she's needed elsewhere." He reclined his chair. "You've been out here longer than I have. How long do you think it will take the Klingons and the Tholians to realize we're on the defensive?"

The captain thought that over for a few seconds. "It depends. From what I've read, the Tholians know the *Defiant* is MIA, but the Klingons might not be aware of it yet. From their perspective, it might seem as if the *Defiant*'s been deployed on a long-range recon. It might be useful to set up some fake comm chatter to make the Klingons think the *Defiant*'s still in action." One side of her mouth pulled into a crooked frown. "Unfortunately, the Tholians already know about the *Defiant,* and they also know just how hard they hit us and the *Sagittarius*. Plus, judging from the size of the armada they have standing by at their border, I think it's possible they've been waiting for a moment like this."

Nogura's concerns increased. "If that's the case, what are they waiting for? They could cross the border any time they wanted. There's nothing we could do to stop them. Why wait?"

"I have no idea, sir." She cracked a sardonic smile. "If you're really that curious, you could hail them via subspace and ask."

"No, thank you," Nogura said. "Something tells me I won't like their answer."

"That makes two of us, sir."

Ezekiel Fisher felt like an invisible man as he forded the commotion of business-as-usual inside Docking Bay 92, located low on the station's central core, just above the lower docking ring. Forklifts buzzed in and out of the open cargo hold of the civilian transport ship *S.S. Lisbon*. The boxy yellow vehicles filled the docking bay with resounding metallic bangs as each one struck the ramp that led up into the ship. Lifting his eyes to take in the vessel at a glance, Fisher found it sorely wanting by more than one measure. It looked like a fat, ugly fish. The only parts of its gray hull not dulled by a patina of scrapes and dents were those covered by mismatched off-white patches whose welded edges reminded Fisher of scar tissue.

Overamplified music echoed inside the docking bay; at first it sounded like raw noise to Fisher, then he realized that was because he was hearing three different songs at once: one from inside the *Lisbon*'s hold; another from one of the forklifts, giving it a peculiar Doppler-shifted quality as it sped past in one direction or another; and one from atop the ship, where a team of grime-covered mechanics and engineers walked across the dorsal hull, scanning it with microfissure detectors and tagging areas in need of repair. A few dozen men of various species worked around the ship, packing or unpacking cargo containers—that is, when they weren't dodging the irresponsibly driven forklifts. Fisher had no doubt that Vanguard Hospital would be treating a number of work-related injuries from this crew in the immediate future. He forced that thought from his mind. *That's not your problem anymore,* he reminded himself.

Navigating the energetic chaos with caution, he slipped through a narrow channel between two tall mountains of stacked cargo containers, following the clamor of voices. As he emerged on the other side, he saw a cluster of people—some in coveralls, others in more formal merchant marine uniforms—surrounding a lean, short-haired woman of Thai heritage. She was in her mid-forties, Fisher guessed, and what she lacked in stature she made up for in intensity. Without the use of a universal translator, she seemed adept at berating each of her people in their native language, whether that was Tellarite, Andorii, Vulcan, or any of a handful of Terran tongues, sometimes switching from one to another in mid-sentence without missing a syllable. While verbally eviscerating one person who would then slink away in shame, she would also be signing paperwork presented by another and silently dismissing a third, complaint unheard.

Enjoying the show from a discreet distance, Fisher smiled.

I know this music. She must be the captain.

He waited until she broke free of her gaggle of people with problems, and then he emerged from the gap between the containers to intercept her on the move. "Captain Boonmee?"

She answered without sparing him so much as a look. "Who wants to know?"

"Doctor Ezekiel Fisher, Starfleet." Boonmee stopped and faced Fisher as he added with his best disarming charm, "Retired." He offered her his hand, and she shook it quickly.

"Captain Khunying Boonmee." She resumed walking. "You've got one minute."

He hurried to keep up with her. "I heard from one of your debarking passengers that you might have an open cabin for the return trip to the core systems."

"As a matter of fact, I do," Boonmee said. "What's your final destination?"

She sidestepped to avoid a speeding forklift, and Fisher lost half a step in the course of not getting run over. He jogged to catch up to Boonmee and replied between gasps, "Mars."

"The good news is, we're actually planning a stop at Mars. The bad news is, the only cabin I have available on this run is our VIP suite."

"Why is that bad news?"

"I usually put it up for auction. Current bid's at eleven thousand." She swatted a yellow-furred Tellarite in black coveralls and let rip a stream of angry Tellarite verbiage. The crewman nodded furiously, then slipped away, grumbling. Boonmee looked back at Fisher. "As I was saying, if you want to put in a bid, you're welcome to, but I'm guessing eleven grand's probably a bit steep for someone on a Starfleet pension."

"I'll pay you twenty to close the bidding and sell me the berth right now," Fisher said. "You can even put me to work if you need a surgeon."

His offer seemed to amuse her. "We have a sawbones, thanks." A narrow-eyed, curious stare. "Twenty grand, huh? You must really want to get home."

"You could say that."

"Make it twenty-five, and you've got a deal."

Fisher nodded. "Sold."

The captain grabbed Fisher by his shirt and pulled him clear of another hot-rodding forklift. She screamed a blistering flurry of Andorii profanities at the vehicle's antennaed blue driver, then made a token effort to brush the wrinkles from Fisher's shirt. "Sorry about that. One more thing: I hope you're not in a big hurry to leave. We're stuck here for at least another three or four weeks, waiting for cargo and passengers coming in from the fringe territories. Can't leave without 'em, since flying empty is just burning fuel for no good reason."

"I understand. It's not a problem. To be honest, yours is the first ship I've found in weeks that had an open cabin for the trip home."

Boonmee smirked. "I wish I'd known that. I'd have charged you more." She held up open palms. "Just kidding. If you're ready to book the cabin, we can head inside and find my XO."

"Sounds great," Fisher said, gesturing for Boonmee to lead the way.

As she escorted him up the ramp and inside the ship, she said, "I don't suppose you play poker, by any chance."

"Just Texas Hold 'em, Omaha, and a few dozen variants of five- and seven-card stud."

She chuckled. "You'll fit right in here, Doc."

An anxious hush settled over the white-jacketed scientists of the Vault who unpacked the first of dozens of shipping containers ferried from Eremar to Vanguard aboard the *Sagittarius*. Ming Xiong watched with anticipation and fear as the researchers handled the twelve-sided crystal artifacts with silent reverence and transferred them to a number of analysis chambers inside the Vault's central containment area. Each dodecahedron would be checked for defects or damage as a prerequisite for inclusion in the next phase of the team's research.

Admiral Nogura stood beside Doctor Carol Marcus a few meters to Xiong's right. They observed the painstaking process from behind the transparent steel protective barrier that separated the master control console from the workstations that ringed the circular isolation chamber, which housed the artifacts. Lieutenant Theriault stood close by on Xiong's left, watching the Vault scientists with equal measures of worry and envy.

Standing apart from everyone else, T'Prynn lurked near the lab's entrance, her motives as inscrutable as ever while she monitored the meticulously choreographed proceedings.

Theriault nudged Xiong with her elbow. "Hard to believe we came back with fifty-five hundred of these things, right? What do you think you'll do with all of them?"

"We're hoping to use the visual scans you made of the Eremar Array to create a similar framework here, but in a far more compact form." Despite the enormity of the find by the crew of the scout ship, Xiong shook his head slowly with disappointment. "I'm still upset the Tholians destroyed the other half of the artifacts before you could recover them. When I think about how much potential each of these objects has, it feels like a major loss to science."

The young female science officer turned a disbelieving stare toward Xiong. "Are you kidding? If you want to talk about a loss to science, shed a few tears for the Dyson bubble that fell into the pulsar. It was ninety-nine percent gone *before* the Tholians fragged it, and I *still* could have spent the next thirty years finding out what made it tick." Her shoulders slumped, giving her a defeated aspect as she looked back at the growing mass of artifacts inside the isolation chamber. "I sure hope those things are worth it, because I'll spend the rest of my life wondering what I might have learned from poking around on those statites."

Beyond the protective barrier, the scientists who weren't directly involved in unpacking the artifacts or configuring them into an array were busy monitoring the first scan results. Deltan theoretical physicist Doctor Tarcoh hovered over a sensor display and pointed out one new string of data after another to Doctor Varech jav Gek. The excitable Tellarite molecular chemist fidgeted madly with each new bit of information, and he seemed to have no idea what to do with his beefy, three-fingered hands, so he just waved them about in between scratching his head or hugging himself, ostensibly to contain his excitement.

Nogura kept his eyes on the activity in the lab as he sidled over to Xiong. There was an undercurrent of concern in his voice. "Lieutenant, are you sure we have enough power and shielding to keep this array contained? I don't want a repeat of what happened to the *Lovell*."

"Based on the readings we made of the first two artifacts, both in tandem and individually, we're certain the new isolation protocols are more than sufficient."

The admiral's salt-and-pepper brow furrowed with doubt. "That's what you and the Corps of Engineers told me before a Shedai turned a *Daedalus*-class starship into confetti."

Xiong clenched his jaw for a moment until he was able to answer his superior officer calmly. "That was because we'd weakened the crystal lattice of that artifact by transmitting an amplified and highly focused subspace pulse into it, while trying to communicate with the entity inside. That's not a mistake we'll make again."

That seemed to appease the admiral. "What do you plan to do with this array once it's finished and operational?"

"In theory, anything the Shedai could have done with their network will be within our grasp," Xiong said. "We can harness the Conduits for everything from force projection to real-time communications across distances beyond the range of the strongest subspace signal. And once we have the Shedai contained, we'll be free to explore and colonize the Taurus Reach, and take our time unraveling the information encoded within the meta-genome."

Carol Marcus stepped up alongside Nogura, in a hurry to join the discussion. "Hang on, gentlemen. I think we need to start by finding a way to communicate with the Shedai we're already holding, before we go looking to snare any more."

Nogura's manner was withering. "With all respect, Doctor, diplomacy isn't high on our list of priorities concerning the Shedai." He turned his back on Marcus, faced Xiong, and continued in a more businesslike manner. "Assuming this array works as planned, what would be the risks to the station in a worst-case scenario?"

As he considered the admiral's question, Xiong was distracted for a moment when he noticed that T'Prynn had moved to stand at the transparent wall of the isolation chamber and was staring intently at the first Tkon artifact they'd ever acquired, the one she herself had helped recover from Klingon forces on a distant planet called Golmira.

Forcing his attention back to the conversation, Xiong said, "A worst-case scenario, from our perspective, would be one that resulted in a massive energy spike from this laboratory's dedicated power plant into the array, compromising the integrity of the artifacts' lattices. In such an event, if they were operating at or beyond their intended capacity, that might be enough to permit the Shedai imprisoned within them to break free, as did the one aboard the *Lovell*. But we have several redundant safeguards against that kind of power spike, sir. Nothing short of catastrophic damage to the system would put us at risk."

"All right," Nogura said. "Proceed as planned, and send me daily status updates. Unless there's a significant development, for better or worse—in that case, notify me immediately."

"Aye, sir."

Marcus stepped in front of Nogura. "Admiral, I have serious misgivings about the operation you're asking us to conduct. Frankly, I don't think we know anywhere near enough about these artifacts to control them properly, and until we do far more research under controlled conditions, I can't approve any plan that calls for them to be daisy-chained together into an array whose functions are not only unknown but also potentially disastrous. Even more important, I have to protest the callous disregard that you and Starfleet have shown toward our Shedai captive. Such barbaric treatment of a sentient life-form is an offense against the laws of the Federation and the principles of Starfleet. Until we establish communication with that being, I refuse to subject it to further experimentation."

Nogura's resolve never wavered, and his eyes betrayed no sign of anger as he met Marcus's glare. "First of all, Doctor Marcus, I have not *asked* the Vault team to conduct this operation, I've *ordered* them to do it. Second, as for your invocation of the laws of the Federation, I see that I must remind you once again that we are not currently *in* the Federation. Third, I do not need you to lecture me about the principles of Starfleet. I am well aware of my oath and my duty. Fourth, and last, you seem to forget that whatever authority you wield inside this lab is nothing compared to the authority I wield over this station. Your concerns are all noted—and overruled." He looked at Xiong. "Lieutenant. Tell your team to construct and activate the artifact array with all due haste, and have Doctor Marcus assist you as necessary."

The admiral walked away while Xiong stood dumbstruck, processing the simultaneous demotion of Carol Marcus and his reinstatement as Director of the Vault, the position he'd held before Marcus's arrival on Vanguard years earlier. He knew the shock and humiliation she must be feeling at that moment, and it took all his training as a Starfleet officer not to look the least bit pleased about the situation. Marcus, however, wore her dudgeon openly, crossing her arms as she fixed him with a smoldering stare. "I suppose you'll want the office back," she said.

"First, I think we should focus on getting the artifacts unpacked and accounted for," Xiong said. Despite his best intentions, he gloated. "*Then* I'll take the office."

18

Captain Kutal entered the main transporter room of the *I.K.S. Zin'za* to find his first officer waiting for him. BelHoQ's lazy stance and saturnine glare radiated disgust as he grumbled, "Has that *yIntagh* Brakk lost his mind?"

"He claims our channels are being monitored and refuses to share sensitive intel over the comms," Kutal said. Before his first officer could protest, he added, "I know it's stupid, but he's the fleet commander. We have no choice but to do this his way." He hooked a thumb over his shoulder at the transporter controls. "Beam over his lackey and get this done with."

BelHoQ stepped back to the transporter controls and activated the system, filling the compartment with the rich hum of charging energizer coils. Kutal kept his true concerns to himself as he faced the platform and awaited Brakk's courier. It had been less than a week since the *Zin'za* and the *baS'jev* had joined Brakk's ship, the *Qu'vang,* as its combat escorts. Brakk had wasted no time splitting up Kutal's and Chang's ships, immediately ordering the *baS'jev* on a long-range reconnaissance patrol while keeping the *Zin'za* close by. Just as Captain Chang had predicted, Brakk—no doubt with prompting from his father, Duras—had pegged Kutal and Chang as hostile operatives of their rival, Gorkon. Regardless, the haste with which Brakk had responded had taken Kutal by surprise. He had expected himself and Chang to be held at arm's length for a few months while Brakk assessed their strengths and vulnerabilities. Instead, the impulsive young commander had gone directly to dividing and conquering.

Even if I respect him for nothing else, Kutal decided, *I have to admire his aggression. But that begs the question: Is he really paranoid about using the comms? Or is this merely a ruse?*

"The *Qu'vang* is signaling ready," BelHoQ said. "Energizing."

A crimson flurry of high-energy particles swirled into view above one of the target pads, and within it a Klingon warrior took shape. Seconds later the glow of the beam faded, and the enlisted crewman stepped down and saluted Kutal with his right fist raised against his chest. "Captain Kutal, I bear a message for you from Captain Brakk." He held out a data card in his left hand. "It is coded for your eyes only, sir."

Kutal took the data card from the soldier. "Naturally."

"My orders are to wait here for your encoded reply."

"Whatever. Stay here. Don't touch anything." Kutal headed for the door and subtly cued BelHoQ to follow him. As they left the transporter room, an armed guard entered to keep Brakk's messenger under watch until they returned.

Neither of them spoke on the walk forward to Kutal's quarters, but as he led BelHoQ inside, the first officer stopped in the doorway. "He said the message was for your eyes only."

"Do I look like I give a damn? Get in here, and lock the door behind you."

BelHoQ secured the door while Kutal crossed to his desk, sat down, and inserted the data card into a slot beside his computer terminal. The imperial emblem, a black trefoil against a red background, appeared on the screen as a guttural, synthetic voice issued from the monitor's hidden speakers: *"State command authorization code."*

"Kutal *wa' pagh SuD loS Hut Doq vagh.*"

"Command authorization accepted." The imperial emblem faded to a vid of Captain Brakk in his office aboard the *Qu'vang*. It was Kutal's opinion that Brakk was far too thin, his face too lean, and his hair too short. Worse, his nose seemed perpetually wrinkled, as if he spent every waking moment afflicted by a foul odor only he could detect.

"Greetings, Captain Kutal. You are a clever man, so I'm sure

you already suspect there is no actual risk of our communica-
tions being intercepted. There are three reasons I have sent you
this message in this manner. The first is that our rank and file
have no need to know of our roles as pawns in the political games
of our betters. The second is that I do not trust you enough to risk
coming aboard your vessel. I have reason to believe you and
your ship were assigned as my escorts in order to spy upon me for
Councillor Gorkon, and possibly to move against me if the op-
portunity should present itself. I do not intend to give you that
opportunity, Captain.

"The third and final reason I have sent you this message will
become apparent soon enough. By now, your ship's internal
comms have been off-line for close to half a minute, and all com-
partments except your quarters have been flooded with neuro-
cine gas."

Kutal tensed and shot a look at BelHoQ. "Get my scanner
from the second drawer."

The first officer retrieved the scanner from Kutal's desk and
activated it as Brakk's recording continued. *"I have spared your*
life this long only because I wanted to thank you personally for
helping me murder your valiant crew. The data card I sent was
loaded with a computer virus. Normally, your ship's data net-
work would have scanned for such a threat and intercepted it,
but by generously providing your voiceprint and command code,
you've enabled my program to bypass your ship's filters and take
control of the intruder-control systems."

BelHoQ showed Kutal the scanner's readout; it confirmed
Brakk's message. "We might be able to reach the nearest escape
pod before the gas takes us," he said. Kutal got up, hurried to his
lavatory, soaked two cloths with water, and tossed one to BelHoQ
on their way to the door.

"Good-bye, Captain," Brakk said from the computer terminal. *"I doubt you'll earn a place in Sto-Vo-Kor for blundering*
into a trap, so I'll look forward to our next meeting in Gre'thor.
Brakk out." The message ended, and the screen went black.

A subtle hiss from the overhead ventilation ducts gave warning that Kutal's quarters were being flooded with the deadly toxic gas. He unlocked the door, which hissed open. Though the air outside his quarters looked no different than that inside, an excruciating stinging assaulted his eyes, which watered instantly even as he squeezed them shut. Kutal and BelHoQ stumbled out into the corridor, holding their breath, mouths and noses covered by the damp rags. Squinting through the pain, they felt their way down the passage and stepped over the corpses littering the deck. Every bit of exposed flesh on Kutal's face and arms felt as if it were on fire as he and BelHoQ staggered the last few steps toward the escape pod.

His hand was poised over the control pad to open the pod's hatch when, out of the corner of his bloodied eye, he noted the blurred profile of a figure standing in the middle of the corridor. When he turned his head to look, he saw a Klingon in an environmental suit, pointing a disruptor at him. Then came a deafening screech and a blinding flash—and, with them, an end to his pain.

If not for his intense aversion to risk and his innate loathing for embarrassment, Brakk might have considered his victory over Captain Kutal and the crew of the *Zin'za* an empty one. But a win was a win, and all that really mattered was that Kutal was dead and Brakk was not, and that all the vital secrets Kutal had possessed about the Taurus Reach would soon belong to Brakk.

Gorkon was a fool to think he could saddle me with such obvious traitors, Brakk gloated. *Now the House of Duras will know what's so important about the Gonmog Sector—and then we'll finally be able to get those Romulan* petaQpu' *to back our rise to power over the Empire.*

Brakk presided over the bridge of the *Qu'vang* from his elevated command chair, his attention fixed upon the main viewscreen's image of the *Zin'za* adrift in space. He was about to call for a status update when his first officer, Nuqdek, appeared. "We've bypassed the lockouts on the *Zin'za*'s protected computer core," he said. "Its contents are being copied to our databanks now. We will have everything momentarily."

"Well done, Commander. Have all our people returned from the *Zin'za*?"

"Yes, sir." Nuqdek seemed troubled. "We've intercepted several subspace messages from Captain Chang on the *baS'jev*. He's trying to reach Captain Kutal."

"What of it? Let him enjoy the silence."

A crewman at an aft station on the bridge called out, "Commander?" When he had Nuqdek's attention, he gave the first officer a single nod. Nuqdek returned the gesture, then said to Brakk, "The databanks have been copied over, Captain. Do you wish to put a tractor beam on the *Zin'za* for its return to Somraw?"

"That hunk of excrement isn't going anywhere," Brakk said.

Nuqdek warily studied the battle cruiser on the viewscreen. "How, then, are we to explain its disappearance?"

Brakk looked down at his first officer. *Some days I just don't understand this man.* "Why should we explain anything, Commander? Space is dangerous. Ships vanish all the time, even imperial warships. Why think the *Zin'za* immune to such a fate?"

"You mean to destroy it, then."

"Of course," Brakk boasted. "I armed its self-destruct system ten minutes ago. After I trigger it, nothing will remain of that overhyped rust pile except dust and memories."

The first officer's discomfort with that news was obvious to Brakk, despite Nuqdek's effort to mask his unease. "Permission to speak, Captain?"

"What is it?"

"I suggest we salvage useful material and munitions from the *Zin'za* before you trigger its self-destruct package. Destroying the ship is obviously necessary for operational security, but it seems wrong to waste parts and torpedoes that could be made to serve this vessel."

He waved away Nuqdek's request. "Absolutely not. The last thing we need is for some overzealous junior officer at Somraw

Station to notice that our weapons bay is stocked with torpedoes from a lot that was used to supply the *Zin'za*." He directed his orders to the bridge officers surrounding him and Nuqdek. "Terminate all data channels to that ship! Helm, reverse thrusters, put us two hundred thousand *qellqam*s aft of the *Zin'za*. Tactical, raise shields." With an oblique glance at Nuqdek, he asked, "Any last words for the fallen?"

For once, Nuqdek was wise enough to hold his tongue. He faced the viewscreen and lifted his chin, a final gesture of respect for the dishonored dead.

The helmsman reported, "We're in position, Captain."

Without ceremony or pity, Brakk pressed a button on his chair's armrest, triggering the *Zin'za*'s self-destruct package. The battle cruiser erupted in an orange-white fireball that quickly spawned several more explosions, washing out the viewscreen for several seconds.

It was the most beautiful vision of destruction Brakk had ever seen. He couldn't help but beam with satisfaction. *Wherever you are, Gorkon . . . you're next.*

Confronted with the latest news from Captain Chang, Gorkon felt as if an oppressive weight had fallen upon his shoulders. "Are you certain the *Zin'za*'s been destroyed?"

"As certain as I can be, my lord." His fury was palpable, even over a subspace channel. *"Brakk claims he sent Captain Kutal and his ship on a routine patrol from which they never returned. Meanwhile, his ship's newest combat escort just happens to be the* Valkaya—*a Romulan bird-of-prey whose captain volunteered its service to Brakk."*

"When was the last time you heard from Kutal?"

"Four days ago. He's missed his last three check-ins. Which would suggest his ship was destroyed while mine was on its own pointless recon mission, as ordered by Brakk." His mien took on a cast of suspicion. *"Why would Brakk have risked so bold an*

attack on other Klingons? What could have made that worth the potential consequences?"

"Most likely, the information in the *Zin'za's* databanks." Gorkon entered commands via the interface panel beside the screen. "I'm elevating your security clearance so that I can tell you this. What you're about to hear is classified at the highest levels."

"Understood, my lord."

"The Empire's interest in the Gonmog Sector is driven by more than a desire for territory and resources. Five years ago, a Starfleet vessel, the *Constellation,* made a discovery that motivated the Federation to build a major starbase far beyond their own borders. It became clear that there was something there that they considered vital to their interests. We soon learned it was related to an extinct precursor civilization, one that had left technology on worlds throughout the sector and complex information concealed inside genetic sequences.

"So far, only the Empire and the Federation have actively pursued the secrets of this ancient race. The Tholians have taken aggressive action to impede both our efforts, for reasons we don't yet understand. Starfleet's scientists seem to have surpassed our own in their understanding of the alien devices, while the Romulans have, until now, apparently been unaware of the reason for this tripartite conflict so far from our respective territories.

"I have reason to suspect Duras and his allies had already stolen a limited amount of information regarding the Shedai. Apparently, that taste merely whetted their appetite. Captain Kutal and the *Zin'za* had been at the forefront of the Empire's investigation of this sector, and they had amassed a significant degree of raw intelligence about the Taurus Reach. Their involvement had been known only by myself and a few trusted contacts inside the High Command and Imperial Intelligence. But it seems Duras became aware of their role, and he took advantage of Brakk's proximity to steal the information from the *Zin'za's* computers."

Chang's intense focus made it clear he understood the gravity of the matter. *"If Brakk has acquired that data, then it most likely has already been passed on to the Romulans."*

"Precisely. Duras and his son might not even grasp the significance of the information until they've already traded it for favors. But once the Romulans learn what's at stake in the Gonmog Sector, they'll stop at nothing to acquire its secrets—most likely by using Duras and his cronies to do their dirty work." Gorkon clenched his fists. He wondered for a moment whether he should share his latest findings, then decided he had so few allies, especially on Qo'noS, that someone else needed to know the truth, just in case something happened to him before he could act on it. "There's something else, Captain: I've gathered a great deal of disturbing intelligence from a number of sources. It seems we have underestimated our foes, and quite badly."

"In what regard?"

He leaned closer to the screen, as if huddling to share a confidence with someone across the table. "The House of Duras has begun consolidating power in the most ruthless and efficient manner I've ever seen. Their operatives are moving against anyone they perceive as a rival, an enemy, or even a mere impediment, and they are using every means possible: assassination, extortion, blackmail, bribery, fraud . . . whatever it takes to make themselves unassailable."

"Have you discussed this with Chancellor Sturka? Perhaps he can—"

"It's too late for that." Gorkon simmered with righteous anger toward his former ally and patron. "I've uncovered evidence that links many recent actions by Duras to the chancellor himself. Apparently, despite Sturka's long hatred of the House of Duras, now that their accumulated wealth and political power has reached a critical mass, the chancellor sees more advantage in allying himself with their treachery than he does in opposing it."

Now even Chang seemed worried. *"How deep are their connections?"*

"Their estates and financial holdings are in the process of merging via proxies, and my sources inside Sturka's House suggest the chancellor and Duras have made secret betrothals for several of their respective scions, to cement the bond between their Houses."

"This cannot be allowed to come to pass," Chang said. *"If their Houses unite, the Duras family will be like a blood tick on a targ's back—entrenched in the highest echelons of Klingon society for generations to come. And Duras would almost certainly replace you as Sturka's chief adviser on the High Council."*

Gorkon wondered if Chang thought him a fool who needed to be told the obvious. "I am well aware of the consequences that would attend the ascendance of Duras. That is why we can no longer wait to take action. Duras and his House are on the offensive, which is when one is always at the greatest risk of being off balance. If we can break his momentum now, and goad him and his House into a mistake when they are the focus of attention and envy, it could be enough to put them back in check for the foreseeable future."

"Whatever service you require of me, my lord, you'll have it. No matter what the cost to myself or my honor, I will not permit Duras to become chancellor."

The declaration coaxed a thin smile from Gorkon. "Your loyalty honors me, Chang."

"I have one concern, my lord, and it's more for your sake than for mine."

"Speak freely."

"If the House of Duras is as powerful, ruthless, and entrenched as you say, we may find that opposing their interests could be considered the same as opposing the chancellor's, or even the Empire's. How do we fight such an honorless fiend without being branded as traitors?"

It was a question to which Gorkon had given a great deal of thought during many an anguished and sleepless night. Now, at the moment of decision, he divined the answer.

"By striking at him from a direction he does not expect."

19

The Wanderer turned her thoughts to stillness, arresting her motion. Her solitary journey to the *Telinaruul*'s bastion in the darkness had been arduous, burdened as she was with a ponderous mass of superdense matter. Her native ability to traverse space—a talent that made her unique among the Shedai—normally entailed shifting only her consciousness and an attendant field of energy. Only a few times before then had she tried to bear physical objects across the interstellar void. Even small and relatively insignificant payloads had proved exhausting. It was a testament to her recent increase in power that she had become strong enough to bear a load such as this.

Lingering in the comfort of darkness, she attuned herself to the invisible energies that transited the ether in all directions. This was but one mystery of the great emptiness—that it was never truly empty. Space-time was abundant with unseen forces and extradimensional pockets of dark power waiting to be tapped, if only one understood how to see the universe's true shape.

She knew she was beyond the reach of the *Telinaruul*'s mechanical sensing devices, ensuring that her next great labor would not attract their attention. In contrast, their presence was a clarion shattering the silence, a white-hot beacon in the dark. High-energy signals poured like a river from their space fortress. Shining brighter than all of it was the presence of the Progenitor, his essence blazing like a sun despite his imprisonment within an artifact of the Tkon.

How arrogant these *Telinaruul* were! Who were they to think they had the right to act as jailers for a being who had been an ancient before their kinds' first ancestors took shape in the primordial soups of their insignificant worlds? To enslave a being who had ruled a spiral arm of the galaxy before their puny races even had language? It was an offense against the natural order.

They will all suffer, she vowed. *Soon, the Progenitor will be free, and they will all know the cold fire of our vengeance.* If forced to choose between emancipating the Progenitor and destroying the station, the Wanderer knew that the freedom of her people's great sire took precedence. Pride demanded that the *Telinaruul* pay for their hubris, but as one of the *Serrataal,* her duty to the Elder One trumped all other objectives and desires.

The Wanderer focused her essence on the block of raw matter she had borne across hundreds of light-years. Her consciousness penetrated its superdense atomic structure, beheld its ultrastable atomic shells, and marveled at its furious inner storm—particles of every conceivable color, flavor, and spin. Manipulating muons and quarks, bosons and neutrinos, she reshaped the matter by will alone, transforming it into an extension of her desire, an instrument of her impending vengeance. This would be slow work, demanding the most painstaking precision and attention to subnuclear details. This was a labor the Wanderer had undertaken only twice before in her countless millennia, though neither instance had been freighted with such urgency as this. On those occasions, the continued existence of the Shedai had not been at stake.

She tried to remember where, when, and how she had learned this delicate art and the arcane science behind it. It was so old a memory that its specifics eluded her. All she could recall was that the process had been imparted to her by one of the elders in the early days of the Shedai's sovereignty over this part of the galaxy. It had been among the final rituals confirming her status as one of the *Serrataal,* those who had been elevated from the churning hordes of the Nameless in recognition of their innate gifts, their inborn worthiness to be counted among the elite. As a Shedai with a name, the Wanderer had earned the right to share in the hegemony's most guarded secrets, the foundation of knowledge upon which their sprawling civilization had been erected. Mastery of these secrets had been her final test of worthiness.

Now the future of all Shedai hinged upon her ability to bend reality's shape to her will, to work the miracle she had been taught two hundred fifty million years earlier, a magic she had worked only twice in the span of an entire revolution of the galaxy. There was no question in her mind that she would succeed. She had vowed to see it done, and its completion was all that stood between her and the sweetness of revenge. It was of no consequence to her that the Sage and the Herald both doubted her ability; she did not require their faith or their approval. Let them mock her and call her youngling; soon she would make them recant their taunts. When the time came, and she proved herself worthy, they would hear the Progenitor's voice in the song, and they would know she had spoken the truth. *I will be vindicated,* she promised herself.

She trapped a quark strangelet in the porous interdimensional membrane and reversed its spin. Atom by atom, the Wanderer molded the mass of collapsed-star core material until it fit the shape of her imagination. For now it was nothing but a superdense blob of heavy metal, squandering its hard-won energy as waste heat and chaotic radiation, its crude form nothing but a prison for its potential—a bastille to which the Wanderer held the keys.

Cloaked in silence and night, she labored alone, paying no heed to time's passage; she would work for as long as it took to finish her task. Sustaining herself with starlight and fury, she felt her thoughts take shape and knew that the hour of her wrath would soon be at hand. When her work was done, she and her kin would free the Progenitor, annihilate the space station, and imbue the galaxy's *Telinaruul* with an old brand of terror, one they apparently had forgotten.

They would be reminded what it is to fear the gods.

20

"What do you mean you've hit a *dead end*?"

Nogura stared down the briefing room table at the sheepish faces of Lieutenants Xiong and Theriault and the glum countenance of Doctor Marcus. He had come to expect results—if not minor miracles—from these three, not excuses, making their latest status update an unpleasant surprise. And it could not have come at a worse time, in Nogura's opinion, what with Starfleet Command breathing down his neck and demanding progress in the ongoing effort to devise a reliable defense and counteroffensive strategy against the Shedai. Seated at the far end of the table, opposite Nogura, was T'Prynn. She seemed distracted and only half present.

Xiong leaned forward, elbows on the table, and slowly rubbed his palms together. "I know it's not what you or Starfleet Command were expecting or hoping for," he said. "But the simple truth is, we've hit an impasse. Lieutenant Theriault and I have gone over all her visual scans of the original array at Eremar, and we've done everything we can to duplicate its form and function inside the isolation chamber. But so far all it amounts to is a really bizarre work of sculpture. The fact is, there are too many variables we don't understand."

"Such as?" The question came out sounding far more flip and confrontational than Nogura had intended, but he had no time to handle his officers with kid gloves.

Theriault leapt into the verbal fray. "For one thing, we brought back only about half the artifacts we found. We don't know if there are specific configurations or numbers of artifacts that work as an array. Maybe we have too few, or too many, or they're grouped wrong. Also, the visual scans I made had tons of interference. We might be missing crucial information."

"The issue might be that we don't know how to distribute power through that many linked crystals," Xiong added. "Or that we don't know the correct frequency or amplitude."

"All good evidence," Doctor Marcus interjected, "that we need to slow down our efforts to turn these things into applied technology, and spend more time on pure research, including making contact with the entity inside the first crystal. I mean no offense to Lieutenants Xiong and Theriault, but I think it was a mistake to even try to link these objects together before we can say for certain what any one of them does individually."

Wearing a mask of skepticism, Nogura shook his head. "That's not an option, Doctor. Besides, we've already seen what these objects can do. It's why we wanted more of them."

Marcus's face reddened. "Really? Are you a hundred percent certain you know what every last one of those crystals does? How can you be sure? We haven't tested any of them. We barely examined them before we started jamming them into a jury-rigged array. What if some of them have microscopic variations in their structures that give them different properties? Or lower thresholds for stress? Starfleet would never be so cavalier with technology of its own making, so why is it acting so carelessly with these products of an unknown alien science?"

"Because this 'unknown alien science' is all that stands between us and a repeat of the attack that turned your lab into a war zone," Nogura said. "The Shedai we captured—and which later escaped—could come back at any time, Doctor. We couldn't track it when it accelerated to faster-than-light speed, which means we'll have no warning of its next attack until it's on top of us. Phasers barely affect it, and we have no other way of containing it. So I'm sorry if your principles feel sullied by our work, but I assure you, it's absolutely necessary."

Chastened, Marcus reclined and crossed her arms, symbolically disengaging herself from the conversation. Xiong held up an open hand in an apparently cautionary gesture. "Be that as it may, Admiral, my team and I need a lot more information before we can proceed. And not just about the array, or the artifacts, but the entire theory behind what makes it work. We need a big-picture understanding of it, as well as the nuts-and-bolts details."

It was a reasonable request, but the thought of any setback rankled Nogura, who knew the Starfleet brass and Federation politicos would give him hell over the delay. "How long do you think you'll need to get the data you need and bring the array on line?"

Apprehensive looks passed between Xiong and Theriault. "It's impossible to say," he replied. "In this case, I have to agree with Doctor Marcus that caution is vital. When we were experimenting on just two of these things, we accidentally blew up eleven worlds—"

"None of them inhabited, thankfully," Theriault interrupted.

Xiong continued, "—all before we realized what we'd done. But now we have thousands of these artifacts, sir. Making them work in unison will take a lot of power—which means the risks of our making a catastrophic mistake are exponentially worse than before. At this stage, I'd recommend operating on the assumption that we have little to no margin for error."

Nogura could tell the problems at hand weren't mere issues of personal motivation that he could rectify with a stern look or a forceful command; he was up against hard numbers and cold realities. "How many members of your team have reviewed Lieutenant Theriault's records of the Eremar mission?"

"All of them," Xiong said. "We've been working the problem from every angle, but because of the interference caused by the pulsar, her tricorder was only able to make basic visual scans. Which means we have no detailed nuclear imaging or spectral analysis."

The elfin redhead added, "We have enough data to build a frame to hold the artifacts, but no idea how to make it start. It's like having hardware with no operating software."

"In other words," Nogura grumped, "a very expensive piece of junk."

"Unfortunately, yes," Xiong said.

Nogura was about to tell the scientists to do their best and then dismiss them, when T'Prynn looked down the table at him and spoke up from the far side of the room.

"Admiral . . . I might be able to help."

Quinn awoke to the sound of two sets of footsteps, the cold touch of a hard surface under his bruised and stubbled cheek, and the grotesque sensation that his guts were filled with boiling mud and rotten eggs. A man's voice announced with bored hostility, "Wake up. You have a visitor." Then one set of footsteps walked away. The angry buzz of a force field generator in Quinn's ears made it clear to him where he was.

He rolled over and regretted moving. A deep pounding ache felt like a lead weight trying to ram its way out of his skull. Each throbbing beat of his pulse made him fear that his abused brain had grown nerve endings just so it could protest what he'd done to it the night before. He groaned pitiably. *Why can't I ever have a coma when I really need one?*

Squinting against the cold, white light of one of Vanguard's numerous, immaculate brig facilities, he labored to focus his eyes. Then he sat up on the edge of the bench and cradled his head in his hands. Hunched over in misery, he realized he'd put his bare feet down in a broad splatter of spilled soup. He hoped it was soup.

"I can hear you breathing, Newsboy," he mumbled, through a vile taste human mouths were never meant to know. With effort, he turned his head. "If you've come to—"

Words failed him as he realized his visitor wasn't Tim Pennington, who had bailed him out so many times that he figured he'd be in the Scotsman's debt for the rest of his natural life. It was T'Prynn, who had recruited him years earlier as a covert civilian operative of Starfleet Intelligence. She stood at ease, hands folded behind her back, exuding a quintessentially Vulcan neutrality. "Hello, Mister Quinn."

He narrowed his eyes in tired contempt. "You're dead to me." He winced at another crushing throb in his temples. "But if it makes you feel any better, *I'm* dead to me, too."

"The arrest report indicates you were ejected from no fewer than six establishments for drunken and disorderly behavior before you were taken into custody." She arched one eyebrow. "You do appear—what's the expression? ah, yes—*worse for wear.*"

Her gingerly mocking didn't make him feel better, but it gave him a reason to be mad, and that helped him focus on something other than how awful he felt. "Goddamn, lady, you got a gift for understatement. I spent all my credit and wound up feeling like phasered shit. It's like I mugged myself, except someone else got the money." Massaging a vicious crick from his neck, he shot a one-eyed glare at the Vulcan woman. "What do you want with me, anyway?"

She seemed unfazed by his blunt challenge. "During your last mission for SI, you witnessed what you described as a 'huge, moving equation' that the Apostate said was the key to the Tkon array. But your final report contained no specific details of that equation."

"I know." He turned his head, growled the foulness inside his mouth into a wad, and spit it on the floor. "Like I said, it was all just a blur. I don't remember the details."

T'Prynn edged closer to the invisible force field that separated them. "I think you could remember much of that equation, Mister Quinn, perhaps even all of it, with my help."

This didn't sound as if it was leading anywhere good. "I know I'll probably be sorry I asked, but what're you driving at?"

"I need you to consent to a Vulcan mind-meld with me."

"Go to hell." He tried to turn away and lie down.

The urgency in her voice stopped him. "Please, Mister Quinn." She waited until he looked back at her, then she continued. "I would not ask you to permit so profound an invasion of your privacy if the security of the Federation and the safety of its people were not at stake."

"Like I give a shit?" Confronted with so much national-security claptrap, it was hard for Quinn not to vent his scorn as laughter. "You assholes have been runnin' around out here for years, breakin' rules, wreakin' havoc, gettin' good people killed—and for what? What've you got to show for it? *Nothing.* 'Federation security,' my ass. What a joke. Hell, for a while there, you even had me playin' your stupid game, flyin' all over hell and creation, lookin' for your little bits o' junk and trackin' down your runaway monsters. I'm *sick* of it."

She looked taken aback by his tirade. "In light of the personal loss you suffered, I can understand your animosity toward Starfleet and the Federation, but that—"

"Dammit, you're not listening to me. I ain't sayin' *no* because I got a grudge with the Federation, and I ain't saying *go to hell* because I give a damn about you invading my privacy. What I'm sayin' is, I don't care anymore. I don't want to do it because I never want to think about that day ever again, as long as I live. All I've done since I got back was try to forget it."

There was sympathy in her voice. "Have you?"

"Have I what? Tried?"

"Forgotten."

He slumped against the metal wall and stared at the light on the ceiling. "Not yet. But I plan to keep drinking till I've killed so many brain cells, I lose my own name."

T'Prynn reached over to the control pad beside the cell and with a few deft taps deactivated the force field. She stepped inside and looked down at Quinn. Her dark eyes had a quality that he would never before have thought to ascribe to a Vulcan: soulfulness. "I understand why you want to forget that day. But I don't need you to recall all of it—only the moments when you saw the machine. Nothing more. If you grant me this request, I will try to help you in return. *Please,* Mister Quinn."

He was too exhausted to argue with her. What harm could it do? He responded with a grudging nod. "Fine, all right. But first, get me someplace else."

"Time is of the essence," T'Prynn said. "This place will serve as well as any other."

"No, it won't."

His defiance seemed to irk her. "Why not?"

"Because right now, you're standing in my puke."

She looked down, confirmed his claim, then met his bleary gaze with her level stare. "You make a reasonable point."

T'Prynn led Quinn inside a plain-looking compartment on an infrequently used level of the station. Everything inside the narrow room was the same shade of Starfleet standard-issue blue-gray. It had no window, being an interior compartment, and its furniture consisted of an uncovered bed atop a platform with drawers, a desk, a chair, and a computer terminal. A small door at the back of the room led to the toilet and sonic shower.

The disheveled ex-soldier-of-fortune edged inside as if expecting an ambush. "Cozy. Who lives here?"

"No one," T'Prynn said. "These are unassigned guest quarters." She locked the door behind Quinn and guided him toward the bed. "Sit there, at the end." As he settled onto the corner of the bare mattress, she pulled the chair from the desk, rolled it to the foot of the bed, and sat down. "Do you understand what a Vulcan mind-meld entails, Mister Quinn?"

"Kind of. It's telepathy, right?"

"It is far more than that. It is a fusion of two minds, a sharing of memory, feelings, and consciousness. Within the meld, we will become one." She lifted her left hand and reached out to touch his face. As she expected, he recoiled slightly. "It will not hurt, I promise."

Quinn looked less than reassured but nodded for her to continue. T'Prynn pressed her fingertips to several key points on his face, tentatively at first, then with a firm but gentle touch. She looked into his eyes and said in a low monotone, "My mind to your mind." He closed his eyes, and she felt him relax—but then, at the first inkling of true contact, his mind withdrew. "It is natural to resist at first," she advised him. "Breathe deeply and let go of your fear. . . . My mind to your mind. My thoughts to your thoughts." He did as she'd instructed, and she synchronized her breathing with his. "Our minds are merging." Closing her eyes, she opened her own psyche to his and lowered her formidable psionic defenses. When she felt the primal undertow of his emotions pulling her deeper inside his consciousness, she knew the meld was complete.

"Our minds are one."

Partly by training and partly by instinct, she interpreted their shared mindscape as a virtual world, an ever-changing theater of memory complete with physical sensations. Focusing her attention on Quinn's mind, she found herself in a shifting panorama of half-perceived drinking binges punctuated by bouts of despondency, physical pain, or self-loathing.

"We need to go back now, Cervantes," she said, gently coaching him. "Take me back to that world where you saw the Apostate's machine."

All at once she and Quinn were inside his last ship, the *Dulcinea,* as it struggled to an emergency landing on a snow-covered mountain ledge. Events melted and bled together, like watercolor paintings being revealed one beneath another as stormy cascades swept away the layers. A hard march knee-deep in snow across a frozen lake . . . an ice cave of dark blue shadows . . . a deep, perilous crevasse into which Quinn's partner and lover, Bridy Mac, had fallen . . . a wall of ice rendered into vapor by a phaser blast . . . and then . . . the machine.

"Slow your perceptions," T'Prynn said. "Let me see the details."

The moment stolen from his mind slowed to a crawl. She stepped past his self-projection to study the complex machinations of the Apostate's creation. Every element was in motion. Each revolved around the core, turned on its own axis, or orbited another piece of the machine. All the pieces seemed to be composed of the same silvery crystal, and they varied in shape from organically curved blobs to aggressively angular and symmetrical polyhedrons. Ribbons of multicolored light snaked through the open spaces, traveling chaotic paths through the mesmerizing order of the machine. At the core was an object that repeated a cycle of transformation, transitioning through multiple complex stellations that all were extrapolated from—and every few seconds reverted to—a basic icosahedron.

Just as Quinn's report had described, waves of warmth radiated from the massive device, which T'Prynn suspected actually had been more of a projection than a physical reality. As she moved closer to it, a galvanic charge rushed over her, tingling her flesh from head to toe.

The scene became blurry as Quinn said, "I think this is what you came to find."

T'Prynn turned to face him as his memory regained focus. A spectral image took shape above Bridy's and Quinn's heads. It was a slowly rotating twelve-sided polyhedron. Circling it were long, complex strings of data—alien symbols, Arabic numerals, equations, and fragments of star charts. Looking more closely, T'Prynn saw that each face of the dodecahedron was etched with a unique alien symbol, all of which she committed to memory.

After a few minutes, she was sure she had found all there was to know from Quinn. Not wanting to prolong his pain any more than necessary, she made the first attempt to pull them both away from this moment and retrace their steps to separate consciousness. To her surprise, Quinn resisted fiercely, as if his mind had chosen to anchor itself.

She turned to ask him if he was all right. He stood in the midst of his own halted memory, gazing at the projection of the late Bridget McLellan. She was leaning against the cavern wall beside the machine, her broken leg wrapped in a crude splint. Quinn was literally beside himself—or the projection of himself—gazing mournfully at his lost love. His grief hit T'Prynn like a crushing force, overwhelming her hard-won stoicism.

"This was the last time I ever saw her," he said, on the verge of tears.

His heartbreak was an abyss, opening wide to devour him, and his pain was so deep that he yearned to let himself plunge into it, to lose himself in it and never return. There was more than sorrow in his heart; there was guilt, and regret, and rage at his own powerlessness—all of it churning into a toxic brew that would eventually consume him from within or drive him to self-destruction just to be free of the torment.

Sharing his pain, T'Prynn felt her own guilt rise like the tide. So much of Quinn's sorrow and heartbreak was her fault. She had coerced him into her service years earlier, used him to hurt innocent people, and even when she had freed him, she had tempted him with a promise of a new life full of adventure and heroism and self-respect.

I could have simply let him go. Starfleet Intelligence did not have specific need of him. Had I not enticed him, he might have been spared this loss.

He shook his head, and she knew he was responding to her thoughts. "Don't think like that," he said. "It wasn't your fault. I wanted this life."

"I can help you," she said.

Her suggestion made him angry. "I don't need your help."

"You need to let her go, Cervantes. You need to make your peace with this loss."

The machine and the cave vanished in a storm of fire rolling up the mountainside while the once-frozen lake boiled far below, swallowing five Klingon warships into its bubbling froth. T'Prynn realized she was reliving Quinn's memory of the explosion that killed Bridy Mac. At the cliff's edge, Quinn crouched behind a cluster of jagged rocks, hiding from the flames. "Screw you! You don't know what I'm feeling! How could you? You're a goddamned Vulcan!"

She reached down, took him by the collar of his jacket, and yanked him to his feet.

As they snapped to a standing position, the mountainside vanished, and they stood facing each other inside an observation lounge overlooking Vanguard's main docking bay. "Do you want to see what I know about this subject?" She grabbed his shoulders and spun him around so that he would see what she saw. Half a second later, the Starfleet cargo transport *Malacca* was split nearly in half by an orange fireball, and it was all T'Prynn could do not to scream.

Quinn stood transfixed, hypnotized as he watched the fiery aftermath of the bombing of the *Malacca,* the bodies and debris tumbling in slow motion as if in a dream, through the airless zero-gravity of the docking bay. His lips moved in tandem with T'Prynn's as she whispered with sad remembrance, "She burns for me."

The fire faded, the observation lounge melted away, and then Quinn stood at the edge of another of T'Prynn's memories, a spectator to her final moments with Anna Sandesjo—the assumed name of a surgically altered Klingon spy named Lurqal, who had been both T'Prynn's double agent and her lover. The two women faced each other inside one of Vanguard's auxiliary cargo bays, surrounded on all sides by a mountain of cargo containers. Anna stood inside one that had been modified to act as a scan-shielded residential module in which she would be smuggled off the station . . . aboard the *Malacca.*

"Just close the door," Anna said.

T'Prynn yearned to reach out to her, to apologize for everything she had done—for using her, betraying her, abandoning her—but most of all for what she *hadn't* done: admit the truth.

I loved you.

She and Quinn were back in the observation lounge. Scorched wreckage and burnt bodies floated past the towering transparent steel window. T'Prynn pressed her hand against it and felt hope and love burn away inside the distant crucible of her betrayal. Tears fell from her eyes as she looked at Quinn, who stared back at her, stricken and mute in the face of her anguish.

"I know exactly what you're feeling," she said.

He lifted one dirty, callused hand and with the delicate touch of a surgeon brushed the tears from her cheeks. He looked almost ashamed. "I'm sorry."

It was a small gesture, but she felt the compassion in it, the unconditional understanding. She took his hands in hers and with a mental push moved them away from their places of pain to one of peace. Vanguard faded away to a Vulcan desertscape by night. "This is a place not far from where I grew up," she told him. "Here I learned the tenets of Vulcan mental discipline. Though I can't teach you all that I know, I can share with you some basic techniques to strengthen your mind and control your feelings, rather than allow them to dominate you."

"Why would you do that for me?"

"To use a human idiom, you and I both 'battle with demons.' Mine are shame and rage; yours appear to be addiction and grief. I cannot cure you of these afflictions, but I can give you an edge in the battle to control your own mind—if you will let me."

He nodded, and she felt his investment of trust in her. "Let's get to it."

When at last the mind-meld ended, and T'Prynn removed her hand from Quinn's stubbled face, hours had passed. Quinn looked at her with a new understanding. Where once he had seen in her a tormentor or a puppetmaster, now he saw a woman who was as much a victim of circumstance as he. But even more than sympathy, he realized what he felt toward her was gratitude.

"I hope I was able to help you," Quinn said as he got up.

T'Prynn stood and smoothed the front of her red minidress. "You have, Mister Quinn, a great deal. Starfleet and perhaps the Federation itself are in your debt."

He chuckled. "You don't say. Well, if someone wants to clear my bar tabs and float me a line of credit, that'd be a right fine way to say 'thank you.'" Noting her reproachfully arched brow, he shrugged. "Just a suggestion. Forget I mentioned it."

He turned and walked toward the door. She spoke as it opened ahead of him.

"Before you go . . ." She waited until he turned back, then she continued. "If you wish, I can help you block out your memories of Commander McLellan. It might make things easier for you."

"No," he said. "I lost her once. I don't think I could take losing her again."

She raised her hand in the Vulcan salute. "Live long and prosper, Mister Quinn."

He smiled at her as he walked out the door.

"Right back atcha, darlin'."

21

"Dammit, Frankie, you've got my word on this!" A host of disapproving stares from strangers scolded Tim Pennington for shouting—a faux pas when using one of Stars Landing's public subspace comm kiosks in the middle of the station's business day. He leaned closer to the screen and continued in an emphatic stage whisper, "The story's one hundred percent legit!"

On the small, round cornered screen, Frankie Libertini looked less than convinced. Her thin lips were pursed, and she brushed a lock of her salt-and-pepper hair from her eyes with a hand whose fingernails looked as if they'd been gnawed on by a rabid badger. *"Tim, let's get a few things straight. First, I didn't ask to be your editor, I lost a bar bet. Second, I don't actually like you. And third, you're not giving me a lot to go on here."*

Hand to chest, Pennington pantomimed a fatal wound to his tender feelings. "Frankie! You don't *like* me? Say it ain't so!" She was unamused, so he turned serious. "C'mon, Frankie! I gave you everything: names, dates, places. Hell, I even sent vids."

"Yes, you did. And I was happy to see they were in focus for a change." Her lips disappeared into a doubtful frown. *"I'm not saying you haven't done some first-rate work over the last few years, because you have. But look at this from my perspective, will you?"*

He was ready to strangle her out of sheer frustration. "What am I looking at?"

"All your sources on this story are confidential. Which I could live with if the whole thing weren't so damned controversial. I mean, if we run with this, and you're wrong—"

"I'm not."

"But if you are," she continued with a silencing glare, *"we*

*could be talking about consequences a lot more extreme than
just you getting booted off staff—though I can guarantee that
would happen so fast it'll make your pretty little head spin."*

An insincere smile seemed the appropriate response. "Thank
you for noticing how pretty my head is. I spend hours making it
like this just for you."

*"Listen to me: this is serious. When this story goes out, if it's
as solid as you claim, heads will roll. And I'm not talking in
metaphors, Tim. You're shining a light on the kinds of people
who don't think twice about solving disputes with duels to the
death."* She pressed the side of her fist to her mouth and looked
away, perhaps debating whether she wanted to say what was really on her mind. Then the look in her eyes turned fierce, and
Pennington braced himself for what he'd known would be in the
offing from the moment he submitted the story. *"The thing is,"*
she said, *"the last time you turned in a feature like this, it was the*
Bombay *story."*

He felt like throwing his coffee, mug and all, through the vid
screen. "That's crap! The two stories have *nothing* in common!"

"Yes, they do, Tim. What they have in common is you. *Not to
mention they're both politically explosive exposés that affect the
Federation's diplomatic relationship with a foreign power, and
they're both predicated on the undocumented accounts of a
bunch of anonymous sources whose stories can't be fact-checked
on our end. The whole thing's a bomb waiting to go off. Give me
one good reason I shouldn't spike it right now."*

Leaning in as if they were locking horns, Pennington said,
"Do it and I'll go to INN."

Pennington derived a perverse satisfaction from watching
Libertini's eyes narrow in contempt at the mention of the Interstellar News Network, the chief competitor of the Federation
News Service. *"You can't do that,"* she said. *"You already gave
the story to us."*

"If you spike it, the rights revert," he shot back. "And my re-
vised contract only gives you right of first refusal—not exclusiv-
ity. I don't do work-for-hire anymore, Frankie." Just to tweak her

temper a degree further, he made a show of examining his own well-manicured fingernails. "So, what's it gonna be? Run it and dominate the next two news cycles, or get aced by INN?"

She rested her head in one hand, distorting the left half of her face into a caricature of exhaustion. *"I'd feel a lot better about this if you'd at least name your sources for me."*

"Sorry, I can't," he insisted. "I promised them all complete anonymity and confidentiality. But I sent you all my hard evidence. You can see for yourself it's rock-solid."

His insistence seemed to have depleted her will to argue. *"All right, fine. It is too good a story to pass up. But I'm warning you, Tim—you've already used up your second chance. If this story goes tits up, you're done as a reporter. You sure you want to take that chance?"*

"Positive. Run it. It's good."

"Okay, hotshot. Look for it tomorrow at the top of the morning feed." As she reached forward to terminate the call, she added, *"I still hate you, by the way."*

"Sleep well, Frankie."

The screen went dark, and Pennington took a sip of his coffee only to find it had gone tepid. He left the kiosk and dumped the quarter-full cup into a waste reclamation slot.

It was late afternoon, and the lanes of Stars Landing were busy with visitors of many species—some dining in small restaurants, others carousing in the pubs, a few shopping at the independently owned specialty shops. Pennington considered making his way to the edge of the ersatz village to grab a late lunch at Café Romano when he felt a sudden flutter of anxiety about the story he had just filed.

It wasn't that he doubted his sources. His information had come directly from Ambassador Jetanien and a well-known, highly placed director at the civilian-run Federation Security Agency. He had taken advantage of connections in Vanguard's intelligence and security divisions to verify the intelligence his sources had forwarded to him, and they had guaranteed him that everything checked out. And yet . . .

He couldn't help but remember how easily and thoroughly T'Prynn had deceived him years earlier after the *Bombay* incident. She had fed him just enough truth to help him swallow her lies, and he had seen his career nearly demolished when his story—despite being essentially correct—was revealed to have been based on a series of easily discredited witnesses and details. He didn't have reason to think she would do that to him again— quite the opposite. But that didn't mean that someone else, maybe someone in Starfleet or the Federation government or even an agent of a foreign power, might not try to fool him again. If he had learned nothing else of lasting value during his tenure on Vanguard, it was that the truth was an infinitely malleable commodity, and that to find it in its unadulterated state required the utmost effort and vigilance.

The more he considered what he had just gotten himself into, the more his hands shook. At a key intersection, he had a change of heart and made his destination Tom Walker's place. Minutes later he strolled in, planted himself on a stool at the bar, and nodded at the comely Irish bartender, Maggie. "Double of Glenmorangie 18, neat, and a Belhaven Ale."

Maggie smiled and started drawing his pint. "Drinkin' two-fisted are ya?"

"It's all right, love—I'm a writer."

She set his drinks in front of him, and he fought not to spill his scotch as he lifted it to his lips. Staring at it, he speculated that he had either just launched his career to the next level—or brought his entire life's work crashing down in flames.

So be it. He downed the double shot in one toss. *Here's to luck.*

In the face of slurs and hissing from his assembled peers, Duras entered the High Council chamber with his head held high, projecting proud defiance.

The chorus of disapproval was practically unanimous; only Chancellor Sturka and his lackey Gorkon abstained from the collective condemnation. Bristling at the public humiliation being heaped upon him but powerless to silence the council's self-righteous spectacle, Duras felt his ears tingle with the heat of shame.

"Traitor!" shouted one, while others called him quisling, spy, or whore. Some spat upon him as he passed through the center of the chamber on his way to his place in the ranks of the Great Houses. Then the throng pressed inward, surrounded him, and harangued him. Cries of "Romulan stooge!" mixed with a medley of epithets in the dim and musky council chamber.

He did not need to ask why he had been cast as the Empire's whipping boy. By the time he had risen from his bed that morning, half the galaxy had seen the latest top story from the Federation News Service: a feature article that accused Duras personally as well as his entire House with numerous specific acts of collaboration with the Romulan foreign intelligence service known as the Tal Shiar. His first instinct had been to dismiss the story as a clumsy attempt at a smear campaign—but then he'd read it.

To his chagrin, it appeared to have been impeccably researched, sourced, and documented. It was replete with names, dates and places of events, accounts of criminal activities perpetrated by Duras and his agents, and the details of promises made by and transactions between both Duras and his Romulan contacts. It had laid bare his House's plan to ally itself with the Romulan Star Empire as a means of seizing political and economic power at home, even if it meant turning the Klingon Empire into a de facto puppet state of the Romulans.

Worst of all, it had revealed his affair with Valina. After surviving the wrath of his wife, confronting the High Council had come to seem like a trifling matter to Duras.

He let them shout their curses and heap derision upon his name until his temper boiled over and he could bear no more. "Silence! Who are you to judge me? Mine is one of the oldest Houses in the Empire! Why would you take the word of *novpu'* over mine?"

Councillor Kesh yelled back, "You deny its claims?"

"Of course I deny them, you fool!"

"If we investigate this ourselves," said Councillor Kulok, "what will we find?"

Duras waved away the accusation. "Nothing!"

Councillor Molok howled, "Because you've buried the evidence?"

"Because there's no evidence to find!" Duras's protestations were met by another long, deafening babel of discord. Spittle flew with the invective, all of it directed at him. Pivoting and snarling like a trapped animal, his bloodlust grew hotter and more bitter until he roared, "Damn you all! Since when does this council believe the lies of its enemy's propaganda machine? Not one soul inside the Empire has ever accused me of such heinous crimes. To think I would debase myself and dishonor my House by betraying the Empire is absurd!" He drew his *d'k tahg* and waved it menacingly at his detractors. "If any of you have proof, present it. If any of you have the courage to accuse me, step forward and draw your blade."

Gorkon's stentorian voice reverberated from the far end of the chamber. "Enough of this. All of you step back. Duras, sheath your blade." The councillors withdrew from Duras with great reluctance. Some glowered at him with contempt while others stared resentfully at Gorkon. When Duras returned his blade to its sheath, Gorkon continued. "Councillor Duras is correct: the slander of a Federation civilian carries no weight under Klingon Imperial Law. The contents of that article are to be considered suspect, and may not be introduced as evidence here."

Duras accepted Gorkon's support with a small nod. "Well said."

"However," Gorkon added, drawing out the word for dramatic effect, "the surprising level of detail in that article does raise a number of difficult questions, Councillor Duras—some of which might be possible to answer with a formal inquiry by Imperial Intelligence."

The mere suggestion had Duras squeezing the grip of his blade and shooting a murderous look at Gorkon. *You arrogant* toDSaH! Swallowing his curses for another time, Duras bellowed to the other councillors, "This is a smear campaign! My House is being framed! Can't you see that?" None of his peers would look him in the eye. Some merely averted their gaze; others turned away from him entirely. He turned in one direction, then another, searching for support but finding none. Even his old friend Kesh had turned against him. Desperate for an ally, he turned to Sturka. "Chancellor! Tell me you haven't been taken in by these outrageous lies!"

"I've heard a great many outrageous lies in recent days, Duras." Sturka's guttural croak of a voice was thick with disdain. "Most of them, I think, from you." He got up from his throne and gathered his long cloak of silvery fur lined with black silk. "Gorkon is correct: This is a matter best remanded to Imperial Intelligence for investigation." He turned his back on Duras and walked away, heading toward his private portal.

Standing beside the throne, looking down at Duras with smug self-assurance, was Gorkon. "Take heart, Duras. If you're guilty of no wrong, you have nothing to fear."

Standing alone in the midst of his rivals, Duras realized Gorkon was the only person in the room who would meet his stare. In that moment, he intuited who it was who had bested him. He snarled at the chancellor's éminence grise. "This isn't over, Gorkon."

Gorkon taunted him with his maddening, wry smile. "Nothing ever is."

Duras turned and marched out of the chamber, vowing revenge every step of the way.

Jetanien greeted Lugok by holding out a large stein as the portly Klingon waddled into his office. "A drink to celebrate our fruitful collaboration," said the Chelon ambassador emeritus.

Lugok accepted it but held it at arm's length. "This isn't a mug of that rotten fruit you like to swill, is it?"

"Don't be ridiculous, old friend. Only the most ungracious host serves his guest an unpotable beverage. You hold in your hand some of the finest *warnog* ever smuggled off Qo'noS. I believe it's of a variety known as *QIp'chech bel'uH*."

The Klingon took a deep whiff of the liquor's bouquet and reacted with delight. "Now *that's* more like it." He quaffed a cheek-bulging mouthful and gasped in appreciation.

"Typically, one waits for the toast before indulging in one's drink," Jetanien said. The mild reproof earned Jetanien a low growl of irritation from his guest. Lifting his own glass, Jetanien continued. "To the truth: may it always come back to haunt our enemies."

"And leave us in peace," Lugok added. "Can I drink now?"

"Go ahead." Jetanien sipped from his bowl of *N'va'a*.

Lugok emptied his stein and set down the empty vessel. "Gorkon and I are in your debt for feeding that story to the human reporter. I'm told that Duras is politically toxic now, and it might be a generation or more before his House regains its former stature."

"That is good news," Jetanien said. "I hope it gives us enough time to steer our two nations toward peace—and keep the Romulans on their side of the Neutral Zone." He waved a clawed manus toward the bottle of *warnog* atop the liquor cabinet beside his desk. "Another?"

"Yes!" Lugok handed Jetanien his stein. He waited while Jetanien refilled it and smiled as he handed it back. "A very generous pour, my friend. You'd make a good bartender."

"Hardly," Jetanien said. "I have no patience for other people's problems."

"I see. You like the idea of serving *the* people, but you don't actually like people."

"In essence, yes." Jetanien savored another long sip of his fermented fruit cocktail while Lugok filled the room with the joyous noise of a deep belly-laugh.

The Klingon slapped Jetanien's shoulder. "You slay me,

Jetanien, really." After recovering some of his composure, he added, "This business with your friend Pennington has given me a new appreciation for a peculiar human phrase."

"Which one?"

"I believe the saying is, 'The pen is mightier than the sword.' That certainly proved true in Duras's case." He took another gulp of *warnog* and smiled. "But I'd still rather go to war with a *bat'leth* than a quill."

Jetanien lifted his bowl in affirmation. "Very sensible, old friend. Very sensible, indeed."

22

The longer he spoke to his supervising officer at Starfleet Command, the more seriously Nogura considered the possibility of early retirement. "All I'm saying," he argued, "is that we should consider giving Doctor Marcus the benefit of the doubt. She has a distinguished record as a research scientist, and she's responsible for many of our biggest discoveries about the Shedai."

Admiral Harvey Severson, a rail-thin, pale-complexioned man of Swedish ancestry, looked back at Nogura over the real-time subspace channel, his affect one of long sufferance that was reaching its limit. *"I don't mean to denigrate your faith in her, Chiro, but this isn't a time for sentimental decision-making."*

"I think my concerns are eminently *practical*."

"Other members of the admiralty don't agree," Severson said.

"Tell me which ones, and I'll talk to them myself. I'm not saying we should close down the Vanguard project. I'm simply suggesting we heed Doctor Marcus's advice to take a step back and make sure we aren't being careless in our approach."

A worried look crossed Severson's face. *"I hope you haven't encouraged her dissent."*

Nogura was almost offended by the question. "Not at all. I've been careful to make clear that I represent the express wishes of Starfleet. But in case you've forgotten—"

"Marcus is a civilian—we know." The senior admiral took an accusatory tack. *"Most of your researchers are civilians, which is one reason we're concerned. If she gets them riled up with her political agitation—"*

"Most of them are too engrossed in their work to pay her any mind."

"What about the ones who aren't?" He lifted a hand to stave off Nogura's reply. *"The point of this is that we can't afford any more delays on the Vanguard project."*

Moments such as this made Nogura feel as if talking to Starfleet Command was about as productive as shouting at the back wall of his office. "I think the point ought to be that Doctor Marcus might be right. We might have pushed this project too far, too fast."

Severson seemed genuinely surprised. *"Forgive me, but weren't you the one in command of Vanguard when a Shedai ripped through it like a battle-ax through a piñata?"*

"I vaguely recall a Shedai attack on the station, yes."

"Spare me the sarcasm, Chiro. You of all people ought to recognize the urgency of the Shedai threat. Do I really need to spell this out for you?"

Eager to hear his superior's latest litany of condescension, Nogura reclined his chair and folded his hands across his lap. "Enlighten me."

"The Federation is hemmed in on all sides," Severson said, lowering his voice as he leaned closer to the screen. *"The general public knows we're butting heads with the Klingons and the Romulans, and a small percentage know about the Tholians, the Patriarchy, and the Gorn. But there are plenty of others the public doesn't even know about yet."*

The implication of Severson's words snared Nogura's attention. "Such as . . . ?"

"Our long-range scouts have reported hostile encounters with several new species. Two in particular, the Breen and the Cardassians, might be real trouble in the next few decades. A few others, like the Tzenkethi and the Talarians, don't seem likely to warm up to us, either.

"Now, add all that to the ongoing threat posed by the current Romulan-Klingon alliance and the fact that the Tholian ambassador just walked away from diplomatic talks in Paris. Regardless of what direction the Federation tries to expand, it's slamming up against foreign powers that don't want us there, and a few that actively want us dead.

"All those threats are potentially disastrous but ultimately manageable, with time, effort, and strategy. Those are enemies we can understand and defend ourselves against, if necessary.

"But the Shedai? They're an angry genie we've let loose from the bottle. It was just sheer, stupid luck that your crew had the resources and expertise to capture the one that hit you. But imagine what would happen if one of those things got loose on a populated Federation planet. Civilian law enforcement and local militaries don't have the technology or firepower to defend themselves against the Shedai. We'd be talking about millions of fatalities, at a minimum. Hell, the only way your predecessor stopped those things was by turning Gamma Tauri IV into radioactive glass. As you might imagine, that's not a solution I'd want to use on planets like Rigel, Vulcan, or Earth. But until you and your team give us something better, General Order 24 is the only weapon we've got against these things.

"So, while I understand the sincere and reasonable concerns that you and Doctor Marcus have raised with regard to the pace of the Vanguard project, I need you to put them aside. We need that array up and working, and we need your team to figure out how to use it, as soon as possible—if not sooner. That's not a request, it's an order. Get it done.

"Severson out."

The screen faded to black as Severson terminated the subspace link. Nogura looked at the ceiling of his office and wondered who, ultimately, history would decide had been on the right side of that argument: Severson or Marcus? At the same time, he knew that in the here and now, the answer to that question was irrelevant. All that mattered was that he had his orders, and like a good soldier, he would follow them—even if he suspected the result would be a catastrophe.

As he sat and brooded, the words of an ancient Earth poem haunted his thoughts.

> Theirs not to make reply,
> Theirs not to reason why,

Theirs but to do and die.
Into the valley of Death
Rode the six hundred.

Nogura looked at the star map on the wall to his left, and his eyes fell upon the dense cluster of icons that reminded him daily of the Tholian armada assembled within prime striking distance of Vanguard.

Into the valley of Death, indeed.

Carol Marcus stood back from the Vault's master control panel and watched Lieutenants Xiong and Theriault. The young Starfleet scientists conferred in excited whispers in front of a huge vid screen as they debated how to apply the new intel from T'Prynn to the alien array. Hours earlier, when the Vulcan intelligence officer had delivered the results of her follow-up debriefing of Cervantes Quinn, Marcus had succumbed to curiosity and pored over the arcane mishmash of symbols, formulas, and molecular models. She had even felt a flush of excitement when she, Xiong, and Theriault had begun to parse the alien syntax—a bizarre fusion of pure mathematics, applied chemistry, and quantum physics. Then she had remembered what they were working toward, and her elation turned to shame.

"Look at this sequence," Xiong said, pointing at the screen. "I think the twelve elements in this pattern correspond to the differences we detected on the facets of each artifact. I think it defines the unique way each facet absorbs or reflects energy."

Theriault pushed his pointing finger aside with her own. "Yes! And this larger sequence tells us which facets to place in contact with one another." She glowed with delight. "Oh, my God! It's an *assembly guide*!" Then realization set in. "You know what this means, don't you?"

"Unfortunately, yes. It means we did this completely wrong."

Xiong stepped away from the screen, put two fingers in his mouth, and split the sedate atmosphere of the Vault with a shrill whistle. His flock of white-coated scientists and Starfleet specialists all looked up at him, their reflex Pavlovian in its perfection. "Everyone! Listen up! I have bad news, and I have good news. First, the bad news. I know you're all eager to start running experiments and testing your new protocols, but all that's going to have to wait—because we need to go in there and take that thing completely apart." Groans of disbelief and disappointment resounded inside the lab, then subsided as Xiong raised his arms and waved everyone back into line. "The good news is the reason why. We have new intel that we think will clear up all the problems we've had bringing this array on line. I want you all to get started on breaking down the array. By the time you're finished, Lieutenant Theriault and I should be ready to give you specific instructions for how to put it back together—the right way, this time." He clapped his hands, breaking the spell of attention. "Let's get to work!"

With varying degrees of enthusiasm and equanimity, the research team trudged inside the isolation chamber and began the delicate, tedious labor of disassembling the makeshift array. Theriault joined in to help speed things along as Xiong continued to study the data on the screen and add more of his own annotations. Hoping this might be a chance to make an appeal to his better nature, Marcus joined him at the master control panel.

"Ming," she said softly. "Can I talk to you for a moment?"

He paused in his analysis and gave her his attention. "Of course, Doctor."

She gathered her courage. "Now that you're taking the array apart, I want to ask you to hold off on putting it back together, even if just to—"

"You know I can't do that," he cut in. "I have my orders. We all do."

The same old argument; it made her want to scream. "I'm aware of that, Ming. But I'm worried about what our work is being used for. And about how it's being used."

Xiong crossed his arms. "We've talked about this. You voiced your concerns, and Admiral Nogura overruled them."

"And you agree with his decision?"

Conflicting emotions played across his youthful face. "It's complicated."

"I understand that." She reached out and gently grasped his arm, hoping a bit of real human contact would help put her point across more effectively than mere words. "But this thing you're building—I think it's dangerous, Ming. It could be used for unethical purposes."

He gently brushed away her hand. "That's true of any technology. A warp drive could be used to accelerate payloads into planets at superluminal velocities. To an undefended planet, a warp drive can be a doomsday weapon. Technologies aren't inherently good or evil."

"Are you sure?" She aimed a troubled look at the array, which had already been stripped of a dozen crystals. "That thing was made to be a prison, Ming. And the research you did on the first two artifacts showed us that when those crystals are occupied, they can be used to generate almost limitless power. They destroyed *eleven* worlds from *hundreds* of light-years away. Does that seem like an ethical piece of technology to you? A weapon that runs on slavery?"

"Those worlds were destroyed by *mistake*."

"Is that supposed to make me feel better?"

He looked flustered. "We checked, Doctor. None of those planets were inhabited. In fact, most of them were lifeless rockballs. No harm done."

"Tell that to the ecosystem on Ceti Alpha V. It was completely destroyed when we blew up Ceti Alpha VI and changed its orbit."

"Well, then," Xiong said, "it's a good thing nobody *lives* on Ceti Alpha V."

She could see he was becoming defensive, but she had come too far to abandon her argument now. "So why is Starfleet covering it up? Did you know they forged new charts of the Ceti Alpha system? They're pretending Ceti Alpha V is actually Ceti Alpha VI! Why?"

"We've been ordered not to talk about that, Doctor. *Ever.*"

"Damn it, Ming, ask yourself why they're keeping it a secret even from their own people. What if it's because some admiral at Starfleet or some politician on Earth wants to see if the array can destroy chosen worlds on purpose? What if they want to make a weapon out of it?"

"They wouldn't do that."

"Don't be so sure, Ming. Power corrupts, and this array is about as close as we've come to absolute power." Turned half away from her, his body language suggested he was ready to shut her out. She changed tactics. "Ming, you're better than this."

"What makes you think so?"

"I read the reports you wrote after you first got here." She leaned sideways to catch his eye one last time. "You did some groundbreaking work. And you used to be a voice for mercy and reason. You represented everything Starfleet claims it stands for. Now you're in charge of a project whose principal objective seems to be trapping and enslaving the Shedai."

His mood darkened. "Actually, our primary objective is to eliminate the Shedai as a threat, for the good of the Federation and the galaxy at large. Studying their technology for new applications is actually our secondary mission."

The revelation horrified Marcus. "So your most human option is slavery, and the only alternative is genocide?" Xiong didn't seem inclined to respond to her outburst, so she added, "The Ming Xiong whose research I admired would never agree to be a party to this."

"People change, Doctor." Determination put a fierce cast on his angular features. "I've seen good people killed, watched nations push each other to the brink of war, and faced an enemy so powerful that I still have nightmares about it. I sent one of my few real friends to her death so we could obtain the intelligence T'Prynn brought us today. I've made more compromises, broken more promises, and shed more blood than I'd ever thought possible. The reasons why don't really matter anymore. I've come too far and seen too much to believe that everything will be all right if only we make token gestures to morality. What matters now is that the whole galaxy seems to be out to kill us, and the Shedai are at the front of the line. So either help us get this array working, or get the hell out of my lab."

Stung by Xiong's vitriolic rebuke, Marcus stormed away, leaving him to his infernal device and willing collaborators. *Those morons at Starfleet Command are going to get us all killed,* she decided. It was time to put a halt to the madness, to plead her case to someone who would listen to reason and intervene before it was too late.

As she opened the secure hatch and left the Vault, she was not surprised to note that none of her so-called colleagues and peers paid the slightest heed to her departure. But she vowed they would not continue ignoring her for much longer.

Sequestered in her private office, T'Prynn drew quiet satisfaction from the comfort of slightly higher gravity and temperatures, and lower humidity and air pressure, than were standard aboard Vanguard—or, for that matter, inside most Starfleet vessels and facilities. She had configured her environmental controls to approximate as closely as possible the climate of her native Vulcan. It was a small indulgence, but one that made her daily work routine more agreeable.

A number of tasks still awaited her attention before that day's duty shift drew to a close. She needed to decrypt a few packets of intercepted Klingon signal traffic, review reports from a handful of recently debriefed field operatives, scan the latest public news from both the Federation and its neighboring rivals for patterns of interest, and conduct a cursory review of the official identity files of all newly arrived visitors to the station to see if any triggered alerts from the biometric recognition systems concealed inside the docking bays and primary corridors.

It was a slow day aboard Vanguard, all things considered.

A soft beeping from the companel on her wraparound desk alerted her to an incoming subspace message on a secure frequency from Earth. She checked the encryption keys, which confirmed the message had originated at the headquarters of Starfleet Command. Following protocol, she tapped in her authorization code to accept the transmission. The Starfleet emblem on her panel's vid screen was replaced by the careworn features of Admiral Selim Aziz, the director of Starfleet Intelligence. His skin was of an especially rich shade of brown, a visible testament to his Tunisian heritage. When he smiled, his gleaming teeth seemed almost blinding in contrast to his complexion. *"Good morning, Lieutenant T'Prynn."*

"Good *afternoon,* Admiral."

His smile faltered, then vanished. *"Ah, yes. I forgot to account for local time aboard the station. My mistake."*

She saw no point in prolonging or capitalizing upon his apparent discomfort at the minor faux pas. "It's of no consequence, sir. How can I assist you?"

"I noted with interest your report of a successful reinterview of Cervantes Quinn. Has the intelligence produced by that debriefing proved useful to the team in the Vault?"

"It has. Lieutenant Xiong informs me the new intel provided by Mister Quinn has been instrumental in the reconfiguration of the array, and it is expected to be of equal value when it comes time to bring the system fully on line."

A sage nod from Aziz. *"Excellent."* He eyed T'Prynn with suspicion. *"I also noticed that your report did not explain how your reinterview managed to elicit this intelligence from Mister Quinn, when your initial interview failed to do so."* He folded his hands and leaned forward. *"Without casting aspersions upon your interrogative methods, I am compelled to ask what made this latest debriefing more successful than the last."*

She had hoped no one would ask about this, but now that Aziz had, there would be no way to avoid an official record of the matter. "A most reasonable inquiry, Admiral. I extracted the information from Mister Quinn's memory by means of a Vulcan mind-meld."

"I see." He thought for a moment, then nodded once. *"From what I know of your people's customs, that can't have been an easy thing for you."*

Giving away nothing with her face or voice, she replied, "It was not, sir."

"I commend you for making such an extraordinary effort, Lieutenant." Concern creased his ebony brow. *"However, it raises troubling questions about Mister Quinn."*

"Such as . . . ?" She focused on masking her alarm at the direction of the conversation.

"My first query would be whether he remembered this intelligence all along but simply chose not to divulge it during his first debriefing."

"No, sir," T'Prynn said with verbal force. "My opinion is that Mister Quinn was afflicted by a psychological block induced by emotional trauma. He was unable to recollect the details of that mission with sufficient clarity due to his distress at the death of his partner."

Aziz pressed his index finger to his lips for a moment, striking a thoughtful pose. *"Would you say that your mind-meld had the effect of helping him overcome that mental block?"*

A small nod. "That would be a fair assessment."

"So his memory of that day's events are now clear in his mind?"

"I think they are, yes. The meld has greatly improved his specific recall."

The admiral's mood turned solemn. *"Most unfortunate."* He paused, seemingly deep in thought. Before T'Prynn could ask him to explain, he continued. *"If his memory had remained unreliable outside of the mind-meld, I might have been able to authorize a simple mind wipe for him and left it at that. But if he recalls the details of the Shedai's technology clearly, even one of our engram erasures won't hide that kind of detailed information from a Klingon mind-sifter."*

"I'm afraid I don't take your meaning, Admiral."

"I'll be blunt, then: Mister Quinn's history of alcoholism and

unstable behavior make him a security risk, especially in light of his recent relapse into binge drinking."

"I've taken steps to help him control his addictions. Given time and support—"

Aziz shook his head. *"It's too late for that, Lieutenant. The intel to which he's had access is too important and the stakes in the Taurus Reach are now far too high for us to risk Quinn being captured and interrogated by a hostile power or rogue political actor. And considering the current downward spiral of his life, I'm afraid he's no longer useful to us as a covert asset, which means we have no compelling reason to spend time or resources rehabilitating him."*

T'Prynn said nothing. She just stared at Aziz and waited until he made it an order.

"Covertly neutralize Mister Quinn at your earliest opportunity. Aziz out."

The admiral terminated the connection without brooking further debate, which was just as well, since there clearly was nothing left to discuss. Quinn's life had been declared forfeit, and T'Prynn had been designated to collect it.

Seeing no other alternative, she began planning the end of Cervantes Quinn.

23

As a general rule, Admiral Nogura preferred to conduct official meetings inside his office. He tried to avoid visiting the other departments under his authority because, in his experience, the arrival of a commanding officer—especially one of flag rank—tended to have a disruptive effect on business-as-usual. Convening behind closed doors also provided the additional advantage of discretion. Put simply, people often seemed more willing to speak their minds in private.

Some matters, however, demanded to be addressed in person.

The secure airlock portal parted ahead of him with a pneumatic gasp, revealing the well-lit, antiseptic environs of the Vault. He lurched through the hatchway, trailed by a quartet of crimson-shirted security officers, and marched at a quick-step through the laboratory, following the shortest possible route to the object of his unbounded rancor. His broken-glass voice boomed inside the hushed hall of science. "Doctor Marcus!"

She casually stroked a lock of her golden hair from her forehead and turned to confront him with an infuriating, beatific calm. "Yes, Admiral?"

He was so enraged that he could barely compose sentences. "What in God's name were you thinking? Going over my head to the Federation Security Council?"

Marcus crossed her arms and lifted her chin with haughty pride. "You made it clear my opinions weren't going to be given due consideration here, so I did what I had to do."

"Except that I *did* give your opinions due consideration, Doctor! Far more, in fact, than you realize or could ever know." He stepped forward, invading her personal space on purpose. "I did all I could to be your advocate to my superiors, but I had to accept that there are larger issues involved than your conscience—or your ego. But that wasn't good enough for you, was it? No, you had to cash in political favors and bring down a shitstorm on all of us. I hope you're happy."

"Far from it." Marcus thrust one index finger in violent jabs toward Nogura's chest, pulling back each time millimeters shy of contact. "What you and your people are doing here, with this array, is both dangerous and immoral! You're enslaving the Shedai, in clear violation of Federation law, and—"

"You're preaching to the choir, Doctor! I agree, this is an ugly situation, but—"

"Ugly! It's unconscionable! It's an offense against sentient beings who have just as much right to live in this universe as we do."

Xiong, Theriault, and the legion of scientists who spent the vast majority of their waking hours inside the Vault gathered around Marcus and Nogura, all of them jockeying by small degrees for the best angle from which to observe and listen. Nogura tried to ignore the pressure that came with an audience and kept his focus on Marcus alone. "Tell me, Doctor, will you defend the Shedai's rights this vigorously after they start slaughtering civilians by the millions? Because that's what's going to happen if one of these things gets onto a Federation world."

"I'm not going to debate hypotheticals with you, Admiral."

"Then I'll tell you something that's *not* hypothetical: I have my orders from Starfleet Command, and those orders are to bring this array on line and make it operational immediately. It doesn't matter what I think of those orders, Doctor. I will see them carried out."

"Even if it means condoning slavery?"

"I'll do it because it means *saving lives*. But, yes, I think there might be a poetic justice in yoking the Shedai to the array after what I'm told they once did to the Tholians."

Marcus radiated contempt. "Answering evil with evil doesn't add up to an act of good."

"Good and evil aren't always options, Doctor. Sometimes all we have to choose from are varying degrees of bad, worse, and completely awful. But we still have to choose." He shook his head. "It's all a moot point now. Your complaint to the Security Council stirred up so much trouble at Starfleet Command that your security clearance for Operation Vanguard has been officially revoked. Ten hours from now, at exactly 2130 hours station time, you and your son will be transferred off this station aboard the transport *S.S. Linshul*."

His proclamation left Marcus looking as if she'd been gut-punched. "You're firing me *and* kicking me off the station?"

"Not me," Nogura corrected her. "Starfleet Command. You took my prerogative out of the equation the moment you decided to circumvent my authority." Looking around at the gathered faces spectating on their contretemps, he added, "Any of you who signed that letter Doctor Marcus sent to the Security Council had better start packing, as well. Because your clearances have also been revoked, and you'll be joining Doctor Marcus at her new assignment."

Angry voices assailed Nogura from all sides, and his security detachment moved closer to defend him, just as they had been trained to do. Over the din of shouting voices, he heard Marcus call for order. As the clamor died down, she yelled, "You don't get to fire us, Admiral, and neither does Starfleet! We're civilians, sent here by order of the Federation Council."

"Starfleet welcomed you to this facility as a courtesy. Now we're letting you know that you've overstayed your welcome, and it's time to go."

"You can't do this!"

"It's done. Be at Gangway Four on the lower docking pylon at 2130 sharp. If you're not there at 2130, I'll send armed security to find you and bring you there. Is that understood?"

She traded exasperated looks with several of her fellow soon-to-be-exiled colleagues, and Nogura could tell from their deepening mood of collective despair that the reality of the moment was finally beginning to take root in their minds. Bewildered and flustered, Marcus pressed one hand to her high forehead as she asked, "Where are we being sent? Back to Earth?"

"No, to a brand-new research station," Nogura said. "A state-of-the-art facility where you can continue your work on your own terms—without Starfleet looking over your shoulder."

That drew a bittersweet smile from her. "Your doing, I suppose?"

"I might have pulled a few strings," he admitted.

She drew a deep breath and relaxed a bit. "Where is it?"

"Orbiting the planetoid Regula, in the Mutara Sector."

All her fury returned at once. "Mutara Sector! That's even more remote than the Taurus Reach! That's practically the middle of nowhere!"

Nogura harrumphed as he walked away. "Don't worry, Doctor. Even at the ass end of space, I'm sure you'll still find *something* to bitch about."

Xiong shouldered his way through the slow-shuffling line of his former colleagues as they trudged in a queue down the gangway to the *S.S. Linshul*. The departing scientists and their family members were burdened with far too much luggage, all of it hastily packed in order to meet their deadline for expulsion from Vanguard. Some of them towed rolling suitcases, others portered bulging duffels on their backs. Most of the banished researchers also lugged overfilled shoulder bags, while the few young children caught up in the mix carted smaller bags and, in a few cases, desperately clutched stuffed animals, as if they feared the Starfleet security personnel shepherding the group aboard the *Linshul* might confiscate plush bears and velveteen rabbits simply out of spite.

Halfway down the gangway, Xiong saw Carol Marcus, who appeared to be traveling light: all she had was an overnight bag over her left shoulder and her tow-haired seven-year-old son, David, clinging anxiously to her right arm. Xiong called out to her, "Carol! Hold up!"

She stopped and turned to face him as he caught up to her. "Ming! What is it?"

"I didn't want to let you leave without saying good-bye."

After a moment of struggling with his pride, he added, "And to say, I'm sorry."

Marcus handed off her son to Doctor Tarcoh, who had been behind her in line. "Kalen, would you take David aboard and show him to my cabin for me?"

The spindly bald Deltan physicist took the young boy's hand in his and smiled at Marcus. "My pleasure, Doctor."

"Thanks." As her son was ushered away, Marcus stepped out of line, set down her bag, faced Xiong, and planted her hands on her hips. "Okay. Sorry for *what,* exactly?"

Xiong let his conscience speak. "For how this turned out." He watched the sluggish line moving toward the transport. "I never thought they'd put you all on a slow boat to nowhere."

"Silly me," Marcus said. "I thought you might've wanted to apologize for selling out your principles and throwing me to the wolves in the name of duty."

"You don't really think that's what happened, do you?"

There was no forgiveness in her eyes. "What do *you* think happened?"

Realizing he might never see Marcus again, he decided to be as truthful as possible. "I think . . . that you took a stand based on your principles. I think you tried to be a voice of compassion and decency in a time and place where those values can get people killed. I think you're a great scientist, and an even better person. And I wish there was some way we could live up to your ideals and still accomplish our mission as Starfleet officers."

"Ming . . ." Her anger melted away, revealing sorrow and disappointment. "You make it sound as if it's an either-or decision, but it's not. Saying we have to pick between security and integrity is a false choice. Cruelty is not the path to lasting peace. It can't be."

"Carol, I think you're missing the point. Starfleet's not doing this because it believes in torture. It's because, whether anyone outside this station realizes it or not, *we're at war.* We've tried to communicate with the Shedai, but they're not interested in talking to us. In almost every encounter we've had with them, they've tried to kill us. Now, I know you don't agree with the remedies we're developing—"

"Remedies? *That's* a lovely euphemism."

Forcing himself not to be baited into a dead-end argument, he took a calming breath and pressed on. "We're doing what has to be done to protect the Federation, and the galaxy."

"I see. You're planning to *commit* genocide in order to *prevent* genocide."

He pushed a hand through his short, spiky black hair. "What do you want me to say?"

"I don't know. Maybe I just want some reason to believe you haven't let your emotions trump your good judgment."

Her accusation rankled him. "What the hell does *that* mean?"

"There's an old saying, Ming: 'Inside every cynic is a disappointed idealist.' You used to be one of the most ethical, principled scientists I knew. But you said it yourself: you saw good people die, and you changed. And I think I know which death it was that changed you."

Xiong turned to leave. "Have a nice trip."

Marcus grabbed his sleeve and spun him around. "It was Bridy Mac. Something inside you changed when she died. I saw the difference in you, Ming. It was like someone flipped a switch inside your head, and you haven't been the same since."

"I'm just applying the scientific method. New evidence contradicted my theory of morality, so I changed my theory to fit the facts. That's how I know I'm doing the right thing."

"Are you sure?" She was pleading more than arguing. "What if you're doing the *wrong* things for the *right* reasons? Would you even be able to make that distinction?"

He felt like she was talking in circles. "Why would it matter?"

"It matters because our actions define who we are, Ming—not just as individuals but as a society. And I'm telling you right now that Starfleet's approach to the Shedai and those artifacts is immoral. Whether it succeeds or fails, it'll demean the spirit of what Starfleet is meant to be, and taint the souls of everyone who's a willing part of it." She seized his hands. "You're playing with fire, Ming. You're meddling with forces that none of us have even *begun* to understand, and you're trying to use them in ways that history will never forgive. Mark my words: this vile experiment can only end in disaster. . . . I just hope you realize that in time to stop it."

Marcus let go of his hands, picked up her bag, and took a few steps down the gangway. She paused and looked back, as if to say a final farewell, but then seemed to think better of it. Without another word she blended back into the line and passed from Xiong's sight as she stepped through the hatch of the *Linshul*.

Xiong walked back inside the lower docking pylon and stopped for a while in the observation lounge overlooking the *Linshul*'s berth. As the *Drogher*-class transport separated from the airlock and navigated away from the station on thrusters, Xiong considered all that Marcus had said, but he kept coming back to her warning: *You're playing with fire*. As the *Linshul* sped away at impulse, Xiong realized where he had heard Marcus's warning before.

It was what his own conscience had been telling him since his first day on Vanguard.

24

Despite having visited the Vault only twice before, Vanessa Theriault thought the lab felt strangely off-kilter without any civilians manning its stations. The few that hadn't been directly dismissed from the project and the station by Starfleet Command's edict had chosen to leave with Doctor Marcus, in a profound demonstration of ethical solidarity. In their place, Xiong had recruited Theriault and more than two dozen of the best scientific personnel from the station and the *Endeavour*. Apparently, the project had been deemed urgent enough that Starfleet Command had approved upgraded security clearances for all those who had to be brought up to speed on the true nature of the Shedai and the objectives of Operation Vanguard.

"We're getting ready to power up the array," Xiong announced. "Everyone stand by and keep a close eye on your readouts. If you see anything that's been flagged as a hazard, speak up." He stepped back behind the clear partition and took his place between Theriault and Lieutenant Stephen Klisiewicz at the master control console. "Initiate start-up sequence."

Theriault, who was tasked with monitoring transmissions and emissions of energy to and from the array, confirmed, "All readings nominal. Throughput is steady, no distortion."

Klisiewicz made a few fine adjustments at his panel. "System interface is up. All checksums are valid, and it looks like we have clear signals from all nodes."

Xiong asked, "How's Node One?"

That was the designation for the array's only occupied crystalline artifact. The operating system Klisiewicz had designed using the new intel from T'Prynn had made it possible to monitor the status of every linked node in the array and identify each by a unique number.

"Containment's solid, boss," Theriault said. "No change in output."

"So far, so good," Xiong said. He rubbed his hands together before setting them back on the master controls. "Okay, folks, time for step two. We're going to slowly increase the power from standby level to what we estimate is the normal operating level. Look sharp."

With one fingertip, he gradually traced the outline of a circle on his panel, and it responded by switching from cool blue to bright red at his touch. A low-frequency hum from inside the isolation chamber sent a sympathetic shiver down Theriault's spine.

"Fifty percent," Xiong said, still nudging the power levels upward.

The deep droning from the array increased in volume and pitch. Crooked bands of blue lightning hopscotched over the linked crystals. Xiong called out, "Sixty percent."

"Interface is still five by five," Klisiewicz said. "Good to go."

Xiong looked left toward Theriault. "Energy readings?"

His request broke the machine's spell over her, and she eyed her gauges. "Pass-through is clean, no distortion. Minor fluctuations in output from Node One." She double-checked the levels against their redlines. "All readings are within rated norms. Good to go."

"Substations," Xiong said, his voice echoing from the lab's PA system, "any red flags?"

The ring of blue-shirted Starfleet specialists all worked in silence, and then Ensign Kirsten Heffron, a much-lauded wunderkind of biophysics and quantum chemistry who had been assigned as the out-station supervisor for this experiment, signaled "good to go" via her console's link to the lab's secure internal network.

"Grab your socks, then," Xiong said, increasing the power. "Seventy percent."

The droning oscillated in an eerie manner, and the high-pitched sound developed a deep contrapuntal undertone that filled Theriault with sensations of dread. The same blue ribbons of energy that danced across the array began to appear spontaneously outside the isolation chamber—climbing the walls, snaking over consoles, and twisting up and around the scientists manning the stations that surrounded the chamber. Theriault arched one eyebrow as she watched an energy ribbon snake over her green jumpsuit. "*That* doesn't look good."

Over the PA, Xiong said in his most reassuring voice, "It's all right, don't be alarmed. It's harmless. The systems are insulated against this, and it'll disperse as it's drawn up to the grounding coils in the ceiling." Moments later, as he'd predicted, the phenomenon ceased, and all that was left were the fear-inducing banshee wails and groans of the machine. "Increasing power to eighty percent."

Theriault shuddered as an intense prickling coursed through her body, starting in her feet and traveling up her spine. It stung her head with heat and left a metallic taste in her mouth. She heard a static-electric crackling, then caught her faint reflection on the transparent shield in front of the master console: her hair was standing on end, floating as if in zero gravity. "This is a new look for me," she quipped. "Also temporary, I hope?"

"It should pass in a few seconds after the array's capacitors catch up," Xiong said. He asked the group, "Everyone all right?" Reports of *status: nominal* came back from every station, and he increased the power. "Coming up on ninety percent."

"We're getting action from Node One," Theriault said as one of her gauges jumped in output. "Signal output is up three hundred percent and climbing."

Excited and concerned at the same time, Xiong asked, "Containment?"

"Locked down tight," Theriault said. "Good to go."

"Ramping up to full power in ten seconds," Xiong said. "Steve, stand by to bring mission applications on line as soon as we have a green signal." Klisiewicz nodded.

As the array thrummed and pulsed to full power, the atmosphere inside the Vault took on a quality that Theriault could describe only as narcotic. Some unknown property of the array, some emanation that Federation science hadn't yet quantified, made the immeasurably powerful device simultaneously hypnotizing and thrilling. It became a labor to tear her eyes from it to monitor her panel's readouts. She forced herself to blink and look away until her focus returned, despite the siren song of the machine's unearthly resonance.

"Full power," Xiong said. "Load mission apps. I want to see what this thing can do."

Klisiewicz launched a series of programs, most of which had been written and designed based only on the first artifact the Vault team had acquired. A number of simulations had suggested that the same control interfaces would be scalable to the much more sophisticated demands of the array; Theriault hoped the simulations proved correct. She didn't want to imagine what might happen if a system channeling as much power as was being fed into the array were to suffer a rapid cascade failure. At the very least, she doubted anyone would ever find her body—or much of the station, for that matter.

"I think I have something," Klisiewicz said. Xiong and Theriault pressed in to watch over his shoulders as he worked at his panel. "This is the program your team wrote for detecting Shedai energy signatures. It can read everything from Jinoteur Pattern sources to passive Conduit responses to living Shedai." He processed a batch of new data, resulting in one enormous cluster of red and a multihued flurry of far-flung specks. "This is what we just picked up with the array."

Theriault squinted to see if perhaps she had missed something other than the dots. "So, what exactly are we looking at here?"

"The blue are Conduits," Xiong said. "The red are living Shedai." He pointed at the cluster. "And it looks like they're having some kind of town meeting."

"It's a Colloquium," Theriault blurted out. Klisiewicz and

Xiong looked at her. "It's what they call it when they gather to make decisions. It's what they were doing on Jinoteur when the *Sagittarius* crashed there."

Xiong sounded worried. "I thought they'd been scattered."

"I guess they got the band back together," Theriault said.

"Most of them, anyway," Klisiewicz added. "We're showing a few stragglers."

Pointing at some of the sidebar menu items on the screen, Theriault asked, "Can you show us exactly where they are in relation to the station?"

"In theory, yes." Klisiewicz entered commands as he spoke. "I'm overlaying a local star map and tactical grid. That should give us a fair idea of where they . . ." His voice trailed off as the composite graphic took shape on his screen. Xiong seemed about to ask what was wrong, but then he, too, stared slackjawed at the display. Growing more alarmed by the minute, Theriault leaned forward to get a clearer view—and regretted it immediately.

"Oh, that is *not* good," she said.

Xiong stood in the station commander's office facing Nogura, T'Prynn, and Captains Nassir and Khatami. The four senior officers stood side by side, their stances and grave aspects giving Xiong the impression that he was facing a rhetorical firing squad. "To be precise," he said, continuing his report, "Lieutenant Klisiewicz made *three* very alarming discoveries."

He inserted a yellow data card into a slot beside Nogura's wall-sized star chart. "I'm sure you all recognize this map of the Taurus Reach." With a tap on one button, he superimposed over the map the Shedai sensor data produced by the array. "Long story short: the blue dots are Conduits. There are a lot more than we thought, and some appear to be within the boundaries of Federation space. That's the first bit of bad news. The second is that the red dots represent living Shedai entities, and it seems like almost all of them still in existence have gathered on Velara II, out by the Pleiades Cluster."

"That puts them roughly three hundred light-years away," Nassir said.

T'Prynn replied, "Three hundred fifteen-point-seven, Captain."

Khatami looked confused. "That's good news, isn't it?"

"No," Xiong said, "because *one* of those red dots"—he magnified the center of the map until it showed one red dot, one blue dot, and a green dot—"is right here."

Nogura's eyes widened. "Please tell me *we* are not the green dot."

"Unfortunately, we are." Xiong added annotations to the image. "There's a Shedai lurking just outside the range of our tactical sensors, and it's got a previously unknown Conduit with it. According to intelligence gathered over the last couple of years, the only Shedai that's known to be able to move freely through interstellar space is the one we captured—and lost—last year." He gestured at the wall monitor. "Well, it looks like you were right, Admiral. She's been holding a grudge, and now she's back."

That news seemed to hit Nogura hard. He walked up to the screen and stared at it, point-blank, as if it would give up secrets if only he looked closely enough. "Options."

"What's there to talk about?" asked Nassir. "We know where it is, let's go and get it."

The admiral shook his head. "It's not that simple."

Nassir verged on raising his voice. "Why not?"

"Because the *Endeavour*'s still under repair," Nogura said. "And while your ship is an excellent scout, it's hardly suited to combat."

Xiong added, "Besides, Captain, we don't even know if our weapons have much effect on the Shedai. The last time we tangled with this thing, we barely scratched it."

"It is also worth noting," T'Prynn said, "that when this Shedai last fled from here, it did so at speeds the *Sagittarius* was unable to match—or even detect. If we attempt to attack it by means of a direct starship assault, there is nothing to prevent it from escaping unscathed."

Khatami seemed to share Nassir's frustration. "So, we do nothing? We just sit and wait for it to take the initiative? For the record, I am *not* okay with that."

"We will act, but not with starships," Nogura said. "This Shedai has committed a tactical blunder, and I don't intend to waste it."

Nassir asked, "What blunder would that be, sir?"

"It chose us as its first target." He returned to his desk and sat down. "If we go out there with starships, all we're likely to do is scare it off. And there's no guarantee its next attack will be here. It could just as well build its next Conduit on a Federation planet. That's not a chance I'm willing to take." He looked at Xiong. "Has there been any evidence of contact between that Shedai and the others?"

"Sporadic bursts of energy between their two Conduits," Xiong said. "Our analysts think the Shedai are testing the new Conduit before putting it into full operation."

T'Prynn asked, "How close do they seem to be?"

"Very. They could be ready to strike any time now."

Nogura nodded. "Excellent. This is the moment we've been waiting for." He stood up. "Arm the array, Lieutenant. Now we attack."

The array's steady rhythm of pulsing sound and its macabre violet aura entranced Theriault, Klisiewicz, and the other Starfleet scientists as they helped Xiong activate its protocols. The air inside the Vault felt charged with their commingled excitement and fear as one monitoring station after another confirmed the array's fully ready status.

"Locking in the coordinates of all Shedai energy signatures," Klisiewicz said. "Calculating resonant attraction frequencies."

"Acknowledged," Xiong said. He looked left at Theriault. "Containment?"

"Node One is secure. Preparing unique node assignments for new signatures."

Xiong checked his master panel. "All signals are clean, no interference. Heffron, ping the Conduits. Verify we have contact on all points."

Beyond the protective barrier, Ensign Heffron keyed in commands. "Transmitting." Several seconds later, she added, "All Conduits responding. The network is active."

Klisiewicz made his final adjustments on his panel. "Resonant frequencies ready."

Theriault added, "Nodes assigned. Containment protocols ready."

A grave nod from Xiong. He wiped his sweaty palms down the front of his shirt, then thumbed open a secure comm to Nogura's office in the operations center. "Admiral, the array is ready. We can initiate Operation Flytrap as soon as you give the word."

"The word is given, Lieutenant. Good luck."

"Thank you, sir. We'll have a report for you shortly. Xiong out." He closed the channel and took a deep breath. Theriault heard him mutter under his breath, "Now all we have to do is make ourselves an irresistible target to every Shedai in the galaxy. . . . What could go wrong?" Xiong blinked, cracked his knuckles, and set his hands on the master power controls. "Okay, everyone, it's game time. Stand by to execute in . . . ten . . . nine . . . eight . . ."

Much to Theriault's dismay, as she listened to Xiong continue the countdown to the activation of the array, she was able to think of a great many things that could go wrong.

Then Xiong said, "Three . . . two . . . one. . . . Execute!"

She and Klisiewicz flipped the final switches on their respective panels.

And the array started screaming.

The mind of the Progenitor stirred in the endless silence, a lone presence in the immeasurable darkness of thought without sensation, existence without form, time without end.

His accursed isolation, his exile into a limbo of his own consciousness, was disturbed by a shriek of primal force and a dis-
orienting flurry of light and energy. It was inchoate, nothing but
noise bereft of significance, a howling torrent of madness and
desire.

Quickly, the chaos was marshaled into order and forced into
shape. The Progenitor dared to indulge a fleeting instant of hope.
Had the Wanderer returned to honor her pledge? Was freedom at
hand? He imagined the unfettered joy of exacting his revenge
upon the *Telinaruul.* . . .

Then came the agony.

Pain with no physical analog reduced the Progenitor's universe to one of horrific psychic torment. It was as if his entire
essence were being ripped asunder, his every thought rent to
pieces, his very being torn in a million directions at once. Never
had he known such grotesque suffering, not even when he'd been
condemned to this private pit of despair.

All he could do was surrender to the brutal energies that assailed him and let their wild surges of power course through him
and bear him away, one mote of consciousness at a time, wearing
him down to nothing, as flowing water reduces a boulder to a
pebble with the passing of ages. He wondered if this was, at last,
his end—being condemned to vanish in a final tide of punish-
ment, flayed to his last iota of existence by a torment beyond his
ken to describe.

For the first time since his moment of self-inception, the
Progenitor was afraid.

Cold and silent, the Wanderer hovered in space above her newly
made Conduit. She reached out with her thoughts to perfect its
final details and make it a flawless portal for the subtle form of
liberated consciousness. Its link to the universe's boundless
reservoir of dark energy was complete, and already she felt the
Conduit's steady emanations of power and harmony.

Soon it would be time to summon the Shedai to take their

vengeance. Before that hour of reckoning, however, she needed to move the Conduit closer to the space fortress. It would be an arduous process, and it would require great patience and stealth on her part not to alert them to her presence. Because the other *Serrataal* lacked her ability to traverse space by will alone, it would be up to her to place the Conduit in contact with the exterior of the *Telinaruul*'s fortress, penetrate its fragile metal skin, and then usher her kin inside. Then they would cleanse its interior of its vermin creators—a prelude for the galactic culling to come.

A wail of terror issued from the Conduit and struck the Wanderer with overwhelming force. Driven by fear and reflex, she made her essence cohere when all she wanted to do was flee. The excruciating shrillness of the signal abated, and then the Wanderer knew what it was that she heard: the Song of the Progenitor! Its message was simple, pure, and clear. He was calling out to her, imploring her to answer his summons, to hie unto him without delay.

This was not the plan, she told herself, even as she felt her essence succumb to the Progenitor's will. His voice was like that of no other Shedai; it was uniquely hypnotic and utterly compelling. Its beguiling melody transited the Conduit and called the other *Serrataal.*

I have opened the way, the Progenitor said. *Gather now and be with me at last.*

The Wanderer felt a surge of elation as she let the Progenitor's voice guide her subtle body of consciousness into the signal stream. *Perhaps he has turned their weapon against them!*

She surrendered to the flow of the Song, expecting at any moment to recorporealize inside the *Telinaruul*'s risibly vulnerable fortress. Only as she passed over the Conduit's final threshold did she detect, in the most ephemeral sense, that something was amiss.

But by then it was too late to save herself—or to warn the others who would follow.

• • •

Waves of panic crashed through the Progenitor's formless prison. Thousands of *Serrataal* voices cried out in bitter fury, **We have been deceived!**

In their flashes of memory he beheld a vision of a molten world where they had massed, and though he had not heard any voice in aeons except that of the Wanderer, he recognized them all, each one by its special timbre and quality: the Sage, the Adjudicator, the Warden, the Herald, and countless others. Still first among them all was the Maker, whose confusion, he realized, had arrived separate from the others. Many of the old voices seemed absent, though, and he soon became aware that the missing were the Apostate and those whom he had counted as partisans.

So, the great war within our ranks came at last, the Progenitor deduced. He reasoned that the Maker and her faithful had prevailed. Or had they? Ages earlier, the Tkon had fashioned this prison of the mind with the Apostate's aid; might this be his great revenge delivered at last?

It did not matter, he decided. At last, he and his progeny were reunited. Together, they would break free of their bonds and renew their patient conquest of the galaxy.

He concentrated, and projected his thoughts through the lattice of united minds.

Be silent. Be still.

Where he had expected obeisance, he found an onslaught of fury and rebellion. **Why did you lure us here?** they shrieked. **You betrayed us! You've led us into bondage!**

He quelled their storm of protest with a command like a supernova.

BE SILENT. BE STILL.

Their bonfire of rage was extinguished. Reverent awe took its place.

The Wanderer's voice pronounced to the darkness, **This is He of Whom I Spoke.**

Thousands of *Serrataal* sought the guidance of the Maker. She opened her thoughts to the Progenitor, and he reciprocated, while the universe without form that surrounded them echoed with the voices of their scions, the elite of those born to rule creation.

Hundreds of voices wondered in unison, **Can it really be He?** Others insisted, **This cannot be. He was only ever a myth, a tale of our forgotten past.** Doubt rippled through the ranks of the *Serrataal*, tainting their enforced Colloquium.

Silence reigned as the Maker and the Progenitor ended their communion.

It is He, she declared.

All their minds opened to him then, yearning to know the shape of his thoughts.

I am He who was before all else, he proclaimed. **He who begat you, tiny godlings. He whose mind is never at rest, whose dreams are the thunder of a million beating wings.**

You are my crashing waves, but I am the sea.

You are my flashes of lightning, but I am the storm.

You are my constant starlight, but I am the darkness.

Together, we shall free ourselves from this abyss of damnation . . . and punish all who dare to think themselves our equals.

My God. Xiong could hardly believe the numbers flying across his computer screen. *It's a miracle the whole thing didn't just melt down.* "Containment status! Report!"

"Um . . ." Theriault was tweaking controls and struggling to get a final set of data points from her own panel. "Containment is holding—barely. All assigned nodes have been filled."

Turning to his right, Xiong shot a hopeful look at Klisiewicz. "Contacts?"

"Nothing but Conduits," Klisiewicz said. "All Shedai signatures clear."

Hearing the news out loud made Xiong exhale with such relief that he almost felt deflated. He leaned forward on his panel, supporting himself with one hand while he used the other to palm the sweat from his forehead and push it back up into his hair. "Holy shit," he said, almost laughing. "We did it! We nearly fried every circuit in here . . . but we really did it."

Klisiewicz leaned over to steal a look at Xiong's panel. "Good lord! Look at the power levels inside the array. Is that where it stabilized *after* we closed the circuit?"

"Yup," Xiong said. "Our new guests are generating all that on their own. It's completely off the charts. I've never seen anything like it."

A comm signal beeped on Xiong's panel. He thumbed open the channel. "Xiong here."

Nogura's voice was quieter than usual. *"What happened down there, Lieutenant?"*

"It worked, sir. We've got the Shedai."

"So, you've recaptured it, eh?"

"No, sir," Xiong corrected. "Not just the one Shedai. We got *all* of them."

A long pause followed. *"Are you certain?"*

"Every last Shedai life sign is locked up inside the array." He traded smiles with Theriault and Klisiewicz, then added, "Shall I send them your regards, sir?"

"By all means," Nogura said. *"And, might I add . . . well done, Ming."*

"Thank you, sir. I'll have a full report on your desk inside the hour. Xiong out." He closed the channel. Half a second later, the Starfleet science personnel crowding the Vault erupted in wild cheers of victory and relief. Some embraced one another; a few clapped.

All that Xiong wanted to do was sit down. If that worked out, he had designs on returning to his quarters and sleeping for a few days, maybe a week. He slogged back to his office—which until very recently had been Doctor Marcus's office, but before that had been his office, a fact that assuaged some of his guilt about reclaiming it—and sank into his chair. He let his body go limp and his jaw slack as he tilted his head back to admire the ceiling.

His chair slowly spun in a half circle, and as the office's doorway drifted into his line of sight, he saw Lieutenant Theriault standing in it.

She seemed reluctant to intrude on him. "Sir?"

"Vanessa, we just saved the galaxy together. You can call me Ming."

"Um, okay. I just wanted to point out that the energy being produced by the Shedai has leveled off, but if it goes much higher for more than a few minutes at a time, we might start to lose containment. It would probably just be a few nodes at first, but . . . well, it wouldn't be good, is what I'm saying."

He rubbed his eyes and sat up. "Okay. Do you have a recommendation?"

"Well, it might sound crazy, but . . . maybe we should put in a self-destruct system."

Xiong chuckled. "It doesn't sound crazy at all. The Vault already has one." He admired the grim practicality of Starfleet's engineers. "It was the first system we installed."

There was no harmony in the Lattice. Alarm and discord flared and spread like an infection through the SubLinks of the armada under the command of Tarskene [The Sallow], and despite the best efforts of Subcommander Kezthene [The Gray], discipline was slow in returning.

All had heard the Song of the Enemy. Its hated tones had filled local space for only a moment, trumpeting distress and hostility to all who had the ability to hear. Then the Voice, so long despised and feared, had been silenced, and its blazing colors, which had flooded the Lattice, vanished like a snuffed flame. No one knew what it meant—Tarskene least of all.

Moving past his subordinates, he activated the subspace thoughtwave transmitter. Projecting his thought-colors via the Warrior Castemoot SubLink, he accessed the InterLink and petitioned the Ruling Conclave of the Political Castemoot for an immediate audience. Seconds passed while he awaited a response, and he labored to cleanse his mind-line of fretful hues. It would not do for him to present ideas clouded by fear or insecurity.

Velrene [The Azure] acknowledged Tarskene's salutation with muddled colors, which Tarskene took to suggest that she and the Ruling Conclave had also heard the Song of the Enemy. Her inter-voice wavered with disquiet. *What news, Commander?*

He projected memory facets shared among his armada's personnel. From thousands of different mind-lines, the Song of the Enemy echoed and stopped. *You have heard it.*

All have heard it. Velrene sent back fragments of countless memory-lines, from worlds throughout the Assembly. *The Voice was heard on every world.*

Tarskene appended his memory-line to the others. *And then it was silenced.*

Is the Enemy gone? Her inquiry was tinted with hope.

Resentment, fury, and fear darkened Tarskene's thought-colors. *Not gone. Snared. By the Federation, aboard its space station.*

Velrene's mind-line fragmented with disbelief, then surged crimson with rage. *It is not possible to contain the Old Ones! They must be destroyed!*

He tried to share soothing hues and calming tones via the InterLink, but Velrene's anger blazed like a wall of lava. *We do not yet know the Federation's intentions. They may yet choose to destroy the Old Ones, for their own safety if nothing else.*

She met his suggestion with sickly hues. *Doubtful. The Conclave must confer.*

A dull gray hum informed Tarskene that his mindwave on the InterLink had been muted. All he could do was wait while Velrene and the other members of Tholia's ruling elite weighed the matter and sought to harmonize their thought-colors.

A mellisonant chiming summoned him back to attention.

Velrene's mind-line radiated resolve. *For now, Commander, hold the armada where it stands, and observe the space station. If the Federation's soldiers destroy the Old Ones and take our vengeance for us, so be it.* Then her inter-voice shimmered with violent intent. *But if they try to steal the power of the Enemy for themselves, that we cannot abide. In such an event, we will have no choice but to act for the good of Tholia—and the galaxy—no matter the cost.*

Tarskene mirrored the colors of Velrene's mind-line with fidelity.

So shall it be done.

25

It had been obvious for a couple of days that something big was happening on the station. Because Fisher was no longer on active duty, no one could tell him anything, but he hadn't needed to hear the news firsthand. He could tell by the way conversations between Starfleet personnel spontaneously halted or sank into whispers as he passed by in his civilian clothes, and by the heightened level of excitement that seemed to be spreading through the crew like a contagion.

There was no point in angling for information; no one would talk. He guessed the chatter was probably related to Operation Vanguard, in which case he was happier not knowing.

At the same time, he saw no reason to sequester himself in his quarters, which were almost bare now that most of his personal effects had been loaded aboard the transport *Lisbon* for the journey home—whenever the hell that ended up happening. Delays of incoming cargo had postponed the ship's departure by at least another week, leaving Fisher with nothing to do but sleep, eat, read, and wander the public areas of the station. He passed most of his afternoons on Fontana Meadow, watching the ad hoc games of competitive sports that tended to spring up on the sprawling greensward that ringed the station's core, enjoying the fragrance of fresh-cut grass, or reading beside one of the pools, surrounded by the astringent odor of chlorine.

He had taken to spending his evenings enjoying the cuisine, wine, and hospitality of Manón's cabaret. In the years he had served aboard Vanguard, he had been there only a handful of times. In the weeks since his retirement, he had been there nearly every night until the house band played its final encore and the bartender enforced the last call. Manón, the club's ravishing alien patroness, an expatriate from a race known as the Silgov, had started calling him a regular. Roy, her bartender, had gotten into the habit of comping every third drink for Fisher—not that he ever finished a third drink. To one degree or another, every member of her staff had gone out of his or her way to make Fisher feel welcome and well cared for within their establishment.

He stepped through the front door that evening expecting to be met by Manón's radiant smile and the cool but funky rhythms of the cabaret's jazz quartet. Instead, the club was silent except for a sad, andante melody from the piano. Every guest and employee faced the stage, their jaws slack, eyes unblinking and glistening with emotion, and all of them utterly silent. Turning toward the stage, Fisher understood why.

T'Prynn sat at the piano, spotlit in the inky darkness, her eyes closed and her features sedate as she evoked from the instrument a somber, mournful tune that Fisher found deeply moving—and also more than a bit haunting in its tragic undertones. It was nothing like the crowd-pleasing music that T'Prynn had played in the past. To the best of Fisher's knowledge, this was the first time she had performed publicly since her return to Vanguard. It fascinated him to see her style so radically transformed.

No one noticed him—or, if they did, they paid him no mind—as he glided through the dining room to an unoccupied table near the stage. Every step of the way he was captivated by T'Prynn's solo showcase. Soft and gentle, the music seemed to spring from her with the simplicity of breath, yet it sounded as if it were in two places at once, bivalent in its nature, harrowing and yet beautiful, touching but also heartbreaking. Though he could not put into words why, he felt certain the song was a work of profound loneliness, an ode to love and mortality, a musical distillation of longing, pain, and shattering loss.

Her song dwindled to a close that felt as natural and elegiac as it was inevitable, and when it ended, the cabaret was heavy with awed silence.

Strong applause came several seconds later, but there was no cheering; the audience responded with reverence and respect, despite seeming more than a bit shell-shocked. T'Prynn left the stage as the clapping tapered off. Fisher's table was along her path, and he beckoned her to join him. She detoured gracefully toward him and settled into the chair opposite his. He flashed a genial smile. "That was quite a performance." When she didn't respond, he realized his remark had been a bit vague. "It was a beautiful piece. What's it called?"

"It was an improvisation. I did not think to title it."

Now he was impressed. "You *improvised* that? That's remarkable!"

She accepted his praise with half a nod. "I am gratified to know you found it aesthetically pleasing." Turning, she caught the attention of a passing server. "Green tea, please."

The waiter nodded and looked at Fisher. "Doctor?"

"Bourbon, neat." Before the waiter could ask him to clarify, he added, "Roy knows the one. Thanks." As the waiter left to fetch the drinks, Fisher turned his attention to the statuesque Vulcan woman sharing his table. "Long time since you played here. What brought you back?"

His question made T'Prynn ruminative. "After being cured of my . . . *affliction* . . . I had changed. Only after I had accepted myself as I've become could I return to my music."

"I think I understand. Change can be traumatic, even when it's for the best."

T'Prynn nodded. "Indeed."

The waiter returned with their drinks and set them on the table. Fisher grinned at the youth. "Put them on my tab." As the waiter departed, Fisher and T'Prynn picked up their glasses. Fisher lifted his in a toast. "To friends and loved ones now departed: may our paths cross again in this life or the next." T'Prynn watched him with curiosity but didn't raise her glass.

"Do you believe in supernatural ideas of an afterlife, Doctor?"

He couldn't tell if her question was innocent or accusatory.

Either way, he saw no need to dissemble. "Not actually, no. The toast is meant more as an expression of hope or remembrance. I didn't mean it to be taken literally." His answer seemed to deepen T'Prynn's introspection. "Why? Do you harbor some belief in a post-physical existence?"

"It is a complicated question," T'Prynn said. "On Vulcan, we have the ability to preserve the essence of a person, their memories and persona—we call it the *katra*—in special arks, so that future generations can commune with them telepathically and benefit from their wisdom. Our philosophers are divided, however, on the question of whether what is contained in the ark is what humans might call a soul, or merely a psychic snapshot of a mind's electrochemical profile at a moment near death. Either way, I know of many who have derived solace from knowing that those close to them have been judged worthy of such preservation by the Seleyan elders."

Her answer gave him much to think about. "I'd never really known much about Vulcan mysticism. It sounds like it has quite a remarkable set of traditions." She didn't answer, so he continued. "I guess it might be nice to think that someone important to us might be able to live on like that—even if it's just a copy or a part of them. And nicer still to think we might not have to be completely erased from reality when we die."

They sipped their drinks for a minute in silence.

"Ultimately," T'Prynn said, "it is the nature of things to pass away. The universe tends toward entropy, and even time itself will eventually end."

Fisher sipped his smoky-sweet bourbon and smiled. "True. But that's why we have to savor life and do all we can to help others enjoy it while it lasts. Because we never know when we'll lose the people we care about, or when our time will be up." He set down his glass. "I think there's an alchemy to life. Call it what you will—circumstance, fate, magic—but it's always felt to me like there's an underlying pattern that brings together certain people in the same place at the right time. You can't force it. It just has to happen. And when it does, when those pieces come together . . . sometimes they make something really special. But part of what makes those mixtures special is that they never last."

T'Prynn seemed to be looking through Fisher rather than at him, and her voice was flat, as if her thoughts were light-years away. "Everything changes. Always."

He nodded. "And everything ends."

PART 3

WALKING SHADOWS

26

"No doubt about it, Chiro, congratulations are in order." The angular jaw and cheekbones of Admiral Harvey Severson looked distorted to Nogura, not by any error of the subspace transmission but by the smile he wore. Nogura had never seen the man happy before.

"Everyone back here on Earth is singing your praises," Severson continued, *"from Starfleet Command to the suits at the Palais. Capturing all the Shedai in one shot is probably the most significant strategic and tactical victory we've had on the frontier in the last five years. I've personally recommended you get another stripe on your cuff for this."*

Nogura couldn't muster much gratitude, because he suspected Severson's parade of praise was merely camouflage for an impending barrage of bullshit.

"I'm glad you're all so happy," he said. "But you could have told me this in writing. So, are you going to tell me what's so urgent that you're spending energy and bandwidth on a real-time channel from Earth, or do I have to guess?"

Severson's jovial mood vanished as quickly as if he'd pulled off a comedy mask—a simile that Nogura suspected contained as much truth as it did poetic license. *"Just because Starfleet Command is happy with you, that doesn't mean they're satisfied with your team. Specifically, the research plan filed by your new project leader is, shall we say,* unambitious.*"*

"I thought its objectives were more than reasonable," Nogura said.

Severson's scathing glower leapt across the light-years. *"We're long past the point of reasonable. Satisfactory isn't going to cut it. We have an edge over the Klingons in the Taurus Reach for the first time in five years, and we're not going to let it slip away."*

Nogura resented the implication. "We're not letting anything slip away, I assure you."

"You're not pursuing the advantage, and that's the same thing. We've had our people evaluate Lieutenant Xiong's research plan, and it's far too cautious for our taste."

Suspecting he would not like the answer, Nogura asked, "Cautious in what way?"

"It reads like Doctor Marcus wrote it," Severson said, as if that were a fault. *"Instead of pushing the envelope on the array's capabilities, it's focused on studying the Shedai."*

"That's not surprising," Nogura said, "considering that Xiong is an A and A specialist."

His answer only deepened Severson's animosity. *"That's all well and good, but it's not what we need right now. Xiong can do as much pure research and write all the history books he wants—* after *he carries out the experiments and operations we've deemed essential."*

"Essential?" It was a simple word, but Nogura knew from experience that when it was spouted by bureaucrats, little that was actually necessary or good ever came of it. "Precisely what are these essential experiments, Admiral?"

Severson relayed a packet of electronic documents via their channel's data subfrequency as he spoke. *"Our experts at Research and Development in New York have put together a set of experiments to test the power-projection capabilities of the array your team built. According to their analysis of Xiong's report, that little gizmo should be able to alter the very shape of space-time from across virtually any distance, at any coordinates we choose."*

Unable to hide his misgivings, Nogura asked, "To what end, sir?"

"Whatever we want," Severson said. *"In theory, we should be able to crush planets into dust, or even just fold them out of existence entirely, by bending space-time in on itself until it vanishes*

into some kind of pocket dimension." He shrugged. *"I didn't exactly follow all the technical mumbo-jumbo, but the end results they suggested sounded pretty exciting."*

"Exciting? I think the word you meant to use was 'horrifying.' Sir."

"Puh-tay-to, puh-tah-to. The point is, Chiro, that's just one avenue of investigation. We also want to run some tests that we think could help advance Doctor Marcus's research into new applications for the Jinoteur Pattern. Ideally, we'd have those datasets ready for her by the time she and her team reach Regula One."

Nogura rubbed his chin. "Two points, sir. First, I'm not comfortable with any of these recommendations. While I understand the enthusiasm the R and D teams have for the work we're doing out here, I think they must have skipped the section of Lieutenant Xiong's report in which he makes clear how fragile the array currently is."

The senior admiral seemed to be losing patience with the conversation. *"You're just being overcautious. I know these things ripped a new hole in your station last year, but that's the past. You need to put that behind you and focus on the present and the future."*

"I believe I am, sir."

"Well, I don't agree. And neither does Starfleet Command. You're sounding all the same alarms you did when we pressed you to bring the array on line in the first place. You were wrong then, Chiro, and the R and D experts are telling me you're wrong now."

"I don't care what your experts are telling you," Nogura said. "The only person I know who deserves to be called an 'expert' when it comes to this array is Xiong. And frankly, I'm inclined to trust his recommendations over yours."

The shift in Severson's bearing was subtle, but Nogura read it clearly enough to know he had just lit the fuse on the man's temper, and that it was about to blow. *"All right,"* said the senior admiral. *"If you won't heed my recommendations, then you leave*

*me no other choice but to make it an order. Admiral Nogura, as
of now, I am ordering you and all personnel under your command to carry out the research plan and experiment schedule
proposed by Starfleet Research and Development and sent to
you by me during this conversation. If your team wishes to run
supplementary experiments, they may, but only after they have
completed the test series prescribed by Starfleet R and D. Is that
understood, Admiral?"*

"Yes, sir."

"Very good." After a moment's thought, Severson asked,
"What's your second point?"

"Excuse me, sir?"

*"A moment ago, you said you had two points. I heard your
first. What was the second?"*

Nogura nodded, his memory jogged. "Ah, yes. Don't ever call
me 'Chiro' again. Nogura out." He stabbed the button on his desk
that terminated the subspace channel, and his screen blinked
back to black, erasing the shocked reaction of Admiral Severson.

Sitting alone with his cold coffee and simmering temper,
Nogura dreaded the reaction from the team in the Vault when he
relayed Severson's orders. As much as Nogura disliked being mi-
cromanaged by the Starfleet brass, he knew that Xiong was going
to hate it far more.

"Are they out of their goddamned minds?" Xiong's dismay escalated as he read each successive page of the proposed experiments and protocols from Starfleet Research and Development.
"It's like they never read a single word I sent them."

He sat behind the desk in his office, which overlooked the
main floor of the Vault. Klisiewicz sat in one of his guest chairs,
and Theriault stood against the wall. All three Starfleet scientists
read from data slates on which was loaded the same report. As
they pored through its contents, Klisiewicz was aghast and Theriault looked perplexed.

"Question," Klisiewicz said. "Do they know that none of our

software for the array is written to do any of this? 'Blowing up planets' wasn't in the original program specs."

"I don't think they care," Xiong said. "All they know is that we did it by accident, so now they want to be able to do it on purpose." He hurled his data slate away, and it cracked against the wall. "Dammit! This is exactly what Carol Marcus warned us about!" He kicked his chair back as he stood, so that he would have room to pace behind his desk. "I told her not to worry, that Starfleet would handle this thing responsibly, that they wouldn't try to weaponize it."

"Got *that* wrong," Theriault mumbled.

Xiong knew her ire was directed at the Starfleet brass, so he let her quip slide. "Yes. Yes, I did. Now we have to deal with this mess."

"You can't let them go forward with these experiments," Klisiewicz said. "Forget that we aren't set up to run any of them. Half of them run the risk of breaching the array."

Theriault added, "He's right. Some of these protocols will drain so much power from the support grid that we could start losing containment."

"What are the odds of that?" Xiong asked.

"Call it sixty-forty for a breach," Theriault said.

The new orders were a total nightmare, as far as Xiong was concerned. If he refused them, he was looking at a court-martial and possibly a life sentence in a Federation penal colony. If he obeyed them, there was a good chance he'd accidentally unleash the Shedai, destroying the station, killing thousands, and possibly subjecting the galaxy at large to innumerable horrors. All he'd ever wanted to do was find out who the Shedai really were, and maybe, over time, get them to shed new light on an entire era of history for which little hard evidence or firsthand accounts remained in existence. Pressing them into service as slaves and turning them into a top-secret superweapon of unimaginable power had not been part of his agenda.

He slumped back into his chair. "Y'know, when Carol Marcus came here a couple of years ago and told me we could use the meta-genome and the Jinoteur Pattern to do things like regenerate tissue or extend our subspace communication range, I thought that was cool. But when she started going on about making planets out of nothing, I thought she might be crazy." He pointed at the data slate in Klisiewicz's hand. "But these orders raise the bar on crazy around here. Compared to what these idiots want us to do, Marcus's plan for spinning dark energy into new planets seems almost quaint by comparison."

"Maybe we need to talk with Commander Liverakos, up in the JAG office," Theriault said. "Capturing the Shedai was one thing. Enslaving them is another."

Her suggestion made Klisiewicz perk up. "Can we prove beyond a reasonable doubt that the Shedai are essential to the operation of the array?"

"Maybe," Xiong said. "Without an occupied crystal, we couldn't interface with the Shedai's network at all. It seems pretty clear to me that without the Shedai, there's no machine."

Eyes wide with hope, Theriault said, "Then that's our case."

"I don't know," Xiong said. "Sounds pretty flimsy to me. And if we're wrong, we could be looking at twenty-five to life. Do we really want to take that chance?"

Theriault reproached him with a cockeyed stare. "Would you rather live with these evil experiments on your conscience?"

"I know I wouldn't," Klisiewicz said. "I think Vanessa's right, Ming. We should ask for a legal opinion from the JAG office. If we have any grounds for declaring these orders unlawful, I think we should tell Starfleet Command to stick them back where they got them."

In his heart, Xiong knew that Theriault and Klisiewicz were right. History was full of casual villains who had rationalized their crimes with the long-discredited excuse, "I was only following orders." Xiong didn't want his name added to the list of those who had tried to hide their own weaknesses of character behind an empty appeal to authority.

"I'm not sure who's going to be angrier," he said. "Nogura or

Starfleet Command." He took a deep breath that did nothing to calm the anxiety-driven bile creeping up his esophagus, then he stood up. "Who's ready to volunteer for a free court-martial?" Klisiewicz and Theriault raised their hands with a comical eagerness that made Xiong smile. "All right, then." As he led them out of his office, he muttered glumly, "Let's go get crucified."

27

Three days sober, Cervantes Quinn had no idea what to do next. His last few months had been little more than a hazy wash of intoxicated mishaps, punctuated frequently by afternoons impaired with hangovers brutal enough to kill a bull moose, and occasionally by stints of a day or more in the brig to "dry out," as the station's chief of security had quaintly put it. Ever since the mind-meld with T'Prynn, he had felt strangely at ease. His body still craved the anesthetic pleasure of alcohol, but now his mind had the strength to refuse its temptation.

Staring at himself in his bathroom mirror that morning, he had marveled at how much damage he had done to his body in so short a time. After spending nearly two years drilling his middle-aged form back into shape, he had reduced himself to a pear-shaped blob of humanity in a tenth of the time. The only thing masking the return of his jowls and double chin was a heavy growth of salt-and-pepper beard whiskers.

After lingering under the soothing warmth of his first real shower in close to a week, Quinn had spent the morning roaming the station's seemingly endless circular corridors, riding its many dozens of turbolifts from the uppermost public levels of the station to its lowest. By midday he had taken to wandering the narrow lanes of Stars Landing, peeking through the windows of shops where he couldn't really afford to buy anything, and averting his eyes from all the places in which he had inebriated and humiliated himself in recent weeks.

Now it was late afternoon, and his stomach growled, his hunger an echo of a more profound emptiness that seemed to define his existence. He knew he wouldn't starve aboard the station, despite being destitute. If the Federation was good for nothing else, one could always turn to it for a free lunch, topped with a heaping scoop of pity and smothered in self-righteousness. They wouldn't foot the bill for a decent meal at Café Romano, but they'd gladly serve him a tray of reconstituted organic slop in their public cafeteria. *I'd rather starve,* he told himself, but he knew that was just his pride talking. When he got hungry enough, he would take their charity and wolf down whatever gruel they gave him. And he might even say "thank you," if he could bear to look anyone in the eye.

Pushing back against the gnawing, acidic sensation in his gut, he crossed Fontana Meadow and admired the rich color of the lawn. It reminded him of Kentucky bluegrass, but it seemed much more resilient in the face of heavy foot traffic and sports activities, which made him wonder if it might be Rigelian mountain grass. The one thing he knew for certain about it was that it made for a very comfortable place to sleep—unless one happened to be there at 0315 when its automatic sprinkler system activated.

His meandering brought him to a halt in front of the lone Denevan dogwood planted at the edge of the meadow, beside a paved walkway that ringed the terrestrial enclosure. In front of the tree was a large plaque of brilliantly polished metal, not yet old enough to have acquired the slightest patina of tarnish, affixed to a large, broad rock. The plaque was inscribed:

> IN PROUD MEMORY
> USS BOMBAY NCC-1926
> "OUR DEATHS ARE NOT OURS; THEY ARE YOURS;
> THEY WILL MEAN WHAT YOU MAKE THEM."

Three years I avoided this spot, Quinn moped, and he knew why. Thinking of the *Bombay* always reminded him of his misadventure on Ravanar IV, a badly planned burglary gone wrong. At the time he had thought the most serious fallout of his botched theft would come in the form of retribution from the Orion crime lord Ganz. Instead, he'd learned that by damaging a sensor scrambler he'd been hired to steal, he had unwittingly exposed a secret Starfleet operation—and that exposure had incited an attack by the Tholians that resulted in the eradication of all life on Ravanar IV, as well as the destruction of the *Bombay* and five Tholian warships.

I made one mistake and sent all those people to their doom. His thoughts fixated on that bitter reflection. *No wonder Karma has it in for me. Nothin' I do could ever make that right.*

Amid the soft patter of distant footsteps and happy voices, he heard one set of footfalls close at his back—and then they stopped. Someone was standing behind him. He turned, half expecting a confrontation. Instead, he was met by the placid presence of T'Prynn.

"Hello again, Mister Quinn."

He stuffed his hands in his pockets and turned back toward the tree. "Hey."

The Vulcan woman stepped forward to stand beside him and regard the dogwood. "Time is of the essence, so forgive me for being brief. It seems my superiors at Starfleet Intelligence have decided that you've outlived your usefulness."

Quinn couldn't help but laugh. "Hell, I could've told them that five years ago."

"I don't think you understand their sentiments," T'Prynn said. "I've been given explicit orders to covertly terminate your life at my earliest opportunity."

Disarmed by her candor, he wrinkled his brow as his lips curled into a crooked half-smile, half-grimace. "You don't say." He let out a snort of cynical amusement and wondered if maybe this wasn't a blessing in disguise. "Can I at least trust you to make it quick and painless?"

"I have no intention of obeying this order," she said. She discreetly slipped a modestly sized vinyl-wrapped packet into his right hand. "I have prepared a new identity for you. It is complete with a long history of good credit, solid employment, shifting residences on several different worlds, and an education similar to the one you earned in your youth."

He sneaked a look at the black-wrapped package in his hand. "And what am I supposed to do with this? Apply for a loan? I think a few folks around here might still recognize me."

T'Prynn seemed mildly irked by his reaction. "Do not be obtuse, Mister Quinn. I have arranged for you to be smuggled aboard a colony ship leaving in an hour from Docking Bay Twenty-nine. It will carry you beyond the periphery of explored space, to the far frontier." She looked back at the tree. "Inside your travel packet is a credit chip encoded with a small fortune. Budgeted wisely, it should be more than enough to finance your new life in exile."

It sounded as if she had thought of almost everything. He eyed her skeptically. "What about my biometric profile? Won't it trip me up if someone scans my DNA or my retina?"

"Normally, yes," T'Prynn said. "However, it appears that when I notified my superiors this morning of your assassination, I accidentally erased your biometric file from all Federation databases, both military and civilian, public and private." She shot him a coy glance. "Officially, you do not exist, and you never have."

Quinn was flabbergasted. He stared at the packet and stammered.

"I . . . I don't know what to say."

T'Prynn offered him her hand. "Say farewell . . . Mister Panza."

He smiled and shook her hand. "Thank you."

Then he stepped away, walking quickly toward Stars Landing.

T'Prynn sounded confused as she called after him. "You have less than an hour to reach your ship. I suggest you go directly there."

He paused and looked back. "Don't worry, I'll make it." He resumed his hurried pace toward the station's civilian center. "There's just one thing I have to do first."

• • •

Tim Pennington smiled awkwardly at the two human civilians, a man and his wife, who loomed over him while he tried to chew his mouthful of food and autograph the top page of a stack of hard-copy printouts of his collected columns and features that they'd thrust in front of him. He scribbled his initials and swooshed a crude circle around them as a flourish, then swallowed his food as he handed the pages back to the husband. "There you go."

"Thanks, Mister Pennington," the man said. "Amazing piece you did on the Klingons!"

A nod and a wave signaled the conversation was done. "Thank you. Have a great day."

Much to his relief, the couple seemed to take the hint and buggered off with their sheaf of papers. It wasn't that Pennington minded terribly being accosted by strangers for his autograph; he reminded himself that he had sought out notoriety. However, it staggered his imagination to realize how many people lacked any sense of boundaries when it came to celebrities of any degree. He'd hardly believed it the first time one of his readers asked to have their photograph taken with him. "With me?" he'd asked. "You're sure? . . . Okay, if you insist." But this was the umpteenth time someone had approached him for an autograph while he was eating at Café Romano, his favorite restaurant in Stars Landing. He was seriously considering punching the next person who interrupted his dinner, just so that poor soul could serve as a warning to others.

Lifting a forkful of soy-and-maple-glazed salmon to resume his repast, he noted out of the corner of his eye another person sidling up to his table, and since it wasn't his white-clad waitress, he assumed the worst. He dropped his fork and turned to face his next uninvited guest. "And what the bloody hell can I do for—" Words logjammed in his brain and left his mouth hanging half open as he saw Cervantes Quinn regarding him with a faint, sheepish smile.

"Heya, Newsboy." Quinn leaned on the other chair at Pennington's table. "Mind if I take a load off?" Pennington motioned for Quinn to sit, and he did.

The waitress appeared as if from thin air and shot a look at Pennington to silently inquire whether he required Quinn's removal. "Can I get you gentlemen anything?"

"I'm fine," Pennington said. He asked Quinn, "Can I buy you a drink?"

Quinn said to the waitress, "Coffee, with cream and sugar, please."

"Coming right up," As swiftly as she'd come, she departed to the kitchen.

An awkward silence stretched out a bit longer than Pennington would have liked. He drummed his fingertips on the table. "So . . . back on the wagon, eh?"

"For the moment," Quinn said. "Reckon I'll take each day as it comes and see if it sticks this time." He looked up as the waitress returned with his café au lait, mumbled his thanks to her, and took a generous sip. "Damn, this joint really makes a fine cup of java."

Sensing an ulterior motive lurking behind the small talk, Pennington eyed his cagy friend. "So what brings you out before the crack of dusk?"

The grizzled pilot slapped a hand to his chest. "You wound me, Newsboy!" They both chuckled at that, and it felt to Pennington like he and Quinn were sharing a wavelength of nostalgia. Quinn took a deep breath and another sip of his coffee. "I came because I'm in your debt."

"Mate, if it's about the money, forget it. I'm bloody rolling in it."

A smile of genuine happiness lit up Quinn's face. "Good for you, man. I mean that. You had a hard run there for a while. You've earned a real payday." Another long sip of coffee, and Quinn's mood turned somber. "But I still owe you, compañero. And I'm not talking about money. I owe you a debt of gratitude. For covering up my mistakes. Apologizing to all the people I insulted on my way down to the gutter. For all the times you made sure I got home alive and didn't end up choking to death on my own puke." He rubbed the back of his head. "I vaguely recall punching you at some point. Did that happen?"

Pennington still felt that night's wound to his pride. "Yeah, mate. That happened."

"Well, then I owe you an apology on top of everything else. All you ever did was help me, and all I did was act like an asshole. And for that I'm sorry, Tim. I really am." He rubbed his hand across his stubbled chin and upper lip, apparently considering his next words with a heavy conscience. "I reckon if I owe you anything else, it's a reason why."

"No," Pennington said. "You don't have to explain yourself, mate. Not to me. After all we've been through, you don't think I understand? I know what she meant to you. Losing her had to be the last bloody straw." He recalled his own lost love, Oriana, who had perished aboard the *Bombay* years earlier. "I've been there, mate. I get it."

The silence that grew between them then was one not of unease but of understanding. For the first time in a very long while, Pennington appreciated the simple pleasure of a friend's company, and realized how much he had missed the easy camaraderie he and Quinn had shared while gallivanting around the galaxy in Quinn's old Mancharan starhopper, the *Rocinante*. They had never wanted for trouble in those days, but neither had there ever been a shortage of fun.

Quinn cracked a bittersweet smile. "So, now that you're all famous and shit, I guess you'll be leaving, right? Headin' home to some cushy job in Paris?"

Pennington laughed out loud, and didn't care that he disturbed the couple at an adjacent table. "Are you daft? Leave Vanguard? And miss out on all the fun? Perish the thought."

"Forget I mentioned it," Quinn said. He glanced at the chrono on the wall of the café, took another long swig of his coffee, and got up.

Wondering if he'd said something wrong, Pennington asked, "Where you going, mate?"

"I got someplace I need to be." There was an enigmatic quality to the light in Quinn's eyes as he grinned and added, "See ya 'round, Newsboy." He left those parting words hanging in the air as he walked away without a backward glance, and Pennington watched his friend's back as he crossed the meadow and disappeared into a waiting turbolift car.

Only many decades later would a nostalgic Tim Pennington realize that was the last that he, or anyone else, ever saw of Cervantes Quinn.

T'Prynn stood at the Hub on the supervisors' deck, in the middle of Vanguard's hectic operations center. Though she did not frequent this duty area, the station's senior officers knew her by sight because of her daily visits to Admiral Nogura's office for intelligence briefings. Consequently, she attracted little notice on those rare occasions when she chose to monitor important station activities from this prime vantage point.

A drone of comm chatter and muted responses from Vanguard's traffic-control team blended into the steady background of computer feedback tones, the hum of the ventilation system, and the hiss of turbolift doors opening and closing at odd intervals. Several sections of the towering viewscreens that wrapped around more than two-thirds of the circular command level's walls displayed civilian vessels of varying sizes and types arriving and departing.

Only one of them was of interest to T'Prynn: the *Zaragoza,* a colony ship of Deltan registry. It was bound for a recently catalogued Class M world that had been named Kennovere by the first civilian team to scout its surface. The planet had been reserved for colonization by a group that wanted to establish a low-tech, agrarian lifestyle with only the slightest intrusion of modern technology; they also had pointedly eschewed any formal political connection with the Federation. It had seemed to T'Prynn like an ideal place to send someone who had reason not to want to be found by Starfleet—or by anyone else, for that matter.

She watched the *Zaragoza* maneuver clear of traffic, taking Quinn away from Vanguard to his new life. Observing the colony ship as it jumped to warp speed, T'Prynn reminded herself that this one act of mercy would not be remotely sufficient to atone for her lifetime of wrongs.

It is likely I will never balance the scales of my own guilt and virtue, she concluded. *But that does not absolve me of my responsibility to try.* As she turned and descended the steps from the supervisors' deck, she permitted herself a moment of private sentimentality. *Live long and prosper, Cervantes Quinn . . . wherever your journey takes you.*

It was possible, she thought as she stepped inside a turbolift, that one day Quinn might forgive her for all the pain she had brought into his life, directly or indirectly. Given enough time, Tim Pennington might forgive all her transgressions, as well. As she recollected all those persons she had harmed over the years who knew that she was to blame for their sufferings, T'Prynn could think of only one who she was certain would never absolve her of her sins.

I will forgive when I can trust myself not to repeat the errors of my past, she vowed, *and not until then.* She didn't know how long it would take her to recover that faith in her own ethical compass, but as she thought of Quinn being ferried away to anonymity and freedom, she felt certain that her own life was, belatedly and at long last, heading in the right direction.

For the moment, that would suffice.

28

Clutching the last feeble straws of his patience, Nogura strode into the Vault backed by JAG officer Lieutenant Commander Holly Moyer and a phalanx of twenty armed security officers. They found Xiong and his cadre of Starfleet science experts waiting for them, standing in a tight formation with folded arms and expressions of hard resolve. As Nogura had expected, this meeting was off to a wonderfully confrontational start. He met Xiong's hard stare. "Lieutenant."

The lean younger man replied simply, "Admiral."

"Let's just cut through it, shall we?" Nogura extended his hand to Moyer, who handed him a data slate. "It's my understanding that you and your team are refusing to obey orders to run the test series requested by Starfleet Command. Is that correct?"

Xiong appeared unrepentant. "That's right."

"On what grounds?"

Nervous looks were volleyed between Xiong and the other members of the Vault contingent, and then Xiong said, "We believe these orders to be unlawful and immoral, sir."

Nogura felt as if he wanted to simply explode. "Mister Xiong, while I understand and can even sympathize with your reaction to the . . . *distasteful* nature of these orders, I am compelled to remind you that they are, nonetheless, orders. Your compliance is not optional."

"And while I understand your legal obligation to uphold the chain of command," Xiong said, "I'm compelled to remind *you,* Admiral, that no unlawful order is valid, and that as Starfleet officers, we are required by regulations to challenge such directives." The other scientists' heads bobbed in cautious concurrence.

Playing the role of devil's advocate was one of Nogura's most despised duties as a flag officer, but his review of the Starfleet Code of Military Justice and the relevant portions of Federation law had left him no choice in this matter. "Tell me, Lieutenant . . . what part of this order do you consider 'unlawful'? Because I don't think you have a case. You're not being asked to do anything others before you haven't done. Crushing a planet might seem radical, but it's not like it's a populated world. It's a dead ball of rock far from the nearest inhabited planet, and it's a confirmed Federation possession. So . . . what's the problem, here?"

"The problem," Xiong replied without delay, "is the role of the Shedai in this fiasco. Their presence inside the array is what gives it the power for this insane exercise. But no one's obtained their consent. The experiment we've been ordered to run uses them as slave labor to make it possible. But we captured them as part of a military combat operation. That makes them prisoners of war—and, as such, they have certain rights under Starfleet regulations, as well as under Federation and interstellar law."

Nogura felt exhausted just listening to Xiong prattle on. "It might interest you to know, Lieutenant, that there's never been a formal declaration of war in the Taurus Reach. Not by us, or the Shedai, or anyone else. At least, not that we've heard of. So we can't very well be holding prisoners of war when there is no war." He scrutinized the isolation chamber with mock intensity. "In fact, if I had to characterize our encounters with the Shedai, I think their actions would better fit the paradigms of insurgents or terrorists. In which case, we're fully within our rights to hold them as hostile nonstate actors, or maybe even as common criminals—both of which are routinely subjected to forced manual labor as a condition of their incarceration."

"At least criminals are entitled to impartial trials before we put them in prison," Xiong retorted, his ghost of a smirk suggesting his delusion that he'd scored a rhetorical point.

"Lieutenant, if I thought it was even remotely safe and practical to release the Shedai, individually or collectively, to face charges before a Starfleet tribunal, I would convene such proceedings with all due haste . . . right after I finished court-martialing you and all your compatriots—a process that will begin *immediately* unless you all give up this hopeless insurrection and proceed with the new experiments, as ordered."

Xiong said nothing, but the mood in the room remained defiant. Nogura spoke past the impassioned young department head and addressed the other Starfleet officers behind him. "Please understand: I don't like being pushed around by bureaucrats any more than you do. But if you don't comply with my orders and start running these tests, I will have no choice but to order all of you taken into custody. You will be court-martialed and convicted. Your careers in Starfleet, and as scientists, will effectively be over. You will be sent to penal colonies—in some cases, for the rest of your lives." He let that hang in the air for a few seconds, then he continued. "The really bad news is that once you're all out of the way, Starfleet Command will send out its own hand-picked bunch of eggheads, who, I have no doubt, will be far less ethical and scrupulous than any of you when it comes to putting this acquired technology through its paces. Frankly, I don't know what they'll do with unfettered access to your work. I'm not sure I want to find out. The real question is: Do any of you want to take that risk? Or would you rather keep this program under your control and be able to pull the plug if it goes too far?"

No one spoke or moved for several seconds. Then, one by one, Xiong's team broke ranks and began drifting back to their work stations, to their cubicle offices, to their private research labs. Finally, only Xiong, Theriault, and Klisiewicz remained. Klisiewicz shifted awkwardly until he caught Xiong's eye. "Ming, I'm sorry, but . . ."

"Go ahead," Xiong said. "It's fine. He's right. Let's get the experiment prepped." He gave a reassuring nod to Theriault, whose embarrassed half-smile shrank to a thin line as her lips folded inward and vanished from view as she stepped away.

Nogura continued staring at Xiong, waiting for an answer. "And you?"

"I'll stay," Xiong said. "We'll have the R and D team's protocols ready for a trial run in a few hours." He stepped forward and stood nose to nose with Nogura. "But as for pulling the plug before it goes too far? For the record, I think that ship has sailed."

"Then it's your job to bring her home in one piece." With a glance he dismissed Moyer and the security detail, then he looked back at Xiong and said sotto voce, "Do your best to make this work, but use your judgment. If it starts to go south, end it. I'll keep the brass and the suits off your back. But we have to maintain the *appearance* of cooperation, or else they'll send us all to some rock with no name and hand this lab to somebody else. Understood?"

A grave nod. "Perfectly, sir."

That was all Nogura could reasonably ask for under the circumstances. "Then carry on, Lieutenant. As soon as you have results, report to my office." He turned and followed the last of the security officers through the hatchway that led out of the Vault.

Nogura's decades of experience as a Starfleet officer told him this entire undertaking was going to end in disaster.

His instinct for danger told him that was an understatement.

Outcast and alone, Ezthene [The Silver] had little sense of how long he had languished in exile aboard Vanguard; he knew only that the passing of time seemed to have slowed to a halt since the death of Nezrene [The Emerald], his fellow expatriate from the Tholian Assembly.

They had come to this place driven by conscience and necessity. She had been a weapons officer aboard the *Lanz't Tholis*, whose crew had survived a close brush with the terrible power of the Shedai thanks in part to the intervention of human Starfleet officer Vanessa Theriault. Ezthene had been one of Tholia's governing elite, a member of the Ruling Conclave of the Political Castemoot. He had seen wisdom in Nezrene's recommendation of diplomacy toward the Federation, and he had risked everything to support her openly to the other members of the Ruling Conclave. The iconoclasts' decision to stand on principle had been their undoing.

Realizing they were no longer welcome among their own people, they had concurred, in a private SubLink communion, that the only rational action left to them was to seek political asylum aboard this Starfleet starbase. To improve the chances that at least one of them would reach Vanguard to share their knowledge of the Shedai and what the Old Ones meant to all of Tholia, they had taken separate routes. Nezrene had evaded pursuit and reached Vanguard in short order, but Ezthene had been delayed for quite some time as an unwilling guest of Councillor Gorkon of the Klingon High Council—along with Vanguard's former commanding officer, Diego Reyes, who, he'd learned, was not so dead as the galaxy had been led to believe.

During Ezthene's absence, Nezrene had helped the Starfleet scientists unlock many of the most arcane secrets of the Shedai's technology. Though she had offered Ezthene well-reasoned arguments for her actions, he remained ambivalent on the subject of whether she had done so in error. But before they'd had the chance to debate the matter to a satisfying conclusion, the Shedai Wanderer attacked the station, and in her mad rampage to reach the laboratory the Starfleeters called the Vault, she'd wrought massive damage to several sections of the station—including Nezrene's half of their environmentally engineered living space. A burst of blinding light and frigid cold had announced the Wanderer's arrival, and then one of her smoky appendages solidified just long enough to cut Nezrene down and leave her broken and twitching.

It had been to the credit of the Starfleet engineers that they had acted with all haste to seal the breach in the bulkhead—though Ezthene suspected they'd done so more to protect themselves than to save him—but there had been nothing that any of them could do for Nezrene. Her life had been snuffed out in a wild flurry of violence, one for which Ezthene was sure there would be no retribution. No consequences. No justice.

Since then he had been alone. Unlike Nezrene, he had never known the cruel touch of the mind of a Shedai, so he had no idea how to help the Federation scientists in their quest to pilfer the

Shedai's ancient secrets. More important, he had not wanted to help them. In his opinion, these long-buried secrets were best left unearthed.

Some days, however, his isolation became so unbearable that he almost considered volunteering himself to help in their experiments, for no other reason than to dispel the crushing boredom and suffocating loneliness of his solitary existence. Most of all, he longed for contact of any kind with another Tholian mind. He wished that he possessed the technical expertise to construct a subspace thoughtwave transmitter. Even the daily waves of vilification he was certain to receive would be preferable to the utter silence that enveloped him.

Instead, he passed the interminable spans reliving moments from his memory-facets, savoring the emotional colors and the harmonious tones of concordance that had once been his norm, the soothing auras of—

Agony split his mind in twain.

Psionic roars of fury washed away all his thought-colors except those of primal terror. Scathing hues of hatred and a cacophonous, piercing shriek disrupted his mind-line and left his thoughts broken and scattered. He knew this sickening dread, this overpowering sensation of being telepathically smashed down and torn apart. This could only be the Shedai.

The brutal onslaught of images beyond understanding, thoughts too alien to comprehend, and truths too horrifying to face swallowed him like the volcanic fires of Tholia reclaiming the husks of its dead. Paralyzed and robbed of vigor, Ezthene collapsed in a trembling mass, cut down as certainly as if a Shedai tentacle had cleaved his thorax in half.

Collapsed on the deck inside his habitat, with his quaking limbs curling inward like those of a hatchling, all he could do was pray for death.

There was no escape from the white-hot sound of rage and the icy touch of enslavement.

The entire Lattice reeled in shock from the violation of Tholia's communal thoughtspace. Every Castemoot and SubLink faltered and collapsed before the Shedai's unstoppable pulse of unadulterated malice. The infinitely variegated hues of billions of Tholian mind-lines blanched and faded, and all the sonorous chimes of harmonized expression fell silent.

Flickering thought-facets recalled the terror of the Shedai thoughtwave they had been forced to extinguish years earlier. That incident had traumatized the Lattice like no other tragedy in all of Tholian history. Now every mind that possessed the Voice knew only fear and suffering, an excruciating violation orders of magnitude worse than its predecessor.

Hereditary memories that had been passed down for hundreds of millennia, ancient knowledge locked in the crystalline molecules of every Tholian mind, suddenly erupted forth, like liquid fires shattering the Underrock from below. Locked in the throes of unspeakable torment, every Tholian throughout the galaxy remembered their ancestors' first moment of sapience: the moment when they understood that their dolor came from the ones known as the Shedai, the Old Ones who had engineered the Tholians for their own purposes.

With the memory came a collective resolve to slay their oppressors and be free.

Silence.

Emptiness yawned in the mind of every Tholian. For the first time that any of them could remember, the Lattice was devoid of hue or tone. The Voice of the Shedai had gone, leaving only the exquisite aching of the void.

Luciferous fury erupted from every level of the Lattice, and bright hues of indignation fountained from every SubLink and Castemoot. Tholians of every age, station, caste, and hue cried out for a war to answer the oppressors' wrongs.

With supreme effort, the members of the Ruling Conclave elevated their mind-lines above the psionic maelstrom engulfing the whole of the Assembly and convened in their private SubLink of the Political Castemoot.

Destrene [The Gray] was the first to compose his mind-line. *The Enemy has risen!*

The thought-colors of Korstrene [The Amber] were tinted with alarm. *Our sensing units on the border have confirmed it: the power of the Old Ones has been unleashed.*

I have opened a thoughtwave to the armada, declared Eskrene [The Ruby]. She tried to project calming hues into the discussion. *We will know the truth of this soon enough.*

Yazkene [The Emerald] scintillated with rage. *We already know the truth! The Federation's soldiers on the starbase did this! They are in league with the Old Ones!*

Dissent swelled within the Conclave's ranks, momentarily drowning out all Voices with deafening waves of scarlet anger. Radkene [The Sallow] rose above the clamor to call for order. *We must be certain before we act. If what we sensed was accidental, we will calm the other castes and remain vigilant. If it was the Enemy's dying thoughtburst, we can rejoice.*

Cynicism and suspicion gloomed the mind-line of Falstrene [The Gray]. *And if it was the Federation taking up the Enemy's standard?*

Then we must avenge, affirmed Narskene [The Gold].

A dulcet chime signaled the inclusion of armada commander Tarskene [The Sallow] in the Conclave's private SubLink. His thought-colors were golden with loyalty but tinged with distress. *Hail and concord, Exalted Ones.*

Velrene [The Azure] answered on behalf of the Conclave. *Harmony and clarity, Commander. What news do you bring of the Enemy?*

The commander projected a series of sensing-unit transcriptions ahead of his reply. *The Voice of the Enemy originated from within the Federation starbase. Interception of their long-range subspace communications has confirmed their use of the Shedai thoughtwave for destructive purpose. Their target appears to have been a lifeless world inside their own space.*

The mind-line of Azrene [The Violet] flickered with uncertainty. *A test? Or a warning?*

Hostile colors coursed through the Conclave. *We should assume the worst,* insisted Radkene. *We gave the Federation a chance to act for the greater good. They failed.*

The will to vengeance within the SubLink flared to a blinding intensity, and there were no colors of dissension. Destrene issued the unanimous judgment of the Conclave.

If the Federation will not destroy the Enemy, we must. Commander Tarskene: Launch your assault—and leave no survivors.

29

A deep groan became a falling hum as the array cycled down to its standby power levels. As the last creepers of violet electricity vanished from the consoles ringing the isolation chamber, Xiong heaved a grateful sigh. *That could have gone a lot worse,* he reminded himself. All the major indicators on his panel had receded from their red-bar warnings to the hairline separating cautionary yellow from "all's well" green.

He asked Klisiewicz, "How was that for operations?"

The *Endeavour*'s black-haired science department chief regarded his own panel with a tired and wary frown. "No errors, no feedback loops, no interference," he said. "As for whether it actually did what it was *supposed* to do, I have no idea."

"Containment's holding," Theriault reported without being prompted, "but only just by the hair on my chinny-chin-chin. If we run this same experiment again tomorrow, I can't guarantee the whole thing won't go up like a bomb and take us with it."

"Noted," Xiong said. "Let's run a full diagnostic and make sure we didn't break anything." While Theriault and Klisiewicz subjected the array, the isolation chamber, and all its related systems to a thorough review as a precaution before conducting more experiments, Xiong left the shielded area of the master control panel and made a quick review of the outer stations' data, so that he could add those findings to his report. He would file a detailed account of the test's success, qualified with all the appropriate caveats and warnings, but he was fairly certain no one at Starfleet Command or Research and Development would pay any attention to anything except whether they had achieved the desired result.

He stopped at an unmanned auxiliary station beside the isolation chamber and compared the readings from several different sensor palettes to see if they had detected any interesting new correlations. As he waited for the computer to finish its analysis, he couldn't help but stare at the array. His eyes were drawn to the web of interlinked crystals, all of which now burned with the wild, kaleidoscopic hues of captive Shedai essences. Though he and the now-departed civilian scientists had mastered the challenge of negating the artifacts' fear-inducing aura, he imagined he could still sense the terrifying energy trapped inside those fragile containers.

Stop, he told himself. *Shake it off. You're freaking yourself out. It's just nerves, is all.*

From the overhead PA came the voice of the station's senior communications officer, Lieutenant Judy Dunbar. *"Ops to Lieutenant Xiong."*

Xiong opened a response channel from the work console. "This is Xiong."

"You have a priority transmission from the starship Repulse *on a coded frequency."*

This was it: the verdict on their insane undertaking. "Patch it down here, please."

"Routing the signal to your office," Dunbar said.

Xiong hurried across the lab, dashing and dodging around the other Starfleet scientists, until he reached his office. He scrambled behind his desk and saw that the signal from the *Repulse* was waiting to be answered on his secure terminal. As he sat down, Theriault and Klisiewicz appeared in his office doorway, and he waved them inside as he opened the channel. The face of the *Repulse*'s youthful commanding officer, Captain Eugene Myers, appeared on his screen. "Captain Myers," Xiong said, coiled with anticipation.

"Lieutenant Xiong," Myers said, his manner guarded. *"My crew and I don't know quite what to make of the readings we've taken for you."*

"Just give me the high points, Captain."

"The high points? All right. For no reason we can determine,

space-time folded in on itself, pulverized Ursanis II—a Class D planetoid—and then the whole mess winked out of existence. Would you care to explain that? Can you explain that?"

"I'm sorry, Captain, I'm afraid all other details of this operation are classified. I presume you and your crew have already been briefed by Starfleet Intelligence?"

Myers cocked one eyebrow with suspicion. *"Yes, we're all painfully aware that we were never here, this never happened, and we didn't see any of what didn't happen. Or else we'll all be living out the rest of our natural lives in a penal colony on Izar's frozen moon."*

Xiong nodded. "Sounds about right. Thanks for your help, Captain. Xiong out." He switched off the terminal, closing the subspace channel, and looked up, wide-eyed, at Theriault and Klisiewicz. "Did you hear that? We just obliterated a planet at a range of ninety-six light-years with the press of a button! Even the *debris* disappeared." He reclined his chair and took a deep breath to slow the furious tempo of his pulse. *"Wow."*

Klisiewicz looked stunned. "I can't deny it's kind of a rush to think we're controlling that kind of power. But all I can think about is what'll happen if it winds up in the wrong hands."

His sentiment seemed to strike a chord with Theriault. "Ming, can you think of a single good reason why Starfleet would need to be able to crush planets from a hundred light-years away? Or even a slightly *not-crazy* reason?" She raised her hands in a pantomime of surrender. "Because I'm drawing a blank, here."

As much as Xiong wanted to bask in the satisfaction of a major accomplishment, monstrous though it might be, he had to admit his friends were right. Nothing about this experiment boded well for the future, and imagining all the ways this technology could be abused filled him with a pervasive dread. "Then I guess the next question—"

The beeping of an internal comm cut him off. He thumbed open the channel. "Xiong."

"This is Jackson" said the station's chief of security. *"I need you up here at Ezthene's habitat, on the double."*

The urgency of the request drew troubled looks from Xiong and his two colleagues. Worried that he already knew the answer, he asked, "Why? What's going on?"

"It looks like our resident Tholian's having a psychotic episode."

Xiong was out of his chair and running for the door. "On my way."

Five minutes later, Xiong dashed out of a turbolift and sprinted the last several meters to the outer hatch of Ezthene's customized habitat. Inside the enclosure, the pressure and temperature were extreme enough to disintegrate most organic matter, and the majority of substances that could survive those elements would succumb to the corrosive effects of the various compounds that served as an atmosphere for their Tholian refugee.

Lieutenant Haniff Jackson waited beside the hatch with Lieutenant Felicia Knight, the station's preeminent expert on Tholian biology. The two of them peered through a ten-inch-thick viewport of specially treated transparent steel. Neither seemed to note Xiong's approach, so he called out, "What's happening in there?"

Jackson stepped aside and motioned for Xiong to take his place. "See for yourself."

Xiong pressed up against the window and peered into the ruby mists of Ezthene's habitat. "Where is he? I don't see him."

"Look down," Knight said.

As indicated, the expatriate Tholian was lying on the deck in front of the inner hatch, below a unique interface panel that had been designed to enable Ezthene to initiate contact with those outside his segregated compartment. His orthorhombic limbs were all curled inward, as if to shield his abdomen and thorax. Xiong asked, "Has he moved?"

"A couple of times," Jackson said. "He alternates between—"

Ezthene sprang from the deck and flailed about in wild, jerking movements. His piercing screech shrilled over the open intercom channel like a diamond drill cutting through duranium. He slammed his body against the walls and the inner hatch, and his ponderous thuds of impact were audible through the reinforced bulkheads. Xiong recoiled by instinct as Ezthene threw himself violently against the transparent barrier.

Hoping to end the tantrum, Xiong reached over and spoke into the intercom. "Ezthene! Calm down, please. It's me, Ming Xiong." Ezthene continued his display, his ferocity undiminished. "Ezthene, can you hear me? It's Xiong. Please respond!"

"The voice!" shrieked Ezthene, his words sounding as harsh from the universal translator as they did in his native language. *"The voice!"*

He kept repeating those same two words, over and over, until Xiong turned off the intercom. "That's not good," he muttered.

Knight turned her baffled stare in his direction. "You know what that means?"

"I have some idea," Xiong said. "But please don't ask. I guarantee you really don't want to know." He turned toward Jackson. "Have you been maintaining surveillance on Ezthene?"

"Twenty-four seven," Jackson said, "just like the admiral ordered."

Xiong said to Knight, "I need your tricorder. Now." She lifted her tricorder from her hip, ducked out from under its strap, which had crossed the front of her blue minidress, and handed the device to Xiong. He handed it to Jackson. "Patch into your security logs and confirm the *exact* moment Ezthene started going berserk. Hurry, please. It's important."

Jackson worked quickly, and several seconds later he said, "His seizure, or whatever we're calling it, began at precisely nineteen seconds past 1622 hours."

"That is definitely not good," Xiong said, feeling as if the floor had dropped out from under him. Inside the habitat, Ezthene ceased his wilding and slumped back to the deck, his narrow limbs once again retracted like a clutching talon around his segmented torso. Xiong reopened the comm channel. "Ezthene? Are you still conscious? Can you hear me?" He thought he heard the scratching sound of a reply from within, but the translator remained silent, so he increased its audio sensitivity. "Ezthene? Can you repeat what you said?"

"Must . . . silence the voice . . . ."

A final twitch and then he was still. Jackson scanned him with the tricorder. "He's alive." He squinted at the tricorder's display, then turned it upside down. "At least I think he is. I can't make heads or tails of his biology."

Knight plucked the tricorder from his hands. "Let me." She checked the readouts, "Ezthene appears to be in a catatonic state. It might be part of his healing process."

Xiong didn't like the sound of that. *"Might* be?"

"It also might be a sign that he's suffering a nervous collapse."

Jackson chided her, "I thought you were an expert on Tholians."

"I am," she said. Then her bravado faltered. "Just not ones that are still alive." She recoiled, hyperactive and defensive. "Well, I never had a chance to study a live one before!"

"Oh, that's just great," Xiong said. He turned off the intercom. "Rest assured, if he dies, you'll be the first person I call." He stepped away to a nearby companel on a wall, entered his security code, and then punched in the code for the Vault.

A soft beep over the comm and then, *"Theriault."*

"Vanessa, it's Ming. Shut down all experiments involving the array, take the interface off line, and route all available power to the containment system."

"Roger that. But what if we get orders to continue?"

"Ignore them. I'll explain why when I get back. Right now, I have to head up to command and tell the admiral why I pulled the plug. Xiong out." He switched off the companel and walked back to Jackson and Knight. "If there's any change in Ezthene's status, raise me on my communicator immediately. And not a word of this to anybody else, understood?"

Jackson's relaxed body language telegraphed his answer: "Whatever you say."

Xiong nodded his thanks and ran for the turbolift.

As the doors closed and he grabbed the control handle to

guide the lift to ops, he wondered who was about to have a worse day: him, Ezthene, or Admiral Nogura.

Pondering the worst-case scenario, he realized it would likely be a three-way tie.

They were all going to lose.

The dire implications of Xiong's news dominated Nogura's thoughts. His headache began a few seconds later, inflicting viselike pressure on his temples. "Are you sure about the timing of the two events? Is there any chance it was a coincidence?"

"It's possible," Xiong said, "but damned unlikely." He pointed at the side-by-side time comparisons he'd routed to Nogura's computer monitor. "At the *exact second* we triggered the pulse that vanished that planet, Ezthene suffered a violent seizure and collapsed, and he's been getting worse ever since. Considering when we last saw this kind of correlation between Shedai-related activity and Tholian meltdowns, I don't think we should be taking any chances."

"Agreed." Nogura didn't need Xiong to elaborate. He'd read the full reports of Operation Vanguard when he'd assumed command, so he was aware of the widespread incidents three years earlier of Tholians suffering simultaneous violent seizures during a brief moment of unshielded emissions from the first Conduit that Starfleet had tinkered with. He also remembered well the subsequent consequences of that early misstep. "The last time the Tholians got worked up like this, they sterilized Ravanar IV and destroyed the *Bombay*," he said. "So what I need to know, Ming, is whether the effects of our experiment were limited to our friend Ezthene—or if we've just taken a torch to a hornet's nest."

"Our best bet would be to check in with someone on Earth," Xiong said. "Maybe the Starfleet liaison to the president, or someone at the Department of the Exterior. If the Tholian delegation to Paris just had a seizure, we'll know we're in trouble."

It was worth a try, Nogura figured. He activated the intercom to his yeoman. "Lieutenant Greenfield, I need a real-time priority subspace channel to the secretary of the exterior."

"Aye, sir. I'll have Lieutenant Dunbar route it to you as soon as we make contact."

"Thank you." He switched off the intercom. "The one flaw in this plan is that the Tholians tend to sequester themselves inside their embassy except when they visit the Federation Council or the Palais on official business. Even if they have felt the effects of our array, unless they were out and about when it happened, there might be no way of confirming our hypothesis."

Xiong's brow creased as he considered their dilemma. "Well, it would take longer to get any answers, but if we had to, we could contact Ambassador Jetanien and ask him to look into it. He might have access to sources of information that we don't."

"Let's hope better options present themselves," Nogura said.

The intercom buzzed. *"Admiral, they need you out here,"* Greenfield said. *"It's urgent."* Nogura and Xiong traded stares of alarm, then they hurried out of his office.

The normally busy atmosphere of ops had become outright frantic. Yellow Alert panels flashed on the walls, and junior officers were scurrying from one duty station to the next, collecting reports and handing them off, each in turn, to Commander Cooper. Nogura cleaved a path through the Brownian chaos of moving bodies, bounded up the stairs to the supervisors' deck, and caught up with the soft-spoken executive officer at the Hub. "Report."

"Long-range sensor buoys have picked up major movement along the Tholian border," Cooper said as he keyed commands into his panel on the octagonal command table. Star maps graphically annotated with fleet deployment information and the positions and headings of known threat vessels appeared on one of the level's enormous, curved situation monitors. "It looks like the armada the *Endeavour* detected is on the move. They've left their space and are crossing the Taurus Reach at high warp—heading straight toward us."

Nogura didn't need to ask what time the armada had started

moving; that much he could now guess. There was a more pressing question on his mind. "What's their ETA?"

"Four days," Cooper said. He lowered his voice, no doubt in the interest of preserving morale for as long as possible. "Admiral . . . Starfleet Command estimates the armada represents more than twenty percent of the Tholians' active combat fleet. They're coming in with more than five times' enough firepower to wipe us off the map. . . . Orders, sir?"

"Show me every Starfleet vessel within four days' travel at high warp," Nogura said, doing his best to project confidence and calm authority. "We need every ship we can get."

Cooper adjusted the deployment information on the large wall screen. It painted a grim picture: there were no reinforcements close enough to reach Vanguard before the Tholian armada arrived. Only two ships, both of which were already assigned to the station, were in range to join the station's defense: the frigate *Buenos Aires* was three days away, and the cargo transport *Panama* was one day out. The *Enterprise* was just outside of response range, and it was also engaged on a high-priority assignment. That left only the *Endeavour* and the *Sagittarius,* both of which were still several days shy of finishing their repairs due to the late arrival of needed parts and equipment. It was an impossible situation, so Nogura had no choice but to start giving impossible orders and have faith in his crew to carry them out.

"Commander Cooper," he said, "I want every engineer and mechanic who can push a tool working double shifts on the *Endeavour* and the *Sagittarius,* starting now. Those ships need to be combat-ready in four days. Recall the *Buenos Aires* and the *Panama,* and start running battle drills. Pull every warhead out of storage and have them in our torpedo bays by 0800 tomorrow. I want all phaser banks checked, rechecked, and ready to give the Tholians a warm welcome."

"Aye, sir," Cooper said.

Nogura held up a hand. "One more thing: I want every civilian ship within three days of Vanguard rerouted here on the double. We'll need them to assist in the evacuation of all civilians and noncombatant personnel." With a nod, he dismissed Cooper to begin preparing the station for battle. Then the admiral left the Hub and stepped over to the communications officer, who sat at her station, nervously twisting a curl of her brown hair around her index finger. "Lieutenant Dunbar." He waited until she looked up at him, her eyes bright with the fear he knew would soon infect everyone on the station, and then he continued. "Work with Lieutenant Xiong to back up all data from the Vault to the main computer on the *Endeavour*. Make sure it stays encrypted every step of the way. Understood?"

"Yes, sir," Dunbar replied. She shot a look at Xiong, who stepped forward to lean over her shoulder and walk her through the process of accessing the Vault's top-secret databanks.

Everyone around Nogura was swinging into action, moving with a purpose, and focusing on their jobs in a desperate bid not to think about the incoming Tholian armada. Nogura wished he had that luxury, but it was far too late for regrets. He hurried down the stairs to the main level and bladed through the frenzy of activity, back toward his office.

As he passed Lieutenant Greenfield, he caught her eye and issued an order on the move. "Tell Captains Khatami and Nassir I need to see them in my office right now."

"Aye, sir," Greenfield replied as the office door closed behind Nogura.

He went back to his desk, sank wearily into his chair, and checked the chrono. It was 1743 hours. By his best estimate, it would take Khatami and Nassir approximately five minutes to travel from their ships to his office. Which meant he had just less than five minutes to think up a dignified and confidence-inspiring way to convey the message, *We are completely screwed.*

30

"Tell me you aren't serious," Gorkon said.

"I most certainly am," Jetanien insisted. He and Lugok stood shoulder to shoulder in the sitting room of the Klingon diplomat's villa outside Paradise City, facing the enlarged image of Councillor Gorkon on the wall-mounted vid screen. "I would not have imposed upon your patience if the matter weren't of the gravest import."

Lugok struck an apologetic note as he interjected, "Forgive me, my lord, but my associate refused to take me at my word when I told him there was nothing we could do."

"With good reason," Jetanien countered. "The Klingon Defense Force has considerable military assets within two days' travel of Vanguard. There is a great deal they could do to affect the outcome of the impending conflict. It is simply a matter of marshaling the will to act."

Gorkon's eyes narrowed. *"Therein lies the impediment, Ambassador. The political climate as it presently exists does not permit such largesse on our part."*

"Yet you saw no such impediment when you sought a favor from me, nor did I shy away from expending political capital on your behalf."

"And for that you have our gratitude," Lugok said.

"But not your reciprocity."

His criticism seemed to stoke Gorkon's temper. *"Do you really think the execution of a low-risk smear campaign on your part merits a costly military intervention on ours? I don't wish to sound callous, Ambassador, but I think you would have to admit the favor you granted and the one for which you've petitioned are far from equivalent."*

The Chelon's frustration mounted, and he struggled to maintain a civil timbre. "Councillor, if your desire to build a foundation for a future peace with the Federation is genuine, this would be an unparalleled opportunity to lay the cornerstone."

The councillor's reply was pregnant with regret. *"It is not the Klingon way, Ambassador. Maybe someday, the Federation will be able to seize such a moment and win a debt of honor no Klingon could ignore. But this is not that day, for either of us."*

Jetanien switched tactics. "If you will not intervene for our benefit, do so for your own."

Lugok and Gorkon exchanged baffled looks, and then the portly diplomat replied, "If the Tholians destroy your space station, that benefits us."

"Are you certain of that? The Tholians have committed a significant percentage of their combat fleet to this attack. If they succeed in destroying Vanguard—"

"I believe you mean *when* they succeed."

Glossing over Lugok's interruption, Jetanien continued, "There will be nothing to stop them from continuing their rampage. The Tholian Ruling Conclave has made no secret of its desire to see the Taurus Reach expunged of all nonindigenous species. Without our starbase to stand against them, they will be able to lay waste more than five dozen colonies in that sector—many of them yours, in case you've forgotten."

Gorkon seemed unmoved by Jetanien's argument. *"We stand ready to defend what's ours, Ambassador. And we have every confidence that your station will inflict serious losses on the Tholian armada before they both go down in flames. Whatever remains of the bugs' fleet after Vanguard is gone should pose little danger to our forces in the Gonmog Sector."*

It took tremendous effort for Jetanien not to grind his chitinous mandible in irritation at having his bluff called so quickly and thoroughly. "Then it's decided: You won't help us."

"If Klingon interests were truly at risk, we would already be en route to the battle. But for me to press the High Council to authorize military aid to your station would put me in a most

untenable position. While I am in your debt for helping me expose the Romulans' corruption of Duras, there is no way I can muster support for defending Vanguard without betraying my own rather questionable ties to a foreign power." A heavy frown deepened the shadows on his face. "*I believe that one day, our nations will achieve a state of truce. Perhaps, in generations to come, our descendants might even stand together in battle, brothers and sisters in arms. But for now, the passions are still too high, and the grudges too fresh, on both sides. Just because we have a common enemy in Tholia, that is not yet enough to make us allies.*" He added somberly, "*May your friends die with honor, Jetanien.*"

Gorkon terminated the transmission, and the screen briefly switched to the red-and-black Klingon trefoil emblem before it faded to black. Jetanien turned to Lugok. "Thank you."

"For what? You've gained nothing."

"Far from it," Jetanien said. "True, my generosity has yielded no immediate boon, and for that I am disappointed—but I am not disheartened, because your Councillor Gorkon has, at least, offered me something else in exchange." He noted Lugok's dubious stare and added, "Hope for the future. I have heard few people speak as passionately for peace as does your lord."

"Let us drink, then, old friend." Lugok walked to his liquor cabinet, opened it, and pulled out a bottle of *warnog*. He filled two steins and carried them back to Jetanien. Handing one of the metal mugs to the Chelon, he raised his own, and Jetanien joined him in clinking the steins together in a toast. "To peace: May we find it somewhere other than the grave."

Gorkon descended the granite spiral staircase at the front of his manor, taking a moment as he neared the bottom to straighten his steel-studded red leather jerkin on his lean frame. He stepped off into the main foyer and looked around until he saw Captain Chang loitering in the entryway to the main dining room, admiring the mounted heads of game Gorkon had felled on various worlds throughout the Empire. "Welcome, Captain! Make yourself at home!"

The captain turned and smiled at Gorkon's approach. "I'm honored to be your guest, my lord. I hope you don't mind that I came early. Your servant let me in."

"I'd have met you myself, but I was quelling Azetbur's latest tantrum," Gorkon said. "I've seen Targhee moonbeasts that were easier to calm. She's become quite the spitfire of late."

Chang grinned. "Teenagers. It happens to all of them when they reach that age. Or so my brothers tell me." They clasped each other's forearms in a fraternal greeting. "Wait until you taste the bloodwine I brought. It's a rare Kriosian bottling from an exceptional vintage."

Gorkon released Chang's arm and clasped his shoulder. "Will it go with *gagh*?"

"I'm sure it will."

"Then we're both in for a treat," Gorkon said, leading his loyal thane down a lavishly appointed hallway toward his private library. "My chef is preparing the most succulent *gagh* in the Empire. This will be a meal worthy of heroes." As they drifted past marble busts of warriors of renown and famed Heroes of the Empire, he added, "I have other good news, as well."

A sly look from Chang. "As do I. But I won't presume to speak out of turn."

Acknowledging the captain's deference, Gorkon said, "I've interceded on your behalf with Chancellor Sturka and General Korok at the High Command. Your name has been placed on the short list for promotion to colonel. I expect it will become official within the year." He landed a congratulatory slap on Chang's back. "We'll make you a general in no time."

Chang stopped and turned to face Gorkon, who mirrored him. "You honor me, my lord. I pledge that my service shall bring glory to your name."

"Of that, I have no doubt," Gorkon said, ushering the captain to follow him inside his library. On the left side of the room as they entered, a long table built from thick, heavy pieces of

Ty'Gokor redwood was strewn with loose papers, open tomes, and hand-annotated star maps. "Now, tell me, Captain: What news do you bring me?"

The captain was ecstatic. "The Gonmog Sector will soon be rid of Starfleet's bloated starbase. Even as we speak, a Tholian armada bears down upon it. In two days' time, there'll be nothing left of it but wreckage and memories."

Gorkon said nothing and withheld all emotion from his face. *News travels quickly,* he realized. Chang's attitude troubled him. Knowing he could not risk asking questions too pointed in their nature, he chose to feign ignorance of the Tholian attack on Vanguard. "What finally prodded the Tholians into action?"

"No one knows, and I for one don't care. All that matters is that they've come loaded for siege, and it promises to be a glorious battle. If not for the risk of being caught unnecessarily in the crossfire, I'd love to be there so I could savor the carnage from my bridge."

Staring out a window twice his height at the deepening purple twilight descending on the distant outline of the First City, Gorkon folded his hands behind his back. "I imagine the Battle of Vanguard will be quite a spectacle. It's rather a shame my old nemesis Diego Reyes no longer commands the station. He would have made the Tholians pay dearly to win the day."

"It would make no difference," Chang said. "Either way, Starfleet and the bugs will pummel each other into blood and scrap, and then the Gonmog Sector will be wide open for us. If we move now, we could dominate that region in a matter of months."

That drew a sidelong glance of dark amusement from Gorkon. "Don't be so confident, Captain. That station might be the Federation's most visible symbol of power in the sector, but it's not their only resource." Dark premonitions crowded his thoughts as he gazed back into the night. "Far from breaking their will, losing Vanguard might actually galvanize Starfleet's commitment to exploring and colonizing the region."

"I think you might be overestimating them, my lord."

"I assure you, I'm not." He turned and paced away from the window. "The Federation is an unpredictable opponent, Captain. It comprises dozens of species on scores of worlds. That gives it complexity and leads to strange interactions. What breaks one of its members emboldens others." He stopped and took his House's centuries-old ceremonial *bat'leth* off the wall. "To understand the Federation, one must think like a swordsmith. Pure metals can have great luster and value—but if you want a supple blade of fearsome strength that's light enough to strike quickly, you need an *alloy*."

Chang eyed the honor blade in Gorkon's hand and smirked. "If the Federation is a *bat'leth*, my lord, then I'm glad our Defense Force is a disruptor: modern, unseen until its moment arrives, and able to deal out death and fire without warning."

Gorkon laughed and slapped Chang's shoulder. "Well played, Captain! *Qapla'*!" He let Chang take a self-mocking bow as he returned his *bat'leth* to its place on the wall above his mantle. Then he motioned toward the open doorway. "But enough talk of the Federation's woes. A feast awaits us, and we'd best not keep my new wife waiting."

"Wise counsel, my lord. Lead on."

They walked together down the hall, back to the dining room, where the kitchen staff was setting out the first course of their meal—fresh *pipius* claws and flagons of *warnog*. Gorkon's wife, Illizar, met them as they entered. "You're late."

"Nonsense," Gorkon said. "We're right on time." His wife shot him a challenging stare, which he weathered in good humor before taking his seat at the head of the table. Illizar took the chair opposite his, and Chang sat halfway between them on one of the table's long sides, facing the broad picture window that looked out on a vista of dizzying sea cliffs and crashing waves.

As Gorkon hoped, Illizar asked Chang to tell tales of his greatest victories and narrowest escapes, and the Captain provided the evening's entertainment by obliging the lady of the manor. But as Gorkon listened to Chang spin one yarn after another of vengeance, cunning, and cold-blooded violence, he wondered if such a man was really the ally he needed for the long work that lay ahead. He harbored no doubts of Chang's loyalty, but unlike Lugok, Chang struck Gorkon as one who might never accept the idea of rapprochement with the Federation. Despite his youth, the man had already amassed a lifetime's worth of hatred for the Empire's greatest rival in local space; such animosity, in Gorkon's experience, was never surrendered easily or without great reservation.

Well, it's not as if I need to make a diplomat of him overnight, Gorkon reasoned. He expected his political agenda would take decades to bring to fruition. *Perhaps, given that much time, I can sway his thinking. Mitigate his bloodlust. Persuade him of my vision for the future.*

Gorkon kept telling himself that, while Chang guzzled one goblet after another of bloodwine and filled the dining room with gales of malicious laughter.

31

Every passageway on the *Endeavour* was crowded with mechanics making last-second repairs through open panels in the bulkheads, ordnance crews moving antigrav pallets stacked high with photon torpedoes, and noncombatant personnel from the station who had been packed like sardines into the ship's guest quarters and cargo bays.

Bersh glov Mog shouldered through the chaos, moving from one urgent repair to the next, checking his crew's work and making sure no important corners had been cut. They had spent the past four days shaving minutes off each bit of overdue damage control, sacrificing perfection in the name of having the ship ready for combat before the Tholian armada arrived. The Tellarite chief engineer didn't know what troubled him more at that moment: the need to tolerate substandard workmanship aboard his beloved starship, or the knowledge that in a few hours there was a high probability it would all be destroyed in a Tholian crossfire.

His snout wrinkled at the stench of melting duotronic cables, and he spun toward its source to see smoldering globs dripping from an open panel in the overhead. "Faran!" He cornered the enlisted engineer's mate who was ducking away from the molten circuit junction. "You can't use plasma cutters near the relays! I've told you a hundred times!"

"Sorry, sir," said the frazzled Efrosian, whose drooping blond handlebar mustache and swooping golden eyebrows were sullied with grime, just like his pale hands and his red shirt.

Mog grabbed an extinguisher from an emergency locker, aimed it, and snuffed the fire before it spread past the slagged junction. Then he tossed the extinguisher to Faran, plucked his communicator from his belt, and flipped open its antenna grille. "Mog to—" He stepped barely clear of a pair of gunner's mates rushing by with another pallet of torpedoes, then tried again. "Mog to Stegbauer. We need a new circuit relay on Deck Five, Section Three."

"Copy that," replied the lieutenant, who had distinguished himself by doing outstanding work under tremendous pressure in the past few days. *"I'll have it back on line in thirty minutes."*

"Good man. Shield status?"

"All back to full except aft port ventral. T'Vel and Burnett are working on it."

Mog nodded to himself. "All right. Impulse systems?"

"Up to ninety percent."

Not perfect, Mog figured, but good enough for now. "Phasers?"

"Still not getting the power we should. We need to swap out the main coupling."

The mere suggestion raised the fur on the nape of Mog's neck. "Absolutely not! We'll never put it back together in time!"

Stegbauer didn't sound any happier about it than Mog felt. *"In that case, the best we can hope for is seventy-five percent efficiency on forward phasers."*

That was not going to be remotely good enough. Mog walked to a nearby wall companel and checked the chrono. It read 1324. "What's the Tholians' ETA?"

"Last update from Vanguard says four hours, nine minutes."

The chief engineer's thoughts filled with unspeakably vile Tellarite profanities. "All right, swap out the main coupling. Pull anybody you need to get it done before 1700."

"Acknowledged. Engineering out." The channel closed with a soft click.

Mog moved on and continued his inspections—hoping as he went that he hadn't just signed *Endeavour*'s death warrant.

• • •

"People, please! Form lines!" Chief Petty Officer Ivan Vumelko was a fireplug of a man, squat and solid, with bulging eyes and meaty hands. In his decades of Starfleet service, he had never been easy to push around. Now, however, with only hours until the expected arrival of the Tholian armada, the paunchy customs inspector felt like a boulder being swept away by a tsunami of panic. "Everyone, proceed to your transports in an orderly—"

Something collided with his protruding gut and knocked the breath out of him. He kept trying to force words out, but all he produced were empty gasps. Civilians and noncombatant Starfleet personnel surged around him, and the flood-crush of the crowd carried him away toward the three small ships parked behind him in the docking bay. Stumbling and fumbling, he weaved through the headlong mass of running bodies until he was clear of it.

Vumelko watched as desperate people scrambled up the gangways of the recently arrived civilian ships, their arms laden and backs burdened with the few personal possessions they had chosen to salvage, only to reach the top and be forced to abandon their duffels and bags in exchange for passage. Every cubic meter of space on these ships had become precious, and only living beings and the bare necessities to sustain them were being taken aboard. A steady rain of luggage tumbled to the deck, each impact reverberating in the cavernous space.

Standing apart as a witness to the madness, Vumelko knew that he was supposed to be heading for one of those transports. Technically, he was considered a noncombatant and had been put on the list for mandatory evacuation aboard the passenger ship *Kenitra*.

He slipped out of the docking bay and sprinted for the turbolift, determined to put his early training as a gunner's mate on the starship *Tamerlane* to good use in a few hours' time.

Evacuate, my ass, he stewed. *If it's a fight the Tholians want, I'll give 'em one.*

• • •

Vanguard's security center was a bedlam of shouting voices and constant alarms. Standing in the center of the chaos, Haniff Jackson felt as if every crisis he resolved spawned two more.

"Tahir, we've got a riot brewing in Docking Bay Sixty-one! Get a squad down there!" Another monitor on the wall to his right flashed a warning. "Holmgren, we've got a GTS in progress! Lower Pylon, Slip Two. Lock down the docking clamps and tell Seklir to get over there, RFN!" He had taken to using the acronym GTS for the offense of *grand theft starship* because the increasing frequency of the crime over the past two days on Vanguard had rendered usage of the formal term burdensome.

More alarms sounded to his left, and he saw several of his deputies were responding to reports of looting in Stars Landing. He shook his head in disgust. *There's nowhere to go, nowhere to fence the goods, and no way off the station with anything more than the clothes on their backs. So what the hell are those idiots thinking?*

The dim ambience of computer screens in the darkness was momentarily washed out by a spill of harsh white light from the corridor as the door opened behind Jackson. He turned to see Ming Xiong enter, and he waved the scientist over to his station in the middle of the U-shaped ring of duty stations. Xiong rushed to his side and sounded winded, as if he had run all the way up from the Vault. "What's up? You said it was urgent."

"I had an idea," Jackson said, calling up tactical plans on his master control screen. "Scuttlebutt on the command deck is that you guys wasted a planet with that gizmo of yours."

Xiong backed up half a step. "I can't discuss that."

"Yeah, yeah, it's classified, I get it. Forget that for a second." He showed Xiong a simulation of the Tholians' likely attack plan. "If we could direct just a fraction of the power from your setup to a handful of key points, we could break their momentum before they—"

"It won't work," Xiong said. "Bringing the array to full power is a risk under the best of circumstances. And the truth is, we just don't have the kind of precision control we'd need to use the array as a close-range tactical system. If we tried to do something like this, we'd probably blow ourselves up in the process."

Jackson held up one hand while he loaded another simulation. "Okay, I thought you might say that. So, look at this. What if you target their fleet right now, while they're still on approach in tight formation? Just hit an area of effect and—"

"The timing on the effect isn't precise to within more than twenty seconds. We could barely target a planet in a slow orbit. No way we can hit a fleet moving at warp speed." He added with a measure of sympathy, "Got a Plan C?"

"Yeah," Jackson said. "Run like hell."

Outside the walls of Manón's cabaret, the residents of Stars Landing were falling victim to the station's spreading contagion of hysteria. Inside the cabaret, Manón packed a few prized possessions into a compact carryall: a rare bottle of Brunello di Montalcino from Earth, an even rarer bottle of Silgov *vasha,* and a smattering of tiny knickknacks she had carried with her years earlier, on the fateful night when she'd fled her homeworld on the eve of its invasion.

Her wanderlust had fired her imagination long before her exodus, but the threat of the Vekhal's arrival in force on Silgos Prime had spurred her into flight. She had forsaken home and noble title for freedom; heritage and the companionship of her own kind for survival. At the time it had seemed an easy bargain. Only after years as an exile did she understand the true cost of her salvation: all her fleeting moments of joy had since been tempered by the bitter loneliness of never again seeing one of her own kind.

She had done her best to fill her days and nights with companions. Ironically, in her opinion, she felt most at home when surrounded by as diverse a population as possible, and nowhere had she encountered a polyglot society on a par with the Federation. Among all the civilizations she had encountered across a span of nearly three thousand light-years, the United Federation of Planets was unique.

Perhaps I would have been happier had I stayed safely within its borders, she speculated. In hindsight, she realized, it was only her emotional need to keep moving, to remain figuratively one step ahead of her memories of the Vekhal, that had driven her to leave her safe haven on Bolarus to open a business aboard a starbase in the perilous no-man's-land of unclaimed space.

In a very short time she had come to think of this place as home, and of its denizens as her friends. Pausing in the doorway before running for her ship, the *Niwlolau Leuad* (which the Federation's ever-obliging universal translator had rendered accurately as "Moonlit Mist"), she lamented that she would never again hear T'Prynn play her baby grand piano, or be regaled by one of Quartermaster Sozlok's ribald tales of misspent youth, or enjoy the succulent delights that her kitchen staff improvised each night, based on whatever fresh ingredients had come in aboard the latest cargo ships. There were few things Manón had ever been part of that had meant so much to her as this place, and it filled her with sorrow to bid it farewell.

Everything ends, she reminded herself. *But for now, I must go on.*

With a light step and a heavy heart, she ran for her ship.

"Get your drink and get out!" Tom Walker stepped briskly down the length of his bar, filling one outstretched shot glass after another in a single, unceasing pour. "One and done! Keep it moving!" He reached the end of the bar and turned back to fill another line of empty glasses being pushed forward. "You've all heard of last call! This is the *very* last call! It's *closing* time, people! One free shot per customer! Belly up and drink up!"

Twenty-five-year-old Macallan single malt Scotch whisky flowed in an unbroken stream, splashing over hands as much as into glasses, and as the patrons were served, they stepped back from the bar, downed their measures of liquid courage, and bolted for the door. There were civilians and Starfleet personnel all bunched together, everyone looking to take the edge off one last time before everything went to hell. At the other end of the bar, Tom's night bartender, Maggie, was doing the same thing he was: bolstering morale one ounce of booze at a time. Whereas he was pouring top-shelf scotch, she had opened up the Gran Patrón Platinum tequila. Tom knew he couldn't take any of this with him, and it seemed like a sin to leave it behind when so many people on this station were so desperately in need of stiff drinks.

"Drink faster, folks!" Tom shouted. "We gotta go! I didn't survive cancer just so I could die in space!" The bottle of Macallan 25 ran dry, so he reached for the Macallan 30—the last bottle on the shelf. He pulled off the pour spout, and resumed his free-for-all last call. Less than a minute later, its last drops fell into a waiting glass, and he hurled away the empty bottle. "Party's over, folks! You don't have to go home, but you'd better not stay here!" He nodded at Maggie, and she grabbed her shoulder bag from under the bar. Tom picked up his half-filled duffel, and together they slipped out the back door and high-tailed it across Stars Landing on their way to his private ship, the *Friday's Child*. He didn't know where the two of them would end up, but he didn't really care—as long as they got the hell away from Vanguard and lived to tell about it.

Tim Pennington had searched every watering hole in Stars Landing, looked behind the bar at Manón's cabaret, and even checked the seemingly never-used officers' club on Level Six, but Cervantes Quinn was nowhere to be found. He couldn't believe that Quinn could have soused himself so utterly that he would have slept through the last three days of evacuation madness aboard Vanguard, but he had run out of ideas for where to look for his friend, so he returned to the first place he'd checked, vowing to start the search over, if that's what it took.

He forced open the door of Quinn's residence in Stars Landing. It was easy, since the portal had remained ajar since the first time he'd broken into Quinn's flat. The barely furnished little bedsit was still empty. The door to the lavatory was open, as was the shower curtain.

"Quinn!" he shouted, thinking he might conjure the old pilot from thin air. "Bloody hell, mate! Where are you? It's time to go, man!" On a hunch he checked the closet, thinking Quinn might have sought refuge there in a moment of drunken logic, but he found nothing except one of Quinn's shirts crumpled on the floor. He turned in a circle, one way and then the other, his eyes scanning the room for clues, but all he gained was a bout of vertigo.

Then he turned toward the door, planning to head back to Tom Walker's place, and found his path blocked by T'Prynn. "If you are searching for Mister Quinn, he has already gone."

"Gone where? When's he coming back? We have to get out of here!"

She stepped forward and gently took him by his forearm. "He will not be coming back, Tim. He has already left the station." She led him toward the door. "It's time for you to leave, while you still can."

He pulled his arm free. "You're sure? That he's safely away?"

"I give you my word: Mister Quinn is well away from here. Now please go."

"I'm going," he lied, jogging away from her. He would make it to his transport; he had enough common sense and desire for survival not to screw that up. But before he left Vanguard, there was one last farewell he needed to make.

Captain Nassir poked his head down through the ladderway to survey the cargo hold of the *Sagittarius*. It was packed from bow to stern and port to starboard with Starfleet personnel from the station who had piled aboard minutes earlier in search of a ride out of harm's way.

Noting the density of their accommodations, Nassir asked, "Everybody tucked in?" There were general murmurs of assent and agreement. Nassir figured this was as good a time as any to break the bad news to his unauthorized passengers. "I think it's only fair to warn you all that this won't be a smooth ride home, folks. This ship's been ordered to help *Endeavour* hold the line, which means we'll be taking fire. Conditions down here can get ugly real fast, so if you have second thoughts about choosing my boat as your ride, you've got thirty minutes to bail out."

He left them to think that over while he climbed the ladder up to his ship's truncated engineering deck and transporter bay. Ilucci and his engineering team were all engaged to one degree or another on repairs to various components of the scout ship's warp core. Nassir caught Ilucci's eye and asked, "What's the word, Master Chief?"

"Five minutes away from being five by five, Skipper."

"Well done. When you finish, go help the *Endeavour* team. They yanked out their main phaser coupling, and they're running late getting a new one put in."

"*Two* miracles before dinner?" The portly chief engineer traded amused looks with his run-ragged crew of enlisted mechanics, then cracked a reassuring smile. "Good as done, boss."

The captain pivoted about-face toward the ship's sensor probe launcher—technically a misnomer, since it was equally capable of launching photon torpedoes. Because of the ship's limited storage space and the difficulty of moving bulky elements from the cargo deck to the engineering deck, it usually carried only probes and no torpedoes. The rationale for that decision was that the *Sagittarius* was not designed for heavy combat. Any threat serious enough to merit a photon torpedo was likely one the *Archer*-class scout ship ought be outrunning.

That afternoon, its entire complement of six sensor probes had been replaced by torpedoes. Junior recon scout Ensign Taryl inspected the new ordnance with her tricorder.

"Do our fish check out, Ensign?"

The Orion woman turned a confused look toward Nassir. "Fish, sir?"

"An old Terran nautical term for torpedoes. I picked it up at the Academy." Waving off the mismatch in their jargon, he inquired, "Are they ready to go?"

Taryl checked her tricorder one more time, then switched it off. "Ready, sir."

"Good. Load one into the tube now. When Vanguard gives the order, I want to be ready to come out swinging."

Ezekiel Fisher haunted the open doorway of his no longer private cabin aboard the *Lisbon*. He had expected to share his accommodations from the moment the evacuation order was sounded, and he had been right: his VIP cabin for one had become a steerage berthing for six. The once antiseptic-smelling compartment had become a sauna of bad breath and sweaty bodies pressed much too closely together.

The loss of comfort and privacy didn't really bother him. He had also taken in stride the news that his personal effects had been removed from the cargo hold and abandoned to make room for noncombatant Starfleet personnel who would be coming aboard at the last possible moment. *Only monsters value things over lives,* he told himself to lessen the sting of the news.

One enlisted crewman after another packed into every free space inside the *Lisbon*. Some of them claimed corners of the mess hall; others staked claims to slivers of space between hulking blocks of machinery. Other than that, there wasn't much talking. Apparently, most of those running for their lives seemed to think there wasn't much left to say.

The tense but muted atmosphere inside the transport was split by the squawk of Captain Boonmee's voice over the ship's PA system.

"Attention, all crew and passengers of the Lisbon, *this is the captain. Admiral Nogura has just sent a priority comm to all ships still docked at the station. Vanguard is asking for trained medical personnel, preferably with trauma experience, to stay and tend the wounded if necessary. I've been asked to emphasize that this call for doctors, nurses, and technicians is strictly voluntary. FYI, we'll be taking off in fifteen minutes. That's all."*

Moments later, Fisher saw two people struggling against the

tide in the corridor, blading and shouldering their way toward the exit. One of them he recognized from Vanguard Hospital—a Caitian nurse named Kiraar. The other was a human-looking male civilian of middling years whom Fisher didn't recognize, but the man carried a telltale black medical bag.

Watching those two force their way upstream against the evacuation filled Fisher with guilt. For several painful seconds he wrestled his conscience, fighting the urge to run toward the crisis as he had for most of his adult life. *I've given Starfleet more than fifty years,* he rationalized. *That should be enough, shouldn't it?* Part of him wanted to believe that, but the better angels of his nature reminded him of what he knew all too well. *If I turn my back now on people in need of a doctor, the last five decades of my life will have meant nothing.*

Fisher dodged past his cabinmates to his bunk, retrieved his medical satchel, and slung it over his shoulder. Then he pushed his way out into the corridor and began his own upstream battle back toward the station he thought he'd left behind.

"Dammit, Admiral, that's a suicide order, and you *know* it! There's no way I'm doing that!"

Nogura was not one to tolerate direct repudiation of his orders by a subordinate, much less in such a vociferous and disrespectful manner, and absolutely never in front of others—and Captain Telvane of the Starfleet cargo transport *U.S.S. Panama* had just committed all three offenses at once, on the supervisors' deck in the middle of Vanguard's operations center.

A sudden shocked hush fell like a curtain as every person in ops turned to see what would happen next. Nogura stepped out from behind the Hub and prowled toward Telvane. The burly, square-headed, lantern-jawed, sun-browned freighter captain towered over the admiral, and yet it was the larger man who seemed to lean ever so slightly away as Nogura confronted him. Rather than raise his voice to match Telvane's outburst, Nogura made his reply cold and quiet.

"This is not open for discussion, Captain. Deploy your ship as ordered."

Digging deep to dredge up the last of his courage, Telvane protested, "My ship doesn't *belong* with a battle group, Admiral. We should be escorting the civilian convoy."

Nogura roared, "Captain! Your ship has a Starfleet registry and a phaser bank! Get back to your bridge and take your ship into battle, or I'll find someone who will!"

"What're you going to do? Court-martial me?"

"No, I'll shoot you dead where you stand." Nogura drew his phaser and held it casually at his side, aimed at the deck. "Make your choice, Captain."

Telvane backed away, a disgusted scowl on his swarthy face. "Looks like I'm dead either way. I hope you can live with yourself, Admiral." He turned and headed for the turbolift.

Nogura holstered his phaser. He didn't worry whether he would be able to live with his decision. He was too busy worrying whether he would live through the next hour.

Pennington sprinted the last several meters to the Denevan dogwood on Fontana Meadow just as a trio of Starfleet botanists, two men and a woman, inserted small, high-tech devices into the soil all around it. "Wait!" he cried. "Not yet!" The three blue-shirted young officers looked askance at him as he stumbled to a halt in their midst and reached for one of the tree's lower branches.

The taller of the men seized Pennington's wrist. "What the hell are you doing?"

"It's all right, mate," Pennington said, raising a small pocket knife in his other hand.

The other male botanist grabbed Pennington's knife hand and told his female colleague, "Call security!" She reached for her communicator and flipped it open.

Struggling to break free, Pennington shouted, "Let go, you wankers! I just want one of the flowers!"

The woman lowered her communicator and looked into his eyes. "Why?"

There was no time for lies. "I lost someone I loved on the *Bombay*. I want the flower as a memento. I don't have anything else."

She put away her communicator and said to the men, "Let him go."

The big man blustered, "Are you crazy? He—"

"That's an *order,* Ensign." Pennington noticed the two men's shirts had no braid on their cuffs, but those of the woman's minidress did—a solid stripe. The men let him go. Not wanting to press his luck or test the lieutenant's patience, he snipped a yellow-centered white blossom from the dogwood's lowest branch, pressed the flower carefully inside his bifold wallet, and tucked it into his jacket's inside pocket. He offered the lieutenant a sad smile. "Thanks."

"You're welcome," she said. "Now stand back." Pennington did as she said, and the other two men did the same. The lieutenant opened her communicator. "Bernstein to *Endeavour*. Ready for transport." She backed up three steps. Seconds later, the tree vanished in a sparkle of transporter energy, leaving behind a perfectly smooth divot in the ground.

From the communicator, a man's voice said, *"Transport complete. The tree's safe inside our arboretum. But you three had better hurry up and head back, because—"*

The station's Red Alert resounded ominously inside the vast terrestrial enclosure. The botanists, and every other person Pennington could see, sprinted for the turbolifts. He ran like hell to keep up and prayed his transport didn't leave without him.

32

"All hands to battle stations," Captain Khatami announced over the *Endeavour*'s PA system, her manner cool and efficient despite the flashing red panels on the bulkheads and the fearful mood that pervaded the ship. "This is not a drill. Damage control teams to alert stations." She closed the channel with a quick jab at the button on her command chair's armrest, then watched Airlock 2 and the surrounding infrastructure of Vanguard's main hangar recede on the bridge's main viewer as her starship navigated in reverse on thrusters.

Lieutenant Neelakanta made some fine adjustments at the helm and keyed the switch for the station's comm channel. "Vanguard Control, *Endeavour*. We have cleared all moorings."

A woman's voice responded from the helm's speaker. "*Endeavour, this is Vanguard Control. Outer doors are open, and you're clear to proceed.*"

"Acknowledged," the Arcturian helmsman said. "Clearing bay doors in ten seconds."

Departure from spacedock normally took twenty-five seconds, but Khatami had seen fast exits such as this many times over the years. Within seconds, the gray curve of the lower half of Vanguard's massive saucer hull dominated the viewscreen from the edges in.

"*Endeavour, you have cleared bay doors. The lane is clear, and you're free to navigate.*"

"Helm," Khatami said, "bring us about, bearing nine one, mark one five. Lieutenant McCormack, raise shields and arm all weapons."

"Shields up," McCormack confirmed. "Phasers and torpedoes armed."

"Charge up the tractor beam, too, Lieutenant," Stano added as she moved to stand beside Khatami's command chair. "It might come in handy."

Khatami looked up at her first officer. "Brushing up on starship combat tactics?"

Stano smiled nervously. "Always worked when I crammed for tests at the Academy." Her forced joviality vanished as the image on the main viewer panned in a swift blur to reveal the *Sagittarius* emerging from the Bay 3 doors directly ahead of *Endeavour*—and, in the distance, a vast swarm of tiny gray specks moving amid the cold brightness of the stars.

Hector Estrada held one hand over the transceiver protruding from his left ear and swiveled his chair to face Khatami. "Captain, the *Panama* and the *Buenos Aires* confirm they're in position and awaiting your orders."

Neelakanta chimed in, "*Sagittarius* is clear of spacedock and moving into a defensive posture on our aft port quarter."

"All ships, proceed to first coordinates as planned," Khatami said. "McCormack, make sure the rest of our battle group has the latest update on Vanguard's firing solution. We need to stay out of their crossfire and force the Tholians into it. Neelakanta, ahead full impulse."

"Full impulse, aye," Neelakanta said over the rising hum of the ship's engines.

Khatami turned toward the sensor console. "Klisiewicz, how's the evacuation going?"

"Ten minutes ago, it was a crisis. Now, it's officially a disaster." To McCormack, he added, "Aft viewer, please." McCormack switched the viewscreen to an image of the steady stream of civilian vessels pouring like a flood from Vanguard's open docking bays and leaping into warp—but there were several vessels still docked at the lower pylons. "Sensors show way too many people inside the station. I think a lot of people just missed their rides."

Stano looked at Khatami. "I'll have all transporters stand by to beam out survivors on your order." She got the captain's nod of approval and stepped away to make it happen.

"Forward angle," Khatami said, and McCormack returned the screen to its default view. The elegant *Miranda*-class frigate *Buenos Aires* and the stout *Equus*-class cargo transport *Panama* were directly ahead, holding position between Vanguard and the incoming Tholian armada. "McCormack, have *Sagittarius* cover zones one and two with the *Panama*. *Buenos Aires* can cover three and four. We'll defend five through eight." She turned and looked back at the communications officer. "Estrada—send the message packet."

Estrada nodded and transmitted a vital signal back to Earth in a coded subspace radio burst: a packet of prerecorded messages by the *Endeavour*'s crew and officers, final missives to be delivered to their loved ones by Starfleet Command in the event that they or the ship did not survive the battle to come. It wasn't the first time Khatami had recorded a possible farewell to her husband, Kenji, and daughter, Parveen, nor was it the first time she had served aboard a ship whose crew had all prepared parting sentiments on the eve of battle. But until now, she had never actually taken the extra precaution of sending the messages home for safekeeping.

That was because, until now, she had never been asked to face down an enemy armada with two warships, a scout vessel, and a freighter.

On the viewscreen, the gray specks grew larger and more distinct with terrifying speed, until the Tholian ships' triple-wedge hulls hove into view like an arrowstorm descending with deadly intent from the darkness. Khatami drew a sharp breath. She felt as if she were standing alone on a beach at night, waiting for a tidal wave to crash down and sweep away all in its path, knowing in her heart that it would be as unstoppable as it was inevitable.

She forced herself to exhale and clear her mind. Making a silent survey of her bridge, she was pleased to see that everyone remained focused and alert. Tensions were high, but her crew appeared resolute. Wiping the sweat of her palms over her black trousers, Khatami was almost hypnotized by the terrifying spectacle of the Tholian armada bearing down on Vanguard.

She couldn't stand to sit still. She stood and paced around her chair as she addressed her bridge crew. "Listen up, everyone. In the next few minutes, any one of you might need to take over at any one of these stations. If the worst comes to pass, one of you might find yourself in command. No matter what happens, know that I have faith in you. Most important, I want you to remember this advice: Whoever's on weapons control, fire for effect. Use the phasers to dimple enemy shields, then use torpedoes to break them. Don't ignore an enemy ship because it's damaged—it can still be used to ram us or the station. If its shields are down, destroy it. Last but just as important, stay alert for the retreat signal from Vanguard. When that sounds, we'll have to beam out as many survivors as we can. The people on that station are counting on us to pull them out before it's too late. I'm counting on all of you to make sure we don't let them down.

"That's all. Man your posts."

As her crew returned to their duties, Khatami returned to her chair and beheld the hundreds of incoming vessels that now filled the forward viewscreen.

She gripped her chair's armrests and grimaced.

Allah help us all.

Most of Vanguard was being maintained by a skeleton crew, but in the operations center, every console was manned. The wraparound screens covering the high walls teemed with images of Tholian warships cruising at full impulse on a direct interception trajectory. Red Alert panels flashed beneath every screen and beside every turbolift, though the wailing klaxon had long since been muted on Nogura's order. The admiral stalked across the supervisors' deck toward the Hub. "Dunbar! Hail the armada commander, tell him we want a parley!"

The communications officer punched commands into her console and shook her head. "They don't acknowledge our hails, sir."

Nogura cursed under his breath. Commander Cooper looked

across the Hub at him. "Do you really think you can talk our way out of this?"

"I'd like to try," Nogura said. He looked back at Dunbar. "Send the following to the lead ship: 'Tholian commander, this is Admiral Heihachiro Nogura. I formally request terms of surrender.'" A hundred wide-eyed stares suddenly were aimed at Nogura from every direction. He looked at Dunbar and ignored the others. "Send it, Lieutenant. See if it buys us any time."

Dunbar transmitted the message as she replied, "Aye, sir."

"Commander Cannella," Nogura shouted across the deck.

Raymond Cannella, the station's heavyset fleet operations manager, looked up from his space-traffic-control station, his fleshy face a portrait in stress, and retorted in his thick, northern New Jersey accent, "What?"

"How many ships are still docked?"

Cannella checked his auxiliary data screen, tracing a line across the monitor with his index finger, then called out, "Twenty-six."

"Tell them all to launch now," Nogura said. "As in, *right this second.* I don't care who or what they're waiting for, they need to go. Anybody left behind will have to beam out with us." The admiral shot an imploring look at Dunbar, who seemed to be listening to a reply. "Well?"

She winced. "You're not gonna like it."

"On speakers," Nogura growled.

The universal translator parsed a screech that made Nogura think of a saw biting through metal bones. *"There will be no parley. No terms. No prisoners. No mercy."*

The noise ended, and Dunbar said, "That's all there is, sir."

Nogura looked back at his bloated fleet ops manager. "Cannella?"

"The last three ships just cleared moorings."

On the towering screens, the Tholian armada split up into attack groups. Each wing of thirty or forty ships peeled off from the main force, shifting course while the rest of the fleet wheeled at high speed around Vanguard, like scavengers circling a dying beast they know will soon become carrion. Nogura steeled himself for the carnage to come. "Cooper, order all gunners to start locking in targets. Take out the point ships first—those will be the leaders."

Cannella bellowed, "All ships away!"

"Raise shields!" Nogura ordered. "Damage control and fire suppression teams to action stations." He opened an internal comm to the engineering levels. "Ops to reactor control. Increase power output to one hundred ten percent of rated maximum."

"Roger that," replied the station's chief engineer, Lieutenant Isaiah Farber.

Cooper tensed. "The Tholians are locking weapons!"

Switching to a coded subspace frequency, Nogura opened a channel to his four defending starships. "Vanguard to all Starfleet vessels: prepare to engage the enemy."

Then came the bedlam of a thousand blows landing at once on Vanguard's shields, and the station's worst-case scenario became a reality: It was under siege.

Nogura knew the battle's outcome was a foregone conclusion.

The only mysteries now were how long it would last—and how many would die.

33

An endless red storm of disruptor pulses converged upon Vanguard. "Evasive!" Nassir ordered, and zh'Firro counterintuitively steered the *Sagittarius* toward the incoming barrage to minimize the ship's profile—and then she accelerated.

Jarring blasts hammered the ship. As the deck pitched and yawed, Nassir clung white-knuckled to his chair and shouted over the clamor of detonations. "Return fire, phasers only!"

The whoop-and-shriek of the ship's phasers was deafening. Unlike larger ships, which had the luxury of isolating their weapons systems from the crew compartments, the *Sagittarius*'s two phaser nodes were just a few meters overhead, on the dorsal hull. Each salvo tortured Nassir's eardrums with piercing, high-pitched noise.

A sudden flare on the main viewer made him wince and shield his eyes. Blue and white fusillades lit up the screen as Vanguard unleashed the full might of its fearsome—and until that moment, never tested—arsenal. Within seconds, the space within twenty kilometers of Vanguard became a hellish chaos of metal and fire. Several dozen high-power phaser batteries lashed the Tholian armada circling the station. Scores of brilliant white photon torpedoes—some in tight clusters, some in wide spreads—tore through the attacking Tholian battle groups. Ephemeral flares revealed the station's shields as salvos of Tholian disruptor fire slammed home. Then tractor beams leapt from the starbase like golden spears, snared half a dozen Tholian cruisers, and dragged them into the station's brutal kill zones of overlapping phaser and torpedo fire.

For a moment, Nassir swelled with irrational hope that the battle might not be futile, after all. Then a crushing blow pummeled the *Sagittarius,* and darkness swallowed the bridge as flames and acrid smoke erupted from the port bulkhead above the auxiliary engineering station.

Tactical officer Dastin attacked the blaze at point-blank range with a handheld fire extinguisher as Terrell hollered, "Damage report!"

Dastin waved a path through the smoke. "Secondary systems are fried!"

The battle on the screen was little more than a fiery blur as zh'Firro guided the ship through wild corkscrew maneuvers at full impulse. The daring young *zhen* raised her voice to compete with the screaming din of the phasers. "Impulse power's down to eighty percent!"

Nassir opened a channel to engineering. "Master Chief, report!"

"Main plasma relay's been hit," Ilucci replied, his voice barely audible over the clamor of shouting voices and straining machines in the engine room. *"We're running a bypass."*

Another near-miss rumbled through the hull. "Make it fast. Bridge out." Nassir closed the channel and twisted around toward the tactical station. "Sorak, how's the *Panama* holding up?"

"Not well," the Vulcan centenarian said. "Her starboard shields are collapsing. She's coming hard about to turn her port side to the armada."

"Give her covering fire until she completes the turn," Nassir ordered. To zh'Firro he added, "Sayna, swing us past the *Panama,* try to draw the enemy's fire." A punishing concussion stuttered the overhead lights and flickered the bridge consoles.

"I don't think we'll have to try very hard," zh'Firro said as she changed course.

Theriault looked up from the sensors. "Bandits, twelve o'clock high!"

"Targeting," Sorak replied. "Firing." Another angry chorus from the phasers, and he added, "Attack group breaking off, heading for zone three."

"Leave them to *Buenos Aires,*" Nassir said. "Find a new target and keep firing."

• • •

Alerts and system failures cascaded across the *Endeavour*'s master engineering console faster than Bersh glov Mog could deploy damage-control teams. He switched from one internal comm circuit to another as he rattled off orders. "Team Four, hull breach on Deck Nine, Section Two! Team Seven, phaser coupling overload, Deck Sixteen, Section Four! Fire Team Alpha, plasma fire on the hangar deck!" He was looking at the status indicator for the secondary hull's port defense screen generator as it toggled from green to red, indicating a failure, and he reached to open a comm channel to the nearest repair team.

A godhammer of concussive force hit the ship and sent him and the other engineers tumbling. Despite his muddied hearing, Mog heard someone call out, "We've lost shields!" Another replied, "Hull breach! Outer sections!"

Mog pulled himself to his feet and stumbled like a drunkard across the heaving deck. "Air masks! Now!" He grabbed the respirator kit next to his station and strapped it on, then lurched across the compartment toward the lockers where the hazmat gear was stored, fighting every step of the way against the random pitching and rolling of the ship. *Damn these weak inertial dampers,* he cursed to himself. Down the length of main engineering, he saw other officers and enlisted men fumbling with their breathing masks.

He reached for the emergency equipment locker.

The loudest explosion he'd ever heard struck him as a wall of sonic energy and threw him against a bulkhead several meters away. As he ricocheted off the wall and collapsed, his black eyes opened wide in shock at the sight of a brilliant crimson beam of disruptor energy tearing through the hull from outside and wreaking fiery havoc as it lanced through bulkheads and filled the air with a terrifying buzz-roar so loud it drowned out the screams of the dying. The heat from the beam singed Mog's mane and beard, filling his snout with the horrid stench of burnt fur. He lifted his arm to shield his face from the jabbing-needle pain of ultraviolet radiation—then the beam stopped, and its harsh buzzing was replaced by the groaning howl of escaping atmosphere. The hurricane-force gale threatened to hurl Mog away into the cold vacuum, but he caught the protruding pipe of a coolant valve and hung on as heavy emergency barriers lowered swiftly into place to contain the damage.

Half a dozen people in the breached sections weren't so fortunate, and Mog watched the horror of their fates register on their faces as they were sucked out into space. A lucky few were close enough to the adjacent sections to escape before the airtight barriers fell. Mog reached out to a Vulcan man who was crawling too slowly, clutched his hand, and with a fierce yank pulled him clear before the barrier met the deck and locked into place.

Air pressure normalized within seconds, and Mog knew there was no time to waste on asking every survivor his or her status. His only concern now was to restore main power, which the disruptor blast had just crippled. He tried to run back to his master console, only to find himself feeling simultaneously lightheaded and dead on his feet. Then he was overcome by nausea and doubled over as he succumbed to a sudden urge to vomit. Spewing sour stomach acid tinged with blood, he heard others around him collapse into bouts of violent emesis.

Coughing and gasping, Mog crawled back to his console and pulled himself upright, even as sickness churned in his abdomen. He reached out to initiate a set of diagnostic checks and saw that his hand was shaking. A cold shiver ran down his spine, and was followed by a fatiguing flush of heat in his forehead that left him panting and dry-mouthed. A single glance at the environmental status gauges confirmed what he already knew: He and the other survivors were just as doomed as those who had been pulled into space moments earlier. They all had been exposed to an acute dose of hyperionizing radiation, far exceeding four thousand rads, as the beam had ruptured the matter-antimatter mix system. Radiation levels inside the engineering compartment were already dropping as automated safety systems kicked in, but it was too late for all of them; the damage was done, and not even Starfleet's best medicine could undo it.

Mog turned around and met his crew's mix of frightened stares and empty gazes. "I won't lie to you. You all know what's happened. But we need to use whatever time we have left to bring back main power, before we lose the whole ship. So snap to!" Fighting back against the hot sensation winding through his intestines, he focused on his master console, started rerouting circuits, and resumed dispatching damage and fire teams.

A minute later, the slightly nasal, New York–accented voice of the ship's chief medical officer, Doctor Anthony Leone, blared from Mog's console speaker. *"Sickbay to Mog!"*

"Go ahead, Doctor."

The doctor was furious. *"What the hell, Mog? Radiation levels in main engineering are off the chart! Get your people out of there!"*

"I can't do that, Doctor. We have to restore main power."

"Don't make me pull rank, goddammit!"

Mog appreciated Leone's aggressive, argumentative style. He'd often thought the wiry little human physician with bulging eyes would have made a fine Tellarite, so he tempered his refusal with admiration. "It won't make any difference, Doctor. There's nothing you can do for us now. We all have an hour left to us, and we plan to spend it working. I suggest you do the same. Mog out." He closed the channel and cut off the comm circuit to prevent Leone from pestering him again. Then he looked back at his weary, dying crew and put on his bravest face. "Move with a purpose, people! The antimatter injector won't fix itself!"

He knew that an ugly, painful death awaited them all in an hour's time.

Until then, he planned to live usefully, or die trying.

Lieutenant Isaiah Farber could barely see through the columns of oily gray smoke drifting through Vanguard's reactor control level, and he struggled to hear over the incessant percussion of energy attacks pounding the station's overtaxed shields.

"Ops, please repeat your last," he said into the comm, "all after 'support.'"

The reply was inaudible amid the tumult of battle, so Farber pressed one ear to the speaker and covered the other with his hand. *"Cut off life support to all unoccupied sections and seal them,"* said Commander Cooper. *"Reroute that power to shields."*

He wondered if anyone up there had any idea what they were asking for. "Ops, we're already pushing too much juice through the shield grid! Any more and we'll burn it out!"

"Admiral's orders," Cooper replied.

"I don't give a damn if they come from God himself," Farber said. "Cook those emitters and you'll have no shields at all." Deep sirens wailed and flashing lights pulsed, which meant another fire had broken out somewhere near the reactor's heat exchangers.

Cooper hollered back with the flustered manner of a man caught in the middle of someone else's argument, *"Then reconfigure the shields to sacrifice the low-value areas."*

"We don't *have* any *low-value* areas!" Farber wished he could punch someone over an intercom channel. "What do you want to leave undefended? The reactor? The fuel tanks? The operations center? The tactical levels? This game's all or nothing, Commander!" High overhead, something resounded with an apocalyptic boom, and the gauges on Farber's master panel started flipping en masse from green to red. "What the hell just happened?"

"Cargo bays are breached," Cooper said. *"Levels Forty-four through Fifty-one."*

Scanning the multitudes of error reports flooding his board, Farber saw something far more serious than damage to the cargo bays. "Ops, we've lost two out of four turbolift shafts in the lower core. I recommend we start evacuating the lower sections—starting with the Vault."

"Acknowledged. Now, get us more shield power, or—" Another brutal impact rocked the station. When the roar abated to a

constant but low rumbling, Farber strained to hear the rest of Cooper's response. Only then did he realize the comm circuits linking the reactor level to the rest of the station had been severed. They were cut off. He grabbed his communicator from his belt and flipped it open. "Farber to ops! We've lost comms! Do you copy?"

Static scratched and hissed from the speaker.

Another explosion, even closer than the last. Half the gauges on Farber's panel red-lined; the rest flat-lined. The broad-shouldered, impressively muscled engineer put away his communicator and looked around, trying to remember where the concealed emergency exits were—because he suspected he and his team were about to need them.

There was no time for triage. Fisher and the rest of the skeleton staff of surgeons, nurses, and technicians in Vanguard Hospital were besieged by a nonstop parade of wounded from all over the station. Every biobed was occupied by the broken, the maimed, the charred, or the bloodied. Plangent wails of suffering filled the air, making Fisher grateful for those moments when the cacophony of the Tholians' bombardment overpowered the plaints of the dying.

There was little to be done for the most seriously wounded. In order to return gunners or engineers to duty, the ones with the simplest wounds were treated and released as quickly as possible, while those who lay in agony, clutching at mangled limbs or trying in vain to stanch mortal bleeding with filthy hands, were treated as invisible. Under ideal circumstances, most of them could probably be saved, but in the midst of combat, they were a liability no one could afford. Their gruesome ranks and imploring voices haunted the periphery of Fisher's perceptions. When he dared to look directly at any of them, he filled with despair and felt certain he had blundered into some unknown circle of hell.

As Fisher bandaged a mechanic's scorched hand, a young Andorian *thaan* in a command-gold jersey bearing a junior lieutenant's stripes sprinted through the hospital's main entrance. "We need medics at Phaser Control Delta!"

Doctor Robles, who had succeeded Fisher as Vanguard's CMO, shouted back, "We only treat the ones who make it here, Lieutenant."

The Andorian was on the verge of hysteria. "There aren't enough people left to man that battery! Give me a medkit and send me back, but give me something!"

Fisher put away his bandage roll in his satchel and replied, "I'll go with you."

Robles shot a poisonous glare at Fisher. "You're needed here, Doctor."

"Sounds like I'm needed there, too," Fisher said as he moved to join the Andorian.

"Get back on the line, Doctor!" Robles looked ready for an aneurysm. "That's an order!"

On his way out the door, Fisher permitted himself a rakish smirk at Robles. "I don't work here anymore, remember? Hold the fort till I get back." The next cannonade that shook the station drowned out Robles's reply full of colorful metaphors, and by the time it faded Fisher and his Andorian guide were in the nearest turbolift and hurtling away to one of the outer sections of the upper half of the saucer, where the phaser and torpedo nodes were located.

He offered the Andorian his hand. "Ezekiel Fisher. My friends call me Zeke."

The Andorian shook his hand. "Fellaren th'Shoras. . . . 'Shor.' "

"Nice to meet you, Shor," Fisher said with a disarming smile. Under his breath he added, "I always make a point of knowing the people I might end up dying with."

The Andorian nodded, as if the sentiment were not utterly morbid. "Most sensible," he said. "If we perish together, I shall vouch for you before Uzaveh the Infinite."

Fisher had no idea what else to say except, "Um . . . thanks."

"You're welcome."

After that, he figured it would be best to just stop talking for a while.

• • •

"One more adjustment," Xiong begged his two remaining colleagues. "If we can equalize the quantum subharmonic frequency across all the nodes, that should do it!"

Sheltered inside the Vault, the most heavily shielded part of Vanguard, Xiong had at first barely been able to tell the station was under attack. Then a devastating blow to the station's lower core had interrupted the supply of primary power to the lab. The secret research center had its own backup power generators, life-support systems, and computer core, but without main power, Xiong had no idea how long the array could continue to contain its Shedai prisoners. All his estimates for the lab's minimum power requirements had been predicated on the simpler setup involving only two inhabited crystals. Now they had more than five thousand of the alien artifacts, all of them except the first packed with multiple Shedai life-forces.

He knew he didn't want to be here when the array's containment matrix failed, but he also knew that the consequences of that would be far worse than anyone outside of Operation Vanguard could possibly imagine. For their sakes, he had to finish this while he still could.

His workstation display flashed with alerts as he struggled to refine his control over the array by making a few final tweaks to Klisiewicz's command interface.

"We need to evacuate," pleaded Ensign Heffron. "Now, before the turbolifts are gone!"

"Just a few more seconds," Xiong said, keying in new lines of code as quickly as he could. "Humberg, do you have that frequency yet?"

Lieutenant Christian Humberg, a thirty-something applied quantum physicist with a compact build and a full head of prematurely gray hair, grimaced as he wrestled with his own set of high-complexity calculations. "I've almost got it," he said. "There! A modulated subharmonic that should enable us to control entropic effects on the quantum level."

"Send it to Heffron." Looking across at the blond ensign, he added, "Kirsten, reset the main emitter to resonate on that frequency. I'm loading the updated command interface into the system now." As he waited for the new software to complete its installation, he looked up at the ominously radiant crystals of the array inside the isolation chamber. He had grown so used to seeing it all from several meters away, through the wall of transparent steel sprayed with a clear compound that acted as a polarizing filter, that he had forgotten how unnerving it could be to stand in the shadow of such awesome, barely yoked power.

"Emitter reset," Heffron said.

Xiong knew he likely would get only one chance to make this experiment work. He hoped for the sake of millions of unsuspecting innocents that his calculations had been correct. "Interface is loaded and stable. I'm bringing the array to full power."

Prismatic ribbons of energy danced over the screaming machine, and a tingle that was part static electricity and part fear crept up Xiong's back. A deep, almost subsonic throbbing pulsed through the deck like a leviathan's heartbeat. Xiong imagined this might have been how it would have felt to be the first mortal to receive the gift of fire from Prometheus.

He engaged the command interface as Heffron and Humberg looked over his shoulder.

Heffron asked, "What are you doing?"

"Pinging all the Conduits in the Shedai network," Xiong said as he worked.

As if fearful of the answer, Humberg asked, "What for?"

Xiong activated the new subharmonic function. "For this."

On his workstation monitor, the constellation of several thousand blue dots began to dwindle, a few at a time at first, then by dozens, and then by scores. Heffron and Humberg both looked perplexed. She pointed at the display. "What does that mean?"

"It means," Xiong said with ruthless satisfaction, "that my program works." He turned and met the bewildered stares of his peers. "Right now, all across the Taurus Reach, all the Conduits the Shedai ever made are self-destructing, shattering into dust. In

a few minutes, there won't be a single node of their former network left in the galaxy."

Heffron looked horrified. "But what about all those planets?"

"It's all right—with the array I was able to target just the Conduits. The planets are fine." He ushered them toward the exit with
broad movements of his arms. "Now go, both of you. Get to the
beam-out point on Level Twenty, before the turbolifts fail."

Humberg held Xiong at arm's length. "Wait, what about you?"

"I need to shut down the array," Xiong said. "I'll be right behind you, I promise. Go." Reassured by his lies, Heffron and
Humberg scrambled out through the main hatchway and started
running. Xiong locked the hatch behind them.

Alone at last with the array, Xiong regarded it with awe and
contempt. He had spent years plumbing the secrets of the Shedai,
plundering their legacy for the benefit of Starfleet and the Federation, and the end result had been this machine, a device of
unimaginable power that he could wield to destroy distant worlds,
but whose principal function stubbornly eluded him.

He had not yet figured out how to make it destroy its Shedai
prisoners.

Realizing he wouldn't have time to unravel that mystery in the
scant minutes remaining to him, he returned to his workstation
and armed the Vault's self-destruct system.

Inside the terrestrial enclosure, the sky was burning.

Smoldering cracks marred the twilight, belying the illusion of
placid heavens. Then the dusk flickered and faltered, revealing
the gray metal interior of Vanguard's upper saucer hull and its
latticework of holographic emitters. A white-hot blister of half-
molten duranium drooped inward, but there was no one left on
Fontana Meadow to see it, no one left to hear the stentorian groan
of hundreds of tons of overstressed metal, the incessant thunder
of high-power detonations tearing their way through the 800-
meter-wide dome.

A fearsome bolt of blinding energy burst through the hull,

raining twisted slabs of scorched metal and charred bodies around its point of impact, just shy of Stars Landing. A shock front of superheated, ultracondensed air vaporized the cluster of buildings in a flash and scoured the deck of its manmade lawn. Driving a ring of debris ahead of it, the shock wave slammed against the station's inner core and blasted in hundreds of transparent aluminum barriers.

Half a second later, the hunger of the vacuum asserted itself and tore the firestorm and every bit of loose matter out through the enormous, glowing-edged gash in the hull. Silence reigned within the sterilized interior of the saucer's upper half, even as another half dozen shining blades of fire ripped through the hull and began carving it into scrap.

"Last torpedo's away!" Terrell called out as he turned from the auxiliary tactical console to face the main viewer. The last photon torpedo aboard the *Sagittarius* streaked away and detonated in the midst of a tight formation of Tholian cruisers, whose course Terrell had deduced while watching them flee from Vanguard's thinning barrage of phaser fire moments earlier. When the conflagration faded, nothing remained of the four ships except debris and ionized gas.

"Good shooting, Clark," Nassir said. Then the image on the screen pinwheeled as zh'Firro steered the slowing scout vessel into another round of complicated evasive maneuvers.

The air in the bridge was thick with the sharp odor of burnt wiring and overheated circuits, and the normal low vibration imparted to the decks by the impulse engines had become a disconcerting clattering and banging, as if they were literally flying the ship apart, one hard turn at a time. Terrell headed aft to check Sorak's targeting protocols and help the old Vulcan coordinate with Lieutenant Dastin, who was using the ship's tractor beam to tow debris into enemy ships and drag enemy vessels in front of Vanguard's still operational phaser batteries.

Theriault cried out, "The *Panama*'s breaking up!"

Turning on his heel, Terrell looked back in time to see the cargo transport splinter with fiery cracks, then break apart amidships before vanishing in a reddish-orange flash. Secretly, he was amazed they—and the *Sagittarius*—had lasted this long. *The only reason we're not dead yet is that the Tholians are throwing everything they have at the station,* he reasoned.

Nassir sprang from his chair to stand over zh'Firro at the forward console. "Swing us around on a wider arc," he said, leaning with one hand on the back of her chair. "We'll need to cover the zones the *Panama* was—"

"Incoming!" Dastin cried.

Total darkness and a sound like the end of the world. Terrell felt himself hurled through the air, as if he'd leapt from a cliff. A blinding eruption and a thunderclap sent him hurtling back in the opposite direction as heat scorched his hair and shrapnel bit into his torso and limbs. He came to a halt when he struck something that he realized moments later must have been another person between him and a bulkhead. Darkness fell again, accompanied by a deep and muddy wash of indiscriminate sounds he couldn't name.

He awoke in a daze to a faraway voice repeating, "Commander! Wake up!" The voice grew closer, louder, and sharper until he recognized it as Doctor Babitz's. Struggling to push through the crushing ache in his skull, he blinked and saw the blond physician kneeling over him, her face lit by the glow of her medical tricorder. "The good news is, you don't have a concussion. The bad news is, the rest of your body looks like it's been through a blender."

Behind her, Theriault watched over her shoulder and held a chemical emergency light stick whose green radiance made the bloody wounds on the left side of her face look black. "Sir, are you okay?" The science officer sounded frightened, but he couldn't say if she feared for him, herself, the ship, or all of them at once.

"Help me stand up," Terrell said.

"I don't think that's a good idea," Babitz said.

"It's an order." Theriault grabbed his right arm, and Sorak took hold of his left. Together, the petite Martian and the elderly Vulcan hoisted Terrell upright and leaned him against the aft bulkhead. Looking around as his eyes adjusted to the darkness, he saw little at first except smoke hanging low and heavy over the bridge. The main viewscreen was gone, the forward bulkhead a charred mess. Then he saw the twisted, burnt remains of the helm console, and the two bodies lying on the deck beside it, both draped with blue emergency blankets: Nassir and zh'Firro were dead. He tried to swallow, only to find his mouth parched and tasting of ashes. "Damage report," he croaked as he staggered to the command chair.

Babitz employed her most motherly voice. "Sir, you need to get to sickbay."

"Later. We're still in combat." When he noticed the doctor's challenging stare, he added with an extra measure of authoritativeness, "You're dismissed, Doctor."

The chief medical officer scowled as she walked away. "Fine," she sniped, "but don't come crying to me when you bleed to death."

Terrell watched her go, then continued trudging to the command chair. "As I was saying: damage reports, people. Let me have 'em."

"Lieutenant Dastin is rerouting helm control to the auxiliary panel," Sorak said, directing Terrell's attention toward port, where the Trill lieutenant was coaxing a damaged console back to life. "Until he does, we're adrift. Shields and phasers are off line, and the tractor beam is down to one-quarter power." A tremor that felt like the result of a glancing attack rocked the ship.

Terrell lowered himself with gingerly care into the center seat. "Communications?"

Theriault replied, "Master Chief's working on them right now."

"I've got helm control," Dastin declared. "Impulse and warp drive both available."

Pale emergency illumination flickered on around the bridge,

and a few seconds later the main bridge lights returned to life and gradually increased to half their normal levels. Ilucci's gruff voice barked from the overhead speakers, *"Hey, bridge. Can you hear me now?"*

"Affirmative, Master Chief," Terrell said. "Report."

"Short-range comms are up, and Captain Khatami wants a word with you."

Apprehensive looks passed between Terrell and his three remaining bridge officers. "Patch her through, Master Chief."

The next voice from the speaker was Khatami's.

"Endeavour to Sagittarius. Do you copy? Please respond."

Thumbing open the reply circuit from the command chair, Terrell said, "We read you, *Endeavour.* Go ahead."

Over the channel, he heard the sounds of battle filter through behind Khatami's voice. The *Endeavour,* at least, was still in the fight. *"What's your status?"*

"No shields or weapons, but we're still mobile."

"Then you need to fall back. Break off and regroup with the convoy."

"Captain, we can still—"

"That's an order, Sagittarius. *Regroup with the convoy.* Endeavour *out."*

The channel closed, leaving Terrell with no choice but to abandon the *Endeavour* and the *Buenos Aires* to the battle. As a soldier, it galled him to be forced into retreat, but he also knew the choice was not his to make—it was Khatami's, and she'd made her decision very clear.

"Helm," Terrell said, "set course for the civilian convoy. Maximum warp until we overtake them, then reduce speed to match them. Engage."

"Aye, sir." Dastin plotted the course and jumped the ship to warp.

"Lieutenant Sorak," Terrell rasped. The Vulcan came to his side. "It seems Doctor Babitz was right. I *am* bleeding rather profusely. I need you to carry me to sickbay, please."

"Aye, Captain," Sorak replied, reminding Terrell that he was no longer the first officer of the *Sagittarius* but its de facto commanding officer. The Vulcan hoisted Terrell forward and out of the chair, then draped Terrell's right arm across his shoulders.

Teetering on the edge of consciousness as he was assisted off the bridge, the acting captain looked back at the shell-shocked Theriault and smiled.

"You have the conn, Number One."

She smiled back as best she was able. "Aye, sir."

Khatami had stopped asking for damage reports when they started coming in every few seconds on their own. The warp drive was down, along with the ventral shields and half the phaser banks. Disruptor blasts and plasma charges struck the ship every few seconds, making it impossible to cross the bridge without being thrown around like a rag doll. The *Endeavour* had become like a punch-drunk fighter: pummeled to within an inch of its life, the only thing that seemed to keep it going was the battle itself.

"*Sagittarius* made the jump to warp," Klisiewicz confirmed.

McCormack waved away the tattered curtain of black smoke drifting between her and the navigator's console. "The *Buenos Aires* is taking heavy damage!"

"On-screen!" Khatami leaned forward as the viewscreen switched to an angle that showed the *Miranda*-class frigate making wild maneuvers in a futile bid to escape a three-way Tholian crossfire. "Target the ship on their starboard flank and fire!"

"Phasers locked," McCormack said. "Firing!" A scathing blue beam lanced upward from the *Endeavour* and destroyed one of the Tholian cruisers pestering the *Buenos Aires,* which veered clear of its remaining pursuers and swung wide to prepare for another attack run.

A bone-rattling crash as plasma charges slammed through *Endeavour*'s primary hull and plunged the bridge into darkness. Half a second later, the lights surged back, but several display screens above the aft duty stations showed only static. Thorsen scrambled across the deck to an open panel beneath the affected consoles. "Hang on," the baby-faced blond lieutenant shouted as he slithered inside the machinery. "I'll have them back up in a few seconds!"

Commander Stano called out, "Brace for impact!"

The *Endeavour* pitched as if it had been struck by the hand of God.

Sparks flew, lights and consoles flickered, and bodies seemed to tumble around Khatami in slow motion, their erratic paths stuttered by the strobing light. When the ear-crushing rumble of the blast abated, Khatami heard Thorsen's screams of pain. She turned to see Stano and Estrada pulling the tactical officer clear of the maintenance area beneath the panels, which were crackling with flames and belching toxic smoke. The explosion had peppered the young lieutenant's face with a flurry of metal shards and scorched it with second-degree burns. Thorsen seemed to want to press his hands to his face but couldn't bear the slightest touch, so all he could do was writhe and scream and bleed. Estrada retreated in horror from his comrade while Stano belted out, "Medkit! I need a medkit, now!"

Klisiewicz bolted from his seat, retrieved the first aid kit from the emergency locker by the turbolift, and ran it to Stano. The first officer pried open the case, pulled out a hypospray and an ampoule of medicine, and injected Thorsen via his carotid artery. Almost instantly, Thorsen ceased his agonized wails and drifted off into a deep and—Khatami hoped—dreamless slumber.

The captain looked at Stano. "How bad are we hit?"

"Pretty bad," Stano said. "They just punched two holes clean through the saucer."

"Load all torpedo bays, and tell *Buenos Aires* to do the same, we'll need them as a wingman when we—"

"*Buenos Aires* is in trouble," McCormack said, drawing Khatami's attention back to the forward screen. The badly damaged frigate took several hits in rapid succession—some from disruptors, some from plasma charges—to its warp nacelles and main engineering section.

"Hector, hail them. Hurry!"

"Aye, Captain," Estrada said, scrambling into action at the communications panel. Seconds later, he turned back toward Khatami. "I have Captain Jarvis on audio."

"Put him on." At a nod from Estrada, she continued. "Captain Jarvis, this is Captain Khatami. What's your status?"

Over the white noise of distress, Captain Andrew Jarvis replied, *"We are officially FUBAR, Captain. We just lost shields, phasers, and warp drive."*

"Withdraw, Captain, we'll cover you. Come about on bearing two eight—"

"Negative. We've still got torpedoes, and I plan to use them. Jarvis out."

"Captain! Belay that!" When she heard no reply, she looked to Estrada.

He shook his head. "They've closed the channel."

Stano pointed at the main viewscreen. "Look!"

The *Buenos Aires* made an abrupt course change and charged directly at the densest cluster of Tholian ships circling Vanguard. Moments later the frigate unleashed a steady torrent of photon torpedoes—and accelerated behind them.

"My God," Stano blurted out, "they're on a *ramming* trajectory!"

Khatami sprang from her chair. "Helm! Get us to the other side of Vanguard—*now*!"

The thrumming of the impulse engines escalated to a high-pitched droning as Neelakanta accelerated the ship to flank speed while guiding it through a dizzying bank-and-roll maneuver.

A brilliant cone of destruction blazed through the Tholian armada, which scattered along dozens of vectors. Phaser and torpedo fire from Vanguard tracked the ships as they were forced out of their holding pattern, and blasted them with ferocious zeal and intimidating accuracy.

Checking the sensor data on the main viewscreen, Khatami realized the battle had already claimed nearly sixty-five percent

of the ships in the Tholian armada. For a moment, she was torn
between despair for the lives lost in the frigate's suicide run and
gloating for the havoc it had seemed to wreak upon the Tholian
fleet. Then she remembered that with the loss of the frigate, the
Endeavour was now the only ship left defending Vanguard. Their
situation until that moment had been bad. It was about to become
much worse.

"Look sharp, everyone," Khatami said. "We're about to get to
the fun part."

Fisher cut through one side of the jammed door to Phaser Control
Delta with a phaser while his Andorian compatriot, Shor, pulled
on the other side with all his considerable strength. As the phaser
beam sliced past the midpoint of the door, the entire thing buckled
and folded outward, and Shor pulled it off its slide track and
hurled it aside. He rushed inside the smoky compartment without
a moment's hesitation and called to Fisher, "This way, Doctor!"

Fisher followed the Andorian *thaan* through the suffocating
haze until they reached a trio of motionless personnel: two humans in their twenties, a man and a woman; and a male Tellarite.
Fighting to breathe and blink away the tears drawn out by the
acrid smoke, Fisher activated his medical tricorder and scanned
the three junior officers. He pointed at the human man. "He's
dead." Gesturing at the other two, he added, "I'll grab her, you get
him."

Shor hefted the portly Tellarite over his shoulder with ease,
while Fisher labored to lift the diminutive woman from her chair
and carry her away from her sparking console. He was several
paces behind Shor and envying the younger officer's vigor as the
bright, fuzzy shape of the open doorway became visible through
the veil of bitter haze.

Just a few steps more to clean air, he promised himself to
keep his feet moving.

He was knocked to the floor by a blast so loud he felt it in his
core, and so hot that it hurt for only a moment until it killed all the

nerves on the back half of his body. Then came the tug of weight-lessness and the sickening sensation of being transformed into a leaf on the wind.

The vacuum of space robbed him of the air in his lungs as he was hurled from the station into the darkness, tumbling beside Fellaren th'Shoras and three people whose names he'd never had the chance to learn. His slow tumble brought the station into view for a few seconds before his vision failed. The mushroom-shaped starbase was crumbling and ablaze, saucer and core alike rent and scarred. One of the massive deuterium tanks on the far side of the station exploded, blasting away a wedge of the saucer and scattering debris to the ends of creation.

Floating like a mote in the eye of eternity, Ezekiel Fisher felt the icy touch of the universe and discovered that death was utterly silent—and every bit as lonely as he'd feared it would be.

Sprawled half-conscious across the Hub, Nogura fought to marshal his ebbing strength so he could pick himself up and carry on. *Get up, damn you,* he cursed at himself. *There's no time for this. Get up or die!* Pain coursed down his spine as he pushed himself upright. Mustering a Herculean effort, he stood straight—then coughed. It was a deep, wet sound from deep inside his chest, and when he wiped his hand across the itch on his upper lip and chin, his palm came away slicked with his own blood. Only then did he notice the throbbing ache of his broken nose.

A hoarse female voice broke the eerie silence in the operations center.

"Admiral, are you all right?"

Nogura turned to see his yeoman, Lieutenant Toby Green-field, herself ragged and bloody, swaying on unsteady feet a few meters away. "I'm fine," Nogura lied. Looking around, he saw fallen sections of the overhead, blasted-in bulkheads, and smoldering consoles heaped with dead officers. At a glance he confirmed that Cannella, Dunbar, and Cooper all were dead, victims of the direct hit that had just crippled the operations center.

Greenfield hobbled over to Nogura, her awkward gait suggesting she had suffered a fractured bone in her leg. "Sir, it's over. We need to abandon the station before it's too late."

The few wall screens that still functioned confirmed that Vanguard and its handful of ships had made the Tholians pay a heavy price for this win—perhaps even a steep enough cost to classify their victory as Pyrrhic. But there was no longer any denying that they had prevailed, and that they now possessed the upper hand in the engagement.

Distant explosions trembled the broken husk of the station, and Nogura felt the grim intimations of Vanguard's inevitable fall with every tremor.

"You're right," he said. "Round up as many people as you can and get to the nearest transporter room. I'll coordinate the evacuations from here."

The feisty young yeoman held up a hand like a traffic warden halting a vehicle. "Hang on. What about you, Admiral?"

"I have a communicator," he said, lifting the device from his belt to prove he was telling the truth. "I'll activate my beacon when the evacs are finished. Now get out of here, Lieutenant. That's an order." He punctuated the command with a stony glare that sent Greenfield limping to the turbolifts. Then he triggered the evacuation alarm and keyed the hailing frequency. "Vanguard to *Endeavour*. Acknowledge."

Captain Khatami answered, "Endeavour. *Go ahead, Vanguard.*"

"Start the evacuation. Get the other ships to cover you, drop your shields, and beam out everyone you can."

After a troubling pause, Khatami replied, *"That'll be a problem, Vanguard. There* are *no other ships—just us. And if we drop our shields now, we're as good as dead."*

34

The *Endeavour* shook as if afflicted with a palsy. Wave after wave of Tholian strikes were swiftly buckling the shields, filling the ship with staccato reports and grave echoes. Half the panels on the bridge had gone dark, and Khatami had lost count of how many hull breaches had been reported in the mere minutes since the battle began. But despite the fact that her ship felt as if it was disintegrating around her, her mind was focused on the dilemma of the few hundred souls still clinging to life inside the core of the fractured and rapidly imploding Starbase 47.

Over the comm, Admiral Nogura's gravelly voice had become even more rough-edged. *"Captain, we're cut off from the lifeboats, and the Tholians would destroy them, anyway. We need immediate beam-out!"*

Another resounding boom rocked the ship and dimmed the lights. As the bridge crew stumbled back to their stations, Klisiewicz left the sensor console to join Khatami and Stano in the command well. "Sirs, we have to go *now*. We can't take another direct hit."

"Unacceptable, Lieutenant," Khatami said. "I won't leave those people behind."

Klisiewicz grew insistent. "When our shields fall, we won't be able to help anybody—and all the refugees we already have on board will die with us."

"Hang on," Stano said, waving Klisiewicz back from the command chair. "We've already lost ventral shields, and the transport array is on the ventral hull. Roll that side toward the station and reroute all power—"

"We're already *doing* that," Klisiewicz protested. "Captain, we only have a few seconds until we get hit again. We need to withdraw before—"

His prediction came true before he finished his warning. A brilliant flash on the main viewer was followed by a violent lurch of deceleration, as if the *Endeavour* had slammed bow-first into a planet. Funereal groans of distressed metal and distant roars of explosive decompression resounded through the bridge, and Khatami knew instinctively that *Endeavour*'s shields were gone and that the underside of the saucer section had just suffered a massive breach.

The idea of saving her ship by deserting Admiral Nogura and the others on Vanguard sickened her, but as a starship captain her first duty was to her vessel and crew, and circumstances had left her no other choice. "Neelakanta, set a new course. Rendezvous with—"

"New sensor contact!" McCormack interrupted. "Starfleet transponder!" She spun around to face Khatami and Stano, brimming with excitement and hope. "It's the *Enterprise*!"

The navigator switched over the main viewer angle to reveal the *Endeavour*'s sister ship cruising into the fray at full impulse, its shields fresh, phasers blazing, and torpedoes flying in a steady stream. Within seconds, the *Enterprise* had broken through the circling formation of Tholian warships and interposed itself between them and the war-torn *Endeavour*. Almost instantly, the percussion of Tholian attacks battering *Endeavour*'s hull faded away.

Thank Allāh for mercies great and small, Khatami prayed. "Hector! Hail them!"

"Already got 'em," Estrada said. He patched the signal to the main screen.

Captain Kirk appeared on the main viewscreen, his often boyish mien now one of keen intelligence and efficient professionalism. *"What's your status, Captain?"*

"We need cover so we can beam survivors off the station," Khatami said. "Can you buy us five minutes?"

Kirk nodded at someone off-screen, then replied, *"You'll have*

*. And I hope your pilot's as good as mine, because we'll have to
*e almost on top of you to pull this off."

"We can avoid hitting the station as long as you don't hit us."

Kirk smiled. *"Deal. We'll follow your lead.* Enterprise *out."*
*The viewscreen blinked back to the distressing sight of Vanguard
*flame.

"All right, Neelakanta, time to earn your pay," Khatami said.
"Take us under what's left of Vanguard's saucer for cover, roll our
belly toward the station, and give me as tight an orbit of the core
section as you can. And don't make any sudden moves, because
Enterprise will be mimicking our every move right above us."

The Arcturian's wide eyes belied his calm reply of "Aye,
Captain."

Khatami opened a comm channel from her armrest. "All
decks, this is the captain. Transporter rooms, start beaming survivors off the station."

T'Prynn emerged from the emergency access stairwell to find
the operations center a smoking heap of rubble littered with
corpses. In the middle of it all, elevated above the destruction,
was the supervisors' deck, where Admiral Nogura worked while
hunched awkwardly over the Hub. "Admiral," T'Prynn called out
over the sepulchral drumbeat of explosions ripping through the
station. "What are you still doing here?"

"Directing the evacuation," Nogura said without taking his
eyes from his work. "Why aren't you at your evac point?"

She clambered over the heaped debris, skipping from one to
the next with preternatural agility. "Sir, this center is no longer
secure. Another direct hit and you will be killed."

"Then you shouldn't be here, either," he growled.

Two running steps and a leap propelled her to the railing of the
supervisors' deck, which she vaulted over, and she landed behind
Nogura. "Sir, I must insist you leave this task to the auxiliary
operations center and beam out immediately."

"I can't," Nogura said, relaying transport coordinates to the

Endeavour like a man possessed. "Aux ops lost its comm link. This has to be done from here. And now that our core's breached, *Endeavour* needs our help to lock in the signals through the interference."

To her chagrin, the admiral's argument was eminently logical.

An uncomfortably close blast rained sparks and debris from the ceiling at the room's edge. T'Prynn realized that Nogura had paid the explosion no mind. "Sir, as a flag officer—"

"This is my command. I don't leave till my people are safe. If that means I go down with the station, so be it. Now get to your evac point, Lieutenant. That's an order."

"Yes, sir," T'Prynn said. She turned to leave—then pivoted back with a dancer's grace, clutched the vulnerable nerve cluster between the admiral's neck and shoulder, and held him as his body went limp and sank to the floor. "Forgive me, sir." She took his communicator from his belt, activated its emergency beacon, and tucked it back into its pocket. Then she stepped back several paces and watched as Nogura dematerialized in a golden shimmer of light and a mellifluous hum of sound. As soon as the transporter effect faded, she stepped forward, took his place at the Hub, and continued relaying transport coordinates to the *Endeavour*.

The station's survivors had gathered at a dozen dedicated emergency transport sites, each capable of beaming up to five people at a time. Two transport cycles had been completed already. She could only hope the station would hold together long enough to complete the last three cycles necessary to finish the evacuation, now that the station's weapons had been knocked out and its shields were contracting and intermittently stuttering out.

Then she noticed one personal transponder that was nowhere near an emergency site, and when she verified that it was in the Vault, she knew it had to be Ming Xiong.

Fear and hatred coursed from the array like a river in flood. Cracks propagated through its matrix, filling the Vault with its delicate symphony of fracturing crystal. The containment system burned out one subsystem at a time while Xiong stood mere meters away, finishing the preparation of the laboratory's self-destruct system. Overriding its security protocols had taken longer than he'd expected; it had been designed to require at least two senior personnel's command codes to authorize the self-destruct, but he was the only one left, so he'd hotwired it.

The terror quotient inside the lab escalated on a logarithmic scale as the array's myriad safeguards broke down. Xiong couldn't say what was more to blame—the Tholian attack or the obvious struggle of the Shedai to break free of their crystalline prison. He decided the cause didn't matter. No matter how hard he tried to focus on entering the final command sequence for the self-destruct, every instinct he possessed screamed, *Run! Get away from there!*

His hands shook above the console, and his mind was empty of everything except fear. *No,* he told himself. *It's not real. It's just beta waves from the Shedai. It's an illusion.* He closed his eyes and fought to ignore the unearthly dirge that groaned from the mysterious alien machine, but it was no use. He felt the Shedai's hateful emanations in his gut; they invaded his thoughts with whispers of interminable pain and suffering to come, cruel fates aborning for one and all.

Just a few more seconds, he berated himself. *That's all it takes.* He thought of the billions of innocent civilians on worlds throughout local space, not just in the Federation but across all the currently explored sectors of the galaxy's Orion arm, and he imagined the brutal horrors that would befall them if even a single Shedai escaped alive from the array. His sense of duty granted him a brief instant of clarity, and he pushed through his fear long enough to enter the final arming sequence. The computer screen flashed COMMAND AUTHORIZATION VERIFIED—SELF-DESTRUCT SEQUENCE ARMED. Then the system prompted him to set a countdown.

Somewhere inside the array, he heard one of the crystals shatter.

His communicator beeped twice on his belt. Keeping watch
over the crumbling array, he pulled out his communicator and
flipped it open. "Xiong here."

*"Mister Xiong, this is Lieutenant T'Prynn. Are you ready for
transport?"*

The first narrow tendrils of dark energy snaked out of the
machine's core. Primal fear rooted Xiong in place and left him
paralyzed. Watching the black liquid creep upward, he knew it
would be only a matter of moments until it shattered another
crystal, and another—then all the Shedai would break free, and
there would be no hope of ever containing them again.

T'Prynn's voice cut through the dire wailing of the Shedai.
"Mister Xiong! Do you copy? Are you ready for transport?"

Startled back to his senses, Xiong replied, "Negative. I . . .
have to finish something."

"The rest of the crew is being beamed out as we speak. En
deavour *is holding position until all personnel are accounted for.
How long until you're ready?"*

An entire row of crystals shattered and rained to the floor in
shards. A vast cloud of unnatural black smoke roiled inside the
isolation chamber, its inky swirls swimming with violet motes of
energy, its entire mass seething with violence and malice.

Xiong fought the temptation to trigger the self-destruct sequence right then. Instead, he forced himself to patch in a feed
from Vanguard's passive sensors, revealing the positions of the
Endeavour and the *Enterprise,* the circling mass of the Tholian
armada, and the escaping convoy of civilian vessels escorted by
the *Sagittarius.*

"Tell them I won't be coming," Xiong said.

It was the only choice he could live with. If he set a long-
enough delay on the self-destruct timer to permit the two *Consti*
tution-class starships to reach minimum safe distance, he
couldn't be certain the escaping Shedai wouldn't disable the system after he left. If he triggered it now, he would doom the two
starships and everyone aboard them to a fiery end. His only way
of making sure he'd contained the threat he'd helped awaken

three years earlier was to stand over it and personally drag it down into oblivion.

"Captain Khatami refuses to leave you behind," T'Prynn said several seconds later. *"Stand by while we establish a transporter lock on your communicator."*

Cracks began to form in the transparent enclosure of the isolation chamber, the wall of triple-reinforced transparent steel that the engineers had assured him was impenetrable.

Xiong realized the *Endeavour*'s crew would never abandon him as long as there remained a chance that they could pluck him from danger, and he had no time to explain the true nature of the threat before them. He couldn't take the chance that they would steal him away and leave the Shedai free to terrorize the galaxy for another aeon.

He dropped his communicator to the floor and crushed it under his heel. Putting his weight into it, he ground the fragile device beneath his boot until nothing remained but broken bits and coarse dust.

Inside the isolation chamber, the array collapsed like a house of cards in a gale.

A symphony of shattering crystal filled the air.

Then came the darkness.

T'Prynn watched Xiong's communicator signal go dark, and then its transponder went off line.

Over the comm, one of the *Endeavour*'s transporter chiefs was in a panic. *"Vanguard! What happened? We've lost your man's signal!"*

"Stand by," T'Prynn said. "I'm trying to isolate his life signs using the internal sensors, but he's inside a heavily shielded area of the station."

"Make it quick," the chief said. *"We're being told it's time to go."*

Massive interference from the starbase's overloading reactors and numerous radiation leaks from battle damage made it difficult for T'Prynn to get a clear reading from the station's lower core levels. Then the signal resolved for a moment—long enough for her to confirm that the Vault's antimatter-based self-destruct system had been armed, and that the secret laboratory was awash in the most concentrated readings of Shedai life signs she had ever witnessed.

If Xiong was doing what she suspected, then speed was now of the essence.

A final check of her panel confirmed that all the other personnel who had made it to the evac sites had been beamed out. She reopened the channel to the *Endeavour*.

"We've lost Lieutenant Xiong," she said. "Retreat at maximum speed as soon as I'm aboard. One to beam up. T'Prynn out."

Kirk swelled with admiration for his crew. Asked to do the impossible, they had carried it off with aplomb, unleashing the *Enterprise*'s formidable arsenal against the Tholian armada despite being locked into a circular flight pattern with no margin for evasion or error.

Even as the ship had lurched and shuddered beneath a devastating series of disruptor blasts and plasma detonations, chief engineer Montgomery Scott had kept the shields at nearly full power, and helmsman Hikaru Sulu hadn't wavered an inch from the close-formation position Kirk had ordered him to maintain between the *Enterprise* and the *Endeavour*. Ensign Pavel Chekov's targeting had been exemplary—not only had he dealt his share of damage to the Tholians, he had even picked off several of their incoming plasma charges, detonating them harmlessly in open space several kilometers from the ship.

Every captain thinks his crew is the best, Kirk mused with pride. *I know mine is.*

Lieutenant Uhura swiveled away from the communications panel. "Captain, we're being hailed by the *Endeavour*. Captain Khatami's given the order to withdraw at best possible speed."

"Then it's time to go," Kirk said. "Sulu, widen our radius,

give them room to break orbit. Set course for the convoy, warp factor six."

Spock stepped down into the command well and approached Kirk's chair. "Captain, sensors show the *Endeavour*'s warp drive is off line. She will not be able to stay with us."

"Sulu, belay my last." Kirk spun his chair toward Uhura. "Get me Captain Khatami."

A thunderous collision dimmed the lights and the deck pitched sharply, sending half the bridge crew tumbling to starboard. Kirk held on to his chair until the inertial dampers and artificial gravity reset to normal. "Damage report!"

Spock hurried back to his station and checked the sensor readouts. "Dorsal shield buckling. Hull breach on Decks Three and Four, port side."

Uhura interjected, "I have Captain Khatami, sir."

"On-screen," Kirk said. As soon as Khatami's weary, blood-stained face appeared on the main viewscreen, Kirk asked, "How long until your warp drive's back on line, Captain?"

The transmission became hashed with interference as *Endeavour* weathered another jarring hit. Khatami coughed and waved away smoke. *"Any minute now. Go ahead without us."*

"With all respect, Captain: Not a chance. Signal us when you're ready for warp speed. We'll cover you till then. Kirk out." He glanced at Uhura and made a quick slashing gesture, and she closed the transmission before Khatami could argue with him. "New plan. Sulu, stay on the *Endeavour*'s aft quarter and act as her shield until they recover warp power. Chekov, concentrate all fire aft—discourage the Tholians from chasing us. Spock, angle all deflector screens aft. Everyone else, get comfortable; we're in for a very bumpy ride."

35

Billions of radiant specks swam in the frigid darkness that surrounded Ming Xiong. Demonic howls and wails assailed him, but his eardrums were still ringing with tinnitus from the sharp crack of the isolation chamber's reinforced door exploding away from its frame and pealing the distant bulkhead like a church bell.

He couldn't bring himself to scream as the Shedai erupted in a torrent from the isolation chamber and gathered around him in a great cloud, a storm of ice and shadow. His mind was numb, his very existence reduced to a state of inarticulate horror. All he could do was cling to his pedestal-shaped console and watch the real-time sensor readouts.

The *Enterprise* and the *Endeavour* were still too close to the station for him to risk triggering the self-destruct system. *Why haven't they gone to warp?* He feared with each passing moment that he might have to condemn them to share his fate.

At the same time, except for a small force of ships that were pursuing the *Endeavour* and the *Enterprise,* the Tholian armada was redeploying into a close-range heavy bombardment formation around the station. As devoutly as Xiong wished he could have left this matter to them, he couldn't trust their weapons to even affect the Shedai, much less guarantee their destruction. Worse, their impending barrage might damage the Vault's self-destruct system enough to prevent it from unleashing its maximum yield at the moment of detonation, so he would have to trigger the autodestruct package as soon as they resumed fire on the station, regardless of whether the *Endeavour* and the *Enterprise* had escaped the blast zone.

And still, all he wanted to do was run.

A dark flash of motion, a black blur in the shadows, and he felt the sharp bite of an obsidian blade as it slammed through his torso. His knees buckled, and then he felt as if he were standing on rubber legs. Blood, warm and tasting of tin, gurgled up his esophagus and spilled over his chin. He looked down and saw the broadsword-sized, jagged-edged mass that had impaled him. Following its edge back toward its source, he saw that it became translucent within a meter of his body, and after that it gradually changed states, first to a dense liquid and then to a tenuous mass of vapor extended from the great cloud of Shedai.

The tentacle jerked back, yanking its black blade from Xiong's body in an agonizing blur that left him clutching at his belly with one hand and hanging onto his console with the other. Where he expected to find his blood and viscera spilling out, he found a freezing cold mass of quartzlike stone covering his wound. Then he felt its deathly chill traveling across his skin, and he realized it was spreading. An icy, stabbing sensation inside his gut alerted him to the substance's cancerlike progression through his internal organs. Cold suffused his body, and he felt his strength ebbing along with his body's heat.

Then he became aware of other presences, distinct entities, drawing near to him. Hunched giants of smoke and indigo light, they wore auras of arrogance and malice like crowns of evil. The unholy host of spectral figures pressed inward. Then one spoke with a voice that wed the roar of an avalanche with the fathomless echoes of a Martian canyon. **"Foolish little spark."** Rich with condescension, its Jovian baritone shook the station. **"What made your kind think it could ever contain such as us? You are but glimmers in the endless gaze of time. Weak minds trapped inside sacks of rotting flesh and fragile bone. You are nothing."**

Xiong wished he had some irreverent reply, some witty retort for its taunts, but all he had was a mouthful of blood and a body shivering with hypothermia and adrenaline overload.

"So? Who are you?"

"I am the Progenitor, the wellspring of all that is Shedai. First among the elite."

"Good for you."

He stole a look at the console. *Endeavour* and *Enterprise* remained at impulse. *Come on. Go, already!*

The Progenitor loomed over him, its countenance one of perfect darkness, a black hole surrounded by sickly hues and pestilent vapors. Its approach sent frost creeping across Xiong's console. **"All your worlds will pay for your trespasses. Your kind will learn to fear us like never before."** A tentacle of smoke coiled around Xiong's throat and solidified into a substance that felt like solid muscle sheathed in cold vinyl. Then it lifted him up against the ceiling and started choking him by slow degrees. **"Beg for mercy, and I will grant you a swift death. Defy me, and I will keep your consciousness alive to witness every horror and atrocity we visit upon your pathetic Federation."**

The Tholian armada was in position. Its final siege was only moments away.

Xiong could barely feel his hands as he clutched at the Progenitor's black tentacle. Looking down in terror and anguish, he glimpsed his console, which was now blanketed by a paper-thin layer of frost. He could no longer see the sensor readout's fine details, but he could still see two bright blue points of light that he knew were the escaping Starfleet ships.

Then both dots vanished from the display. *They've made the jump to warp!*

He forced out a desperate whisper, "Mercy . . ."

The Progenitor dropped him. He rolled as he hit the floor, coming to a stop in front of his console. Fighting past the torturous sensation of a hundred needles of ice drilling through his intestines, Xiong fought his way back to his feet and slumped against his console. He had planned to do so as a ruse, but it had become a necessity.

"So," the Progenitor mocked, **"it's to be a quick death, is it?"**

Xiong looked up at the Progenitor and flashed a bloodied grin. "You have no idea."

He pressed the autodestruct trigger, and his pit of darkness turned to light.

Bruised and aching, Admiral Nogura stepped out of the turbolift and onto the bridge of the *Endeavour,* only to be brusquely shouldered aside by the ship's surgeon, Doctor Anthony Leone, and one of its nurses, who together carried out an unconscious and maimed young lieutenant on a stretcher. "Out of the way," Leone said, his nasal voice tolerating no argument. The short, sinewy physician seemed to regard Nogura not as a flag officer but as an obstacle.

The turbolift doors hissed closed behind Nogura as he inched toward the center of the bridge. Captain Khatami appeared to have suffered her fair share of lacerations from airborne debris. Blood trickled down from above her hairline and seeped from a cut beside her right eye; numerous bloodstains tainted her gold command jersey in flecks and streaks.

Apparently having caught sight of Nogura out of the corner of her eye, Khatami swiveled her chair toward him. "Admiral, are you all right?"

"I'm fine. Though I might have to court-martial Lieutenant T'Prynn. Again."

A curious look. "For what?"

"Saving my life," Nogura grumbled.

Khatami looked slyly amused. "Good luck getting a conviction for that."

"Did you finish evacuating the station?"

"Yes, sir, thanks to Kirk and the *Enterprise.* We—" A sudden flash on the main viewer snared her eye and snapped her back into command mode. "Klisiewicz, report."

The science department chief stared with haunted eyes at the sensor display. "It's Vanguard, Captain. It blew up and took most of what was left of the Tholian armada with it."

The image on the main viewscreen changed to show an incandescent cloud of fire blooming against the starry sprawl of deep space, its rolling blazes littered with chunks of the once-mighty starbase and the broken husks of dozens of Tholian warships. Within seconds the storm of superheated gases had already begun to dissipate into the endless darkness.

The autodestruct, Nogura realized. *Xiong must have triggered it from the Vault.* He descended into the command well. "Are there any Shedai life signs, Lieutenant?"

"Negative, sir. Only a few Tholian life signs, and they're retreating at warp speed."

Khatami remained on edge. "What about the ships chasing us?"

McCormack replied, "They're changing course, sir. Breaking off and heading back toward Tholian space at warp eight."

That news seemed to bring a wave of relief to everyone on the bridge except Nogura. He stared at the fading glow of the antimatter-fueled explosion that had just wiped Starbase 47 and every remaining member of the Shedai out of existence, and wondered whether, in the long view of history, this five-year covert operation would be deemed a success or a failure, and if the innumerable lives sacrificed in its name would be hailed as heroes and martyrs, or as victims of a national-security misadventure run amok.

Ultimately, it didn't matter, he decided. It would fall to future generations to judge this undertaking and its consequences with the benefit of hindsight. There was nothing left for him to do now but file his final report as the commanding officer of Starbase 47 and await new orders.

Officially, as of that moment . . . Operation Vanguard was over.

EPILOGUE

A BRAVER PLACE

CALDOS II

Pennington sat in the stern of Reyes's narrow skiff, clutching the gunwales with both hands. His coat was pulled tightly closed, and his legs stretched toward the middle of the small boat. Reyes sat facing him on the center bench, rowing the five-meter-long watercraft with slow, powerful strokes through the limbo of predawn fog that surrounded them. Reyes's oar blades cut gentle wakes, and the handles creaked inside the oarlocks. It was impossible to see more than a few meters in any direction, and all Pennington saw was the rippled water of the lake.

"You really didn't have to do this," Pennington said.

Reyes's long hair swayed with the tempo of his rowing. "Yes, I did."

"I could have waited another hour for the ferry."

The former Starfleet officer drawled, "I just wanted you out of my house."

Pennington chuckled. "Suits me. You were out of whiskey, anyway." Except for the soft splash of water against the boat and the wooden groans of the oars, the world seemed utterly still. Then, even though he couldn't yet see the mainland, he caught a faint scent of pine and a distant lilt of birdsong from the vast sprawl of virgin forest that ringed the lake.

Exertion deepened Reyes's respiration, and his exhalations added ghostly plumes to the morning's heavy shroud of pale vapor. Catching his breath, he asked, "So, I meant to ask: What was the fallout from the Tholians attacking Vanguard?"

"Less than you'd expect." Pennington dug his hands into his coat pockets to keep them warm. "The Tholians made a stink in Paris about 'the crimes of the Taurus Reach,' or some such twaddle. The Federation Council passed off the attack as a 'benevolent Tholian intervention' to help Starfleet contain the Shedai threat after an accident aboard the station."

Reyes chortled and cracked a cynical smile behind his salt-and-pepper beard. "And who blew the lid off *that* lie? You or the Tholians?"

"Neither. Starfleet started jamming and censoring all transmissions out of Tholian space, and the editorial board at FNS ran with the official spin from the Palais." He strained to see anything through the fog, mostly as an excuse to avoid eye contact with Reyes as he added, "That was when I handed in my resignation and went to work for INN."

"And they broke the story."

"Nope. They'd been co-opted, too." The memory still made him angry. "Sometimes, I think the whole galaxy's in on the lie, and I'm the only one left who cares about the truth." Suddenly recalling that Reyes had been court-martialed years earlier for helping Pennington expose some of Starfleet's shameful secrets, he added, "Present company excluded, of course."

A dour glance let him off the hook. "Naturally." Reyes looked down at the compass resting between his feet and adjusted his stroke to make a minor correction in the skiff's course. "Speaking of which, whatever happened to my successor?"

"Just what you'd expect for a man who had a Watchtower-class starbase shot out from under him: He got promoted." That drew a short but good-natured laugh from Reyes, and then Pennington continued. "Since I know you're probably dying to ask, Captain Khatami and the *Endeavour* are exploring the Taurus Reach, and so are Captain Terrell and the *Sagittarius*."

Reyes looked pleased. "Seems only fair, after all the legwork they did." He glanced over his shoulder, as if he expected to find something there, then he turned back toward Pennington and continued his slow-and-steady rowing. "Did you keep tabs on anybody else?"

"Everyone I could," Pennington confessed. "Doctor Marcus and her civilian partners are in some top-secret location—nobody really knows where—doing God-knows-what. Probably learning how to stop time or turn old chewing gum into black holes. Your old pal Jetanien's still living on that backwater rock, Nimbus III. When I asked him why, he said he was there 'for the waters.' Rumor has it the old turtle's finally lost his mind."

A thoughtful frown. "What about T'Prynn?"

"No idea," Pennington said. "Vanished into her work at SI, along with every last shred of proof the Shedai ever existed. I figure at least some of those artifacts must have been taken off the station before it went up in flames, but I'll be damned if I can find any trace of them."

"Probably all boxed up in a warehouse on some airless moon at the ass end of space. I doubt they'll ever be seen again—at least, not in our lifetimes."

"Maybe that's for the best," Pennington said. "I just wish I could find a lead on my old mate, Quinn. He not only disappeared, he erased himself from history, like he was never born."

Reyes stopped rowing to mop the sweat from his creased forehead with the sleeve of his insulated red flannel shirt. "Take it from me, Tim: some people don't *want* to be found."

Pennington grudgingly saw the wisdom in Reyes's point. "I know. It's just my nature to dig at these sorts of things."

The older man resumed rowing while eyeing him with open suspicion. "True, but you don't usually do it for free. At least, you never used to. So . . . who paid you to dig *me* up?"

He tried to deflect the question. "Who says anyone did?"

"FNS? INN?" When he realized no confirmation or denial was forthcoming, he seemed to grow concerned. "The Orions? . . . The Klingons?"

Realizing his reticence had unnecessarily alarmed Reyes, Pennington held out a hand to cue him to stop. "No, no, nothing like that, I promise. If you must know, I'm here on a personal contract. I'm acting more as a private investigator than as a journalist, to be honest."

Behind Reyes, the mainland dock appeared from the fog—a dim suggestion of a shape at first, then a dark gray outline slowly growing more solid. As Reyes guided the skiff to a halt alongside the mooring posts, a shadowy figure on the dock became half visible through the leaden mist. Reyes stood to secure the skiff for Pennington's departure with his back toward the unannounced traveler on the dock, and Pennington said nothing as he climbed out of the narrow boat and took a few steps toward the mainland. Then he stopped and looked back.

Reyes turned and climbed onto the dock—probably to bid Pennington farewell and safe travels, the writer surmised—only to find himself speechless.

He faced Rana Desai, who stood and gazed back at him, and in their eyes Pennington saw an affection undimmed by their years apart. Neither of the estranged lovers said anything. Ever a willing martyr to romantic illusion, Pennington imagined the two were so attuned to each other's feelings that they had no need of words.

Desai graced Reyes with a bittersweet smile. His eyes misted with emotion. He beckoned her with one outstretched hand. She went to him. He lifted her off her feet and swept her into a passionate embrace. As they kissed, Pennington turned and walked away, granting them some well-earned privacy.

Arriving at dry land, he looked back. Desai was in the skiff with Reyes, who rowed them slowly away toward his island, into the veil of fog. Watching their details fade into the mist, Pennington knew that they, like so many other figures both noble and tragic, despite being deserving of honor and remembrance, would be forgotten by history. Their names and deeds would sink into obscurity, borne away by time's ceaseless current.

He reached inside his jacket, took out his wallet, and opened it to admire a single white blossom, a token of love and memory, a memento of life as it once had been.

Let the world forget, he consoled himself, tucking his wallet back inside his coat and walking back toward town. *I'll remember.*

HERE ENDS THE SAGA OF

ACKNOWLEDGMENTS

There's a lot I want to say in this space, because for me this was very special undertaking, the culmination of a seven-year literary journey that has meant a great deal to me both personally and professionally. First, I want to thank my wife, Kara, for her support and patience over the past several months. She has been my muse, my cheering section, and my sounding board as I wrote the manuscript for this novel. I would have been lost without her.

I also am grateful to my friends and creative partners in the *Star Trek Vanguard* series. Marco Palmieri, with whom I developed the *Vanguard* concept seven years ago, and who edited the first four volumes of the series, has been a terrific mentor, guide, and collaborator. His creativity and passion inspired me to challenge myself and craft a more thoughtful work than I had ever attempted before. Authorial duo Dayton Ward and Kevin Dilmore helped make this series the best it could be by infusing it with their vision, talent, and hard work. Our friendly game of one-upmanship, which informed many of the twists and turns of the series' early installments, made writing each new *Vanguard* novel a true joy and a labor of love. Thank you, guys, for making this all more fun than I could ever have imagined.

I'd be remiss if I failed to acknowledge two other remarkable visionaries whose artistic contributions are as integral to the *Vanguard* series as those of the writers and editors. I speak, of course, of designer Masao Okazaki and digital artist Doug Drexler. Masao designed the exterior and interior of Starbase 47, a.k.a. Vanguard, as well as those of the *Archer*-class scout ship *U.S.S. Sagittarius*. It was Masao's designs that brought both the station and that plucky little ship to life in my imagination; than you, Masao, for making these places "real" to me. Doug, course, is the man who transformed Masao's designs into th series' striking CGI cover renderings. Each time we saw one Doug's covers, Marco, Dayton, Kevin, and I would all be blow away—and then we'd collectively wonder, "How will he ever to this one?" And then, whenever the next book in the series cam along, he did. You are a master without equal, Doug. Thank yo for making ours some of the finest-looking novels on anyone bookshelf.

Lest I forget, my sincere thanks also go out to all the editor who have worked on the *Vanguard* series over the past seve years. In addition to Marco, this roster includes Margaret Clar Jaime Costas, and Ed Schlesinger. Thanks also to one of our mo ardent fans, the knowledgeable John Van Citters, our licensin contact at CBS Consumer Products. And, lest I not get my royalt checks on time, I offer my gratitude to my agent, Lucienne Dive for dotting my I's, crossing my T's, and vetting the pesky fir print in my publishing contracts.

Keeping one's facts straight is one of the hardest things to d when writing for such a vastly developed shared universe as *Sta Trek*. As such, I am indebted to the many fine sources information that help me remain in step with both the series canon and the vast web of continuity shared by the current line o novels: *The Star Trek Encyclopedia* and *Star Trek Chronology* by Michael Okuda and Denise Okuda; *Star Trek Star Charts,* b Geoffrey Mandel; and the wiki-based reference website Memory Alpha and Memory Beta.

Because music is so integral to my creative process, I wish to thank the composers whose work served as my touchstone on this final literary odyssey in the *Vanguard* saga: Clir Mansell (*The Fountain*), Ramin Djawadi (*Game of Thrones*) Hans Zimmer (*Sherlock Holmes*), Alan Silvestri (*Beowulf*) Bear McCreary (*Battlestar Galactica*), and Cliff Martine (*Solaris*).

Lastly, my thanks belong to you, the readers of the *Vanguard* ⁀ies. Your passion for this series not only made it possible to ⁀ep it going for eight books to its natural conclusion, it made ⁀worth doing in the first place. So, until next time—live long ⁀d prosper.

ABOUT THE AUTHOR

David Mack is the national bestselling author of more than twenty novels and novellas, including *Wildfire, Harbinger, Reap the Whirlwind, Precipice, Road of Bones, Promises Broken,* and the *Star Trek Destiny* trilogy: *Gods of Night, Mere Mortals,* and *Lost Souls.* He developed the *Star Trek Vanguard* series concept with editor Marco Palmieri. His first work of original fiction is the critically acclaimed supernatural thriller *The Calling.*

In addition to novels, Mack's writing credits span several media, including television (for episodes of *Star Trek: Deep Space Nine*), film, short fiction, magazines, newspapers, comic books, computer games, radio, and the Internet. He also co-authored Bryan Anderson's nonfiction Iraq War memoir, *No Turning Back: One Man's Inspiring True Story of Courage, Determination, and Hope.*

Mack's upcoming novels include a *Star Trek: The Next Generation* trilogy and a new original supernatural thriller. He resides in New York City with his wife, Kara.

Visit his website, www.davidmack.pro, and follow him on Twitter @DavidAlanMack and on Facebook at www.facebook.com/david.alan.mack.